PENGUIN BOOKS

SAHYADRI ADVENTURE: ANIRUDH'S DREAM

Deepak Dalal gave up a career in chemical engineering to write stories for children. He lives in Pune with his wife, two daughters and several dogs and cats. He enjoys wildlife, nature and the outdoors. His books include the Vikram–Aditya adventure series (for older readers) and the Feather Tales series (for younger readers). All his stories have a strong conservation theme.

A
VIKRAM–ADITYA
STORY

SAHYADRI ADVENTURE

ANIRUDH'S DREAM

DEEPAK DALAL

PENGUIN BOOKS
An imprint of Penguin Random House

PENGUIN BOOKS

USA | Canada | UK | Ireland | Australia
New Zealand | India | South Africa | China

Penguin Books is part of the Penguin Random House group of companies
whose addresses can be found at global.penguinrandomhouse.com

Published by Penguin Random House India Pvt. Ltd
4th Floor, Capital Tower 1, MG Road,
Gurugram 122 002, Haryana, India

First published by Tarini Publishing 2010
Sahyadri Adventure: Anirudh's Dream was published by Silverfish, an imprint of Grey Oak Publishers, in association with Westland Publications Private Limited 2013
This edition published in Penguin Books by Penguin Random House India 2022

Inside illustrations: Anusha Menon
Some illustrations have been adapted from photographs and maps appearing in *Bombay: The Cities Within* (Sharada Dwivedi, Rahul Mehrotra), *Bombay to Mumbai* (Marg Publications), *The Taj Magazine* (vol. 37, no. 1)
Geographical inputs and map illustration: Dr Sanjeev Nalawade
Map sketching assistant: Pradnya Apte

10 9 8 7 6 5 4 3 2 1

ISBN 9780143449423

Typeset in Adobe Caslon Pro by Manipal Technologies Limited, Manipal
Printed at Replika Press Pvt. Ltd, India

www.penguin.co.in

For my dear departed mother and father—wonderful parents who blessed my unusual career choice.

PREFACE

Aditya's father always maintained that Pune's National Defence Academy (NDA) ranked amongst the best colleges in the world. An air force pilot and ex-student himself, he often boasted of the Academy's incomparable sports facilities.

'Forget about your standard sports,' Aditya had often heard his father say. 'You know what I'm talking about: cricket, football, hockey, golf, basketball, tennis; several colleges have facilities for those and of course, so does the Academy. But tell me . . .'—his eyes would always sparkle at this point—'how many colleges have stables of their own, with a hundred horses, mind you? How many can lay claim to having a world-class sailing facility? And here's the icing on the cake: where can you find a college that has its own airstrip with real aircraft to fly?' He would then rub his hands with glee. 'The Academy is the best. It has to be. Because right there, on its fabulous 8000-acre campus, India's finest are trained for a career in the armed forces.'

With a glowing recommendation like that, it was hardly surprising that when offered to spend his summer holidays at the Academy, Aditya grabbed the opportunity and invited his best friend Vikram along too.

Having travelled to the furthest corners of India, excitement and adventure were commonplace for Vikram and Aditya. Yet, in spite of their experiences, nothing could have prepared them for the bizarre incidents that would befall them at the Academy and its neighbouring range of hills, the Sahyadri.

It was at the Academy, on a storm-riven lake, that Vikram bonded with a boy named Anirudh Dongre. There was nothing remarkable about Anirudh. He was an ordinary teenager at best. But on an excursion to the Sahyadris, Vikram discovered that there was more to him than met the eye. Then Anirudh inexplicably fell into a dream. The dream profoundly affected Anirudh and he confided its contents only with Vikram. So startling and incredible were Anirudh's revelations, that they altered Vikram's understanding of reason and reality forever.

This is the story of Anirudh's dream and the strange events that unfolded in Pune, Mumbai and the splendid hills of the Sahyadri.

PART 1

THE SAHYADRI

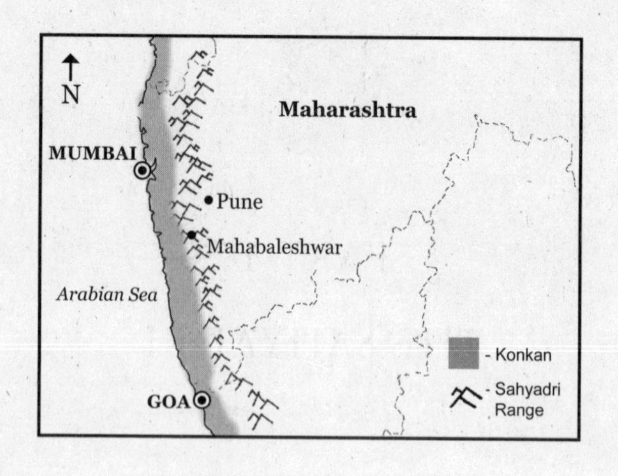

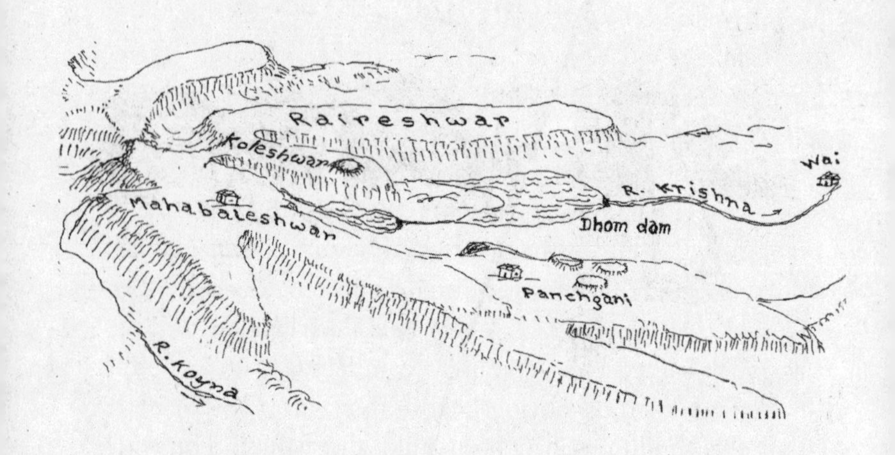

Sketch of Mahabaleshwar Region

(Not to scale)

ANIRUDH

Anirudh and Vikram had been cast together as partners in the Inland Water Championship, a sailing race held annually on Pune's Khadakwasla Lake. Vikram hadn't chosen Anirudh as his partner. Anirudh's fear of all waterbodies, whether large or small, was common knowledge, and Vikram hadn't exactly been pleased when he was assigned as his partner.

Vikram had resigned himself for the worst, convinced that he was slated for a last-place finish amongst the fifty boats taking part in the regatta. But, surprisingly, their ranking at the end of the first two days was a commendable thirty-seven. Anirudh's performance on board couldn't be faulted. During the races—two held each day—Anirudh had responded to Vikram's commands, successfully battening down his obvious fear of the lake. It had helped that the conditions had been mild and balmy. The sun had shone fiercely from a deep blue sky and the wind had restricted itself to a gentle breeze. But on the last day of the race, the weather turned.

The regatta—hosted by the illustrious NDA—was always slotted in the first week of June, in part because the period coincided with a major seasonal change in Pune and its surrounding areas. It was the time of the year when the monsoons invaded the skies, propelling wind and turbulence and deluging the parched land with eagerly awaited rain. The monsoons did not disappoint that year. Holding fast to their anticipated date, they shadowed Pune's skies on the final day of the regatta.

It was midway through the morning race that clouds began to fleck the skies and a strong wind swept the lake. This was greeted with wild cheers and jubilation. For sailors, the wind is an essential element of their sport—just as snow is for skiing. The cheers grew ever louder as sails flapped, masts creaked and fifty boat prows cut swifter through the water.

On board Vikram's boat, however, the raging wind inspired a diametrically opposite reaction. Seated on the gunwale, Anirudh appeared to freeze. His dark features turned pale and his limbs frosted over till their pliability was little different from blocks of ice. The dramatically altered conditions worried Vikram too. Unlike his classmate, Aditya—a top-notch sailor—Vikram's abilities were only average. A disturbing swell was making its presence felt on the water and he wasn't sure he could handle the blustering wind.

A scary incident all but sank his waning morale. It happened at the final buoy, where he had to perform a gybe turn. The boat swung wildly and Anirudh screamed as he almost toppled overboard. Vikram lost control completely as the sail spun wildly. But luck was on his side as somehow—even later he had no clue how—he regained the sail and brought the boat back on an even keel.

Vikram could only pay attention to Anirudh later when the boat was powering along on a far reach. His partner's face had shrunk dramatically and it was clear that he was in a state of terror. Although Vikram attempted to encourage him, Anirudh was too far gone. Vikram couldn't blame him as the conditions were frightening indeed.

Waves were battering the boat, drenching the boys and flooding the deck. The lake was transformed, its placidity a distant memory now. It bucked and heaved fiercely and the wind slapped deafeningly against the sails. Of the fifty boats that had set sail, five did not complete the race, capsizing along the way. Surprisingly, Vikram and Anirudh finished well, an exhilarating twenty-fifth they learnt later.

As he drew near the shore, Vikram noticed a crowd on the jetties. Spotting Aditya and his partner Kiran in its midst, he waved as he docked his boat.

Aditya came running, face flushed, hair wild and bobbing. 'We came second!' he shouted, pumping his fists in the air. 'We almost won the race.'

'Wow!' exclaimed Vikram. The boat rocked as he rose carefully to his feet. 'That's incredible. Way out! Congrats.'

A beaming Kiran came striding as Vikram and Aditya exchanged high fives. 'We almost won,' he crowed. 'Just one boat length. One teeny-weeny boat length. That's all we were beaten by.'

'Yeah!' exclaimed Aditya. 'One miserable boat length.' He turned to Kiran. 'We won't let that happen again. It's going to be us in the final race, right? We're going to win.'

A bearded sailor slapped Aditya on his back. 'If anyone can do it, it's you guys.' It was Umaji, one of several contestants from Goa. 'Your boat simply took off when it began to blow. That was an awesome performance. Keep it up and the final race is yours.'

Aditya bounced on the jetty, performing a jig. 'The wind!' He waved a fist. 'We have wind. A real wind. No more of that namby-pamby sailing of the past two days. And it's going to blow stronger. Look. The clouds are getting darker.'

Indeed, the heavens were blackening. Clouds were pouring in from everywhere, rapidly obscuring the remnants of blue in the sky. The gathering mass harboured the promise of rain and turbulence, conditions that brought out the best in Aditya. The boy was blessed with a rare ability to read and anticipate the vagaries of the wind. On board a boat, he responded instinctively, adjusting rudder and sail to draw that elusive extra power that talented sailors alone could tap.

Aditya's partner, Kiran Kale, was no less a sailor. Kiran hailed from the same school as Vikram and Aditya. After passing out, Kiran had gone on to train as an officer in the armed forces, gaining admission to the NDA. The successful pairing of Aditya and Kiran had been a last-minute affair. Having known about the regatta—a highlight of NDA's sporting calendar—Vikram and Aditya had registered for it as partners in advance. Shortly after their arrival at NDA, they had stumbled upon their old school buddy and Aditya had wanted to team with Kiran. Vikram hadn't objected, believing that the pairing could be a medal-winning combination. It was then, to fill in for Aditya, that Anirudh had been assigned as Vikram's partner.

Vikram hadn't been paying attention to Anirudh while he chatted with his friends. It was only when Kiran and Aditya drifted away with the other sailors that he noticed his absence. It was dereliction of duty on Anirudh's part to leave without helping de-rig the boat, but Vikram wasn't particularly annoyed. Vikram's mild reaction owed to the feelings of guilt he bore at his inept handling of the boat. Anirudh's discomfiture was a result of his incompetence. So he believed.

Vikram set about bailing the water that had collected in the boat's hull. He de-rigged the sail and wrapped it carefully. It was during his final inspection of the boat that he heard a shout and looked up. Aditya was striding down the jetty towards him, a large smile on his face. Behind him, matching Aditya's gangling six-foot length was a tall figure, a dark-skinned girl with hair neatly brushed back.

'Chitra!' yelled Vikram, his face lighting as if the sun had pierced the clouds.

The girl broke into a delighted smile and the jetty creaked and swayed as they rushed towards each other and hugged.

'You haven't changed one bit.' Chitra laughed, pulling back. Her voice was strong and her laugh throaty. 'Look at you . . . the last one to leave, carefully stowing away his gear, as always.'

'If it's news to you, neither have you,' responded Vikram, staring at her. 'No lipstick, no powder, no make-up. But wait a minute, you look taller than last time.' Vikram bent low, inspecting her footwear. 'No . . . it isn't heels, you never wear them.' Vikram shook his head, sighing. 'Your folks must be fed up with you. It's only been four months and you have grown. Never mind. It's wonderful to see you again. But what happened? We were expecting you earlier. Where were you?'

'In the Sahyadris, she claims,' Aditya said. 'An expedition to search for snakes.'

'Hey,' protested Chitra, 'I'm here for work. Get that into your heads. I have to do what my boss at the Snake Park tells me. It isn't my fault that we had to leave for the mountains on the same day you arrived. We got back this morning and I've come straight here to meet the two of you.'

It was a matter of coincidence that the boys and Chitra were together in Pune. After a tumultuous holiday together on the Andaman Islands, they had split up, Vikram and Aditya returning to school and Chitra staying on. While there, she had sought admission to a college in Chennai to study zoology and had been accepted. But college did not commence till late July and she had time on her hands. Chitra's passion in life was the pursuit of reptiles, snakes in particular, and Pune's famed Snake Park was an institution she had always dreamt of working at. She had applied for a summer job and only after her application had been confirmed did she learn that the boys were also coming to Pune.

'What a wind,' said Chitra, looking about her as they ambled companionably down the jetty. 'I wish I could have taken part. These races look like so much fun.'

'We had registered you,' said Vikram. 'But you chose to go searching for snakes. Sorry, there's only one race left now.'

'Dumb choice,' smirked Aditya. 'Snakes! Yuck. Doubly stupid considering what she's missing.'

'Hey!' protested Chitra, stopping dead. 'Don't knock it, Aditya. There's nothing wrong with searching for snakes.' Chitra always reacted sharply when people spoke insultingly about her beloved reptiles. But the boys were looking at each other and laughing.

'You're having me on again, I see,' she breathed. 'Just you wait, both of you. You're going to have to spend time at the Snake Park, in the snake pit; I'll see that you do. And I'm going to drag you to the Sahyadris to find snakes. Neither of you is going to get away from me.'

Chitra cut an impressive figure as she stared indignantly at the boys. Though not classically beautiful, she was tall and superbly fit, like an athlete—an all-round decathlon athlete, with sturdy shoulders, strong legs and washboard abs. Passers-by were casting glances at her. Amongst them was Kiran, who Vikram hailed and introduced.

Though Vikram wanted to spend time with his friends, he excused himself.

'If you're looking for Anirudh, he's with his mom,' said Kiran. 'The poor guy is in a funk. I don't see how he's going to sail the next race.'

'It's okay,' said Vikram. 'That's what I intend fixing. I'll give him a pep talk . . . set him right.'

'That should do the job,' said Aditya. 'Vikram's the motivational sort. He's good. Does it all the time at school.'

'Hold on,' said Kiran. 'I didn't make myself clear, sorry. It's not about motivation. He doesn't intend to sail, he made it clear to his mom. She told him not to worry and promised to speak to his dad on his behalf.'

Vikram stared open-mouthed at Kiran.

Kiran nodded his head in sympathy. 'You got a problem, dude.'

Vikram's expression turned grim. 'That's not done. He can't back out—not from a commitment. He's got to finish what he started. I'll see to it that he does. Sorry, Chitra, you'll have to excuse me. I'll catch you guys later.'

Vikram was upset. So disturbed was he by Kiran's revelation that he barely spared a glance for his surroundings as he set about searching for Anirudh.

NDA's sailing facilities were nestled in a pleasant anchorage known as Peacock Bay—aptly named after the colourful birds that were common in its wooded environs. But the bay's charming setting wasn't its most prized asset, it was the equipment stored there—a hoard so rich that it fulfilled every sailor's fantasy. From the tiny Optimist class of boats to large, clumsy whalers, the club possessed an incredible array of sailing vessels. Adding to its plenitude were kayaks, windsurf boards, speedboats and even jet skis.

Aditya and Vikram would have sacrificed anything—friends, girlfriends, even their precious holidays—to have such a fabulous lake with all that incredible gear in their backyard. The tragedy of it was that Anirudh, the most reluctant sailor Vikram had ever met, had it all. Not only that; Anirudh's father, Commander Vikas Dongre, was the officer in charge of the sailing club.

Vikram chafed at the unfairness of the world as he crossed to a grassy flat behind the jetties. An enormous tent had been erected there to shelter the regatta spectators, but by now it had emptied, and Anirudh and his mother weren't amongst the handful lingering there. Anirudh's father's office was tucked away behind an enormous shed that housed large naval equipment. Vikram found Anirudh there, in a room with sparse furniture, along with his mother and father.

Commander Dongre was a big man with a dominating personality. Outfitted in a smart naval uniform and sporting a snow-white beard, he looked handsome and distinguished, quite the opposite of his son who stood beside him with his head bowed. Anirudh was short and small, his build resembling that of a jockey. He was shorter than even his mother by a couple of inches. Whenever he saw the family together, Vikram wondered where Anirudh had acquired his rich nut-brown complexion, as both his parents were fairer than him.

When Vikram entered, the commander's pale features were flushed with anger. Beside him, Anirudh's mother, Smita Dongre, a slim, long-legged woman, was looking as if all the woes of the world were heaped on her shoulders. Her hands were working furiously as she clutched and twisted the strap of her handbag.

Commander Dongre looked up at Vikram. 'You are out of luck, young man,' he said, his tone blunt and abrupt. 'You don't have a partner for the final race. My son has backed out and his mother supports him. Finishing something that's been started doesn't matter to either of them, leave aside trifles like courage and valour. A puff of wind is enough to blow away family pride.'

Smita Dongre was a pleasant-faced lady with large dimpled cheeks and heavy lips. She prised open her ample lips in protest, but Vikram interjected before she could speak. 'Can I have a word in private with Anirudh, please? As his partner, I'd like to talk to him.'

The commander shrugged. His wife nodded. Her grey eyes were filled with unshed tears. She tried unsuccessfully to smile.

Aditya and Anirudh's families had known each other for years. Their fathers had met as young men at NDA and had graduated together as officers. As luck would have it, after several years of service, Commander Dongre had been posted back to NDA. Aditya had been delighted at the news of the posting and had chosen to spend his summer holidays there. Vikram had tagged along and the two of them were guests of the commander and his wife.

As they stepped out of the commander's office, it struck Vikram that even a week together at Anirudh's home hadn't sparked any kind of chord between them. There was something about Anirudh's make-up, a kind of stand-offishness, which kept him at a distance from others. Even two days together in a cramped sailboat hadn't changed things. Anirudh was still an acquaintance rather than a friend.

Vikram settled Anirudh in a quiet area, on a patch of grass overlooking the lake. The wind snatched at their clothing and tore at their hair. White waves danced on the grey surface of the lake. Vikram grimaced inwardly. The weather certainly wasn't aiding his cause.

Vikram wasted no time, pitching into Anirudh in a no-nonsense manner. 'This is not happening, Anirudh. You can't back out of the race. No one does that. Your dad's absolutely right. It *is* a matter of pride.'

Anirudh did not speak. He stared in strained silence at the lake.

'You have to finish what you started, Anirudh,' went on Vikram. 'There's just one more race. Five out of six are done. The conditions are different, I agree. But that's part of the game. We have to take the good with the bad. We could capsize—'

Anirudh started violently.

'That's what's bothering you, isn't it? You'll have a life jacket strapped on, in case you're forgetting. The jackets we wear aren't fashion accessories. They have a purpose. They keep us afloat in case we capsize—'

Anirudh flinched again.

'Look, Anirudh, it's a lake we're sailing in, keep that in mind. This is not the sea. There's a difference . . . a huge difference. We have a shore here on every side of us. If things go wrong and we find ourselves in the water, swimming to a shore is as easy as walking there when you have your life jacket on. I'm not saying this just to make you happy . . . it's true, believe me. Put your faith and trust in your life jacket. That's what they're for.'

Vikram paused, but Anirudh did not respond. He sat rigidly, imitating an iceberg to perfection.

Shrugging, Vikram resumed his monologue. 'All right, Anirudh. I want you to listen to me. There are two things you have to get straight. The first is that I'm not going to let you back out of the race. I'm not! Get that into your head. I'll drag you to the boat if I have to.'

Anirudh started.

Vikram narrowed his eyes. 'Oh yes. I mean what I say and your dad will help me if you put up any resistance.'

Vikram paused, waiting for his threat to sink in. Then he softened his gaze and toned down his voice. 'The second thing I want you to know is that I am here to help you. The whole world knows you have a problem with water. You haven't kept it a secret, have you?' Vikram smiled. 'Now, here's my proposal. We're going to solve your problem—you and I together. I want you to trust me. I'll be there beside you if anything goes wrong. That's a solemn promise.'

Anirudh's gaze had dropped. He no longer stared at the lake. His head was down and his eyes were welling with tears.

'You confound me, Anirudh. Yes, you truly do. You are fantastic with horses, absolutely the best rider I've ever come across. And I'm not the only one who says so. Everyone at NDA would agree. I've seen you play polo and I've seen you jump on horseback. No ordinary person can do what you do. It takes a lot of courage. For someone who can exhibit such bravery on horses, your present breakdown makes no sense at all.

'Everyone has fears, Anirudh. Each and every person on this planet. If people say they don't, they're lying. There's nothing shameful about being scared. You think soldiers aren't afraid when they go to war? Of course, they are. Yet those same frightened men obey their call of duty. They go and fight; some even win medals. You think Virat Kohli did not fear fast bowlers when he started? He did. Every cricketer is afraid of getting injured. But Virat overcame whatever fears he had, and in spectacular fashion too. What about you, Anirudh? You are a natural with horses, but think back to your first time on horseback, your first jump. You must have been scared like everyone else. But you overcame it, didn't you? What I'm telling you, Anirudh, is that your fear of the water is no different. I want you to understand that this fear too can be conquered.'

Anirudh had gone still. Even though his gaze was directed at the ground, Vikram knew he had his attention.

'I am going to share with you a terrible fear that I had. It still troubles me. I haven't overcome it, but I've learnt to deal with it, and my life is that much more bearable because of it.'

Vikram drew a breath. 'My worst shortcoming is my fear of heights. I don't speak about this to anyone. No one other than my dad and Aditya knows. I have always been terrified of heights—so bad that even looking down a mild slope could reduce me to a shivering wreck. It was horrible. And like you, I hated myself for my fear. It was particularly agonizing for me because my first love is mountains and trekking. My phobia was hellish. It choked me. I felt hobbled, as if with chains. I was robbed of my greatest pleasure. You wouldn't believe how miserable I was—far worse than the condition you are in now.

'But I changed all that. Yes, I did, Anirudh, and I did it by forcing myself to confront my fear. After a particularly bad trek, I sat myself down and thought about it. I thought long and hard and concluded finally that I couldn't allow my fear to come between my passion and me. That was the turning point. It didn't happen overnight, I can tell you. Overcoming a phobia is far more complex than a simple mental decision. I had to recondition my mind, sweep away the cobwebs that had muddled my brain since childhood. It's all about combating the self, and I taught myself to battle hard. My legs would shake so fiercely that I would often collapse. My chest would freeze and my breathing would halt. Nightmares would haunt my sleep . . . but I persevered and I succeeded.'

Anirudh's head was up. He was gazing at Vikram, eyes riveted.

'I've shared my problem with you, Anirudh.' Vikram paused. 'It's your turn now.'

Anirudh swallowed. A storm of emotions buffeted him. Hesitancy and fear were obvious, but chief amongst them was shame. His lower lip began to shake. Then, with great effort, he spoke. He started hesitantly but gained confidence as Vikram looked on encouragingly. What started in trickles gained momentum and Anirudh's wretchedness gushed forth, pouring out as if a valve inside had been unplugged. Water terrified him, he confided, staring at his feet. He loathed himself for his weakness, but there was nothing he could do about it. Anger flashed in his eyes. 'I hate my fear. I hate it! It shames me.'

Vikram spoke soothingly. 'Your fear is natural. You aren't the only one. Almost everyone I know is scared of water.'

'You don't understand,' he said brokenly. 'My fear isn't rational. You have no idea what it's like. No one understands, least of all my father. He tossed me into a swimming pool when I was a baby.' Anirudh shuddered. A vein twitched on his forehead. 'I still get nightmares about it.

'You know what my father is like. Fear is a weakness for him. It has to be banished. Mom tried to stop him when she saw I was suffering, but he brushed her aside. Dad is a natural in water. He is brilliant at every water sport. He was a national-level water polo player. He represented India in swimming meets and he is one of India's best sailors. For him, it wasn't just about my learning to swim. I had to be the best—it was a matter of pride. Dad forced me into the water every day. I learnt how to swim, but my fear refused to go away. In fact, it became worse. Later, Dad tried to teach me how to sail too, but I wasn't up to it. Dad knows now that I will never be like him. But he is bitter about it. You think I wanted to take part in this regatta? Not a chance. It was Dad who bulldozed me into participating.'

Anirudh paused, choking back tears.

Vikram waited.

'I've tried my best. You have seen how I have performed these last few days. I managed to put my fears behind me, and it was a wonderful feeling. I thought I had freed myself of my terror . . . but it wasn't as simple as that. I know now that I was only fooling myself. The weather was good the first two days. It's different now. There are waves and . . .'

Anirudh shook, 'the wind . . .'—he swallowed—'my fear . . . it's back . . . I can't control it. There is a storm out there on the lake and the boat can capsize anytime.'

Anirudh's face darkened, matching the shade of the clouds. He lowered his voice and Vikram had to strain his ears. 'My worst memory is when a boat capsized on me. It was a mild day and my father was on shore, not paying attention, but the wind gusted suddenly and before I could react, the boat overturned, trapping me underneath. I was in the water and there was this lid above me . . . like a tomb . . . blocking out the sun and the sky.' He trembled. 'Dad says I could have ducked and swum out from under, but that's easy for him, different for others. The hull was like a suffocating blanket above me—'

Anirudh was disintegrating.

'Forget about claustrophobia,' Vikram interjected forcefully. 'Banish that thought from your head. You are not going to be trapped beneath the boat. I'm there with you. We've been sailing continuously for three days. I was shaky this morning, I admit, but we sailed well and nothing went wrong. I can handle these winds. We'll be okay, Anirudh, believe me.'

Vikram spoke at length. He talked about life, about the weather, about sailing and why Anirudh's fears were unfounded. Anirudh needed someone to talk to him. He responded well to honest, heartfelt talk. It was a pity that his father and he were antagonistic to one another. Commander Dongre, as a parent and a champion sailor, was best equipped to deal with his son and restore his confidence. Vikram, as a friend, could only fill in.

Smita, her face pale and drawn, watched the boys anxiously from her husband's cabin. Kiran arrived to call them for lunch, but Vikram shooed him away. He convinced Anirudh that even if the wind defeated him and the boat capsized, nothing could possibly go wrong. He would make sure that the hull of the boat did not trap them. They would float in comfort. Vikram vouched he would make it fun if they were forced into the water. He promised that he would never leave his side.

Anirudh finally consented to take part. His parents were relieved with his decision and when the commander hugged his son, Smita squeezed Vikram's hand. They enjoyed a light lunch in the commander's cabin. Vikram then requested privacy for a nap and convinced Anirudh to rest before the race too. Anirudh's parents left the room and Vikram fell asleep as soon as his head touched the sofa.

STORM-SEALED FRIENDSHIP

Anirudh's face was tense an hour later when Vikram and his father escorted him to the jetties. Commander Dongre watched critically as they rigged their boat. They were almost done when Chitra turned up.

'Is this your friend, Anirudh?' she asked, halting beside them.

The droop suddenly vanished from Anirudh's shoulders. He shook hands with Chitra when Vikram introduced him. 'This is Commander Dongre,' continued Vikram, turning to Anirudh's father. 'He is our host, and this wonderful bay and the sailing facilities are run by him.'

Chitra's eyes lit up. 'Wow! All these boats and your father in charge of them. Anirudh, you are a lucky man.'

'He's making use of the opportunity.' Commander Dongre smiled, covering smoothly for his son. 'Vikram and Aditya have spoken a lot about you, Chitra. My wife wants to meet you too. She wants to invite you to join us for dinner tonight. She's at the spectator tent. Shall we go there? We can watch the last race together.'

Anirudh's eyes weren't dull any more. Vikram didn't try figuring out what had brought about the change; he was simply thankful for having a sunny, helpful partner. Aditya and Kiran's boat pulled away from the jetty. Anirudh yelled and waved at them. Vikram cast off and they followed, their sail fluttering and hull creaking as their boat cut through the dark waters of the bay.

A tongue of land jutted like a breakwater to starboard, sheltering the waters of the bay, and though the lake was only gently ruffled where they sailed, ahead, beyond the protective barrier, there were waves and a deep swell. A strong wind was sweeping the lake and dark clouds were mobbing the sky.

'Prepare yourself,' hollered Vikram. 'Action stations! The wind is going to belt us when we hit open water.'

The lake turned restless and suddenly, like a howling express train, the wind was upon them. The boat shuddered, listing sharply to port.

'Hike out!' screamed Vikram, as he pulled the rudder and trimmed the sail.

Anirudh leaned out across the water, his eyes closed.

The competition had elevated Vikram's skill at the helm several fold and a delicious thrill of accomplishment coursed through him as his Enterprise class sailboat shot forward. The speed of the vessel was heady, the fastest he had ever achieved on a boat. They were scything forward as if jet-propelled.

The upper half of Anirudh's body was hiked out across the water. The brilliant orange of his life jacket contrasted brightly against the asphalt-black water. His long hair was wet and his face seemed calm, exhibiting no sign of fear.

The white wake of their Enterprise boat was one of several streaking the lake. Sails flapped noisily everywhere and whoops of exhilaration reverberated across the lake. Amongst sailors, there is only one climatic condition that stokes wild enthusiasm and excitement: the wind. This was a genuine wind, and its tumultuous presence was conjuring a grand setting for the regatta's final race.

It wasn't long before their boat neared the far shore of the lake. Vikram tacked around and Anirudh responded like a seasoned professional, shifting smoothly to the opposite sideboard and adjusting his body weight perfectly.

An imaginary line between two buoys was the starting zone for the race and boats were already massing there. Their colourful sails seemed butterfly-like as they clustered about the invisible line. The race was to start at 3.30 p.m. and Vikram's watch indicated it was time to join the butterflies and hover between the starting posts.

Loud voices greeted them as they fell in with the boats prowling the start zone.

'We're going to thrash you, Vikram!'

'Give yourself a break, Anirudh, you're shaking like the sails.'

'You're a crummy sailor, Vikram. The wind is going to sink you.'

'Best of luck, buddy.'

Though the banter sometimes sounded coarse, it was always conducted in good spirit. Vikram sparred with his mates as they manoeuvred in tight circles beside the start line.

'You can still back out, Remy,' shouted Vikram. 'You're going to capsize again for sure.'

Pointing at a sail that seemed slightly askew, he cried, 'That's the worst rigging I've ever seen, Gopal.'

Anirudh joined in, shouting lustily. 'You Goa bunch only know how to climb coconut trees. Sailing is far too complicated for you.'

'Anirudh,' sounded a call from port. It was Umaji, the bearded sailor from Goa. 'Look up, Anirudh, look at the sky.' Anirudh turned to look up and Vikram saw his face suddenly blanch. 'Ha, ha!' chortled Umaji from his boat. 'I knew that would get him. Look at him, he's going to be sick.'

Vikram's heart skipped a beat when he looked up. The sky had turned black. So black that it wasn't possible to tell the clouds apart. There was just one band of the deepest darkness he had ever seen. Vikram noticed suddenly that the wind had dropped. There was a thundery feel to the air. It seemed to spark and sizzle, as if electrified.

An angry shout suddenly erupted beside Vikram. 'Watch yourself!'

Losing concentration, he had almost steered his vessel into another boat. A quick thrust of rudder averted disaster. As he opened his mouth to voice an apology, a gun boomed.

The race had begun!

'Hike out,' shouted Vikram, tilting the boat into a beat.

Anirudh leaned out obediently, his body parallel to the water.

Like racehorses fresh from their boxes, boats fanned forward as they crossed the starting line. Though the wind had dropped, it was still strong enough to propel them at a lively speed. The skilled sailors quickly detached themselves from the huddle, speeding ahead and establishing preliminary leads.

A whistle shrieked loudly.

'"Number 29"!' blared a foghorn-like voice. 'Foul for touching "Number 31"; two circles penalty.'

Commander Motivala, the referee, hawk-eyed as usual, had noticed an infringement. In deepening gloom, Vikram spotted the flashing hull of his motorized speedboat as it darted away. The collision had taken place where the boats in front were executing their first tack.

The wind suddenly picked up, doubling in strength. Vikram reacted swiftly, releasing the mainsail and spilling the wind as his boat lurched sickeningly. There was a shout ahead. Looking up, Vikram saw that 'Number 29', in the midst of its penalty, had been caught broadside by the blast. There was no hope for the crew. Struggling to prevent his vessel from suffering the same fate, Vikram managed only a glimpse of the stricken boat as it keeled over.

An ear-numbing explosion detonated overhead. Thunder! The storm was breaking. The wind suddenly went wild. The sail began to thrash and pull. It was as if an alien force was plucking it from Vikram's hands. His arms felt as if they might pop from their sockets, and though he hung on as long as he could, he was forced to let go.

'WATCH OUT!' he screamed.

Anirudh could have lost his head if it had been in the path of the scything boom, but Vikram needn't have wasted his breath as he was seated on the opposite flank of the boat. Unfettered now, the sail generated a tremendous din as it flapped uselessly in the tearing wind. Yet, despite the loss of its power, the boat cruised on at express speed. The jib sail! The tiny jib sail—still tethered to a cleat—was propelling the boat. But the wind was too strong and the jib sail rope was wrenching violently. Vikram reached forward instinctively but held himself. To get to the sail, he would have to release the rudder, which would be suicidal.

'ANIRUDH!' he thundered. It was a cry of despair as he did not expect his partner to react. But Anirudh rose heroically to the occasion. Reaching forward, he yanked the rope from the cleats and hung on to it.

Vikram struggled manfully with the rudder, somehow holding course. The entire boat was vibrating. They were shooting through the water at a dizzying speed. But they were straying off course.

'We're going to have to turn!' hollered Vikram over the banshee-like howl of the wind. 'It has to be now or we will run into the shore. Ready?'

Anirudh's eyes were large as he stared at Vikram, but he nodded.

'NOW!' shouted Vikram, wrenching the rudder and forcing the nose of the boat through the wind. Clasping the jib rope, Anirudh nimbly changed sides as the boat turned and both of them ducked as the mainsail swept across the deck. The jib sail caught the wind, propelling them forward again.

Vikram's tension and fear evaporated. He couldn't believe it. The storm should have alarmed and intimidated him. Yet he was enjoying himself. Anirudh too was smiling hesitantly. Not only had they survived but they had also mastered the crazy wind. The mainsail was thrashing about like an untamed beast. The miracle was the jib sail. The tiny piece of fabric, ineffectual at the best of times, was powering the boat on its own. And what incredible power! It was as if they were on board a jet ski at full throttle.

'Yo! Vikram, Anirudh!'

Though half-lost in the rampaging wind, the voice was unmistakably Aditya's. Probing the murky expanse, Vikram spotted his boat, way up in front, already at the end of the next tack. Aditya was pumping his fist and Kiran was waving. Unbelievably, they were using their mainsail. Vikram was waving at them when their boat and every other boat suddenly vanished.

Rain, like a dark fog, descended on the lake. It was as if sluice gates in the heavens above had been cast open. Thick shafts of water speared down forcefully, like a stinging mist, obscuring everything. The world shrank. Anirudh was reduced to a blur and everything beyond was an inscrutable grey. The lake began to heave. There was a swell, several feet deep, and there were waves. Yet, despite the cloudburst, their sturdy Enterprise soldiered on. Harnessing wind energy equivalent to a high-powered outboard motor, the wisp-like jib sail motored them through the swell, thrusting them over the peaks and hurrying them through the troughs.

The boats about them were simply shadows. There was no trace of the hills surrounding the lake. The shore was probably the darker shade at ground level. The alpha buoy, which marked the first turn of the race, had disappeared. But having sailed so many races, Vikram had a fair idea where it was.

The storm intensified as they tacked from beat to beat, moving steadily upwind. Thunder detonated and when lightning flashed, it momentarily banished the fog of darkness. The flickering bursts unveiled a frightening spectacle. Several boats were down, their crews clinging to their upturned hulls. But an equal number were still upright and tearing through the water.

A few tacks later, a dazzling bolt illuminated the alpha buoy. It wasn't far, and it was clear that they would reach it on their next tack.

Anirudh had seen it too. 'Alpha buoy coming up,' he cried.

'Prepare yourself,' roared Vikram. 'It's going to be tricky. We have to watch that we don't overpower the boat.'

The dark shadow of the shore drew closer as they approached the buoy. The area between the shore and the buoy was where they had to execute the turn. As the buoy drew near, Vikram spotted the white shadow of Commander Motivala's boat. He often took position beside buoys, making sure no one cheated by turning before they reached them.

Vikram saw that Anirudh was ready. 'You're doing great,' he complimented, shouting to make himself heard.

'We'd have been in the water if it wasn't for your grabbing the jib sail.'

Anirudh's crooked smile surprised Vikram. But his smile suddenly froze as the boat ahead of them floundered at the buoy. Vikram steered away from the stricken boat. The shadow of the buoy loomed larger as their boat barrelled forward. They drew parallel with it and then they were past it.

'Now!' bellowed Vikram, yanking the rudder.

Rope in hand, Anirudh leapt to the port side as the Enterprise came to a halt. As Vikram struggled with the rudder, he saw the rope in Anirudh's hand turn taut. The boat was swinging rapidly, far too rapidly. The sail was pulling as if there was a tiger trapped beneath it. They had messed the turn and at their current angle, the wind was bound to overpower the sail.

'LET THE SAIL GO!' screamed Vikram.

But it all happened too fast. One moment the mast was upright and the next it was plunging to the water, with Anirudh hanging on to the sail rope. The boat tilted sharply. Its port gunwale went under and water surged across the deck. Anirudh was already in the lake, flailing above the sunken mast. The tilting deck turned vertical, and faced with no alternative, Vikram turned towards Anirudh and leapt into the water.

'ANIRUDH!' he yelled, his first concern for his partner. Surfacing, Vikram blinked away the water and saw Anirudh still clinging to the sail rope and the cavernous hull toppling towards him. Anirudh's face was terror-stricken and his eyes were shut. He couldn't see the hull and had no idea that his nightmare was fast turning to reality. Vikram had judged his leap from the boat well and was right beside Anirudh. Grabbing Anirudh's life jacket, he pulled with all his strength. The hull was tumbling in slow motion. Anirudh's head was still below it. His eyes were open and he was staring at it. Vikram yanked again, lunging backwards. The hull swept down, gathering momentum. Vikram had time for one more almighty tug, and the boat settled in the water, barely six inches from Anirudh.

Vikram did not let up. He kept pulling, dragging Anirudh away from the upturned hull. When he let go, Anirudh grabbed Vikram's shoulder, fingers digging hard. Vikram turned. Anirudh's mouth was open and he was gagging as the swell kept breaking over his face.

Vikram grabbed his friend's jacket, pulling him closer. 'RELAX!' he shouted. 'Your life jacket's working fine. Don't fight the swell. Float with it. Let it carry you.'

Vikram was pleasantly surprised by Anirudh's response. He was prepared for histrionics and thrashing arms and legs, but Anirudh simply nodded. Though he still clung to Vikram's shoulder, his grip eased considerably. His other hand floated limply and his struggle against the swell ceased.

Around them, the rain and the wind continued as before. The spray from the pounding rain bounced off the water, stinging their eyes and faces. There were waves and the lake was bucking insanely. Continuing the race seemed impossible. Even if he somehow managed to get the boat upright, the waterlogged hull would render it sluggish and the wind would topple it again. And besides, Anirudh was in no state to continue. The race was over for them, decided Vikram. They would have to float and wait for rescue.

The buoy had disappeared. All Vikram could see was their upturned hull; impenetrable darkness obliterated everything beyond. A current was dragging them and it was impossible to tell where they were drifting. The lake waters were surprisingly warm. On board the boat, the rain had stung and the wind had chilled Vikram. But now that his body was submerged, he was actually quite comfortable. It was possible to enjoy the storm, even though he was ensnared in its powerful midst.

Striking a conversation in the thunder and rain was next to impossible. Vikram kept glancing at Anirudh, winking and smiling each time he caught his eye. After a while, Anirudh's grip on his shoulder eased and then fell away altogether. Vikram turned and was flabbergasted to see him smile and wink. Anirudh leaned forward awkwardly, bringing his mouth to Vikram's ear.

'. . . not scared . . .' Vikram could barely catch his words as the swell kicked and reared about them. 'life jackets are good . . . not far from shore.'

Vikram shook his head, not believing what he was hearing. He winked and Anirudh winked back. Vikram laughed and raised his hand and Anirudh reached out, clasping his. It seemed far-fetched, but it was true. On a storm-swept lake, in heaving, frothing water, Anirudh was coming to terms with his fear.

Anirudh did not bother to hold on to Vikram again. They passed time companionably, floating side by side, cocooned by the rain and the lake. Though it seemed like an hour, it was barely fifteen minutes before a rescue boat came for them.

Rafiq, the burly chief tindal, was on board and beside him was a short man in sodden trousers and shirt. The short man seemed uneasy and clearly uncomfortable in the midst of the storm. Taking no part in the rescue, he watched as Rafiq plucked the boys out of the lake. Anirudh had lost his shoes in the water. His legs were distinctly unsteady and he slipped and fell on the heaving deck. Rafiq was busy issuing instructions to the pilot of the boat, and it was the short man who reached out to help Anirudh. The man seemed to freeze when he stretched to grab Anirudh's hand.

One finger on each of Anirudh's hands was permanently bent—a defect he was born with. Vikram saw the man recover and as he helped Anirudh to his feet, he stared at the boy's bare legs. There was a toe missing from each of Anirudh's feet, another birth defect, and the man tottered and almost fell as he gazed. The boat jerked forward, gathering speed, and Vikram attributed the man's lurch to the sudden jolt of the vessel. From the prow of the boat, Rafiq called loudly. The hull of another upturned Enterprise had been spotted. Settling Anirudh gently on the deck, the short man rushed to join Rafiq.

Five other crews were rescued before the boat returned to the bay. There was complete chaos on the jetties. Chitra embraced Vikram. Anirudh's mother clung to her son as if he had returned from a battlefield. His father pumped Vikram's fist and then hugged his son. Commander Dongre couldn't spend much time with them, but before leaving, he informed them that the storm had forced the cancellation of the race. Almost every boat was down and a full-fledged salvage and rescue operation was underway.

Everyone on shore was sopping wet. The awning that shaded the spectators had been snatched away by the winds, explained Chitra. Pulling Vikram aside, she told him how Smita Dongre had turned pale and sick with fear for her son when the winds and the rain had swept the lake. She had broken down when thunder and lightning erupted and the winds breached storm levels. Vikram explained Anirudh's fear of water to Chitra and the guilt his parents must have felt when the conditions turned dangerous.

Rescue boats sped back and forth across the bay and Chitra, Vikram and Anirudh turned anxious when neither Aditya nor Kiran arrived on any of them. They came in finally on the last boat with scowls and anger on their faces. The storm had capsized their Enterprise four times, but on each occasion, with heroic effort and determination, they had managed to right their vessel and keep going. They were certain they could have completed the course, but Rafiq, mouthing dire threats, worried more about his precious boat than their safety, had forced them to abandon the race. It wasn't fair, they protested. They had been denied a golden opportunity to complete the course in the teeth of a storm.

So ended the eventful regatta. Aditya and Kiran finished a laudable fourth in the overall standings. Vikram and Anirudh were proud of their thirty-fifth-place finish. Except for a few minor injuries everyone had been lucky to escape the storm. Every boat had capsized during the final race and several had to be junked because of the damage they sustained.

The commander took the loss of his boats philosophically. It was worth it, according to him. The boys had been privileged to witness such a storm from ground zero, he said. Vikram, Aditya and Kiran were entirely in agreement with him, and to the commander's everlasting amazement, Anirudh endorsed his sentiments too. It had been an incredible adventure for the boys, but for Vikram and Anirudh, the experience had been far more profound. On the storm-riven lake, a friendship that would last a lifetime had taken seed.

MONSOON PLANS

It was retired Colonel Ishwar Arora, a close friend of Commander Dongre and Aditya's father, who hit upon the idea of a monsoon trek.

Commander Dongre instantly approved his suggestion. 'Trekking is a great idea,' he said. 'The perfect antidote to sitting here and crying about the weather.'

It had been raining continuously for two weeks. The storm on the lake had heralded the much-awaited arrival of the monsoon. Like a marauding army, a legion of angry dark clouds intruded the skies, entrenching themselves over Pune and the neighbouring Sahyadri Mountains. The invasion was sudden and complete. Where once there had been blue skies and sunshine, now there was darkness and a ceaseless flood of rain.

It was evening and sure enough, rain was moistening NDA's extensive campus located at the western edge of Pune, where the level expanses of the Deccan Plateau yield to the hills of the Sahyadri Range. The commander's home was tucked in a lush green corner of the campus. The boys and the officers were unwinding on his bungalow's veranda after an energetic session at the squash courts. Smita Dongre and Chitra were present too. Chitra was mildly grumpy as she had arrived late on account of the traffic-choked roads of Pune city, and had missed out on playing with the boys. Smita Dongre, however, had enjoyed a lively contest with them. Calm and relaxed, she betrayed none of the exertions she had wrung her body through, humbling Vikram first in a heady game of squash that could have gone either way, and then successfully countering Aditya's challenge, holding him to a hard-fought draw.

'The monsoons are the best time,' continued Ishwar, buoyed by his friend's support. 'Finest season of the Sahyadris. It's the rains. They transform the landscape. The monsoon wind is special too. It can sweep you off your feet if you're not careful. And there's mist everywhere with the clouds descending on the mountains. It's so beautiful. It's hard to imagine till you actually see it.'

Ishwar Uncle, as Aditya addressed him, was the third in a company of staunch friends that included Commander Vikas Dongre and Aditya's father. The trio had bonded at NDA where they had been batchmates, and their attachment to one another, despite the years, was still as fresh as the day they had first met.

Anirudh wasn't particularly impressed. 'Sure,' he said. 'Of course, since we aren't aquatic we'll have to burden ourselves with raincoats and boots and hats to fight off the rain. Enjoyable for fish and ducks, I'm sure. For us too, that's if we develop scales or webbed feet.'

Smita frowned at her son. 'Anirudh! There's no need to speak like that.'

'Look at the rain, Mom. It's hopeless, we'll get washed away.'

'He's right,' said Ishwar, placating Smita who was glaring at her son. 'It's certainly too wet right now, but I've checked the Met report and it forecasts a break in the weather.'

'That's great news!' exclaimed Aditya. 'Perfect. We could start skydiving then.'

Skydiving was Ishwar's passion, one of many adventurous pastimes he loved. Although middle-aged, Ishwar was gifted with strength and extraordinary athleticism. After passing out of the Academy, he had been a key member of several army expeditions that had conquered the peaks of the Himalayas. In the later part of his career, during a stint in an elite commando division, Ishwar had developed a passion for skydiving. The sport had captivated him, and with a view of starting an adventure sports company specializing in aerial recreation, Ishwar had put in his papers barely a month earlier, retiring from the Services to pursue his goal. He owned a house in Pune, not far from NDA, and had only just returned from Delhi after completing his retirement formalities.

Ishwar dismissed Aditya's skydiving plea. 'The weather has to be far more settled for skydiving. Sure, you want to be airborne, Aditya, but I have things to worry about. Mundane matters like safety. Inconsequential to you, no doubt—but if ignored can not only threaten your life but also pull the curtain on my career as an instructor even before it has begun. Your eagerness is blinding you, young man. Push back on the pedal a bit. Relax. There are other pleasures in the Sahyadris. Blink and you will see them. I'll repeat once more—the Sahyadris are magnificent during the monsoons. Explore them.'

A bearer wearing a white apron and carrying a tray laden with cups and a kettle, stepped on to the veranda.

Smita spoke in Marathi. 'Here,' she said, smiling and pointing at a table. 'Pour us the tea please, Salim.'

There was a pause as they waited for Salim to serve everyone. Salim was the short man who had rescued Vikram and Anirudh after their boat had capsized. Unlike on that stormy day when he was soaked to the bone, Salim looked smart now in white clothes and an apron. A grey beard masked the lower section of his face. Thick salt-and-pepper hair was brushed neatly behind his ears.

Salim had secured a job at the Dongre household thanks to Rafiq, the tindal who served at Peacock Bay. Aware that the Dongres were short-staffed, Rafiq had sent Salim across on the day following the storm.

'I'm for trekking,' declared Vikram, pitching for the excursion after Salim departed. 'Chitra can't stop harping about Torna. Let's climb the mountain.'

Chitra's face lit up. 'Great idea!' she exclaimed.

Torna was one of many spectacular forts that guarded the summits of the Sahyadri Mountains. Chitra had scaled and explored the fort during her expedition with her colleagues at the Snake Park and had raved about her experience to the boys.

Aditya lifted his eyes to the sky. 'Vikram is always the guy with the ideas, isn't he?'

'You are perfectly right, Aditya,' said Chitra, ignoring Aditya's sarcasm. 'And his ideas are good, unlike yours. What say we make it an overnight trip? There's a temple up there with a roof that will keep us dry. It'll be fun.'

Aditya snorted. 'Don't get taken in by Chitra, Vikram. The fort's just an excuse to search for your slithery friends, isn't it?'

The mention of snakes caused Anirudh to flinch, not very noticeably, but Vikram, who was sitting beside him, saw. He also saw Smita turn and glance at her son. Her hands twitched in her lap.

Chitra stared irritably at Aditya. 'I don't know what you're trying to get at,' she snapped. 'Of course, I'll search for snakes, but what's that got to do with the trek? Torna is a fabulous fort. Everybody will enjoy it, believe me.'

Ishwar endorsed Torna unreservedly. 'Great choice,' he affirmed. 'Torna is awesome. The best fort in the region, my personal favourite. I've tried to tempt the Dongres to climb it, but they've always found a reason not to.'

'Here we go again,' said Commander Dongre, pretending to yawn. 'This guy's always going on about us, Smita.'

'And with good reason,' said Ishwar. 'You can't deny I've tried, Vikas—almost every fortnight—but not once have I managed to drag even a single Dongre to the mountains, not even Anirudh.'

'Hey!' protested Anirudh. 'That isn't fair, Ishwar Uncle. Not like I sit at home and do nothing. I ride, you know.'

'Sure, you ride. You Dongres are a gifted bunch. Sport is imprinted in your genes! But it's the mountains I'm talking about and it's only excuses I get when it comes to the Sahyadris. Your family has been posted at NDA a year already and not once have any of you accompanied me.'

Commander Dongre shook his dignified grey head. 'I'll have you know, Ishwar, that I am an officer and a sailor, and my wife, as a professor at Deccan College, handles a demanding job. We're both working, not retired like you.'

A smile flitted across Ishwar's face. 'I'm going to make you a wager, Vikas.' He paused theatrically, like a magician about to conjure a magic trick. 'This audience is my witness,' he declared. 'Hear this, everyone. I'm willing to bet five thousand rupees that neither you nor Smita will accompany the kids even this time.'

Smita tapped an elegant hand on her forehead. 'This man sure missed out on his true profession. What a melodramatic performance. He should have been on stage.'

'Hear, hear!' applauded Commander Dongre, clapping loudly.

'Grown-ups,' said Aditya in an undertone, winking at Vikram.

'I heard that, Aditya,' said Smita, glowering at him before turning to Ishwar. 'This break in the weather you speak of,' she went on, 'when is it supposed to take place?'

'In a couple of days,' replied Ishwar. 'Maybe even tomorrow.'

Commander Dongre snorted. 'You've got it all wrong, Smita. This man isn't just an actor. He's an unashamed rogue too. That's the most one-sided bet that's ever been proposed. You know darned well, Ishwar, that there's a delegation from Kazakhstan visiting NDA next week and that the Commandant has cancelled leave for senior officers while they are here.'

Ishwar dismissed Commander Dongre's protestations with a contemptuous wave. 'And what's your excuse, Smita?' He turned to her, a smug expression on his face. 'Wait, let me guess. You are the professor of history at the illustrious Deccan College of Archaeology. It's exam time at your college. It's got to be exams. And sitting in Delhi I knew about them, just as I knew of the Kazakhstan delegation as your husband alleges.'

Smita laughed. 'You're a rascal, Ishwar, enjoying yourself at our expense as usual. Three students are defending their PhD theses this week. There's not a hope of me getting even a half-day off. I have to be there, but—' she paused, smiling sweetly, 'but you, Mr Dependable, will be there as always and can look after them.'

The smile exited Ishwar's face. 'I'm busy too this week,' he said, his voice suddenly sheepish. 'That's why I've been trying to rope you two in.'

Commander Dongre hooted loudly, clapping his hands. 'That's rich!' he cried. 'Really rich, coming after your holier-than-thou attitude. Who's ducking the mountains now?'

Ishwar looked reprovingly at his friend. 'It might come as a surprise to you, Vikas, but even retired officers are busy. I have to start a business and there's tons of paperwork to be done, which simply cannot wait.'

'Wow!' exclaimed Aditya, turning to Chitra and Vikram. 'No adults. Count me in, guys. I'm certainly coming along.'

'And Anirudh too?' asked Chitra, turning to him.

Anirudh shuffled his legs. 'I haven't ridden in a while; there's been no opportunity. Good weather will give me—'

Commander Dongre turned on his son. 'No excuses!' he snapped harshly. Too harshly, thought Vikram. 'No riding for you. You are going with them whether you like it or not.'

Anirudh's mother reacted swiftly. 'It's a great opportunity, son,' she said in a gentle voice that sharply contrasted her husband's. 'Your friends are with you. You will all have a good time together.'

'We certainly will,' said Vikram. 'My dad has said that the Sahyadris are great. Ishwar Uncle and Chitra can't stop raving about them. We'll have a blast, Anirudh.'

'And don't forget we have Chitra with us,' chipped in Aditya. 'She'll look after us. No snakes, no problems . . . nothing to worry about.'

Chitra stared at Aditya, unsure whether he was being sincere or sarcastic.

'Is it necessary to stay overnight?' inquired Smita. 'Torna is a day trek, everyone says. You can return by evening.'

'No!' exclaimed Chitra. 'That will reduce the outing to an ordinary walk. It's the staying-the-night part that's fun.'

Smita clenched her hands. 'Then you'll need somebody to look after you. You can't spend the night out on your own.'

Chitra goggled disbelievingly.

'Come on, Smita.' Ishwar shook his head. 'Stop being a grandmother. They are old enough to stay out on their own. Didn't these kids camp in the Andaman Islands and the Himalayas? Torna will be a piece of cake for them.'

Smita's eyes flashed. 'Keep out of this one, Ishwar. You have no idea what it's like to be a parent! An adult has to accompany them.'

Commander Dongre backed his wife. 'I know what happened to these kids in the Andamans, Ishwar. They landed themselves in serious trouble. The same story in the Himalayas, they got away by the skin of their teeth. His dad, Abbas—' the commander pointed at Aditya, 'sent them to me with firm instructions: "Look after them like little children".'

Chitra gaped at the commander. Aditya and Vikram looked incredulously at one another.

'Come off it, Vikas,' said Ishwar. 'That's rubbish. Abbas worries too much. Use that head of yours instead. Look at Aditya and Vikram. They are capable and confident young men. Their expeditions to every corner of India have seasoned them. And have you seen a stronger and more competent young woman than Chitra? A little bit of danger . . . tricky situations . . . what's wrong with that, it's what makes men and women out of them.'

'Ishwar,' said Smita, in a measured voice, as if addressing an errant schoolboy. 'If I wasn't aware of your background, I might have heeded your advice. However, I happen to know of the umpteen times you've risked your life during wars and how you readily volunteer for frontline assignments—the more dangerous, the better for you. Your deeds are all very creditable and have won you several medals, but they also illustrate your bindaas, couldn't-care-less attitude to danger. I'd be the biggest fool on this planet if I heeded your advice regarding the safety of children. The youngsters are our responsibility while they live with us. They are going to require an escort and if we don't find one, their expedition is as good as off.'

Looking skyward, Ishwar raised his hands in surrender.

Chitra's face had turned red. Aditya breathed deeply. Vikram felt cheated. Anirudh alone seemed to perk up.

Commander Dongre snapped his fingers. 'I have an idea. What about Salim? He is from the area. He says his home is near Mahabaleshwar. That can't be too far from Torna. He could be their escort.'

Smita pursed her lips uncertainly. 'He seems all right, but he's new . . . We don't know him well enough.'

'Rafiq vouched for him,' countered her husband. 'Speak to Salim, Smita. He could solve our problem if he agrees to the outing.'

Smita stood up. Easing her way through the tangle of chairs, she made her way to the hall.

Aditya sat up. 'How about Kiran? He lives in Pune and has holidays till the Academy opens again. I'm sure he'll come along if I ask him.'

'By all means,' said the commander. 'He's a good boy, a final-term cadet. Ishwar, what do you think?'

'A sixth-termer would be an asset to any team,' said Ishwar. 'No question about it. The boys are young and strong and trained for handling whatever comes their way.' A smile came to him and he winked at the boys and Chitra. 'The kids don't have to restrict themselves to one night if they have him along, Vikas. They can extend their trip and explore other areas if they have an NDA cadet with them.'

Commander Dongre chuckled. 'Don't push it, Ishwar. You have Smita to contend with.'

Chitra crossed to where Vikram and Aditya sat while they waited for Smita to return. 'Did your dad really speak about us like that?' she asked Aditya. 'To look after us like babies?'

'He did,' admitted Aditya.

'You can't blame him, can you?' said Vikram. 'It is the truth. We keep getting into trouble.'

'Yeah,' sighed Aditya. 'Dad wasn't kidding. I was told that we can do what we want in NDA, but going out requires adult supervision. I'm not hopeful about the trek. I wouldn't bet on our being allowed to go. The commander seems okay, I think, but Smita Aunty is a tough one.'

'She's a toughie all right,' agreed Chitra. 'I can tell.'

'Then let's be philosophical about it if we're not allowed,' said Vikram.

'Philosophical, my foot!' exploded Chitra. 'We're not children.'

'Look, I feel as bad about this as you do, Chitra,' Vikram spoke placatingly. 'But NDA's not the worst place to be stuck in. We're spoilt for sporting choice here—cricket, football, hockey, squash, badminton, tennis, basketball—name your sport and we can play it here.'

'You're forgetting the horses,' grinned Aditya. 'There are loads of horses here and polo grounds too.' He turned to Anirudh. 'You better teach us how to play polo if your mom cancels the trip.'

'His mom isn't cancelling the trip,' said Smita, striding into the room. 'It was never my intention. Vikas and I aren't rakshasas. All we're insisting upon is adult supervision. You can all thank Salim. He has agreed to accompany you . . . so it's settled. Come on in, now. I'm serving dinner early. Chitra has to get back.'

And so their trip to the Sahyadris was finalized.

TORNA

The Sahyadri Mountains that lie to the west and south of Pune were once the home of the great warrior king Shivaji. Their brooding cliffs, their spiny ridges and their deep, winding valleys were his childhood playground, and it was in their embrace that he achieved his manhood. He knew every intricacy of their rugged terrain and could effortlessly hide entire armies in a chasm of rock or fold of mountain. A combination of his famed bravery and his intimate knowledge of the area rendered him invincible, as the sultans and emperors of his time discovered to their cost.

Several forts straddle the summits of the Sahyadris, many of them predating Shivaji. Recognizing their significance, the astute king refurbished and strengthened their fortifications. Employing his celebrated military acumen, he brilliantly exploited their strategic potential to repulse and rout vastly stronger armies. Located in the heart of his kingdom, Torna was Shivaji's first fort, the launch pad of his epic military campaign.

A pleasant evening drive from NDA through farmlands and green countryside brought Vikram and his friends to a pass, from which they dropped into a lush valley bounded by mountains whose summits were buried in cloud. One of the mountains was Torna, and though Chitra identified it for the boys, the tenacious cloud, as if safeguarding a mythical realm, refused to reveal its fortified contours. A village with tile-roofed dwellings and a sparkling temple dome nestled at the base of the mountain, and after a short ride across the valley, they turned on to a bumpy road that terminated not far from the freshly painted temple. Chitra directed the driver along the final stretch, halting the vehicle at a deserted square, skirted on one side by bland government buildings and simple tenements on the other.

'This is it,' she said, stretching as she stepped out of the car. 'The village of Velhe. Our climb starts here.'

Amongst the government buildings stood a concrete cabin with a rusted signboard identifying it as a police station. The door and window to the cabin were open, but it seemed unmanned as there was no light inside. Opposite, stood a low flat structure, a restaurant according to the panel above it. A short man with a disproportionately large pair of spectacles perched on his nose stepped out of the restaurant and greeted Chitra with a smile and folded palms.

Bowing politely, Chitra engaged the man in conversation. When she was done, she turned to the others. 'This is Anand, the proprietor of the restaurant,' she announced. 'He serves *asli* local khana, but since it's late and we're carrying packed dinner, I told him we'll pass for now, if that's okay with everyone.'

Kiran looked up at the overcast sky. 'The light isn't going to last. I'm all for starting immediately.' He turned to Anirudh and added unnecessarily, 'That is, of course, provided our friend here doesn't need a break to have some milk.'

Chitra glared at Kiran, her features darkening into a scowl.

Aditya spoke before she could dash off a retort. 'I'm going to run all the way to the top,' he said, eyes sparkling. He turned to Kiran. 'Let's race each other like old times at school.'

Chitra spun angrily on him. 'Don't make me laugh, Aditya. Torna isn't a Jack-and-Jill sort of hill that anyone can sprint up. The climb is more than 2000 feet and spread over several kilometres. There will be no race. We're all going to stick together.'

Kiran shook his head. 'No, we won't,' he said. 'I'm not going to hang about waiting for laggards.' He stared pointedly at Anirudh. 'We'll race if we want to. What's your problem?'

Chitra controlled herself with visible effort. 'There is a problem,' she breathed. 'A huge problem and I'm surprised you haven't worked it out for yourself. You forget that only Salim and I know the way. Not only that but you choose to ignore the fog on the mountain and the fact that it's going to get dark very soon. There's enough space on this mountain to lose an entire army, and what's more, something you should know, is that the final section is vertical with sheer black cliffs, not the best place to get lost on a wet foggy night. It makes a lot of sense to stay together. Now, if you don't mind, I have to talk to Anand here. Instead of wasting whatever daylight we have left, I suggest that the rest of you put your gear together while I chat with him. Arrangements have to be made for our driver, Shankar. He's staying behind to look after the car.'

Chitra was not someone to be trifled with when she was angry, and though Kiran was smarting at her dressing-down, he turned away and helped Aditya and Vikram unload the car. There was chaos for a while as rucksacks, bottles, flashlights, jackets, caps and walking sticks rained down on the tiny porch of Anand's restaurant. The mess, however, was quickly sorted out, with everyone claiming their gear.

As Vikram inspected his rucksack, he wondered whether inviting Kiran along could be a decision they might regret. Kiran's unconcealed contempt for Anirudh indicated so. Although he was likeable, Kiran had a peculiar code governing his friends. For him, personality was all-important. Failure, timidity and helplessness were traits Kiran could not stand. He had shown his intolerance to them when he had been appointed prefect during his final year at school. Those who were go-getters and achievers were okay in his book; in fact, he openly favoured them. Ordinary plodders were acceptable to Kiran, but received no favours. Hesitancy, uncertainty and fear—all starkly visible on Anirudh—were characteristics Kiran abhorred. Poor Anirudh, he had never wanted to be part of the excursion. Unhappy and visibly downcast since leaving NDA, he had drawn a constant stream of snide remarks and scorn from Kiran.

While Vikram mulled over the problem of Anirudh and Kiran, Salim stood quietly to one side watching amusedly as the boys carefully kitted themselves in fancy jackets and expensive waterproof clothing. His dress for the evening was only marginally different from his daily wear—his trousers making way for a faded white dhoti wrapped about his legs. For protection from the elements, he had brought along a simple plastic raincoat that reached only as far as his knees. Wrapping up the contrast was his overnight gear—a plastic bag fastened to a stick—so elemental that it seemed like a remnant of prehistory, when compared with the stylish rucksacks bristling with a welter of fancy pockets and straps that the boys possessed.

Chitra had brought several walking sticks along, which she distributed when everyone was kitted out and ready. Kiran, Vikram and Salim gladly accepted theirs, but Aditya and Anirudh were reluctant till she casually informed them that the sticks were useful in case of snakes too, at which they promptly collected theirs.

The village square was curiously empty. The police chowki remained unattended and other than Anand, there was not a single villager about. While they bade goodbye to Shankar, a herd of buffaloes shuffled silently into the square. Salim waited for the big black animals and their tiny master—a skinny boy with sticklike legs—to pass before starting.

A mud track wound forward, leading them past small nondescript dwellings. Light shone inside the tiny homes and smoke issued from their roofs, yet the street, if the mud track could be called one, was quiet and empty, like the square. A smell permeated the area, a mix of soil and manure, sharp but not unpleasant.

As the weight of his rucksack settled on him, Vikram stared enviously at Salim's lightweight pack dangling from the stick on his shoulder, wishing he had packed as economically as the villager. At least he was better off in the shoe department, he mused, staring proudly at the expensive lightweight boots with special treading that his father had bought him. Salim wore simple plastic sandals with flat un-treaded soles.

Passing quickly through the village, they entered fields and soon their path was blocked by a fast-flowing stream of muddy water. Chitra, who had forged ahead of Salim, forded it without hesitation, wading through the knee-deep torrent. Vikram grimaced as he crossed. Cold water flooded his shoes, turning his socks into sodden rags. As he squelched along on the other side, water trapped in his shoes, Vikram couldn't arrest a growing conviction that even in the shoe department Salim scored over the rest of them, as his sandals, in contrast to their hi-tech footwear, permitted the annoying wetness to drain out.

A short march brought them to a labyrinth of rice fields carved skilfully from the lower slopes of the mountain, and after a hike along the meandering bunds that partitioned them, they arrived at the foot of the first challenging slope. Kiran and Aditya shot up the incline with Chitra keeping pace behind. A gap opened up as Salim and Vikram slowed down for Anirudh, who was finding the going difficult. Anirudh's speed declined steadily, his inhalation quickly turning to gasps, and when they topped a rise, they halted considerately, giving him time to catch his breath.

A magnificent panorama of cloud, mountain and water stretched before them. High above, like a bashful bride, Torna still veiled her features, shrouding them in thick and lustrous swathes of cloud. Beneath her mists, Torna's slopes were dark and steep. There were folds and cracks in the mountain where water tumbled in spiralling strands. Far below, a massive ledge projected from the mountain and water that poured on to it from above surged off its sheer edge in a series of spectacular waterfalls. That same water rushed on, flashing through forested gorges, losing its untainted purity as it did so, turning brown and slushy. Further down, on the lower section of the mountain, it entered the rice fields, where the cleverly planted bunds trapped vast quantities, flooding the terraced soil into lagoons of muddy broth.

It seemed to Vikram, as they resumed walking, that they had entered a damp and watery world. The only sound—besides their laboured breathing—was the splash and tinkle of tumbling water. Water gathered in puddles at their feet. It soaked the dark rock that crusted the mountain. It speckled the rippling meadows of grass with a flood of tear-sized droplets that sparked when they caught the light.

Vikram's brow was soon wet with perspiration. Aditya and Kiran spearheaded the assault on the mountain, striding way up in front while Anirudh, like a weighty anchor, held up the rear. Anirudh's progress was inexplicably slow, surprising even Vikram. No doubt they were all carrying heavy packs, but Anirudh had proved at the squash courts of NDA that he was no slouch. Could it be that the oncoming night was troubling him? Was the threatening cloud and the prospect of camping out affecting his morale? Vikram couldn't imagine any other reason. Not that Vikram minded. He was always for sacrificing speed for enjoyment, and Anirudh's snail-like gait presented him ample time to admire the forbidding cloud-wrapped panorama.

Chitra, however, was torn between her natural desire to compete with the boys and her fear of the group severing dangerously apart in the fast-dwindling light. Like a mother hen struggling to discipline her disorderly brood, she kept darting up and down the mountainside, yelling dire threats at Kiran and Aditya, and cajoling Anirudh forward. Unable to cope, she finally ordered a halt halfway up the mountain, below the dark edges of Torna's misty veil.

Kiran was waiting for them on a level section of the path, hands on his hips and a determined gleam in his eye. His tone was defiant. 'Aditya and I are going ahead,' he announced when Chitra and Vikram halted beside him. 'You lot can hold back, but we see no reason why everyone should suffer because one of us has legs that would shame even a slug. We'll see you at the fort.'

Kiran was mutinous. It was clear that he and Aditya had run out of patience. Chitra could understand their point of view, but night was falling and their demand could compromise safety. The impasse would have to be handled tactfully.

Chitra leaned on her walking stick. 'Firstly, a slug doesn't have legs,' she corrected with a smile. 'Second, you don't know the way. And third, there's the mist and it's getting dark. I've said this before and I'm repeating myself. The only sensible option is to stick together.'

Aditya's face was blood red, and it wasn't the exertions of the climb that had brought on the shade. 'That's your opinion,' he erupted, rebellion seething in his eyes. 'We've dawdled long enough, Chitra. Spare us your sermons. This is no way to climb a mountain. Even you know that. We're going ahead whether you like it or not!'

'Maybe you should ask Salim for his permission,' interjected Vikram. 'It was made clear to us that he is in charge of our group. What are we bickering for when we have the captain right here?'

Although Kiran shot Vikram a look of irritation, the soldier in him acknowledged the wisdom of the proposal. He turned to Salim and addressed him in Marathi. Salim heard him out and after glancing at Anirudh, who lay flopped on the grass, and casting his gaze up and down the darkening mountainside, he replied.

Not understanding a word, Vikram stood to one side, observing Salim as he spoke. In spite of not interacting much with the villager, his respect for the man had mounted the past few days, especially after he had single-handedly achieved the impossible, persuading his employers, a doubting Smita Dongre in particular, to lengthen their excursion to the Sahyadri.

Salim's village wasn't far from Torna and Vikram had been present when he had requested permission to drive them there after their Torna visit. As expected, Smita had refused. Salim, however, had ably subdued her apprehensions. In a manner belying his mild and submissive behaviour, he had astutely deflected her misgivings, managing to convince her that visiting remote villages was necessary and that exposure to rural life would benefit the youngsters. Anirudh too had succumbed to his impressive powers of persuasion and hadn't kicked up a fuss at the lengthening of an excursion that held no joys for him.

Even as he chatted now with Kiran, it was evident that he was no pushover. At one stage, Kiran was sharply rebuked for losing his temper. Vikram watched as Kiran humbly apologized and after a long conversation that followed, Salim appeared to relent.

When they finished, it was a relieved Kiran who turned to face them. 'Man . . . this guy drives a hard bargain. He has agreed to split the group, but those of us in front have to stay together—no racing, that's the condition. Chitra, you have to come with us, that's another condition. Salim says he'll look after Anirudh, bringing him along behind. Vikram can climb with them if he wants to.'

'But—' protested Chitra.

Kiran cut her off. 'Salim is a local. He knows these mountains better than any of us. He has assured me he'll find his way up. Ask him.'

Salim smiled. Speaking in Hindi, he said, '*Fikar mat*, memsahib. We will reach the top on our own. It is better you go with your friends, they might get lost.'

Chitra stared for a moment, then shrugged. 'Okay, we'll split up. Vikram, I'll feel more comfortable if you stay back with Salim and Anirudh. Hope that's okay with you?'

Vikram grinned. 'You know me. I'm in no hurry at all.'

Chitra flashed him a smile. 'Couple of things you need to know before I leave. The climb is fairly easy except for two sections. The trickiest is the final bit when you enter the fort. There's a narrow crack between rocks that leads vertically upwards. Negotiating it will be difficult as it will be dark and the rocks are wet and slippery. But I'm carrying ropes and I will fix a belay for everyone, so I wouldn't worry too much about it. The other section you need to know about is an exposed ridge just above us. My friends at the Snake Park, with good reason, have named it "Cellphone Alley".'

'Cellphone what?' asked Kiran.

'Cellphone Alley,' repeated Chitra, grinning. 'Even I wondered at the name when I first heard it, but you'll understand very soon why it is named so. There's a wind that strikes the ridge from the west and it blitzes you as if something wailing its lungs out has attached itself to your ear. But it's not your ear you have to look out for, it's for yourself, as the wind can sweep you off your feet if you aren't careful. I'm telling you because the ridge can be hazardous if you aren't prepared. Forewarned is forearmed. That's it then. There are several gates on top, they call them *darwazas*. We'll be waiting at the final one. Look after Anirudh. Any questions?'

Vikram shook his head. Kiran and Aditya were already displaying signs of impatience. Chitra hurriedly bade goodbye and turned away.

'Catch you on top,' shouted Aditya, waving.

'Get tough with your leaden-footed companion,' yelled Kiran in parting. 'Else you won't make it till sunrise tomorrow.'

Vikram waved and when they disappeared around a bend, he shrugged off his backpack and squatted beside Anirudh.

The cloud cover was unchanged on the mountains, but to the west, it had turned patchy and as Vikram rested on the wet grass, the setting sun broke through, casting orange incandescence. The mountains bloomed green in its watery light, and the raindrop-strewn grass winked fairy flashes till a bank of spoilsport cloud overpowered the sun again.

To the east, the panorama was far darker. The mountains were shadows. Yet in spite of the deepening gloom, it was still possible to discern the boundary of the Sahyadri Range, where the mountains tapered and merged with the flat plain of the Deccan. A patchwork of lights was visible on the distant plateau, and as he stared at its blurred shadow, Vikram found it hard to believe that a significant number of scientists and geologists worldwide were convinced that the fiery birth of the Deccan plateau was to blame for the extinction of the dinosaurs.

In the tranquillity of the darkening night, the theory seemed improbable, laughable almost, yet geological studies indicated that the plateau was forged 65 million years ago during a period of unprecedented volcanic activity, when a plume—a fountain of molten rock several thousand miles wide—parked itself beneath the Deccan, spewing lava and smoke for many thousands of years. The intensity of the eruption is believed to have devastated the earth, wrapping it in a veil of volcanic ash so thick that it blocked the rays of the sun, triggering the extinction of the dinosaurs.

On the windswept slopes of Torna, Vikram thought it awesome to even contemplate that he sat not far from one of the most cataclysmic geological eruptions the earth had ever known.

A bout of shivering interrupted Vikram's ruminations. A wind was stirring the mountainside, swirling and harrying the mists. A bush nearby shook and Anirudh, who was leaning against a rock, jerked upright. Salim, after a cursory glance, looked away. Vikram, drawing his cue from the villager, relaxed, but Anirudh turned apprehensive from then on, darting nervous glances at the bush, and he rose without a murmur when Salim announced it was time to move on.

Vikram adjusted his pack, settling it evenly on his shoulders as he fell in line on the narrow path behind Salim. They climbed steadily for a few minutes and after cresting a ridge, a howling wind set upon them. Before Vikram could blink, his cap was snatched from his head. Struggling to stay upright, he watched despairingly as his headgear soared skyward before spinning into the valley below.

Anirudh stumbled, unprepared for the onslaught. The ridge wasn't particularly wide and Vikram watched in horror as the wind dragged his friend to the edge. Vikram couldn't rush to his aid as he himself was struggling to keep his footing. But Anirudh managed to halt his perilous slide, head bowed and body crouched, almost touching the ground.

Salim and Vikram scurried towards him, their backs bent low. But when they arrived at his side, he brushed off their assistance. He stood composedly, body tilted forward, perfectly balanced, countering the wind. His clothes flapped noisily and his hair flailed behind him, like sea anemone tendrils in a current. There was a strange expression on his face, an expression Vikram interpreted as of someone who had roused himself from a long slumber.

While they watched, Anirudh bowed his head. Then he stepped forward, unmindful of the wind, as if the rampaging tempest was a mere breeze. He was gone in a flash, travelling into the wind, body angled expertly, tapping its cyclonic strength to propel him along, halting finally at the far end of the ridge. Bent almost double, Vikram floundered against the whiplike blast, struggling to Anirudh's side. Salim arrived before Vikram. Silver hair streaming in the wind, the villager was staring at Anirudh whose arms were outstretched like wings, a rapturous smile emblazoned on his face.

Anirudh's features were aglow. Vikram saw wonder, disbelief and joy on his face. But transcending all his emotions was pure, unbridled excitement. It was as if he had discovered something miraculous.

'Look!' shouted Anirudh, pointing down into a valley that had been hidden from their gaze. 'That waterfall. I know it. I have seen it.'

Far below, on Torna's western slopes, a waterfall spiralled lazily from a cliff edge. But unlike typical waterfalls, this was the strangest spillover Vikram had ever set his eyes on. The frenzied wind was disrupting its earthbound stream, blowing it sideways in mid-fall and spinning it around with such force that the waterfall doubled in a loop around itself so that not a single drop fell to the ground. It was as if he was gazing down on a pitched battle between wind and water in which the wind emerged victorious, achieving the impossible, suspending the plummeting stream in space and neutralizing gravity.

The contest between wind, water and gravity was an enthralling one. Anirudh gazed at it as if it were the most marvellous spectacle he had seen in his life. Salim, inscrutable as always, was staring alternately at the spinning waterfall and Anirudh.

Vikram turned away from them, looking about him. The ridge they crouched on—like a land bridge—connected them to the hulking Torna massif. A band of shifting darkness—the cloud zone—hovered barely a hundred feet above, obscuring the climb ahead. He watched in fascination as tendrils of cloud, like threads of fine silk, were whipped across the ridge at jet-stream velocities by the all-powerful wind. The tempest thundered about him, clutching at him with unseen fingers. He felt as if he were in the sky, seated in an aircraft battling turbulence and cloud.

The sun had set behind the mountains and darkness was creeping everywhere. Though exhilarating, the ridge was not the safest spot to linger on. He reached forward, tapping Anirudh's shoulder.

Anirudh turned. 'Watch the wind take me!' he shouted, comprehending Vikram's unspoken intention. And he was gone, careening along like before, using the wind to propel him along.

Salim outstripped Vikram as they hurried after Anirudh. The going was nowhere as easy as Anirudh made it out to be. The wind mounted a ferocious attack, striving to sweep Vikram off the ridge. He staggered, he stumbled, he fell and he crawled on all fours when it teetered him towards the edge.

Then suddenly, the wind was gone, vanishing without the semblance of a warning. The ringing in Vikram's right ear ended abruptly and he discovered he could stand without effort. Although his eyes conveyed that the exposed ridge lay behind, it was the thunderous silence that was the clearest indicator that Cellphone Alley had been successfully traversed.

Mist embraced Vikram now, draping grey curtains about him. His world shrank, and his vision was stripped of colour and dimension. So thoroughly did the vapour swallow him that he could have sworn he was underwater. There was a band of darkness ahead and as he stumbled towards it, the outline of a tree emerged. It was a tree shorn of leaves, its branches bare and twisted like gnarled fingers, bent and misshapen by the wind. It looked unearthly in the gloom, and his heart recoiled when he spied shadows beside it. His breathing eased when he saw that the shadows were his friends, not some wraithlike demons as his nervous brain had conjured.

Salim turned wordlessly and resumed their journey. Anirudh winked unexpectedly and flashed a smile before falling in line behind the villager. Vikram followed, his heart throbbing.

Night had fallen. Vikram and Anirudh flicked on their headlamps. The mists scattered their puny light, etching eerie haloes around their heads. The path led steeply upward and their breathing turned heavy. They worked their way through a band of slippery rock before entering a forest of shadowy, head-high bushes. At one point, where the path bent back on itself, the wind suddenly huffed, spinning the mists aside, and Vikram saw a plunging chasm of darkness barely an arm's length away. An involuntary shudder racked him as the mists poured back, blotting out the precipitous fall. Vikram found himself leaning towards the mountain wall thereafter, and he noticed Anirudh slanting similarly too.

A drizzle enveloped them, hampering visibility further. Salim ascended fast and Vikram wondered at Anirudh's new-found vigour as he energetically kept pace with them. The rushing sound of water grew steadily louder as they climbed, and they found themselves fording ankle-deep run-offs that streamed across their path. After a long, wet and slushy ascent, the rain withdrew and Vikram, lifting his gaze, saw that rocks had replaced the bushes they had been tramping through.

From high above, a disembodied voice clamoured through the mists and Salim bellowed in response, startling Vikram. Salim chattered in Marathi, and the voice, which Vikram placed as Kiran's, hollered a rejoinder. They resumed their climb. Salim walked faster and Vikram, fatigued as he was, mentally applauded Anirudh as he uncomplainingly kept pace with them. Soon, a warped circle of light was visible, bobbing in the mists above.

A big smile split Kiran's features as they drew level with him beneath a dripping wall of rock. He was bundled in his waterproof jacket and his hood was pulled back, revealing his short military-cropped hair.

'Good show, gentlemen. I thought I'd have to wait forever, but it's not even been a half-hour. Congratulate yourself, Anirudh. You deserve it, buddy. That was an impressively fast climb.'

Anirudh nodded, acknowledging the unexpected compliment. But he pointedly refused to look up or smile.

Vikram shook the wetness from his hair. 'Salim didn't halt. Not even once, and Anirudh walked like a champ. It was some climb. Are we done?'

'Almost,' grinned Kiran. He pointed up into the misted darkness. 'The fort darwaza is about a hundred feet above, but the dangerous bit that Chitra spoke about lies in-between. She wasn't pulling our legs when she said it's treacherous, but she's rigged the rope she promised, making life a lot easier. Once you're through that stretch, you are in the fort.'

Monstrous shadows loomed perpendicularly above, churning Vikram's stomach. 'Where are Chitra and Aditya?' he asked, diverting his thoughts from the alarming ascent ahead.

Kiran snorted. 'Where do you think? Searching for creepy-crawlies, of course. Chitra found some geckos on the fort walls—small yellow creatures, disgusting if you ask me. Aditya wasn't excited at all, but Chitra dragged him along. They are somewhere between the first and second darwazas, shining their flashlights on the walls.'

Salim was standing patiently to one side. He looked up when Kiran addressed him.

There was a rope curled at Kiran's feet. While Kiran chatted with Salim, Vikram directed his torch beam at the rope. Spinning the beam about, he followed the rope as it snaked up a set of dripping rock-hewn stairs that rose giddily into the night. Water flashed as it spilled in dribbling streams down the sharply inclined rock. A bat darted across his beam, clicking loudly before vanishing into the gloom of the night. Vikram clamped his teeth, stemming an involuntary shudder.

Kiran had finished his exchange with Salim. 'I saw flashlights on the slope as I descended,' he said, explaining for Vikram's benefit. 'Two lights and they weren't far behind you. Salim says it could be other trekkers like us, which makes sense, but if true, it could pose a problem, as there's only one roofed shelter on top. The rule is whoever's there first gets to use it. We should start moving if we want to avoid the prospect of a long, wet night.'

Anirudh was standing beside Vikram, looking up. Unlike Vikram whose insides were fast turning to jelly, his expression was unruffled, as if it were a stroll through a park ahead, not a precarious ascent up a tower of dripping rock. He started forward without hesitation the moment Kiran conveyed the necessity of a quick ascent.

Vikram felt his chest constrict as Anirudh scrambled up the rock. Even the act of watching someone on a cliff edge was sufficient to fan Vikram's vertigo. Shafts of dread lanced his veins. He swallowed, suppressing the demons inside him, refusing to let his phobia get the better of him.

Kiran whistled. 'Look at him go,' he cheered. 'He's not even using the rope. What did you do, Vikram? You guys have worked a miracle on Anirudh.'

Vikram did not answer. He lowered his gaze, staring at his boots. Fear was a great equalizer. The irony of the moment was not lost on him. When they had first met, it had been Anirudh who had choked on his fear. Now it was the turn of his nightmare to strike.

Kiran waved him forward. 'Move along,' he said. 'Flash your torch when you get to the top. Salim and I will follow then.'

Vikram grasped the rope. The slit-like stairs were no more than scratches in the cliff wall. The workmen who had gouged the rock face had done a rudimentary job at best. Their handiwork was uneven, and the wind and the rain had cracked and split what remained of their toil. Making matters worse was the layer of moss and slime that coated the stairs, like a film of soap. Vikram clung to Chitra's rope as if his life depended on it. He climbed slowly, feeling carefully with his boots, transferring his weight only after rigorously testing his foothold. He was acutely aware that he was surrounded by a void of nothingness, permeated only by air and moisture, vapourous entities incapable of supplying handholds but perfectly suited for swallowing him whole if he suffered the misfortune of losing his footing. Sweat poured from Vikram and his hands turned clammy. He worked on his breathing, struggling to control the galloping palpitations inside his chest. Chitra's rope was a godsend. Despite its reassuring presence, Vikram refused to look back or down the slope. He stared fixedly at the wall, working his feet and climbing steadily.

Soon dark walls appeared, enclosing the stairs. Vikram looked up. A massive stone gate loomed above, wedged in a crack in the mountain wall. Anirudh stood inside it, looking down on him. But there was no welcoming smile on Anirudh's lips. He was waving frantically instead, his face shrunken with horror.

Vikram was in mid-step, his entire weight on the rope, when it suddenly lurched. The motion wasn't an ordinary quiver like the nudge of the wind—it was a vicious, powerful tug instead that launched Vikram clear off the cliff face. Vikram screamed as the rope swung him out into the void, dangling him in space, before slamming him back against the rock. He reeled in shock and horror as the rope twitched like a serpent, tossing him back and forth. He had to let it go. But he couldn't. Fear glued his hands to it.

'LET IT GO!' screamed a voice above him.

Vikram stared. Anirudh had lowered himself on to the stairs. His hand was outstretched, reaching for him. Vikram let the rope go. But his timing was wrong, his judgement clouded by fear. His scrabbling feet searched desperately for a foothold. His hands grasped at the slimy rock, slipping and skidding on its slick surface. Vikram screamed in despair as his fingers failed to anchor him, sliding instead with the pressure of his weight. A vice-like grip seized his hand. For a moment, Anirudh bore his entire weight. The shoring was vital, allowing Vikram's flailing feet to find a footing. A heartbeat later, his free hand wedged itself in a crack. Anirudh held him, his hand rock steady, a divine anchor.

'YOU OKAY?' shouted Anirudh.

Vikram nodded, unable to speak.

'I have to let you go.' Anirudh's voice was urgent. He was staring down, beyond Vikram. 'Don't look back, but we have to move. NOW!'

Anirudh released Vikram's hand and scrambled up, pulling himself across the fort gate. Vikram followed far more warily, his pace curbed by fear.

'MOVE,' bellowed Anirudh. He knelt and yanked Vikram over the last stretch, depositing him on firm, level ground.

Vikram had hardly recovered when the sound of doglike panting reverberated in the enclosed gate area. Chitra's rope was jerking and quivering as if a rampaging bull was tethered to its other end. Vikram raised himself to peer out across the gate when a shadow shot forward from its gaping mouth, smashing into him and bowling him over.

'Salim!' Anirudh's yell was despairing.

The shadow stumbled to its feet. Vikram caught sight of a strip of cloth wrapped about the shadow's legs. Plastic shoes encased its feet. The plastic shoes blurred into motion. Salim was gone, sprinting through the gate. Anirudh sprang forward a moment later, dashing after Salim.

Vikram leapt to his feet, ready to follow Salim and Anirudh, but the frenzied see-sawing of the rope distracted him. He paused, staring down the open void of the gate and his blood froze. There were three shadows on the nightmarish stairs. Two were a short distance below while the third was way down, at the foot of the incline. The close-at-hand shadows were rolling and squirming as if locked in combat. Grunts and swear words issued from them as they rained a string of kicks and blows on one another.

The pitched battle was the most heart-stopping sight Vikram had ever laid his eyes on. A scene so absurdly dangerous that if it weren't unfolding beneath him, he could have sworn he was in a movie theatre. A physical encounter was hazardous enough on level ground, but on a knife-edged cliff, it was certain death for the loser, if not for both the combatants.

Vikram's heart sank as he identified one of the shadows.

Kiran!

Vikram did not pause for even a moment. Kiran was in mortal danger. One mistake . . . a single slip of hand . . . and he would be gone, lost forever. A fist-sized stone lay at his feet. Stooping, he swept it up. But even as he readied to fling it, he held back. He couldn't risk a throw. Kiran and his opponent were entwined together. He turned his attention to the second shadow, the man at the start of the stairs. He was climbing to assist his friend. Shifting his aim, Vikram let fly.

The man was far below, yet Vikram's aim was true. The stone connected solidly with his head, stunning him. There was a loud, agonized scream. The shock of the impact knocked loose the man's grip on the mountain and he fell. He bounced against the cliff before crashing with a sickening thump on to the flooded landing where the climb began.

The pitiful scream skewered Vikram's heart. He trembled in shock at what he had done. The scream decisively ceased the murderous battle. The shadows disengaged. Kiran shot upwards to the gate. His opponent scooted down to his stricken comrade.

Vikram's nerves were on edge. Footsteps pounded behind him and he spun around, ready to defend himself. But he needn't have worried. The newcomers were Chitra and Aditya. They arrived breathlessly by his side a moment before Kiran hauled himself through the gate.

Voices erupted, blabbering all together.

'What's going on?'

'Salim was attacked. Anirudh said to help.'

'Kiran—' There was shock and concern. 'What's wrong? You look like a ghost.'

Kiran collapsed to his knees. Chitra and Aditya grasped his arms. Kiran leaned against them and they staggered as they supported him.

'He was attacked,' said Vikram. 'The men are down there. Look.'

Kiran's assailants were clearly visible. One was kneeling and the sight of the second one sitting lifted a terrible load off Vikram's shoulders.

'Attacked?' Chitra stared at Vikram as if he had gone crazy. 'What on earth for? Why would anyone want to attack Kiran?'

Kiran spoke, his voice unsteady. 'It wasn't me. It was Salim . . . They were after Salim.' He paused, struggling to calm his breathing. 'We were down there waiting for Vikram to finish the ascent . . . They attacked without warning, jumping on Salim. I punched one of them hard and Salim broke free. He took off, shooting up the stairs. They tried to follow him, but I wouldn't let them. We slugged it out. One of them pulled a knife. I backed off, running up the stairs. The man followed, coming after me. I kicked the knife from his hands, but he wouldn't let go. We fought. Then there was a scream and he suddenly dashed off.'

'I threw a stone,' Vikram filled in. 'The second man was climbing to help his friend. The stone hit him and he fell.' Vikram swallowed. 'He fell sickeningly. I . . . I thought he was dead, but he's sitting up now.'

'You fought on the stairs . . . those vertical stairs?' Aditya's voice dripped incredulity.

Kiran dropped his head. 'I thought I was gone. Chitra's rope saved me.'

Aditya was shocked into silence. So was Chitra. No one spoke.

It began to rain.

Vikram shone his torch through the mists to the men below. Kiran's assailant was assisting his accomplice to his feet. The injured man stood up, leaning on his friend. The man was hurt, unable to move on his own. His mate helped him, placing an arm around his shoulders. They walked slowly, the wounded man hobbling.

Chitra turned to Kiran when the clouds swallowed the vanquished duo. 'Are you hurt?' she asked, flashing her torch on him.

Kiran rose slowly to his feet, assisted by Aditya. 'I'm bruised all over,' he said, running his hands gingerly down his sides.

'There's blood,' said Chitra.

'Nothing serious, just scratches and bruises. Antiseptic cream should handle it. Thanks, Vikram. That missile of yours couldn't have been better timed. I don't know what would have happened if the fight had gone on.'

Vikram patted Kiran. 'Your NDA sergeants would have been proud of you. That was life-and-death stuff.'

'Life-and-death stuff . . .' repeated Chitra. 'Are you sure they were after Salim, Kiran? It doesn't make sense.'

Kiran flexed his arms tentatively. 'I'm dead certain. The men weren't interested in me. Why would they be?'

'They could have been thieves?' said Chitra. 'Thugs out to make a quick buck.'

Kiran shook his head. 'You should have seen Salim. The look on his face would have convinced you. He was frightened to death. He raced off like a hunted animal when I put up a fight. Those men were after Salim. He'd be lying if he denies it.'

'Did you see Salim?' asked Vikram, turning to Chitra and Aditya. 'He ripped through here like a flying monkey, knocking me over. Anirudh shot after him.'

'We did,' said Aditya. 'That's how we knew something was wrong.' He turned to Kiran. 'You're right about Salim. The man looked as if he'd seen a ghost. He babbled at us in Marathi. We didn't understand, but his fright was obvious. We were all set to come down here, but he refused to let us leave his side, not wanting to be left alone. Then Anirudh came tearing along. He relieved us and we came here as fast as we could.'

'Let's go find them,' said Kiran. 'Come on. It's pointless hanging about here.'

They trooped out of the doorway, turning their backs to the black cliff walls. Stairs led upwards. There were walls around them now, constructed from blocks of pockmarked black stone. Tufts of grass grew on the walls in the crevices between the blocks. But the vegetation did not in any way detract from the solidity of the barriers, which had been designed with the obvious goal of withstanding cannon fire. Vikram wondered how many monsoons they had weathered. Many hundreds for sure, and though they had been erected in the days before cement, they stood proud and firm, a testimony to the workmanship of those bygone days.

They came presently to the next darwaza, a massive door encased in a sturdy frame, Torna's second line of defence. Anirudh and Salim were waiting beside the door, sheltering from the rain in a small portico behind.

Chitra walked on without halting. 'No point stopping,' she said. 'The temple isn't far ahead. We'd be wasting time here. We can talk there.'

No one objected. They followed Chitra, sloshing along a flooded mud track that climbed far more gently than the incline they had grown used to. Mist rolled thickly about them and rain fell, spattering noisily on their jackets. After a short walk, they came to a level area and a wall emerged from the cloud. A single glance was enough to reveal that this wasn't a fort wall. It was narrow and cemented and would certainly have crumbled if targeted by cannon fire. Chitra led them around the wall and they came to a stone platform with a simple hut erected on it. The door of the hut was open and a light shone. There were tiny lanterns inside and they illuminated a wall hung with framed portraits of Shivaji together with those of holy deities.

They entered reverently, Kiran and Anirudh prostrating themselves before the deities. The rest bowed respectfully and then unburdened themselves, stacking their rucksacks against the walls.

Chitra issued a stern warning. 'Don't mess the place up. Spread only your carry mats and sleeping bags. Vikram and I have the food. We'll hand it out.'

Food consisted of sandwiches and cold biriyani, which they ravenously helped themselves to. Anirudh collected his and Salim's share, and the two of them sat separate from the others, eating and talking quietly to one another.

The rain intensified while they devoured their meal, pitchforking to the earth, its fury amplified by the tin roof that reverberated thunderously above their heads. The entire hut shook as the wind howled, and Vikram thanked his stars that their journey was over. It was dark and cold inside the temple. The food, however, was appetizing, and chocolates and biscuits were passed around too.

'Any prospect of further hostilities?' asked Chitra when the meal was done.

Vikram crushed his paper plate and stuffed it in a garbage bag. 'I don't think we need to worry,' he said. 'The man who took a tumble is in no condition. He's nursing more than just bruises for sure; could be a couple of broken bones too. The other guy already got a taste of what Kiran is capable of and he knows there are four more of us to deal with. I don't think he'll risk anything. What do you think, Kiran?'

Kiran helped himself to a slab of chocolate. 'The fellow Vikram nailed is knocked out for sure. The man I fought with didn't strike me as an idiot, and only an idiot would pit himself against so many of us. My guess is we're safe.'

It was time to talk to Salim, yet no one spoke. They busied themselves with preparations for the night. The rain eased and the uproar on the roof slackened to a more civilized drumming. The wind dropped too, but it constantly reminded them of its lurking presence, heaving every now and then at the roof and door.

Anirudh displayed little interest in his friends, hobnobbing only with Salim, with whom he shared several lengthy exchanges. They spread their night-gear to one side of the hut, at a distance from the others. It was when everyone was tucking themselves into their bags that Anirudh finally spoke.

'Salim is unhappy and upset,' he said. 'He doesn't want to talk now, but he wants me to convey his thanks to you, Kiran, for saving him from those men.'

Kiran smiled. 'He ought to know that Vikram helped too,' he said. 'There could have been trouble if he hadn't dealt with the other man.'

'Kiran's being modest, Anirudh,' said Vikram. 'He's the one who saved Salim. It's understandable that Salim doesn't want to speak, but we think he should. It's important we know who those men are. This is no small matter, the assault was murderous in intent. Kiran could have been seriously injured.'

The light from the lanterns illuminated Anirudh's features. It struck Vikram as he gazed at him and Salim that their skin tones were identical, the same nut-brown colour.

'Salim understands everyone's concern,' said Anirudh. 'But he wants you all to respect his silence, it is a personal matter.'

'Has he told you anything?' asked Aditya.

'That has nothing to do with his request, Aditya. He doesn't want to speak about it. He's asking for your understanding. And no, he hasn't told me.'

There was a brief silence. The wind gusted, pummelling the temple door.

Chitra stirred. 'He's going to have to speak sometime. We have to report this. He should know that.'

Vikram yawned. 'Leave it for tomorrow. Let's respect Salim's wishes. We're all tired. Not the best time for an argument. We'll talk at breakfast.'

Not everyone agreed with Vikram. But it was late and they were exhausted. No one pressed the issue. Chitra secured the door with strong climbing rope. They bid each other goodnight and it wasn't long before they slipped into exhausted slumber.

THE ABANDONED DWELLING

The next morning brought no change to Salim's stance. They had quit the hut shortly after first light, and after an uneventful descent under an overcast sky, had returned to the restaurant where Anand, its genial owner, had served them a sumptuous breakfast. It was after the meal, while they were relaxing over cups of hot chai, that the topic came up. Salim demonstrated no inclination to talk and Anirudh stood in as his mouthpiece once more.

Chitra objected instantly. 'Matters like this shouldn't go unreported. There's a police chowki right here. Torna is under their jurisdiction. Salim must talk to them.'

They were the only customers in the restaurant. Though it was morning, lights had been switched on, as the sky outside was grey and gloomy. A fan spun slowly, circulating damp air. They were seated around a large steel table. Salim sat quietly to one side, beside Anirudh.

'Salim does not dispute your point of view,' said Anirudh. 'He will report the matter. He promises to do so, only he doesn't want to do it now. He prefers to leave it for later when the excursion is over.'

'What sense does that make?' asked Kiran. 'Chitra's right. This is where the incident happened and so, the police chowki here is the right one. He must report here.'

Anirudh shook his head. 'Salim doesn't see it that way. He is taking us to his home today. This is a happy day for him. He doesn't want to spoil it.'

Aditya lowered his teacup. 'Are you taking sides with Salim? It sounds to me as if you are. The two of you were up half the night whispering to one another.'

Anirudh looked scathingly at Aditya. 'Not half the night. You wouldn't know in any case. You were snoring the whole time. We both woke early and since we couldn't sleep, we talked, if you must know. He was eager to speak to me about his village. Anything wrong with that?' He turned away, miffed. He gazed at the others, as if challenging them, and then calmed when no one opposed him. 'My mother called this morning,' he continued, his tone more settled. 'I respected Salim's wishes and didn't mention a word about last night. He's hoping the rest of you stay silent till we return.'

Chitra wasn't the sort who gave in easily, especially on matters of principle. 'I'm willing to consider his request,' she consented, 'but Salim must explain why he doesn't want to speak. If his reasoning makes sense, sure I'll respect his wishes. But first, he has to tell us.'

'I'll try to explain,' said Anirudh. 'Villagers hate dealing with the police. They can be very tough on them and Salim has had bad experiences before, so bad that he still gets nightmares from them. As I said, today is a happy day for him as he is returning home. He doesn't want to spoil it by being forced to spend it with the police. It's as simple as that. He wants to be in good spirits while we are at his home. He's only asking that he delay the reporting . . . One day is all he requests. He's hoping everyone will cooperate.'

Vikram stared at Salim. Though he did not understand English, Salim was obviously aware they were speaking about him. His dark face was expressionless as always, and his eyes stared fixedly at a portrait of Shivaji on the opposite wall.

Vikram shrugged. 'I don't have a problem,' he said.

Chitra stared angrily at him.

'It's not my quarrel,' defended Vikram. 'It's Salim's and if he doesn't want to speak about it, that's fine by me.'

'And what about justice and law?' Chitra asked heatedly. 'Are you going to let a pair of murderous thugs get away scot-free? Is that also okay by you?'

'It isn't right,' admitted Vikram. 'But he's assured us he will report the matter when we get back. He's scared of the cops and doesn't want to spoil his homecoming. I respect that.'

Chitra snorted loudly, venting her dissatisfaction at Vikram's stance.

Vikram raised a pacifying hand. 'It's obvious this is troubling you a lot. So, here's a suggestion. It was Kiran who fought to save Salim. He's the one who risked his life. Let's leave it to him. We'll do whatever he thinks is right.'

Chitra deliberated a moment, then nodded assent. 'I'll accept that,' she said.

Kiran wiped his mouth with his shirtsleeve. 'That was clever, Vikram, shifting the responsibility to me.' But he smiled, relieving his remark of animosity. 'I'll have to talk to Salim first. Give me a moment.'

A lengthy conversation ensued, conducted entirely in Marathi. Salim's eyes were white and large. Emotion finally intruded his deadpan features as he spoke with bouts of intense passion. Anirudh listened intently but did not contribute a word.

Kiran finally turned to his friends. 'For some reason, he's frightened to talk to the cops here. He's not telling me why. But he's scared, genuinely scared, that's the impression I get. As Anirudh said, today is a happy day for him, and he doesn't want to spoil it.' Kiran shrugged. 'I don't really have a problem as long as he does report the matter, and he has promised me that he will. So it's okay by me.'

Kiran's stand settled the debate. Although Chitra wasn't convinced, she did not press the matter further.

Upon questioning Anand and Shankar, they learnt that a car had parked at the square shortly after they departed the previous evening. A white Innova. Neither of them could remember the number plate, but Shankar was certain it bore a Mumbai registration. The passengers, both men—one lanky and tall, the other bearded and heavy—fitted the description of the thugs who had attacked Kiran. The vehicle had driven off sometime during the night because by morning when Anand returned to the square, there was no sign of it. Although hardly enlightening, this was all the information they could muster. Chitra left her mobile number with Anand, requesting him to call if there was further news.

They pulled out from Velhe Village under a sky unchanged from the previous evening. Still bashful, Torna refused to lift her veil, her modesty exasperating Vikram, as he still had no clue of the mountain's features, even after a night on her summit. He would always remember his experience on Torna though, especially the cyclonic winds of Cellphone Alley and the harrowing vertical section that led into the fort. Maybe the mysteries of Torna's wild slopes would draw him back someday.

The landscape their vehicle trundled through was unchanged like the sky. There were fields and orchards and groves of trees. Sprinkled across the valley, like pencils embedded in the earth, were the tapered domes of temples, heralding the presence of villages from afar. Cows grazed on green hillsides, villagers and bullocks toiled in fields, and children waved as they drove by. Water flashed in muddy streams on the roadside and on the hills, beneath the mists, it cascaded over cliff and rock, sparkling white and pure. The country road looped and twisted, snaking serpent-like between endless fields of rice till they came at last to a broad highway.

Chitra, Kiran and Aditya chatted ceaselessly, discussing gadgets, music, movies and sports. Vikram chipped in every now and then, during intervals when he was not engrossed by the landscape. Anirudh and Salim sat amidst the luggage at the back, apart from the others, heads together like schoolboys, chatting quietly. Salim was composed, his face untroubled, as if the attack of the previous evening had never taken place.

Curiously, the interaction between Salim and Anirudh was almost entirely one-sided, Salim speaking and Anirudh listening. Anirudh's attentiveness was absolute: face intent, eyes focused, ears tuned—like an apprentice monk absorbing the wisdom of a Zen master. Salim talked ceaselessly, as if he were a politician on a podium, until Shankar turned the car off the highway, on to a village road, at which he announced they were passing through the historical village of Wai that lay at the foot of the popular hill stations of Panchgani and Mahabaleshwar.

Wai was a long, rambling village with narrow roads, inhabited by cows and pedestrians in equal number. The houses were a mix of graceful old-world homes, standing side by side with apartment blocks of the boxlike variety. They passed quickly through the village, entering fields once more. Soon they came to the long, low wall of a dam and when they drove around it, they spied a huge lake whose waters were grey and dimpled, reflecting the colour of the gloomy sky.

Chitra stared out of her window, taking in the breathtaking expanse of water. 'That's some lake,' she whistled.

Aditya was equally impressed. 'Look at that water, Vikram,' he cried. 'We should have brought windsurfing boards along.'

The streamers of froth furrowing the lake surface were an indication of the wind raging across its dark waters. The conditions were perfect for windsurfing, and Vikram too wished they had brought boards along. The lake was similar to Khadakwasla where the regatta had been held, except that it was larger. Even the mountains were bigger here.

They were taller and more extensive, forging an enormous barrier to one side of the lake.

'Krishna Nadi,' announced Salim. 'They have dammed the River Krishna here.' He pointed to the misted mountains that stretched above like the Great Wall of China. 'Look there, you can see Panchgani and further down is Mahabaleshwar.'

High up on the wall of mountain, a scattering of houses was visible, half-hidden by the mists.

'Wow!' exclaimed Kiran. 'That *is* Panchgani. Salim has got it right. What a view. I've never seen it from this angle . . . Where's Mahabaleshwar now?'

Salim pointed to the distant edge of the immense mountain plateau. 'Mahabaleshwar is there, but you cannot see it. It is far and hidden by the mists.'

Mountains towered everywhere about them, and interestingly, instead of peaks, their crowns were elongated into plateaus, a feature distinctive of this section of the Sahyadris. Amongst the elevated tablelands was the fort of Kinjalgadh, but Salim could not identify it for them, as its head was hijacked by cloud. The other famed fort of the region, Kamalgad, was wreathed in mists too. The entire valley was overwhelmed with cloud, yet despite the absence of the sun, there was light on the hill slopes—a blaze of luminous green that mocked the sun, twinkling with an effulgence that was its very own.

They drove along the lake, tracking its northern bank, crossing it finally where its width narrowed to a bridgeable length. The road then turned away from the lake towards a phalanx of mountains that walled a green valley. After a short drive through fields, a banyan tree appeared and beside it was a large shed-like building with a compound in which children were playing.

'My village,' declared Salim. 'Vashivale.' He pointed to the mountains barring the path ahead. 'The plateau above is called Koleshwar. We will be climbing there today and if the weather is good, I will take you to Kamalgad later in the evening. The walk is long and will take time, so if it is okay with everyone, I would like to start climbing immediately.'

'What about food?' asked Chitra, gazing at the mountains. 'We'll all be hungry soon. There's only forest up there as far as I can see. Shouldn't we eat before setting off?'

'There is a settlement on top,' said Salim. 'Dhangaar tribals live there . . . very poor, but generous and hospitable. I'm carrying supplies and they will cook for us. We will rest on top and eat there and then walk to Kamalgad.'

The bitumen road yielded to a mud track, and they were bounced about as Shankar steered the vehicle over rocks and potholes that would have done the craters on the moon proud. They laboured through trees and fields and mountains. Everywhere about them, like an untiring orchestra, thrummed the refrain of rushing water. A muddy river thundered not far from them, its waters swollen with the run-off from the surrounding mountains. Green fields flanked the river on either side. Above, there were steep slopes and waterfalls and bands of dark rock veiled by cloud.

They drove past mud houses, a temple and a lone shop with no customers. As they bounced through a grove of bamboo, Salim pointed to a slope on their right, 'My house,' he said. 'It is behind the trees, where the hillside flattens. I will take you there when we return from Kamalgad.'

Exiting the village, the road entered fields once more. They were driving to the head of the valley, where the mountains converged in a crescent of green walls. The road began to climb, gently at first, then sharply, before terminating at a temple with a large pipal tree beside it.

'Leave your heavy gear behind,' instructed Salim, stepping out of the car. 'Shankar will look after it. Carry only what you need for the day, and water.'

To one side, a footpath led to a line of simple houses, roofed with tiles. Opposite the parking area was a flat concrete structure, which Vikram guessed was a school, as children were playing there. Their presence attracted a crowd, mainly children, who gathered around them as they extracted their gear from the car. Their cherubic faces rippled with delight when Chitra brandished a can of sweets. There were smiles all around as she handed them out.

Salim, for some reason, seemed to be in a hurry. Surprisingly, it was Anirudh who was ready first and the two of them set off, cutting through the houses, to the incline behind, not waiting for the others. They had advanced considerably up the mountain by the time Chitra finished distributing the sweets.

'What's come over Anirudh?' asked Kiran, as they waved goodbye to the children. 'Has he guzzled a magic potion or what? The guy's energy has doubled. He's climbing like a monkey. Look at him go.'

It was true. Salim and Anirudh were shooting up the hill.

'It's the Salim effect,' said Aditya, staring up the slope. 'The man seems to have some kind of hold on Anirudh. At NDA, Salim was his mother's helper and Anirudh was his usual self. But here, in the hills, it's different.'

'Like school chums, aren't they?' said Chitra. 'Best-buddy sorts who stick together and keep everyone else out.'

'Yeah,' said Aditya. 'Sitting in corners. Whispering to one another, as if they have secrets no one should hear. That isn't the loner Anirudh I know. Salim has worked some kind of magic on him.'

Vikram held the same view. Something had certainly come over Anirudh. But the change wasn't only Anirudh's strengthening bond with Salim. According to Vikram, the makeover of Anirudh had commenced the previous evening, at Cellphone Alley. The incident was stark in Vikram's memory, when with the wind threatening to blow him off the mountain, Anirudh's face, instead of shrivelling with fear, had inexplicably blazed with a dazzling radiance. That was the moment that had changed Anirudh, transforming him from a lazy, sullen trekker into an able climber with creditable ability and energy. There was no rationale to Vikram's reasoning, yet he believed that the wind and the spinning waterfall, in some unaccountable manner, had triggered Anirudh's renewal.

'I was wrong about him,' said Kiran, as they scrambled up a denuded stretch of slope. 'He can certainly climb.'

'It's a bit late to be wrong about him,' breathed Chitra. She paused, panting with exertion. 'You weren't particularly pleasant to him yesterday, were you?'

'He deserved it!' Though Kiran shot back his answer, his tone was defensive. 'He was behaving like a two-year-old missing his mama.'

Vikram shook his head. 'You were offensive, Kiran. You came down too heavily on him. A little patience and understanding would have helped.'

They ascended quickly, but Anirudh and Salim stayed comfortably ahead. The climb wasn't as easy as Vikram had hoped it would be. The slopes were knuckled into folds that lengthened their expanse, and their gradients were deceptively steep. As the fields and the village dropped away, a splendid panorama unfolded beneath. The lake was a brushstroke of grey in the distance. Bordering its shore were trees and fields and the sinuous road they had travelled upon. The entire sprawl of the road was visible, including the point at which it veered away from the lake, turning into the mountain-locked valley where Salim's village was located. Vikram saw that the phalanx of mountains was shaped like a horseshoe and that the valley was larger than he had thought. Salim's wasn't the only village nestled inside the valley; three temple domes scattered across its breadth indicated the presence of an equal number of villages.

Every inch of the mountainside was wet and green, no different from the slopes of Torna. The ground was slushy, the grass damp and the vegetation saturated. Water cascaded from the encircling mountains, converging on the muddy torrent that split the valley along its length. Far below them, a single row of tiny homes probed forward like an extended finger, terminating at the head of the valley.

Vikram pulled up suddenly. 'Hey!' he exclaimed, staring at the huts below. 'Look at that house. How on earth did something so fancy get there?'

The others halted, staring at where Vikram pointed. At the head of the valley, where it narrowed like the prow of a boat, was a house so different from the rest that it drew their gaze the moment they spied it. Located some distance from the others, its size alone set it apart, and instead of four simple walls and a roof—the norm in the valley—its lines were grand and extravagant, like that of a country villa. It looked thoroughly out of place in the nondescript village, like a gem amidst a bed of stones.

'That's not a hut,' said Chitra. 'It's a mansion. Someone has spent a lot of money.'

'Yeah,' grunted Aditya. 'But also ran out of money. Look at how run-down it is.'

The house was in a bad way, its state of disrepair obvious. Tiles were missing from its roof, a portion of a wall had collapsed, its garden was infested with vegetation, and a film of green coated its fine walls.

'Some villager probably,' said Kiran. 'Must have made a lot of money and then gambled it away.'

'No villager would have constructed such a house,' said Vikram. 'It isn't just money that has gone into the house. There's design too. Not village design, I can tell you. The structure is colonial, if you ask me. Could be some British official in the days of the Raj who built it. Salim should know.'

'Speaking of Salim,' said Chitra, looking up the mountain, 'he's way ahead and moving fast. Come on! We don't want to lose him in the mist.'

The path was narrow, little more than a mud track. It looped in bends around the mountainside, rising continuously. Later, at a fold in the mountain, they crossed a water run-off where they waded through a knee-deep torrent, balancing precariously on slippery rocks. The water was clear and clean, and they spotted crabs splashing hurriedly away. The armoured creatures were large, the size of regular sea crabs but coloured differently, their shade approximating that of the brown soil of the mountain. As they climbed, Vikram, to his surprise, discovered that the crabs weren't restricted to the water run-offs. They ventured freely on the slopes, prancing up and down the hillside.

They climbed rapidly and the tapestry of mist drew closer. They lost sight of Salim and Anirudh as they tramped through a dense grove of trees, and Vikram was beginning to worry when suddenly they came upon them on a flat verge of mountainside at the very edge of the cloud ceiling. They were standing close together beneath a tree, halfway down a grassy expanse of rock and soil, with their heads bowed. A wall of black rock rose perpendicularly behind them, its upper section lost in cloud.

Threads of fog floated across the mini plateau as they tramped towards Salim and Anirudh. No one spoke. There was a stillness and sobriety to their bearing that silenced Vikram and his companions. For some reason, Vikram felt as if he were gatecrashing a funeral. It was as if the swirling vapour was wreathed in a cloud of sadness.

They halted at a respectful distance near a broken stone wall. Salim and Anirudh were standing beside the remains of what had once been a dwelling; a modest one, constructed from stone and little else. The entire structure had caved in. All that stood of it now were its outer walls, each in varying stages of collapse.

Vikram shivered. It was cold up here. The mini plateau was wild and desolate, not the most suitable spot to build a home unless the purpose was to shun human company. The only sound was that of the wind and the tinkle of tumbling water.

Neither Salim nor Anirudh acknowledged their arrival. They stood like a pair of bereaved family members grieving the loss of a loved one, and once again, Vikram was struck by the likeness between them. Not only was their skin colour the same but their height and build—both short and slight—were comparable too.

A lengthy period of silence elapsed before Salim finally turned to them, his head still bowed.

'You left us behind,' said Chitra, a touch of reproach in her voice.

Salim blinked and Vikram was taken aback to see that his cheeks were stained with tears. 'I'm sorry,' he apologized in Hindi. 'You weren't far behind. I was sure you would find your way. I wanted to spend some time here on my own.' He shuffled his feet. 'This is where my brother once lived. He died many years ago.'

'Oh!' Chitra gulped. 'We're sorry. We can wait if you like.'

Salim looked up. 'It's okay. I have paid my respects. You have climbed quickly and are tired. We will rest here a while. The summit is not far.'

The break was welcomed by all. Chitra and Aditya sprawled on the ground, shrugging their backpacks from their shoulders. Kiran extracted his water bottle and drank deeply.

Vikram wandered towards Anirudh. 'Is anything the matter?' he asked, halting at his side.

Anirudh turned away. 'Nothing,' he said, brushing his face. There were tears on his cheeks too.

'You can tell me,' said Vikram. 'I won't speak to the others . . . you know that.'

Anirudh walked away.

Vikram followed. He pulled a water bottle from his pack and offered it to Anirudh who swigged deeply before handing it back.

After a lengthy silence, Anirudh spoke. 'Salim and I have been talking . . .' he said.

'I've noticed,' said Vikram, swallowing water.

Anirudh stared at his shoes. 'I'm sure everyone has; the others must have enjoyed gossiping about it.' He smiled, raising his head. 'We've talked so much that I feel I've known Salim all my life. We've spoken about everything you could think of. I told him about my family. He told me about his people . . . his parents and his brothers. Life hasn't been easy for him. It never is, I guess, when you don't have much money. It was his youngest brother who lived here and he loved him dearly, more than the rest. He wanted me to be by his side when he paid his respects to him.'

Anirudh reached for Vikram's bottle and gulped a mouthful. 'I experienced the strangest feeling in my life, Vikram, as I stood beside Salim. An absurd emotion overwhelmed me, as if I had known the man who had lived here. Salim began to cry and so did I. There are all kinds of sensations going through me, and I don't know what to make of them. I'm getting strange vibes from this place . . . from this entire mountain. It's like I have been here before.'

Vikram blinked, not sure how to respond. But Anirudh was gazing expectantly at him, as if seeking a response. 'Maybe it's Mahabaleshwar and Panchgani that you are recalling,' ventured Vikram. 'The hill stations can't be very different from this mountain. This place could be triggering memories of holidays with your folks.'

Anirudh shook his head. 'I've never visited Mahabaleshwar. Our family is not the travelling sort. This is my first time in the Sahyadris, you know that.'

There were tiny yellow flowers amidst the grass. Vikram bent and plucked one. 'What happened to you yesterday?' he asked. 'I'm talking about the waterfall and the wind at Cellphone Alley—something came over you there.'

'You noticed?' Anirudh grinned. 'I had a hunch you might have. All the absurdities, the craziness . . . the contradictions, began there, on that windblown slope. I told you I've never been to the Sahyadris and yet, I was certain I had seen that waterfall before. Not the Cellphone Alley one, mind you, but a similar one where the wind terminates the flow and circles it about. This is the madness, Vikram. How could I, if I haven't been to the Sahyadris before? It doesn't make sense. Even the hurricane wind. You saw the way I handled it. Somehow I knew how to tackle it, to use it to propel me along. How did I know? Where have I seen wind-driven waterfalls? Why does this mountain feel so familiar? What's going on?'

Vikram had no answer. Maybe the fact that the expedition was Anirudh's first foray into the wild could provide an explanation. It was also possible that his mind was acting strangely because he was missing his parents and home, but Vikram could hardly share such speculation with him.

'We'll talk about it later,' said Vikram instead. 'Try and ignore what's going on upstairs.' Vikram pointed at his head. 'Just enjoy the walk. Come on, Salim has started already.'

Salim and Chitra were walking towards the dark cliffs. Kiran and Aditya strode behind. Shouldering their packs, they hurried forward and fell in line.

KOLESHWAR

The cliffs drew near. Water dripped from their weathered walls and moss blossomed in their folds. There was a grove of trees leading to the cliffs, and Salim had just entered them when he halted and turned. Vikram and the others spun about too, their attention drawn by the same noise that had alerted Salim.

Vikram inhaled sharply. There were shadows at the far edge of the plateau. Though the mist obscured them, it was obvious that the shadows were upright and two-legged and that they were rushing towards the cliffs. The attack of the previous evening sprang to Vikram's mind.

Salim . . .

Vikram turned, looking for the villager, but Salim had already bolted, shooting up the path like a hunted hare. Anirudh took off too, sprinting after him.

'There's eight of them,' said Kiran, his voice conversational, as if the advancing shadows were as harmless as the wafting cloud. 'We have a repeat of yesterday, only there are more of them this time round.

I'm not sure I'll be able to manage them on my own. Ideas, anyone?'

'Only one!' yelled Vikram. 'Follow Salim! RUN!'

Chitra hesitated only a fraction of a second. Then she turned and ran. Kiran waited for Vikram and Aditya to pass before following.

A mud path, swamped with slush, led steeply upward. It was dark and gloomy and they could hardly see. They had entered the mists, and the forest canopy shadowed the existing light even further. Salim and Anirudh weren't visible, but the stampeding commotion of their flight was audible.

Chitra set a scorching pace. Voices rang behind them and feet thudded on wet earth. They flashed past boulders, leapt across fallen logs and swept through obstructing vegetation as if it didn't exist. Vikram could hardly see. Sweat blurred his vision and the mist and the forest encapsulated everything with gloom.

Around a bend, cliffs appeared before them once more. Vikram despaired as a wall of solid rock barred their way, but Chitra shouted, pointing at the mist-shrouded cliff. There was a shaft-like gap in the towering rock and Chitra rushed towards it. Vikram looked up, gaping as he followed. A passage, about a metre wide, sliced upwards, tunnelling through the cliffs. The rock lining the passage was smooth and so finely weathered that it was impossible to tell whether the shaft was natural or man-made. Steps had been hewn from its base and rain had rendered them slippery. Even as he slipped and stumbled, Vikram marvelled at the rock corridor. Whether natural or carved by man, it was a magnificent passage through the cliffs.

Traversing the rock, he emerged on a level section of the mountain. The cliffs were below them now. There was grass and mist and a blustering wind. Salim stood a few yards away, his face ashen. He was staring in despair at Anirudh, who for some reason had sunk to his knees. Anirudh's expression—in complete contrast to Salim's—was jubilant and resplendent, like the joy of a blind man whose vision had been restored.

Salim was pleading with Anirudh, urging him to rise, but Anirudh was steadfastly ignoring his pleas.

'Do something,' urged Chitra, looking pleadingly at Vikram. 'This is ridiculous. Fine time to choose. We are running for our lives and he flops to the ground. Get him moving. You're the only one he listens to.'

Vikram knelt beside Anirudh.

Kiran called urgently and Chitra moved away, joining him and Aditya.

'This shaft is fantastic,' panted Kiran, gazing at the rock fissure at his feet. 'It's a passageway that can easily be defended. All we need is stones. The corridor is narrow and long, without any cover whatsoever.' He pointed down the fractured cliff. 'We can easily target the men as they climb. All it will take is two of us to defend the area. One to collect stones, the other to hurl them. Aditya and I can hold the men. The rest of you can run and get help.'

Chitra dismissed the idea outright. 'Forget it. We have to stick together.'

'Aditya,' called out Kiran. 'Quick, help me gather rocks. Heavy ones. A handful will do for now. We're going to pelt those guys. We'll make them regret chasing us.'

While his friends scrambled about collecting rocks, Vikram shook Anirudh by the shoulders.

Anirudh's face was flushed a deep red. His eyes were on fire and his chest was heaving. 'I know this place,' he gasped. 'This . . . this is the gateway to the plateau . . . the gateway that Rustom never let me cross.'

Chitra strode to where Vikram knelt beside Anirudh. 'Rustom!' she fumed. 'Who on earth is Rustom? He's gone mad . . . delirious.' She stamped her foot in frustration. 'Snap him out of it, Vikram. Slap him if you have to. DO SOMETHING!'

Kiran had positioned himself at the head of the passageway. There were five grenade-sized rocks at his feet, and Aditya was rapidly swelling his arsenal.

Anirudh was babbling. 'The waterfall is here . . . the one that the wind sweeps back . . . this is where I had seen it. There are forests, cliffs, caves. This is where Rustom and I lived for months. I know every inch of this place—'

Anirudh was prattling nonsense. Only a few minutes earlier, he had said he had never set foot in the Sahyadris, now he was proclaiming he had lived on this mountain for months. This was the worst possible time to turn delusional. Vikram raised his hand and slapped his friend hard on his cheek.

At the plateau entrance, Kiran tensed.

Two men were tearing up the rock corridor. Kiran's heart leapt as he recognized the tall figure up front. He grinned. The man was the same long-limbed assailant who had accosted him on the cliff, the very person he had a score to settle with. Clasping a rock, he took aim. His missile missed his intended target, bouncing off the wall, inches from the man, but it ricocheted, striking him on his chest and sending him tumbling on to his comrade behind him.

Vikram's forceful blow had worked on Anirudh. The rapturous expression on his face had evaporated and he had risen to his feet. He was looking about now, eyes alert, absorbing what was happening around him. Salim stood beside him, holding his arm.

While Kiran and Aditya showered rocks down the passageway, Vikram crossed to the verge of the grassy expanse they stood on, and halting short of its edge, surveyed the cloud-filled void beneath. As he had expected, cliffs—the very same ones they had seen from the lower plateau—guarded the shelf of mountain they stood upon. The cliffs were unassailable, like the walls of a fort. Kiran was right. The narrow gateway to the summit plateau could be exploited to their advantage. Controlling the gateway was the key. Whoever possessed it could block access and defend the summit.

Vikram turned. Salim was pulling Anirudh's hand. Anirudh was arguing with him and gesturing towards the passageway entrance where Kiran, Aditya and Chitra crouched.

Then Salim turned and ran.

'STOP HIM!' shouted Vikram.

Chitra and the others jerked their heads around.

Anirudh stood undecided, his gaze alternating between his mates and Salim's flashing rump. 'I'm going after him,' he yelled. Taking to his heels, he sprinted after Salim.

'Vikram!' shouted Aditya. 'You and Chitra go with them. Kiran and I will stay and defend the passageway. They've backed off already. There's no way they can get through. We can hold them off indefinitely. Go! Go with them and get help.'

Vikram stood undecided.

Chitra forced his decision. 'Makes sense,' she yelled. 'They can fend the men off while we get help.' She began to run. 'Come on,' she urged, looking back at Vikram. 'Don't just stand there. MOVE! We don't want to lose those two.'

Vikram made up his mind. 'Best of luck, guys!' he shouted. 'Hold the fort.'

'Punny!' shouted Aditya, laughing.

'We'll be back,' cried Vikram. Waving, he dashed after Chitra.

The mist hadn't swallowed Anirudh and Salim yet, but it was on the brink of doing so. They were visible, but barely, at the edge of a shadowy line of trees. In spite of the restrictive presence of the mist, a certainty was building inside Vikram that they were on the summit plateau of the mountain. The cliffs were below them now. Nothing towered above them any more. They were running across rolling highlands. The shadowed line of trees drew steadily closer. They soon entered them and Vikram knew he was in a forest.

There was a stillness inside that Vikram was familiar with—a stillness that only forests could conjure. Not a breath of wind. Only trees. Enveloping him, shrinking his world. Water dripped and leaves spiralled to the ground. The trees here were different from those on the lower slopes—shorter and rooted further apart, branches hanging low, snaking crookedly everywhere, interlocking above to create a canopy that screened the sky. It was dark and the mist hung in wisps. He couldn't see Salim and Anirudh, but he could hear them as they crashed through the forest. The forest floor was layered with leaves, and the thump of running feet was clearly audible.

Vikram had penetrated a short distance into the forest when a burst of gunfire brought him to a halt.

The gunshots took Kiran and Aditya by surprise too, sending them headlong to the ground. They had been making merry till then, flinging stones every time a head popped into the corridor. The furthest their pursuers had managed was only a handful of steps before beating a hasty retreat beneath a barrage of well-directed missiles. But the advent of a gun loaded with live bullets dramatically altered the equation.

Kiran stuck his head into the corridor and hurriedly withdrew it as a bullet screamed past his ear. He managed a glimpse down the rock shaft, however, and the sight he saw sent him tumbling backward.

'RUN!' he shouted. 'They are swarming up the stairs. It's no use. Rocks can't protect us from bullets. We cannot hold them back.'

Aditya sprang to his feet. He started instinctively after Vikram and the others, but changed his mind. He would be leading the men to his friends if he did so. There was cover on the right, a line of trees along the cliff edge. He sprinted towards them with Kiran following.

In the forest, the gunfire had ground everyone to a halt.

'ANIRUDH!' screamed Vikram.

The reply was instantaneous. 'I'M HERE!'

'WAIT THERE!' yelled Vikram. 'Wait for Chitra and me.'

Vikram caught up with them after a short run. Salim's face was sick with fear. In contrast, Anirudh's eyes were alight, his features remarkably free of alarm given the circumstances.

Chitra was taut with horror. 'Do you think—?'

Vikram's response was sharp. 'Of course not! Kiran and Aditya are too smart to get shot.'

'Bullets—' Shock replaced the horror on Chitra's face. 'What's going on?'

'Only Salim knows,' said Vikram grimly. 'Leave it for later, there's no time now.' He paused a moment, gathering his thoughts. 'Kiran and Aditya have been driven off. That's for sure. The gateway is open and they will be coming after us. We have to run.' He turned to Salim. 'Where do we go?' he asked in Hindi. 'You know this mountain. Is there another way down or is there someplace where we can safely hide?'

Salim was experiencing difficulty speaking. His jaw was quivering, in the manner of a child about to break into tears. 'They will kill us . . . they killed my brother. Now it is my turn—'

Chitra cut him off. 'Salim!' she bellowed. 'Stop babbling nonsense. Is there another way down?'

'There is a place we can hide!' blurted Anirudh. 'A cave. A cave shielded by a waterfall. I know where it is. No one will find us.'

Vikram and Chitra stared at each other. This was not the time for absurd propositions.

Vikram drew a breath. 'Look,' he said, 'we have a situation on our hands. If you don't mind—'

Vikram never completed his sentence. Anirudh turned away. Grabbing Salim's hand, he pulled the villager and began to run.

'STOP!' howled Chitra.

But Anirudh refused to pay heed. He dashed forward, sprinting at an angle to their original bearing, Salim racing behind.

'Idiot!' cried Chitra, frustration writ on her face.

Vikram grabbed Chitra's hand. 'Follow them! Come on. We have no choice.'

Anirudh ran like a man possessed. He tore forward without the slightest hesitation, as if he knew exactly where he was going. Salim, his dhoti filthy with mud, ran behind. The absence of ground vegetation allowed them to rush at full speed, dodging only tree trunks and vines that hung from them. Despite the damping effect of water on the leaves, the noise of their flight crackled like a forest fire. Vikram kept glancing behind, checking whether they had been discovered. For a while, there was no sound of pursuit, but Vikram's chest turned cold when voices rang behind them.

Chitra's face was grim. 'They've found us,' she panted, looking behind.

'I don't see them,' breathed Vikram, turning his head. 'They must be far behind. They won't catch us.'

'They will if we keep running behind that hallucinating fool!' exclaimed Chitra. 'We're insane to be following him.'

Chitra was mad at Anirudh. She would have walloped him if she could. But her frustration was of little consequence, as they had no choice in the matter. Anirudh was racing through the forest with the speed and nimbleness of a deer, and fleet-footed as they were, Chitra and Vikram were having difficulty keeping up with him.

All of a sudden, there were no trees. The forest had fallen behind like a roof retracted. An undulating plateau, shrouded by cloud, stretched before them. Anirudh kept going. The ground was covered with hip-high vegetation and a strong wind swept the mountain. It was raining, but they hardly noticed as they were soaked already. There was a pain in Vikram's stomach, but he ignored it. His breathing was laboured and his legs felt as if they were laden with all the muck and slime on the mountain.

Soon, the vegetation gave way to an area of scattered rock and grass. They splashed through puddles, forded streams and stumbled over inclines. They entered a bowl-shaped arena with curved sloping flanks. At its deepest point, Anirudh located a bubbling stream and rushed along its rocky bank.

Vikram kept glancing back as he ran. The rain and the fog were working to their advantage, limiting the range of view, but despair seized him when the fog lifted briefly and he spotted shadows in the distance. Anirudh had seen the shadows too and he suddenly changed direction, abandoning the stream and climbing out of the bowl depression.

'The fool has no idea where he's going,' panted Chitra, as Anirudh charged down a fractured incline.

Vikram kept silent. A feeling was building inside him that Anirudh knew what he was doing. And not just that, he was also deliberately misleading their pursuers. Vikram's hunch proved true when after a long ramble through sloping country, arcing in a wide circle, Anirudh zeroed in on the stream they had been following earlier.

The wind was blowing stronger now, its intensity comparable with that of Cellphone Alley. It flung rain in their faces, forcing them to slant their heads away. When it gusted, it rocked them, seeking to blow them off their feet. It chilled their cheeks and cut through their soaked clothing.

Clouds were whipping above their heads in woolly flurries when Anirudh finally halted. The stream flowed nearby, rushing over rocks and pebbles. It was tumbling fast now, but the roar of the wind drowned the sound of its flow.

Anirudh breathed heavily. Although exhausted, his face was vibrant and his eyes burned like the sun on a cloudless day.

'We are at the plateau's edge,' he panted, when they gathered about him. 'There are cliffs ahead and a sheer fall to a valley far below. The cave . . . the one I spoke of . . . is here on these cliffs. Nobody will find us there.'

Chitra stared witheringly at him. 'How would you know?' she queried in a voice so sharp that it could have sliced a brick.

'I know,' said Anirudh simply.

Chitra turned wrathful. 'Enough of this lunacy!' she erupted. 'You've gone bananas. You are delirious, mad. We've tolerated your fantasies long enough, but no more. We have to find a way down, to the valley, where we can get help. Now! Before the crazy men with their guns find us.'

Anirudh's hair fluttered in the wind. 'There is no way down from here,' he said.

Chitra spun about, turning to Salim. 'Why are you allowing him to lead us?' she cried. 'You're the one who knows this mountain. You brought us here. You are our guide. Show us the way down.'

Salim was in a state of mental collapse, in no condition to guide anybody. 'There . . . there is no way down,' he stuttered. 'Those men will kill me. The cave—' He turned to Anirudh, hands folded. 'Find the cave, Anirudh baba. Those men are ruthless. Find it quick or they will kill all of us.'

Chitra stared incredulously at Salim.

Vikram reached out and held her shoulders. 'Give Anirudh a chance. We've run out of options.' He looked at Anirudh. 'A cave would be perfect if there is one. Show us where it is. Fast. Those men aren't far behind us.'

Anirudh turned and strode towards the stream.

Despite the distance the stream had traversed, its waters were still clear and pure. Anirudh ran along its banks, body angled to ward off the wind.

The going turned more arduous. The wind assaulted them, driving at them with a force that threatened to flatten them. It was as if a jet aircraft was directing its exhaust at them. The gale blasted their ears and drove a stinging flow of droplets that forced them to drop their heads. The droplets grew in size and intensity as they stumbled behind Anirudh, till it felt like they were being sprayed by a fire hose.

Blinking, Vikram raised his head. The spray wasn't plummeting from the heavens; the rain hadn't intensified into a storm. It was the stream instead. The wind was hoisting the stream, airlifting its flow, swivelling it about and arcing it back at them. The edge of the plateau was only metres ahead. The stream was gushing towards it, but not a single drop flowed off its edge. Vikram experienced a tremor of elation. Anirudh had found the wind-terminated waterfall he had promised. Maybe the cave he spoke about existed too.

There was a shelf of black rock to their right. Anirudh forded the stream and crossed towards it. The shelf rose upwards at a sharp incline. Anirudh ascended the rock. The others followed, cresting the incline and descending the other side. The wind magically dropped. It was volubly there one moment, howling and screaming at them, and it was gone the next, as if a door had been slammed shut. Vikram felt numb. The sudden silence was deafening. He could stand without effort. There was no need to lean into the wind. He could hold his head up and see, though there wasn't much to look at except cloud and the weaving edge of the plateau. Anirudh had brought them to the spot where the plateau altered its orientation. The shelf of rock was the turning point, the juncture where the plateau curled upon itself, bending sharply backwards, almost at right angles to its earlier direction.

There was rock everywhere about them now. They were standing on the very cliffs themselves, their boundary a stone's throw ahead. Anirudh ran to the edge. The others stood back as he strode along the brink as if searching for something. He halted and, dropping to his knees, signalled them to join him.

Vikram held back while Chitra and Salim knelt beside Anirudh. He watched as they leaned forward and craned their necks over the edge, gazing where Anirudh pointed. Vikram's legs began to tremble. It was becoming chillingly apparent that Anirudh's cave lay over the edge.

Chitra rose and crossed to Vikram. 'There's a ledge down there. I can't see any cave, but he says the ledge leads to it, to the windward side of the rock shelf, beneath that revolving waterfall. I'm beginning to believe him. He seems to know what he's talking about.'

Vikram felt his breath catch in his chest. 'I'm not going down there,' he breathed.

'I don't know whether you have any choice,' said Chitra. 'That spur of rock is a great screen, but if those men come around it, which they are bound to at some point, you'll be forced to. Hang on. I'll go check where they are.'

While Chitra hurried to the rock incline, Vikram studied the plateau boundary. The reason the raging wind had suddenly died became apparent to him. The cause was two-fold. The rocky shelf itself protected the area, but more importantly, the plateau changed direction at this juncture, looping away from the wind.

Anirudh halted by Vikram's side. 'There used to be a forest here,' he said. 'There were trees that came almost to the cliff edge, but they are gone now.'

There were only fern and shrubs in the area Anirudh referred to. A forest would have provided cover, but the hip-high vegetation that existed wouldn't conceal them. It was becoming agonizingly clear to Vikram that they had run out of options. The cliff and Anirudh's cave were fast turning to frightening reality.

The puzzle of Anirudh's knowledge of the plateau confounded Vikram once more. But even as he turned to question him, he saw Chitra waving frantically and rushing down the shelf towards them. She was mouthing words, not speaking them. Her face was distressed, the urgency obvious.

Anirudh caught Vikram's arm, dragging him along. 'Come on! There's no time to waste. We have to get down.'

Salim had already slipped over the cliff edge. He seemed to be suspended in mid-air, only the upper half of his body visible. Vikram battled Anirudh's hand, pulling back as he neared the rock boundary. Mercifully, there was no wind. The presence of clouds also helped as it screened the magnitude of the drop. Still, Vikram's legs were quaking.

Freeing himself from Anirudh, he halted well short of the cliff edge.

Anirudh faced him. 'Remember the lake? You told me there that you had conquered your fear of heights and I believed you. I put my faith in your words. Prove them now.'

'This is different,' protested Vikram. 'The cliff edge is a matter of life and death.'

Anirudh shook his head. 'This is no different, Vikram. It's only upstairs here that you have a problem.' Anirudh pointed at his head as Vikram had earlier done. 'Back at Khadakwasla, I too felt I could have died on the lake. You spoke to me then. You instilled confidence in me and I trusted you. I'll supply the confidence now. You have to trust me.'

Anirudh clasped Vikram's hand once more, and leading him forward, halted barely a foot short of the edge. Prickles of sweat beaded Vikram's brow. His insides heaved, as if beset by a storm. Breathing turned painful as his chest contracted. It was as if the maelstrom of cloud that confronted him was an ocean. It dizzied him like a restless sea. He was swallowing, struggling to repel a surge of light-headedness when Chitra arrived, breathless.

Her face was stiff with urgency. 'They are almost here . . . too many to fight. We have to hide. Now! Fast!'

Anirudh addressed Chitra. 'Salim's gone ahead. Follow him. I've told you where the cave is. Go slowly. The ledge widens further on and it gets easier. The wind will strike when you turn the corner, but by then the ledge will be much wider so there shouldn't be a problem. I'm bringing Vikram along.'

Chitra lowered herself off the edge. 'See you at the cave,' she said in farewell. 'Don't waste a moment. They could come around the corner any minute.' She dropped away, descending without fear. She vanished from view, her waist and shoulders first, followed by her head, and then she was gone.

'I'll go,' said Anirudh. 'I'll stand on the edge and help you. Place your weight on me. It doesn't matter. Have confidence. I will support you.'

Vikram battled a wave of nausea as he watched Anirudh drop over the edge. On hands and knees, he crawled forward. Mustering the remnants of his battered courage, he leaned his head over the edge.

There was an outcropping below. It was more than a foot wide and Anirudh's feet were planted on it. There was nothing but emptiness beneath. His stomach churned.

'Move towards me,' instructed Anirudh. 'That's it. Now turn.'

Vikram was in a trance. His mind had blanked out. He was grateful it had done so because if it were alert, it would never have permitted him to lower himself to the ledge beneath.

Anirudh assisted him. Reaching down, he guided Vikram's feet, installing them firmly on the ledge.

Anirudh spoke in an unhurried voice. 'The slope is gentle. You won't face a problem. I'm turning. Place a hand on the wall, the other on my shoulder. Hold tight and follow me.'

Vikram did as he was told. The cliff walls were dark and wet. Tufts of grass sprouted in cracks in the wall.

Anirudh spoke comfortingly. 'Easy,' he said. 'We're in no hurry. Nobody can see us now.'

It was true. Their heads had dropped below the rim of the plateau. Vikram considered asking Anirudh to halt as they were screened from view and safe from their pursuers, but only for a moment, till his gaze slipped to the cloud void to his right. His breath turned to ice in his chest. The cave was safer.

The ledge descended, weaving along the cliff wall, widening as it did so.

Vikram walked in a trance.

Anirudh spoke, his voice gentle and encouraging. 'Congratulations, Vikram. You've done it. The knee-shaking portion is behind you. Now it's a stroll.'

Vikram grimaced. Stroll! He would have laughed if he were in a better frame of mind. Anirudh couldn't have chosen a more absurd adjective to describe the nerve-racking journey. Yet he couldn't deny that the ledge was widening and settling his nerves. His knees weren't knocking any more, and a semblance of control was returning to his legs.

Except for the vertical face of the cliff wall, there was only space and cloud around him. He knew now what it felt to be a bird, and it was a wonderful feeling. Raw, crisp sensations were rising inside him, emotions he would never have thought possible. To his everlasting astonishment, he discovered that he was enjoying himself. He felt liberated. Like an eagle, he was one with the sky and the cloud.

The setting was wild and incredible: the racing cloud, the grey void, the dark, dripping cliff walls, the ledge and the tufts of grass waving in the wind. Vikram had entered the realm of birds, a world that was known only to mountaineers and those blessed with stout heads and hearts.

But Vikram was not stout-hearted. His fragile confidence was being shaken again. A shrieking noise—steadily increasing in power—was rattling him. The wind. It was howling with a frenzy that was certain to blow him off his perch.

Anirudh halted. 'The wind's going to hit us around the corner, exactly beneath the waterfall. Don't worry about the waterfall. You saw it earlier, above. There's not a drop falling. The wind's holding it back. The cave is right there, carved into the wall beneath the waterfall. Prepare for the wind. Crawl the final distance. It's easier that way.'

There was a bend in the cliff wall ahead. The wind wailed its warning well before they reached the turn, and both Anirudh and Vikram were on their hands and knees when they rounded the curve.

The wind struck them with appalling force. Vikram crouched, flattening himself against the ledge. Water, a fine mist, whipped his face. Anirudh was holding the cliff wall and rising to his feet. There was a crack in the wall beside him and Vikram spotted movement inside the cavity. Chitra was there, reaching out with her hand. Anirudh grasped it and with Chitra's aid clambered into the cave.

Vikram looked up. There were white tresses of water above. But the wind was blowing them backwards. The fine mist raining upon him was the fractional flow that escaped the wind. Chitra was signalling. He crawled towards her and reached for her hand. Secure in her grip, he rose and scrambled into the slit-like aperture of the cave.

The first, most striking feature of the cave was the absence of wind. It was still inside, like a shuttered room, a haven of calm after the tempest outside. The second was the almost complete absence of light. Darkness pressed on him like the lid of a coffin.

'Don't move!' hissed Chitra. 'You could break a leg. The floor is uneven. Remember the caves in the Andamans*? There could be crevasses here. Back off slowly . . . just a bit. My torch is giving me trouble. I need the light from outside to see what the matter is. It's supposed to be waterproof, but the rain seems to have . . . AAARGH!'

Chitra screamed suddenly.

Vikram wasn't sure what terrified him more, Chitra's scream or the sudden burst of sound and movement above his head. But he understood immediately what had transpired.

'It's all right!' he cried. 'It's a bat! There are bats in the cave.'

'Dumb animal!' hooted Chitra. 'It could have killed me. Stupid creature.'

'Keep a lookout,' cautioned Vikram. 'There could be more. I have a torch too. Wait . . . I'll pull it out.'

Vikram unzipped his jacket and groped inside for his torch.

'My torch,' Chitra muttered grumpily. 'I dropped it . . . brainless bats—' She ducked again as another shadow

---

* Refer to *Andaman Adventure: The Jarawa.*

whizzed past, barely an inch from her face. 'Get that torch of yours out, Vikram,' she shouted. 'These creatures are spooking me.'

'Take it easy,' snapped Vikram. 'It's wrapped in plastic and I don't want to drop it. Do you want two lost torches?'

'Sorry,' replied Chitra, her tone suddenly contrite. 'Take your time . . . all the time in the world. Don't drop it, whatever happens. Anirudh . . . do you have your torch with you?'

There was no reply.

Several bats winged out of the cave.

Chitra called out again. 'Anirudh . . . answer me . . . where are you?'

Vikram carefully unwrapped his torch and gripping it firmly, switched it on. A bright beam lanced forward, piercing the darkness. The cave was a cavernous one, much larger than its slit-like opening suggested. It was as if someone had gouged a massive chunk of the mountain, leaving an enormous empty space behind. Dark walls rose about them, fusing above in an uneven ceiling, every inch of it carpeted with endless ranks of dark, dangling creatures. A cacophony of high-pitched clicks erupted as Vikram ran his beam over them.

Vikram hurriedly lowered his beam. The cave floor was notched and uneven, as Chitra had anticipated. Jagged fissures split its rocky floor.

'ANIRUDH!' yelled Chitra. 'I told you it is dangerous to move. Stop! There's a crevasse behind you . . . and . . . FREEZE.' Chitra screamed the last word.

Vikram swung his beam about.

Anirudh had traversed far into the cave. He stood poised beside a dark, gaping chasm, his back to it. But it wasn't the chasm that had triggered Chitra's alarm. On a rock beside Anirudh, inches from his feet, lay a coiled, sinuous creature, its head raised, hood puffed. Vikram's blood ran still.

A cobra.

'Don't move,' warned Chitra. The shrill edge of her tone was gone. Panicking Anirudh could prove disastrous. One backward step and the chasm would swallow him. 'The snake won't harm you . . . as long as you don't move. I can handle the snake. I'm coming. Cobras are harmless unless threatened. It's not going to attack you . . . just remain still.'

Anirudh stood paralysed, his mouth frozen in a soundless scream. Chitra edged forward. Silence reigned inside the cave. Outside, the wind heaved and there was the patter of rain. Anirudh's shadow was large and deathly still. Chitra's crept forward.

Salim babbled something in Marathi. Vikram and Chitra had no idea what he said, but the fear in the villager's voice was evident.

'Quiet!' hissed Chitra. 'Don't panic him.'

But Chitra's warning was too late. Anirudh's right foot edged shakily backwards.

'STOP!' cried Vikram.

'ANIRUDH!' screamed Chitra.

Shadows flickered on the cave walls. The participants in the ghastly drama were moving. Only the snake did not budge. Anirudh's half-illuminated torso shifted as he stepped backwards.

Chitra lunged despairingly forward. Anirudh's foot descended, expecting support. But there was nothing, only empty space. Anirudh screamed as he lost balance. His body tumbled in slow motion. It hung suspended for a moment, and then he was gone, swallowed by the chasm.

PART 2
ANIRUDH'S DREAM

Pain and shock of the kind Anirudh suffered can sometimes trigger unusual events. Only in rare cases, when the strands of fate and destiny entwine, do dream and reality merge as one. So it was with Anirudh.

> 'Dreams are true when they last, and do we not live in dreams?'
>
> —Alfred, Lord Tennyson

IRFAN

First, there was pain. A frightful all-consuming pain. It was as if a volcano had ruptured in his head and bubbling lava was scorching the passageways of his brain. Desperate to douse the fire inside, he heaved, twisting mightily, but his muscles refused to obey. He opened his mouth to scream, but his lips were locked, as if taped by gum, and though he exerted powerfully, he couldn't budge them. To his horror, he discovered that it wasn't just his lips; his legs, his hands, his arms, his shoulders—every joint, every sinew, every tendon—had ceased to function. His body for some strange reason had packed up on him. He couldn't muster even a twinge of response. Yet, in a cruel pairing of sensory associations, though his systems had shut down, his agony raged unchecked.

Torment consumed him. A million ants with knife-edged teeth feasted in his head. It was too much to bear. He prayed for his consciousness to release him. Even death was preferable to the suffering inflicted on him. His stomach heaved. His lips unlocked as he retched. He struggled to close them, but as before, they refused to heed his urging. The pain spread now, shifting from his head to his guts, his bowels, his intestines. The torment abandoned his head, relocating to his abdomen. The ants morphed into a school of fish. They sped turbulently inside his gut, churning his innards. As he endured this fresh assault, he felt a stirring in his numbed brain. The gut-wrenching sensation was familiar. Improbable though it seemed, he felt he was on a boat, pitching on a storm-tossed sea.

A soundless scream reverberated in his head. No! Anything but the sea! The sea was his most terrible failing, his worst fear. He prayed for the pain to return to his head. The biting of the ants were gentle prods compared to the misery of the ocean. But the marauding fish continued to inhabit his stomach, circling relentlessly, speeding faster with each passing minute. A fresh rush of despair engulfed him. Another of his nightmares had come true. He was on the ocean, trapped on a boat in a violent storm.

A dim light penetrated the fog that blanked his vision. It was a dismal light, grey and morbid. A dreary sky took shape above, packed with clouds. The clouds reassured him, bestowing a faint sensation of relief. The sky had been turbulent and troubled by clouds a while ago—before the pain had struck. Maybe he was pulling out of his nightmare, surfacing from his trauma. The boat and the storm were untrue, a figment of his imagination.

Then he saw something slanting above him. It was a pole: a worn, weathered pole with a cloth attached to it. The cloth was white and lines of stitching ran spidery patterns across it. The cloth was large, like a tent, and it was straining as if some mighty force was welling against it. His exhausted brain identified the flapping cloth. It was a sail and the slanting pole a mast.

His ears had been wrapped in eerie silence since the torment had begun. But they pulsed with noise suddenly, confirming his darkest fears. There was the deafening crash and hiss of an angry sea. Adding to the tumult was the roar of the wind, the creaking of the mast, and the thunderous flap of cloth and sail.

Sensation returned abruptly to his body. His teeth began to chatter uncontrollably. He was cold and wet. He discovered he could move again. His limbs responded to his urgings. He could toss and turn. His lips opened wide as a tortured moan escaped them. The sky was spinning, so was the sail and the mast. He pressed down on his eyes, screwing them shut. Maybe if he kept them locked the nightmare would abate. But there was no relief. He despaired as the cold, the retching and the misery persisted. Time passed. Miserably. Painfully. Finally, a deep weariness swept over him and a liberating all-encompassing darkness released him.

He had no idea how long it was before he opened his eyes, but even before he did the wretchedness returned. The crash of the sea and the flapping of the sail assaulted his ears once more. An unaltered cloudy sky appeared, but this time, in addition, the hazy image of a face hovered above. A most extraordinary feeling overcame him as he stared at the face. It was a countenance he had never set eyes on before. He was certain that it was unfamiliar, but in a confounding twist of reason, the face was not only familiar but beloved too. The nightmare was befuddling his brain. How could he describe a strange face as familiar and beloved when he had never set eyes on it before?

The face belonged to a boy. He was thin with delicate clear-cut features. In spite of the gloom, he seemed pale, his complexion not ordinarily fair, but sickly white instead. His skin was smooth, with just a hint of beard and moustache. His nose was small and perfectly shaped. His eyes were large and brown, reflecting a mix of concern, love and friendship.

A hand reached out with a damp cloth and he felt his face being swabbed and cleansed. A bottle was placed gently on his lips and he gagged and pushed it aside. But the boy with the beloved face persisted, forcing water down his throat. Then the bottle was removed and loving hands massaged his arms and legs.

He lay sprawled on the restless deck, supine, unwilling to move, certain that if he raised himself he would retch and his head would spin absurdly again. He closed his eyes and, as if bidden by him, the encompassing darkness returned. For the first time since the ordeal had begun, he felt pleased, as if he had accomplished something. By simply exerting himself, he had managed to pull out from a depressing portion of the nightmare. There was no mistaking, however, that the nightmare was ascendant, in complete command. It had him in its grip. Yet, at the same time, it was flashing signals that it was easing up. The darkness had provided tantalizing glimpses of better times: of horses, of fun, of a city, and a life that intrigued and excited him.

Maybe the ordeal wasn't a nightmare. Maybe it was a dream. Certainly no ordinary dream. He was sure the images it conveyed were true, only that they portrayed the experiences of another person, transporting him to another consciousness, another life. The dream had a story to tell. It was the story of a life that had long ceased, but a life that in some inexplicable way was connected with his.

The dream nudged him gently, willing him to move on. But he resisted. The pain and the sickness had drained him. The encompassing darkness was soothing, and he wanted nothing more than to drift in its snug emptiness. He wrestled the dream, attempting to keep it at bay. But even as he opposed it, the dream impressed upon him that it was in a tearing hurry. There was to be no dilly-dallying. It might permit him a degree of navigational control, but there would be no recess; it had a mission and it would drag him relentlessly forward, unravelling the life it intended he know.

The name the dream bestowed upon him was Irfan. It informed him that Irfan was fifteen years old; that Irfan loved horses and that he was pathologically afraid of sea voyages. Nothing wrong with that: the age was correct, horses were indeed his passion and he hated anything to do with water.

Irfan . . . it was only momentarily that the name sounded odd. Then almost at once, Irfan seemed natural. This caused him to panic because all traces of his real name vanished and the calling Irfan stuck fast in his head. His name! How could it slip his mind? It was his identity: the word that embodied him, the calling that personified him, and yet in a flash it was gone.

Now he was Irfan.

No! Something deep inside him rebelled. Though he was powerless, a prisoner of the dream, he wasn't going to abandon his real self. The dream might dictate he was Irfan, but that wasn't true. On this issue, he would oppose the dream. He would flow along with the dream; live the life it revealed. But he was an observer, a bystander staring through a looking glass. 'Bystander'. Yes, 'bystander' would do. Till his real name slipped back into his consciousness, 'bystander' was how he would address himself.

Thwarted only briefly by his tantrum, the dream, like a fast-flowing river, claimed the bystander once more, sweeping him along in its turbulent midst. But peculiarly, as if the river course was familiar to him, there were many things the bystander knew the instant the dream began.

An encyclopedic knowledge of Irfan, every incident from his birth to the present moment, was known to him. He knew that Irfan's mother was no more; that she had died in the year 1844, when he was three years old. She had passed away in their home town of Mahabaleshwar. A poisonous snake had bitten her and she had collapsed and died within minutes. The year 1844 was significant in that not only was it the year Irfan's mother had died but it was also the year his father, Mohammed Aziz, devastated by his wife's passing, had quit Mahabaleshwar.

Irfan knew his father as a deeply religious man. Mohammed Aziz was a God-fearing soul, a man who was a firm believer in destiny and fate. He often told young Irfan that his migration to Bombay was a fate he had never desired but was forced to accept. Allah had decreed that his wife must die and so it had come to pass. Allah had been kind thereafter, securing him a job and his son an education. Allah was great; whatever his will, Mohammed Aziz unquestioningly abided by it.

It so happened that Mr Brown, a British saab, was holidaying in Mahabaleshwar with his family at the time Irfan's mother died. The Browns lived in Bombay and vacationed in Mahabaleshwar each year during the hot season, employing Irfan's father as their horseman. Mr and Mrs Brown were kind people. Shortly after the passing of his mother, they had invited his father to work permanently for them, and that was how Irfan, still a child then, had come to Bombay.

The Bombay revealed by the dream, however, was very different from the Mumbai the bystander was familiar with. Most confusing was the Fort located at the very heart of this Bombay. As far as he knew, there was no Fort in Bombay, yet not only was this strange Fort the most prominent edifice in the city but it was also the focal point where business, trade and all activities of consequence were conducted. Located near the southern tip of Bombay, it was a huge Fort, fronted by the sea on one side and a large open space called the Esplanade on the other. The walls of the Fort were grim and black and encircled by a deep moat.

The Fort had been built by Englishmen and their trading company more than a hundred years earlier when the islands of Bombay were unsafe and vulnerable to plunder by marauding armies. The Maratha power—hostile and implacably distrustful of the British—was at its peak then and the seas that surrounded Bombay were infested with pirates. By Irfan's time, however, the Maratha power had been vanquished and the entire coastline was firmly in the hands of the Englishmen and their powerful trading enterprise, the East India Company.

Two centuries of British rule had transformed Bombay from a collection of swamp-ridden, mosquito-infested islands into a flourishing city, home to a burgeoning population of energetic, industrious and enterprising citizens. Traders, craftsmen, artisans, boatbuilders, adventurers and businessmen poured into the city from the vast Indian hinterland and from around the world. There was no port on India's west coast, or for that matter, along the entire rim of the Arabian Sea that could match Bombay's eminence. Dhows from Arabia, steamers and tall mast boats from Europe, vessels from the Mediterranean, from Siam, from China, from Japan, from Africa and the Dutch Indies, crowded Bombay's magnificent harbour. At her sprawling bazaars, the vessels stocked their holds, loading cotton, spices and produce from the shores of India, and setting sail from the city's sun-drenched shores, they ferried their precious cargo to every port in the known world.

People of every possible colour, of every religion and caste inhabited the thriving island city. Amidst the marketplaces and in its winding gullies could be spotted the jebela of the Arab, the sweaty suit of the European, the elaborate costume of the wealthy Jew, the shining dark skin of the Abyssinian, the pale complexion of the Parsee, and the oriental features of the Chinese.

Yet the Bombay of Irfan's time was still a fledgling city, infinitely smaller than the sprawling metropolis the bystander was familiar with. Though crowded in the areas surrounding the Fort, it was still wild and green in its extensive heartland and far-flung regions. Panthers roamed the forests of Malabar Hill and the occasional tiger could still be spotted, swimming the harbour or prowling the fringes of the city. There were rice flats in Byculla, coconut plantations at Mahim, forests at Matunga, and the sea breached vast areas, flooding the channels between the original seven islands of the city.

It was to this city that the dream guided the bystander. The encompassing darkness brightened as the bystander willingly allowed himself to be led forward. The pain in his head had gone and his sickness had dwindled to a ghastly memory. The raging sea, the voyage and Irfan's misery lay in the future. The dream, for reasons known only to itself, had opened out of sequence, but it was correcting now. The darkness brightened further and he discovered that he was on the northern shores of Bombay, on a deserted beach fringed by coconut trees.

Irfan was a boy of medium height and build. The bystander was jolted by a stab of wonder as he set eyes on him for the first time. Even though the face he was gazing at was certainly not his, he experienced the uncanny sensation that he was staring into a mirror. The dark eyes, the rounded forehead, the crooked nose and flat cheeks were so familiar that it could be a mysterious twin he was gazing at. But the bystander quickly discovered differences. Irfan's fingers, unlike his bent middle digits, were long and smooth, each of them perfect. Irfan's colour was darker too and the skin on his face was fleshier, more weathered and robust.

Irfan was wearing dark cotton robes that reached to his knees and there was a cap that fitted tightly on his head. He was seated on a towering splinter of rock on a sloping shore. A moist wind was blowing from the sea, dampening his brow and whistling noisily through the palm trees behind. Large breakers, capped with foaming crests, surged across a curving beach, thundering as they streaked and frothed over the sand. In spite of the booming surf, from the sea thrummed a noise that equalled if not exceeded the roar of the elements.

There were birds on the water. Seagulls. An immense cackling swarm studded the sky and the sea. Their white plumage powdered the sea, flashing like snow on the water. Above, in the air, they cavorted in dense clouds so thick that they blocked the light of the sun, swirling like mists in the air.

The beach had been empty and quiet when Irfan had last visited. There had been no gulls then. That was just after Nariyal Poornima, the festival that celebrated the withdrawal of the monsoon. Now, several weeks later, Bombay's mild winter had set in and the gulls had returned, as they always did at this time of the year.

But Irfan hardly saw or heard the birds. His mind was elsewhere in a distant land, lost in thought. Clutched in his hands was a brown envelope with letters. The precious contents of the letters had so absorbed him that hours had flashed by without him noticing. Although he knew every carefully inked word by heart, he plucked them out again, carefully, so as to not lose them to the gusting wind, and scanned them once more.

Dear Irfan,

Our passage through the sea was dull and boring. There was nothing to do except stare at the water and the sky, and at night, the stars. Not a day passed without us wishing you were on board the steamer with us. We could have had so much fun together. Peter misses you terribly and so do I.

The only enjoyable leg of our journey was our halt at Cairo where we saw the great pyramids. It is difficult to believe that a civilization many thousand years before our time could build something so monumental and enduring. The pictures Mr Hunter showed us in his books cannot do justice to their magnificence. I hope that one day you will be able to see them too. It is a shame that you refuse to travel by sea, Irfan. You must overcome your fear, if only to see the world. You have no idea what you are missing. We didn't either, till we sailed the seas for the first time.

England is very different from India. Peter doesn't like it here because it is rainy and cold. It doesn't rain as hard as it does during the monsoon, but the clouds never seem to go away. I miss the sun and the blue skies of Bombay. Here, it is gloomy and cold.

Ealing is a very small place. Fewer people live here than those in Bombay's Fort. There are many trees where we live, but most have lost their leaves and appear dead and skeletal. Everyone says the weather is going to turn colder and that depresses me, but the prospect of snow is exciting and makes the cold bearable.

Peter hates school here, but it isn't that bad except that the teachers are frosty, much like the weather. There is no one amongst the staff who can compare with our sunny and cheerful Mr Hunter.

It is late now and Mother wants me to go to bed. Peter is fast asleep. He hasn't been well these past few days. He has caught a cold, a nasty one, which bothers me because at night his coughing sometimes sounds frighteningly like the convulsions that often seize Mother. Thankfully, the doctor who looks after Mother says there's no cause to worry and that he will get well soon.

As I end, I am reminded of Mother's nostalgia for the home she left behind in England when she first came to India. I remember, in particular, her words about never realizing how much you love a place till you leave and travel far away.

How true her words are. I miss you terribly, Irfan. I miss Father too and also our wonderful home in Bombay. I long for its warmth, the murmur and smell of the sea, and the wonderful green of our garden. I must end now.

Your loving friend,
Ralph

The second letter was from Mrs Alice Brown, Ralph and Peter's mother. When Irfan lifted the sheet, he pressed it to his nose. The flower-rich scent of her perfume was his most powerful memory of her. But there was no trace of her on the neatly penned note. He breathed only the salt and the sea.

Dear Irfan,

I thought continuously of you when the children were enjoying the great pyramids in Cairo. Irfan, you must teach yourself to overcome your fear of the sea. It will be a shame if you restrict your view of this great world to Bombay. There is so much to see, to learn and to discover.

You must travel, Irfan. Your father's dearest wish is to take you home to Mahabaleshwar, but you constantly deny him. You must understand that, like Craig and I, your father is getting old now. It will gladden his heart if you fulfil his desire. Undertake the journey. Gather your courage, banish forever your dread of the water. Do it for my sake.

I trust you are enjoying your new school. I know the teachers are not of the standard of Mr Hunter who tutored you and the twins these past years. Yet, you must attend, as the learning will keep your mind fresh and alert. The effort is worth your while. It will benefit you when your tuitions resume, following our return to Bombay.

I know our parting has hurt you deeply, Irfan. Our leaving was thrust upon us. But God-willing my health will be restored soon and the boys and I will return. Have faith and pray for us and be assured that I will never abandon you; it is a promise that I have made to your sweet and wonderful mother.

With deepest affection,
Alice Brown

The letters were the first Irfan had ever received. No one had written to him before. Yet, instead of evoking excitement, their arrival had unsettled him. Emotions he had managed to bury deep inside had been roused and he had thought that he would break down and cry.

It was Mr Craig Brown, the father of the twins, who had delivered the envelope to him. Mr Brown had come home from office for lunch, on the hour as he always did, driven in his handsome black carriage by Irfan's father, Mohammed Aziz. Then, as was his habit, after handing his hat, gloves and cane to his manservant, he had retired to his favourite armchair in the veranda. But that afternoon, the manservant, instead of fetching him his drink, had been dispatched to summon Irfan. Mohammed Aziz had been leading his horses to the stables when Irfan arrived and he had halted, watching as Mr Brown, with a kindly smile, handed the envelope to his son.

Irfan's hands had quivered as he held the envelope. Conscious that he was being watched, Irfan had swallowed, smothering an all too familiar sensation that was welling inside him. Tears had blurred his eyes, and terrified that his emotions would get the better of him, Irfan had stumbled blindly away. His feet had led him instinctively to the stables, where he had sought his horse and ridden away with the unopened envelope tucked safely inside a pocket.

The quiet beach on the shores of Mahim was Irfan's favourite hideaway. Ralph and Peter too had loved this unfrequented corner of Bombay. Surprisingly, when he had arrived at the black rock and read the precious notes, the flood of tears he had braced himself for never emerged. The very beach itself had impaled his wounded heart, arousing memories of joyous afternoons with the twins. Remembrances of their favourite pastime of speeding their horses on wet sand—hooves pounding, mud flying and blond hair billowing in the wind—had flashed before his eyes. Yet, in spite of the burning sense of loss, not a single tear had moistened his eye.

Irfan wondered why the tears hadn't come. He had shed more tears during these past few weeks than in his entire life. Could his inexhaustible supply have finally dried up? Or could it be that he had overcome the misery of his friends' departure?

His father had said that time would heal his pain. Mohammed Aziz had assured him so on that fateful morning at the docks as a steamer bore his precious friends and their mother away. Irfan hadn't believed his father then. How could he? His tender childhood world had been destroyed. Ralph and Peter weren't ordinary friends; they were his best friends, the only friends he had ever known. They had promised they would return, but that was to be a year later. Like the lengthening wake of the London-bound steamer, an impossibly dark and friendless existence had stretched ahead of him. The despair had been overpowering. A torrent of tears had flowed from him and he had wept for days on end. He had believed then that the tears would never cease, yet now, they had dried. Maybe soon, as his father had said, the pain would dwindle too.

Irfan discovered that his thoughts, for the first time, could dwell on his friends and their mother without the mortification of tears and misery. He sat transfixed, his mind many thousands of miles away. Neither the charm of the secluded beach nor the squabbling throng of birds distracted him. Visions of a cold and clouded land floated before him. He explored a tiny town with steeples and churches and a handful of residents. He drifted through forests with trees that had no leaves. And in the chill and the gloom, he came to a tiny cottage—like the ones in Mr Hunter's books—with a sloping roof, a large chimney and wooden floors. A radiant light shone from the cottage, dispelling the winter gloom. Inside, it was warm and wonderful, and fast asleep beside a roaring fireplace were his precious friends and their beloved mother.

The cloud of birds thinned, fragmenting and finally dispersing as the sun fell into the sea and the sky turned scarlet and gold. The seagulls were gone when Irfan finally snapped out of his reverie. With a start, he realized how late it was. A long journey home awaited him. His father had warned him to start early. Bombay's roads weren't safe in the dark.

He dropped to the ground and hurrying across a sloping strip of sand, entered the gloom beneath the swaying canopy of palms. An angry snort greeted him. Blinking, he spotted the sprightly shadow of his horse, Mohini. The animal turned away as Irfan approached, a sure sign that she was angry. Lowering her head, she pretended to browse the unappetizing yellow grass beneath the trees. Mohini was a handsome cream-coloured mare with a high head and flowing mane. Irfan had liked her the moment he first set eyes on her at the stables at Bhendi Bazaar. Though Irfan rode Mohini wherever he went, she was not his horse. She belonged to an Arab horse-trader named Ismail. Irfan helped out at Ismail's stables, and the horse-trader had obliged him the use of the animal in return for his services.

Mohini was upset. She had been neglected for hours and was determined to make a show of her displeasure. A flock of egrets, wings flashing orange and red in the twilight, settled in the swaying palms as Irfan stroked the horse and whispered apologies in her ear.

The call of the faithful carried faintly on the evening breeze, reminding Irfan of his unsaid prayers. He had hoped to visit the mosque in the village of Mahim on his way home but had delayed too long at the cove. He remembered then that there was a blanket in Mohini's saddlebags, thoughtfully packed for him by his father. He retrieved the blanket and, much to Mohini's disgust, returned to the beach. Spreading the cloth on a patch of clean brown sand, he placed it to face a few degrees north of the crimson patch of sky where the sun had buried itself. The sea grew dark and twilight faded as he recited his prayers.

Mohini rebuked him with a fresh snort when he returned. But surprisingly, she submitted to him, grudgingly allowing him to tighten her saddle and mount. The wind eased and died as Mohini trotted away from the shore. Bats swooped low and crickets crooned noisily. Visibility improved as he came to an open area where he found the mud track that would lead him to Byculla. After an open section, the track entered a plantation of palm trees again. He passed a crossroad and then a pond with buffaloes wallowing quietly in dark water.

Mohini snorted as they approached a banyan tree standing somewhat incongruously amongst the palms. Something had disturbed the horse and alert to her signal, Irfan narrowed his eyes, squinting at the gloom beneath the banyan's heavy canopy. He noticed movement beside the massive trunk of the tree. Mohini nervously hurried forward, but Irfan tugged her reins, forcing her to halt.

RUSTOM

Peering at the darkness, Irfan picked out a shadow. Edging his reluctant mount forward, he saw that the shadow was short and slight. Staring, he discerned a boy, standing bent, his shoulders drooping. Despite the lack of light, it was clear that the boy was distressed.

Irfan cleared his throat. 'Err . . . is something the matter? Can I help?'

The boy sobbed quietly, his body shaking. Irfan waited, unsure. He calmed Mohini as she fidgeted.

The boy spoke finally, his voice interspersed with sobs. 'They stole my money.' He gulped heavily. 'Two men . . . they . . . they took my horse away . . . left me here.'

Irfan restrained Mohini as she pulled determinedly at the reins. 'I'm riding to the Fort,' he said. 'If you are headed that way, I can take you home or to the police if you like.'

The boy looked up. His headgear was a rounded hat, worn typically by Parsee boys. His tear-streaked face was pale. He nodded miserably, stifling a sob.

Dropping to the ground, Irfan helped the boy on to the saddle and mounted behind him. Mohini tossed her head, upset at having to carry double. Irfan spoke quietly to her. He turned her around and spurred her into a canter.

The boy's name was Rustom and he lived in the Fort. Clinging tearfully to the saddle, the boy unburdened himself. The stolen money belonged to his uncle, Mr Palkhivala, who owned a business that fabricated palkis and horse carriages. Rustom had delivered a carriage to a trader who lived at Mahim barely an hour earlier. The transaction had taken longer than he had expected, and it was late by the time the trader paid him. It was on his return, while passing the banyan tree, that the robbers had struck and made off with the money, taking his horse along too. He was certain that his assailants were Parsees. Although they had worn masks, their accent and traits were typically Parsee.

'My uncle—' the boy's voice trailed away. Sobs choked him and Irfan had to hold him as he crumpled in the saddle. 'He . . . he will never forgive me. The money is gone . . . his horse lost. He will throw me out and I will have no home.'

But they found the horse. It had been abandoned several miles ahead and they came across it grazing quietly by the roadside. With the recovery of the mount, Irfan's services were no longer required, but the dispirited boy seemed incapable of looking after himself, and he tearfully thanked Irfan when he offered to escort him home.

They moved quickly through the deepening night. Mohini ran swiftly, eager to return home. From the palm groves of Mahim, they entered the dark and empty flats of Byculla. Avoiding the crowded inner town areas, Irfan chose the deserted expanse of Grant Road. They sped their horses along the elevated and empty thoroughfare, coming finally upon people—a crowd of carriages and their drivers beside the road's famous theatre. Several carriages were parked opposite the theatre gates, their attendants lounging alongside, waiting for their saabs who were being entertained inside. Irfan and Rustom pressed on, making good time through the pleasant tree-lined areas of Cavel and Girgaum. Very quickly, they emerged on the open plain of the Esplanade.

Irfan slowed Mohini to a walk and Rustom's weary mount readily eased its gait. The Esplanade was Irfan's favourite area. Its immense open spaces never failed to lift his spirits. He breathed deeply, enjoying the cold wind sweeping in from the sea. But for the stars and a sprinkling of lights in the distance, there was darkness everywhere. The sea was a blur of shadow to one side. Although at that distance, the Fort was lost in shadow too, needles of light from the tightly packed buildings behind its walls betrayed its hovering presence. There were lights on the Esplanade grounds too, pinpricks of radiance that flocked like fireflies beside the Fort's Church Gate. The lights indicated that they had made it back in good time. The Fort gates were still open and people were out enjoying the evening.

After a long traverse across the Esplanade's flat plain, the lights drew nearer, and as they approached the Fort, Irfan wondered whether Rustom's uncle was one of those who fancied evenings on the Esplanade. The Esplanade was a popular recreation ground for those who lived inside the Fort. Its windy open spaces drew large crowds in the evenings, but it was mostly Parsees who lingered on after the sun had set. Evenings on the Esplanade were a ritual for many of their community. They brought along mats to recline upon and lanterns to see in the dark. Rustom, however, gave no indication that his relatives were about. He huddled miserably in his saddle, head firmly down as they approached the flickering lights.

The evening revellers were in good cheer. Parsee hats bobbed everywhere. Several of the mats were crowded. On one, a solemn-faced Parsee gentleman was surrounded by a group of youngsters squatting obediently at his feet, their faces engrossed, imbibing his every word as he read from a book. On others, families were sprawled, and Irfan's nostrils twitched as the aroma of bhajia and chutney wafted deliciously from plates spread before them. There were people playing chess, slouched over their boards, frowning at their pieces in the dim light of their lanterns. Children shouted and scurried everywhere and men in long robes strolled companionably.

Weaving through the throng, they came to the massive outer gate of the Fort. It was an impressive structure, tall enough for an elephant to walk through. Passing through it, they trotted their horses along a mud path to a moat with a bridge that led to a second gate manned by armed sepoys. The soldiers leaned idly against the gate walls, not sparing even a glance at Irfan and Rustom. They rode on to Church Gate Street, the broad avenue that led into the Fort. The road was virtually deserted with only the odd pedestrian shuffling along its cobbled surface. A smart carriage driven by a handsome Arab steed clopped past as they came to Saint

Thomas's Church, the spired structure that the street drew its name from. A short ride brought them to the imposing building where the Fort police station was located.

There were only two men on duty inside: one, an Indian constable dressed in a blue tunic and a bright yellow turban, and the other, a British officer with a brown topee on his head. A young boy stood at one side pulling a rope that turned a *pankha* above the British officer's desk. The officer was reading a book. He flicked an eye at Rustom and Irfan when they entered and then reverted his attention to his book. The Indian constable displayed an identical lack of interest, but Rustom halted before him and tearfully related his story.

Irfan stood respectfully to one side, beside the door, studying Rustom in the lamplight as he recounted his misfortune. The tufts of hair that peeked from under his cap were short and dark. His features were childlike, with dark, large eyes and a perfectly formed nose, faultlessly straight without any bumps or curves.

Something niggled at the bystander and in a flash, he knew what it was. Rustom's face! He had seen it before . . . on the boat, in that horrid snatch of the dream. The boy who had lovingly tended to Irfan while he lay sick on the deck was none other than Rustom. His voice was the same too, soft like a whispering breeze, only now it was distressed as he tearfully recounted the robbery to the indifferent constable.

The constable played with a pen, rolling it back and forth on his table as Rustom ploughed painfully through his story, his misery only mounting with the man's uncaring attitude. Irfan heard the march of footsteps behind him and stepped aside from the door. An English officer wearing a dark coat and leather boots entered. He stared at Rustom as he crossed briskly to a door opposite where the English policeman sat.

Placing his hand on the doorknob, he looked down at the policeman. 'What is the boy's complaint, Hoskins?' he queried, his voice crisp and businesslike.

Hoskins looked up, slowly, as if the angling of his head involved an inordinate amount of effort. 'I wouldn't know, sir. Ganesh is attending his complaint, as you can see.'

The officer drew a fierce breath. 'You are the senior officer, Mr Hoskins. It is your duty to attend to all who enter here. A native boy delivering a complaint does not absolve you of your responsibility. I have made this clear to all my officers, and I shall do so one last time for your sake. I want a report on the matter. Now!'

Hoskins lowered his book, refusing to look his senior officer in the eye. He rose sullenly and hitching his trousers, crossed to the constable's desk.

Irfan cleared his throat. 'If I may, sir,' he said, addressing the senior officer. 'The boy has been robbed in the coconut groves near Mahim, sir.'

The officer turned, eyes bright and keen, and Irfan quickly related Rustom's ill-fated adventure.

The officer stroked his chin as Irfan detailed the robbery. He removed his topee revealing a full head of black hair.

When Irfan finally completed his story, he slammed his topee on Hoskin's table. '*Every night*!' he exclaimed. 'Like dastardly wolves, they strike every night. I have deployed more men, increased patrolling . . . yet they get away . . . *always*. There's more to this than meets the eye; something is wrong here . . . something rotten. It's as if the wolves have a master. An impostor who always knows where my men are.' He turned to Rustom, who was on the verge of a fresh bout of tears. 'Young man, I cannot assure you that I will nab the culprits and get your money back, but I shall do everything in my power. I shall work my force as hard as possible. Have you given my men all the details?'

Rustom nodded wordlessly.

'Then go home. Your friend—' he turned to Irfan. 'I didn't get your name, son.'

'Irfan Mohammed, sir,' replied Irfan.

'Your English is very good, Irfan. Where did you learn to speak like that?'

'A private tutor, sir. An Englishman by the name of Hunter taught me, sir.'

The officer stared. He stroked his chin once more. 'Where do you live, Irfan, and what is your father's name?'

'I live at Colaba, sir. My father is Mohammed Aziz. He is a coach driver and horseman. He works for an English saab named Mr Brown.'

The officer gazed intently at Irfan, who shuffled his feet, uneasy at the scrutiny he was being subjected to. 'Did your family once live in Mahabaleshwar?'

Irfan started, taken aback. 'Yes, sir. But that was long ago. Why do you ask, sir? Do you know my father?'

The officer nodded slowly. 'Yes, I do. I met him many years ago in Mahabaleshwar, when I was stationed at Satara. Your father would remember me. Tell him that the Superintendent of Police, Charles Forjett sends him greetings.' There was a pause as the officer gazed at Irfan.

He started to say something, then checked himself. 'Look after your friend,' he sighed instead. 'He needs help. Take him home.' He turned away, striding to his room. 'Hoskins,' he barked. 'Come to my room, I need to speak to you!'

Rustom was in a bad way. He started to shake when they stepped on to the street. 'He's going to throw me out,' he whimpered. His cheeks glistened as tears spilled from his eyes once more.

Irfan stared, puzzled. 'Who's going to throw you out?'

Rustom's jaw began to tremble. 'My uncle, Bejan . . . Bejanbhai Palkhivala. He hates me. He detests my living in his house. I have lost his money. Now he has the perfect reason to throw me out. But . . . but where will I go? I have no home.'

'What about your parents?'

Rustom shook his head miserably. 'I don't have any. My sister . . . she is married to Bejanbhai . . . she brought me here last year after my parents died in Porbandar. But my uncle has never been happy at my being here. I have always been the uninvited guest, the outsider. Now—' Rustom wrung his hands.

Irfan spoke spontaneously, his words unbidden. 'Come and stay with me. I live alone with my father. We have space. Don't worry about your uncle, we'll look after you.'

Lamplight caught Rustom's eyes. His tears shone like stars. 'You are so kind,' he mumbled.

It was obvious that Rustom was in no condition to help himself. Irfan grabbed his arm. 'Come on. I'll walk you home. You have to face your uncle. Be brave. Don't worry if he throws you out. I am there for you.'

Bazaar Gate Street, the thoroughfare that led to Rustom's home, was awash with light and noise. Sailors were in town that night. Irfan could tell by the loud singing and coarse laughter spewing from the bars that lined a section of the road. Shop shutters were hurriedly being downed, a sign that trouble could be brewing. Drunken brawls were common in this part of the Fort, especially on nights when groups of boisterous seamen prowled the town.

At a crossing, as Rustom turned towards a dark lane, Irfan suddenly halted. There was a bar at the corner with large doors and several chairs and tables. Irfan had spotted a familiar face in its smoky interior. Leaning back at a table, cigar in mouth and mug in hand, was Ismail the Arab horse-trader, Irfan's boss, the man who owned Mohini, his horse. Ismail had traded his Arab robes for European clothes and a smart hat. Though his apparel altered his appearance, there was no mistaking his shrewd, narrow face and sharp, intelligent eyes. He was in a jovial mood and beside him sat three equally happy white men.

Although it was well known that Ismail enjoyed alcohol, this was the first time Irfan had actually seen his boss in a tavern. The horse-trader's reputation as a man who enjoyed the good life didn't bother Irfan, but it deeply troubled his father who firmly believed that an irreligious ungodly man like him was a bad influence on his son. Irfan made a mental note to avoid mentioning what he had seen to his father, as the horse-trader and Irfan's job were a simmering source of friction between father and son.

Rustom lived in a lane off Bazaar Gate Street. The street was noisy, dimly lit and skirted on either side by buildings. He halted at a shop at the foot of a building with long balconies. A large clock, its frame engraved with silver, occupied prime space at the centre of the shop, and there were display cabinets filled with watches and clocks of all shapes and sizes.

'Is that your uncle?' asked Irfan, staring at an elderly gentleman inside wearing a Parsee cap.

Rustom shook his head, eyes awash with tears again. 'No. We live on the floor above.'

The Parsee gentleman had seen them. 'Rustom *dikra*!' he exclaimed worriedly. 'What happened, why are you crying?'

Rustom's inhalations were deteriorating to gasps. He squared his shoulders, as if steeling himself. Then he strode towards a doorway to one side of the watch shop. A staircase led steeply upwards and Irfan and the Parsee gentleman watched as he disappeared above.

'What's wrong?' queried the gentleman. 'The boy seems scared to death.'

The man listened attentively as Irfan narrated the events of the evening. Irfan was halfway through his story when furious shouting erupted from above. A male voice thundered uproariously, drawing the attention of passers-by too. It ranted wrathfully and though Irfan didn't understand Gujarati, the language of the Parsees, it was clear that choice abuses were being heaped on poor hapless Rustom. Interspersed with the tirade were pleas and sobs, and when several minutes later there was a pause, a female voice, shrill and imploring added to the commotion.

The Parsee gentleman translated helpfully for Irfan. 'Palkhivala is furious and wants to kill Rustom and if the pandemonium above is anything to go by, he must have tried. Now Palkhivala wants to throw Rustom out, but his wife Naheed, Rustom's sister, has begged him not to. She is sure that the police will find the money. Mr Forjett is the new Superintendent of Police. She says he is a good man.'

'Forjett will find the money!' declared a bespectacled man who had halted beside them. 'He is a sincere policeman. If anybody can recover the money, it is he.'

'Rubbish!' snorted another, with hairy sideburns. 'All policemen are useless. Robberies take place every day under their very noses. Only fools venture out of the Fort after dark. It is unsafe. The police strut around in their uniforms doing nothing.' He scowled and added darkly. 'If you ask me, it is the police themselves who are involved.'

'Have patience,' exhorted the bespectacled man. 'Forjett is already making changes in the force. Give him time. Mark my words, he will solve this case.'

Drawn by the ruckus, a crowd was gathering beneath Palkhivala's balcony.

'Palkhivala has been robbed,' shouted a man dressed in a white dhoti, delighted by the news.

'Serves him right,' whispered another, wielding an umbrella. 'Mean and stingy. Have you seen the way he treats his nephew?'

'It's the nephew who lost the money,' informed the man with the dhoti.

'There will be trouble then,' said the man with the umbrella. 'Bloodshed. The family is heartless. The boy will be thrown out.'

'Not if the money is recovered,' said the Parsee gentleman from the watch shop. His head was half-turned, ears cocked to the ranting above. 'Naheed has pleaded for her brother. She has persuaded her husband to wait a week. If Forjett doesn't recover the money by then, the boy will be thrown out.'

'Then he is as good as gone,' cackled the man with the sideburns. 'The police will never catch the culprits.'

The noise and fury above was abating and the crowd began to disperse, some shaking their heads, others tittering and passing derisive comments. It was time for Irfan to leave, but he lingered, feeling deeply for Rustom.

The Parsee gentleman was staring at Irfan, looking him up and down with the air of a housewife gauging the quality of groceries at a bazaar. 'You could do with a watch,' said the man, obviously impressed by what he saw. 'Step inside, I have the best selection of watches and clocks in Bombay. Come, have a look, you don't have to buy.'

Irfan excused himself, explaining it was late and that he had to return home.

The man waved expansively. 'Come another time. You will always find me here. My name is Ghadiali, Minoo Ghadiali. My *dukaan* is the best and most trusted in the Fort. You are a friend of Rustom's. For you, there will always be a special price.'

Irfan smiled and hurried away. Collecting Mohini, he rode quickly to the Church Gate. The former island of Colaba where he lived was a five-minute ride across the narrow causeway that now connected it to the Fort. Giving Mohini full rein, Irfan galloped home.

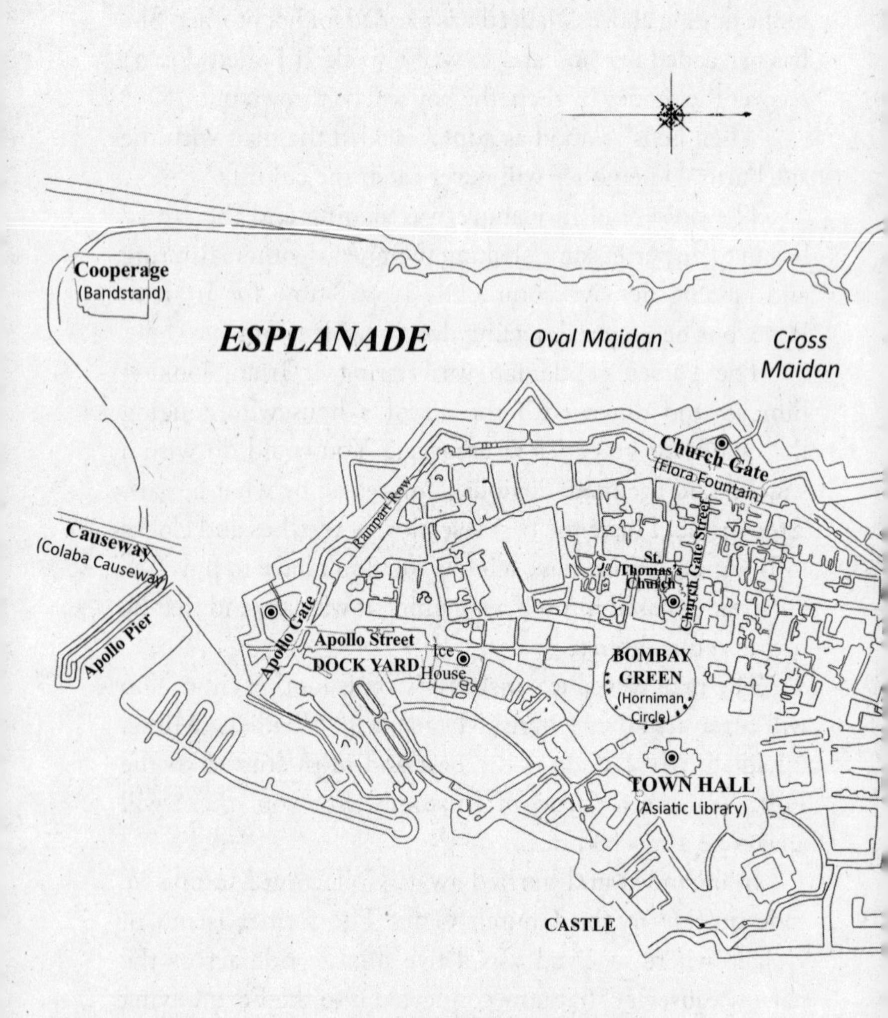
ARABIAN SEA
Cooperage
(Bandstand)
ESPLANADE
Oval Maidan
Cross Maidan
Church Gate
(Flora Fountain)
Rampart Row
Church Gate Street
St. Thomas's Church
Causeway
(Colaba Causeway)
Apollo Pier
Apollo Gate
Apollo Street
DOCK YARD
Ice House
BOMBAY GREEN
(Horniman Circle)
TOWN HALL
(Asiatic Library)
CASTLE
BOMBAY HARBOUR

PLAN of the FORT and ESPLANADE of BOMBAY, 1827

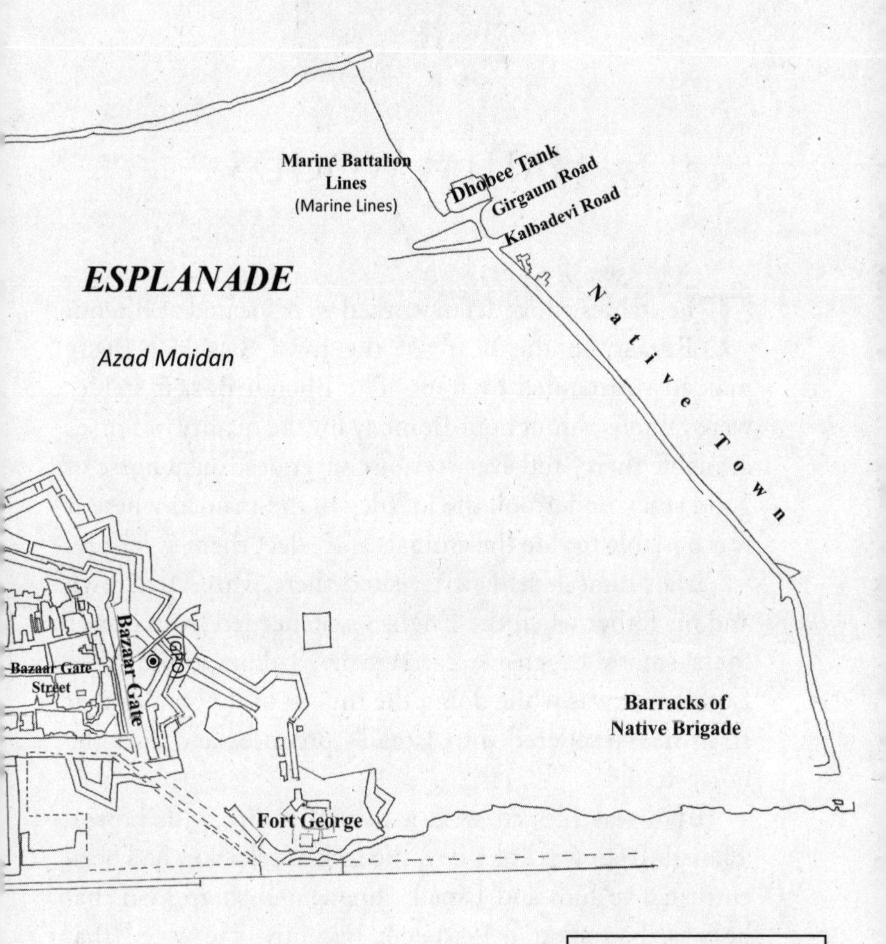

Bold - 19th century details
Light - Present day features

MAHIM WOODS

The stables where Irfan worked were located at Bhendi Bazaar, in the heart of the town, beside a dusty maidan surrounded by trees. The Bhendi Bazaar stables were famous throughout Bombay for the quality of horses available there, and every serious buyer desiring a horse of good stock undertook the journey to the maidan where it was possible to ride the animals and select them at leisure.

Irfan himself had first visited there with Mr Brown and his father when the English saab needed fresh horses for a smart, expensive carriage he had imported from London. It was while doing the rounds of the stables that Irfan had wandered into Ismail's premises and met the horse-trader.

Irfan was blessed with a natural ability with horses. Though Irfan was but a boy, the task of selection had been entrusted to him and Ismail, shrewd and sharp man that he was, had spotted his talent instantly. He noted that the gentlemen accompanying Irfan exhibited complete confidence in the boy's judgement, and in addition, his horses—moody and quick-tempered with strangers—behaved like house pets in Irfan's presence. Within minutes of entering the stables, Irfan connected with his charges in a manner no one else ever had—the animals gathering eagerly about him, rubbing against him, nickering softly and welcoming him as if he was one of their own. Ismail had promptly offered Irfan a job. Irfan had accepted impulsively but had been forced to decline, as his father, Mohammed Aziz, rejected the offer, making no secret of his contempt for the horse-trader. Irfan had dutifully abided by his father's wishes. In any case, he did not have the time as he was caught up with tuitions each day along with Ralph and Peter.

Ismail, however, was not the sort who gave up easily. A shrewd businessman, he had perceived that Irfan's talents could boost his profits considerably. Despite stiff opposition from Mohammed Aziz, he had dropped by their home often and showered Irfan with gifts at every opportunity. Irfan was also invited to the stables whenever a fresh consignment of horses came in. The period following the arrival of his animals was critical for Ismail as the sea journey from Arabia invariably upset his delicate charges.

Distressed animals fetched a low price; the rapid restoration of their vigour and health was crucial to his profits. It was for their timely revival that Irfan's skills were invaluable. Irfan had helped at the stables whenever he could, flattered by Ismail's perseverance. Finally, when Mrs Brown and the twins departed, Ismail, sensing an opportunity, baited Irfan by offering him the use of Mohini, and despite the certainty that his decision would provoke his father's anger, Irfan had accepted a full-time job at the stables.

On the day after his meeting with Rustom, Irfan reported as usual to the stables, only to discover that his services were not required. Ismail's nephew, Taufeeq, an indolent Arab boy with sleepy eyes, explained that the boat from Zanzibar, which had been expected for some time now, had been spotted that morning entering the harbour. A consignment of horses was on board, and Ismail would be held up at the docks the entire day. He had left instructions for Irfan to report early the next morning.

The horse-trader's absence suited Irfan just fine. Rustom's tear-stained visage had haunted Irfan through the night, and as he sleeplessly tossed and turned, an idea had struck him. The unexpected holiday provided a fortuitous opportunity to follow up on his hunch.

Waving goodbye to Taufeeq, Irfan trotted Mohini away. The Bhendi Bazaar road bustled with its usual complement of cows, pedestrians and horses. Piloting a straight path was impossible, yet Irfan did not steer Mohini, trusting her to pick her way through the confusion and crowd. Irfan's mind was engaged elsewhere, occupied with his father's bizarre and unwarranted reaction to his encounter last night with the police chief, Mr Charles Forjett.

Forjett had been unduly kind and helpful the previous evening. He had spoken cordially of Irfan's father and had even extended a greeting. Forjett was an important white man in a high office and at the very least, Irfan had expected his father to feel proud to be associated with such a powerful man. But Mohammed Aziz's response had been exactly the reverse.

His voice had quavered with fierce resentment. 'So, he remembers me,' he had whispered. 'And well he should. For Allah will punish him and he shall always carry the burden of guilt for what he has done.'

Irfan had been taken aback. 'But Forjett spoke kindly of you, Father!' he had exclaimed. 'Why is it that you are upset? People say he is a good man.'

'*Good man!*' His father's eyes flashed and to his amazement, Irfan saw they had filled with tears. 'There are no good white men in this land. They work only for themselves. They care nothing for us. They are the superior race. We are only cattle to them—animals that have no rights. A white man can get away with murder, but there is no justice for simple people like us.'

Tears trickled from Mohammed Aziz's eyes after his outburst.

Irfan had stared, dumbstruck. His father was a stern-faced man who rarely displayed emotion. He had never seen him shed tears.

An oil lamp illuminated Mohammed Aziz's stocky frame. Irfan had inherited his father's dark eyes, crooked nose and rich brown complexion. The black hair on Mohammed Aziz's head was peppered with flecks of grey. A dense beard covered the lower half of his face. Though only middle-aged, he looked old and frail in the flickering glow of the lamp.

'It is well that Forjett remembers me,' continued Mohammed Aziz. 'If there is even a grain of decency in the man, his deeds in Mahabaleshwar should haunt him for the rest of his life. Men like Forjett make empty promises. He will not help your unfortunate friend. Do not place faith in his words. Don't get fooled by him as I once mistakenly did.'

'But why, Father?' Irfan queried, thoroughly shaken. 'What did he do to you? I don't understand.'

But Mohammed Aziz had refused to elaborate. 'Forjett stirs painful memories. I have spoken enough already. In Mahabaleshwar you will learn of his treachery, but since you refuse to travel there, you will never know. I don't want to hear Forjett's name again tonight. Help me with the horses so we can go to bed.'

Irfan puzzled over his father's dislike of the man as the congested market area fell behind. Forjett had been courteous, attentive and helpful. Rustom's plight seemed to have genuinely angered him. His promise of help hadn't sounded empty—not by any stretch of imagination. Yet his father had taken a strong stand against the policeman. If he was to be believed—and his father never lied—an injustice had taken place many years ago; one which Forjett was somehow connected with. The memory of the incident was so bitter that his father had shed tears. His father's emotion-wrought reaction was inexplicable, his hostility deeply troubling, more so because Forjett's sincerity had impressed Irfan.

Soon Irfan was amidst the paddy fields of Byculla. Although lush and green during the monsoons they were brown and dusty now, having been harvested a month earlier. The fallow fields shimmered in the midday heat and there was hardly a soul to be seen on their rolling expanse.

Presently, Mohini came to a fork and chose the track that led to Mahim. After a quick ride, they entered coconut groves and it wasn't long before they reached the banyan tree where they had found Rustom. A forest of palm trees, trunks arching gracefully, surrounded the solitary banyan. It was midday now—a time when people were about—and yet the area was dark and quiet. By evening, when the light waned, the spot would be ideal for robbers and criminals.

Several stubby toddy trees with prickly fronds stood amidst the coconut palms. Irfan carefully studied the toddy trees, scrutinizing the area beneath their crowns, and as he had expected he spotted earthen pots nailed to their trunks. The toddy trees and their earthen receptacles were crucial to Irfan's hunch. The pots had been placed there by Bhandaris—local toddy tappers—who collected the toddy that seeped from the incisions they carved on the knuckled bark of the trees. The Bhandaris climbed the trees every evening to collect their pots, which by then had filled with sweet toddy juice. The robbers had ambushed Rustom at dusk. It was possible that a Bhandari toddy tapper could have been on one of the trees at the time the thieves had struck and witnessed the hold-up. Irfan's plan was to find and question the local toddy tapper. Noon was the best time to search for the Bhandaris as it was the period when they rested before their evening work.

The pond he had ridden past the previous night was just ahead. Trotting Mohini forward, he came upon it around a bend. Buffaloes wallowed lazily in its green water, and at this hour, children splashed and played there too. On inquiry, Irfan was told that there was a hut deep inside the grove. It was located beside another smaller pond, and a Bhandari tapper lived there with his family.

The tapper was fast asleep when Irfan located the hut. His fat wife was squatting on the mud floor outside, grinding spices. Throwing Irfan a suspicious glance, she rose and woke her husband. Blinking, the man stepped out adjusting a dirty turban on his head. He was thin and spindly, half the width of his wife, and he wore only a loincloth with a sickle dangling from a thong at his waist.

A dog wandered out of the hut while Irfan explained the purpose of his visit. It barked fiercely when it saw Irfan. Unfazed by its hostility, Irfan knelt as he spoke and when he held out his hand, it came grudgingly forward and allowed itself to be petted. The dog was wagging its tail and enthusiastically licking Irfan by the time he completed his narration.

The Bhandari regarded Irfan with dark, unfriendly eyes. 'Several policemen were here this morning, inquiring about the same incident,' he said.

Irfan looked up in surprise. Forjett was holding to his promise.

'It is unusual that they came,' continued the Bhandari. 'Robberies are common on this road, but the police never bother. This is the first time they have taken the trouble of investigating and I pray it is the last. They call themselves policemen, but in truth they are ruffians. They didn't ask questions and were least interested in solving the robbery. The rascals bullied me for free toddy instead. They mentioned this man that you spoke of . . . this Forjett. They did not have nice things to say about him.'

Irfan patted the dog absently. 'Did you tell them anything?'

'No. And I have nothing to tell you either.'

Irfan stared at the man. 'You were up there in the trees?'

'Yes, I was.'

'You saw the robbery! I know you did! You saw what happened. You must help me. My friend is in need. He will be thrown out of his home if the money is not recovered.'

The Bhandari looked away. 'Please leave,' he said, his voice firm. 'I mind my own business and I have nothing to say.'

Irfan stared at the man. He opened his mouth to plead, but the Bhandari cut him off with a wave of his hand. The man's face was set. His threatening stance indicated he was no longer welcome.

Irfan's hands fell from the dog as he rose to his feet. The Bhandari stared steadfastly at the ground, refusing to look Irfan in the eye. There was a movement from the hut. Turning, Irfan saw the Bhandari's large wife. Her eyes were round and white as she gazed at him from its dim interior.

The dog whined and followed Irfan as he dejectedly walked away. Mohini backed off when she saw the dog at her master's heels. But Irfan whistled softly and the horse held its ground. The dog sniffed the horse briefly before returning its attention to Irfan.

Irfan sighed as he fondled the dog. 'Pity your master isn't as nice and sociable as you,' he muttered.

Irfan rose and grasped Mohini's reins. He stroked her mane, preparing to mount, but paused when he heard footsteps.

'Excuse me—'

It was the Bhandari. Irfan turned to face him.

'My wife thinks I should talk to you.' The spindly man paused, looking Irfan up and down. 'My wife says that you have a way with animals, and she respects people who are good with them. Our dog hates all visitors. He attacks viciously and scares them away. But he made friends with you and he doesn't mind your horse. My wife believes you are a decent boy who wants to help his friend. You are not like the police.'

Irfan waited as the man paused again. The veil of hostility had lifted from his dark eyes.

'Before I speak, you must promise me you won't tell anyone, not even the police. No one should know that it is I, Madhukar Bhandari, who has passed information to you.'

'I promise,' said Irfan, holding his breath.

'There were two men who attacked your friend. I saw them waiting. I was at the top of a tree, not far from them. The men were Parsees, I could tell.'

Irfan's pulse quickened. 'Who were they? Can you identify them?'

The Bhandari shook his head. 'I don't know who they were. I have witnessed many robberies on this road, but I have never seen those men before. There was another man, however, a large, fat Parsee. He came with the men but did not take part in the attack. He spoke to them telling them what to do and showed them where to wait. He left soon after; long before your friend arrived on his horse.'

Irfan spoke urgently. 'Can you identify this man?'

'He is big. One of the largest men I have ever seen. His skin is fair, like all Parsees, and there isn't much hair on his head. I heard the men talking to him. They called him Modi, Mota Modi. I have seen this man before . . . several times. He is an evil man. He never takes part in a robbery, but he has set up many.'

Irfan shifted rapidly from one foot to another. 'This is great news!' he exulted, unable to contain his excitement. 'I don't know how to thank you. Mr Forjett will nab this man for sure. Your information will save a good boy; his gratitude will always be with you.'

Irfan's joy had no effect on the Bhandari. His face remained emotionless, if anything, it turned anxious. 'You must keep your promise, young man,' he said. 'You must not tell anyone that it was Madhukar Bhandari who had spoken to you. Many ruffians pass this way and horrible things happen on these roads. We live here alone. We don't want any trouble.'

The Bhandari's wife had stepped out from the hut, bangles jingling.

Irfan bowed low before her. 'Thank you, madam. You won't regret your kindness. There will be many blessings for you. Not just from the boy you have helped but also from others who will be spared once this man is punished. Don't trouble yourself worrying. I shall never disclose my source of information. You have my word.'

The lady smiled. The Bhandari and his wife waved as he rode away. The dog accompanied Irfan for a distance, loping beside Mohini, but Irfan pushed his horse into a gallop when they reached the road and whining sorrowfully, the animal fell behind.

Irfan rode Mohini hard, easing up only when they neared the busy bazaar area. Irfan directed Mohini along the centre of the road, hastening her past pedestrians, carriages and bullock carts. Entering the Fort from its busy Bazaar Gate, he hurried to the police station.

Forjett was closeted in his cabin and after a short wait, a constable led Irfan in. The police chief was bareheaded. Sunlight from an open window highlighted his sturdy bronzed features. Though pale, his complexion was darker than most of his countrymen. His jet-black hair was swept neatly behind his ears and his moustache was thin and trim.

Inviting Irfan to sit, he regarded him with keen eyes. He listened intently to Irfan's story, occasionally drumming his fingers on the table. His eyes lit up when Irfan uttered Mota Modi's name. 'Modi again!' he muttered, his fingers rattling away. 'I have heard his name before. There were two robberies where victims named him . . . and now, again.'

'Modi is the mastermind, sir. I cannot reveal the source of my information, but I swear by Allah it is true. Modi has been involved in several hold-ups. The man never takes part himself, but he plans the robberies.'

Forjett stared at his desk, tapping it absently with a pen. 'Twice before I have sent my men to investigate allegations against Modi; twice they have returned with long faces and empty hands. The same thing happened today. Is there any conspiracy, I wonder?'

'Sir, if I may,' said Irfan respectfully, 'your men visited the area this morning. But from what I heard, they showed no interest in solving the case.'

Forjett dropped his pen, his fingers curling into a fist. 'You have confirmed what I suspected. The investigation was nothing but a sham. The problems I have inherited are far worse than I imagined. The rot in my force has set deep.' The officer banged his fist against his desk, startling Irfan. 'I will personally work on this case. That's the only way this man will be stopped.'

Forjett rose, reaching for his hat. 'Find your friend, the one who was robbed. Stay with him. Remain in the area. If there is good news, I will deliver it today.'

Irfan followed respectfully as Forjett marched out of his office. Outside, after checking on Mohini, Irfan walked down Bazaar Street, searching for a meal. At the roadside stalls, he gulped down a snack of kebabs and bhajia and then strolled to the section of the Fort where Rustom lived.

FRIENDSHIP

Mr Ghadiali, the friendly watch store owner, spotted Irfan as he neared the building with the long balconies. 'Dikra, you have returned!' he greeted, waving his arms grandly. 'I knew you would. My watches and clocks are the best in Bombay. Come inside, dikra, I know exactly what a smart boy like you needs.'

Inside, the walls and cabinets of the tiny shop were crammed with a bewildering array of clocks and watches. Fancy imported timepieces with carvings and gold trimmings shared the walls with simpler local models. With a flourish, Mr Ghadiali picked a handsome watch with a long chain. 'This one is ideal for you,' he spouted exuberantly. 'Imported from England. Strong and heavy. Shockproof and rustproof. It's even got an alarm to wake you every morning. It's yours for a special price because you are Rustom's friend.'

Convincing Mr Ghadiali that he had come to search for Rustom and not for a watch wasn't easy. Only after displaying several watches and proudly showing him his first-rate repair facilities—two men bent over a table cluttered with watches in various states of dismemberment—did Mr Ghadiali finally disclose the information Irfan sought. 'You disappoint me, young man,' he said regretfully. 'All these wonderful timepieces and you show interest only in Rustom.' He sighed. 'You won't find your friend here. His uncle is in a foul mood and the boy is sensibly avoiding him. You could try the *bagicha* at the Green. I have seen him there often, especially in the evenings. Come again, dikra. A well-dressed lad like you can certainly do with a stylish watch.'

Irfan thanked Mr Ghadiali and hurried away, eager to be off before another 'wonderful' watch struck the store owner's fancy.

The southern region of the Fort, where the Bombay Green was located, was very different from the northern section. While the northern precinct, particularly the locality where Rustom lived, was riddled with narrow lanes and packed tightly with buildings, the southern area was airy and open, and the shops and buildings, spacious and elegant. Europeans and the British preferred the genteel environs of the Fort's southern confines. Here there were graceful homes, plush offices, grand administrative buildings and first-class hotels.

Walking down Hornby Row, a quiet residential street that bordered the Fort's western walls, Irfan soon reached the fortified defences of the Church Gate. As it was afternoon the road leading out of the Fort was deserted and the sepoys who manned the gates were nowhere to be seen. Church Gate Street was silent and mostly empty, with only a few Parsee storekeepers squatting idly beside the entrances of their shops. Passing beneath the tall, elegant steeple of the church, he soon came to the open expanses of the Green.

The Fort Green was a huge oval-shaped maidan, brown and dusty for the most part, with scattered patches of withered grass lending colour to its drab expanse. At its centre, however, grass grew thickly beside a domed canopy, under which stood a statue of an English nobleman. A circle of buildings surrounded the Green, the most prominent of which was the Town Hall, distinguished by its grand staircase, soaring columns and palatial façade. There was a well at the near side of the Green and alongside the well were gathered several carts. Each of the carts was drawn by bulls and was equipped with a colourful canopy that provided shelter to a deck area beneath. Bombay's commuters—for whom the carts were intended—were absent at this hour, and while the bulls rested, their masters squatted in groups, playing cards and chatting idly.

Two trees provided shade near the well and Irfan spotted Rustom beneath them. He was sitting alone, hunched disconsolately, chin resting on his knees. He wore a torn and faded Parsee tunic and pants. Drawing closer, Irfan saw that his eyes were red and his face was streaked with tears.

Despite his tears, Rustom managed a smile for Irfan. He rose in greeting, but Irfan pressed him down and squatted beside him.

'I didn't get a chance to thank you last night,' mumbled Rustom, brushing his cheeks with mud-soiled fingers.

'I'm sorry. I was upstairs and—' he swallowed, his voice faltering.

Irfan patted Rustom. 'Don't worry yourself. I understand. Your uncle has a loud voice—like a ship horn.' Irfan grinned. 'The entire street could hear him.'

Rustom laughed bitterly. 'Everyone knows what happened. The robbery has provided much gossip and entertainment. People amuse themselves by passing nasty remarks. They are whispering that it was I who stole the money, and that I have cooked up a story to cover up the theft. I've never had many friends. But even the few I trusted have turned against me.'

Irfan kept silent.

'It's all so hopeless,' choked Rustom. 'What will I do when my uncle throws me out? I don't want to leave Bombay.'

Irfan placed an arm around Rustom's shoulders. 'You don't have to. I meant what I said yesterday. You can stay with my father and me till you find a home.'

Rustom looked down at the grass, tears moistening his cheeks again. 'You are so kind . . . you don't even know me—'

Irfan raised his hand suddenly, pointing at the statue at the centre of the Green. 'I see a ganna-wallah there,' he said cheerily. 'Come on. You've been sitting here too long. I'll buy you some sugar cane.'

Irfan rose and strode away, not waiting for Rustom. The Parsee boy followed, stumbling listlessly across the maidan, arriving beside Irfan only after he had purchased the sugar cane. The vendor, a dark-skinned man wearing a white cap and dhoti, had cut the cane into manageable chunks and wrapped them in rolls of paper. Irfan handed a roll to Rustom and they settled in the shade beneath the statue's canopy. The boys chewed the block-like chunks, enjoying the sweet and sticky juice.

Rustom's expression was still woebegone when they were done with the ganna.

Irfan stared sternly at him. 'There's no need to be so miserable. You'll make yourself sick if you cry all day long.'

Fresh tears gathered in Rustom's eyes. 'It's easy for you to speak. You don't know what it is like to be alone in the world and not have any friends.'

Irfan tossed a stone at a crow that was pecking at the remnants of their ganna. 'You're not the only one who doesn't have friends,' he said. 'It might surprise you, but I don't have any myself—not a single one.'

Rustom turned disbelievingly to Irfan.

'It's true,' asserted Irfan. 'I've only known two friends all my life and both are gone. They went away to England recently, leaving me friendless and alone.'

'There must be others,' said Rustom, not convinced. 'Everybody has friends.'

Irfan made a scoffing kind of sound. 'Not if your friends are white-skinned.' His voice was so unexpectedly bitter that Rustom stared. 'Not if you possess privileges others are jealous of. You spoke just now of people turning against you. It's a new occurrence for you, but not for me. What you experienced today is only the start. You have no idea how bad it can get.'

Rustom stared blankly at his companion. 'I don't understand.'

Irfan sighed. 'It's a long story—' He paused, reluctant to go on, but changed his mind. 'Maybe I should tell you. My story might cheer you. Your misery could lessen when you understand that your plight is no different from mine.'

Irfan turned silent. Plucking grass, he tossed the blades in the air and watched them float to the earth.

'My father is a horseman,' he began. 'It's an ordinary job, like that of any servant. He works for a rich English gentleman named Mr Brown. My father tends the horses the Brown family owns and he drives their coach, riding Mr Brown to work each day. He looks after Mrs Brown's needs too, attending to her shopping, sightseeing and taking her to her friends' homes. The Browns are wealthy and several servants work for them. There is a cook, an ayah, a dhobi, a *bheesti* for water, a mali, a lamp cleaner, a sweeper and many others who take care of the daily chores. The Brown mansion, called Seawind as it borders the shore, is large and we servants live in the huts and stables in the backyard. Many of the servants have young children like me. You would expect those children to be my friends. I have grown up with them. We used to play together during our childhood. But today, I cannot count even a single one of them as a friend. It isn't that they just aren't friends—that would be okay by me—but what's worse is that they hate me. They hate me because I have privileges. It burns their hearts that I alone enjoy these privileges and that they have none.'

Irfan paused.

'Go on,' said Rustom, his mind distracted from his problems at last. 'What kind of privileges?'

The crow was still pecking at the remnants of their ganna. Irfan tossed another stone at it, but it ducked and held its ground.

'I possess incredible privileges, Rustom. I enjoy freedom and opportunities no other Mussulman boy from a poor family can dream of. Look at me. I'm an ordinary native boy, like any other. Yet the Browns treat me as one of their own, like a family member. The Browns have two children—twin boys—by the names Ralph and Peter. Mrs Brown adores me and Ralph and Peter are my best friends. My skin is dark and my religion is different from theirs, yet I am a member of their household. I eat my meals with the boys, I sleep over with them whenever I want, I go on outings every evening with them . . . I do as I please. My special privileges extend to education too. The reason I speak English so well, with the correct angrez accent, is because I was educated alongside Ralph and Peter by a private English tutor.'

The crow hopped as Irfan tossed another stone at it.

'Why are they so nice to you?' asked Rustom.

'I knew you would ask,' sighed Irfan. 'Everyone does . . . but the truth is that I don't know. I honestly don't. Their kindness to me is so uncalled for that even other angrez people, friends of the Browns, think it odd.' Irfan laughed. 'Their friends find my liberties distasteful and have openly told Mr and Mrs Brown so, but they have never cared. Their friends stopped sending their children to play with Ralph and Peter, but even that didn't matter. The Browns stood by me.' Irfan blinked suddenly, his eyes glistening in the sunlight. 'As a child, I thought nothing about my privileges. I was too young to know better. Much later, when I became aware that I was "different", I started questioning my father. But my father was of no help.'

Irfan sighed again, staring sightlessly at the defiant crow. 'My privileges came at a terrible cost. Every other child—these were my friends, mind you, my childhood mates—was barred from entering the house. They were servant children and were treated accordingly. It was only *I* who was different. No one knew why and never was an explanation forthcoming. It was only natural that they turned jealous, spitefully jealous. It was the elders who turned against me first. Their children soon followed. I lost all my friends. I was cast out by my own community. You might not believe me, but it's true—for ten years now, maybe more, I have had no friends.'

'You have the English boys,' said Rustom.

'They've gone,' said Irfan flatly. 'Mrs Brown has been sick for many months. Her illness turned worse, forcing her to return home for treatment. Almost overnight I lost my mates, my brothers, and the lady who was like a mother to me. The bottom fell out of my life. I was inconsolable. I wept for a month. Everything had come to an end and life wasn't worth living. That is what I thought then. But it wasn't so. Life goes on, as I discovered. I found myself a job last month. I have my own horse now. I learnt to get by without friends. You have to learn too, Rustom, and the faster you do, the better for you. I don't want you to cry like

I did. Yesterday's disaster is not the end of the world. Face up to life. Be brave. You have to be strong. When you are strong, everything will get sorted, trust me.'

Two more crows arrived. They drove the earlier crow away and settled beside the ganna remnants. Rustom stared at Irfan, his eyes bright and intense. Something new reflected from Rustom's big brown eyes, a stirring Irfan hadn't seen before.

Scenting success, Irfan pushed on. 'Mrs Brown took me aside the day she left. My pathetic condition had affected her and though it was she who was sick, she spoke words of hope to me. She said that even in the darkest moments, a star always shines. Have faith, she told me; have faith and strength, and you will find the star. I haven't seen one yet, Rustom. But I'm sure I will and if you stay strong, so will you.'

A pensive silence prevailed thereafter. As time passed, the road that straddled the Green finally showed signs of life. Evening was upon them and work at the docks and offices was ending for the day. Pedestrians appeared, their numbers swelling quickly. They swarmed the road, dodging horses and carriages that drove imperiously by. Business suddenly perked for the bullock carts beside the well. Weary wayfarers engaged them and their numbers steadily dwindled till only one, a cart with a broken wheel, remained.

After a while, Irfan rose and helped Rustom to his feet. Enjoying the cool of the evening, they strolled towards the Town Hall at the far end of the Green. Crossing the busy road, they settled on the Hall's expansive staircase. Children played on the stairs, running up and down and shouting and calling to one another. Their ayahs—oblivious of their ebullient charges—huddled in a corner, trading gossip.

The Hall held happy memories for Irfan. As a child, he had spent many enjoyable evenings on the staircase, frolicking with the twins. Irfan experienced a twinge of emotion as an English lady wearing a pretty summer dress walked past with two boys in tow. The boys were fair-haired and young, achingly like Ralph and Peter.

Rustom, who had been silent since Irfan's pep talk at the Green, suddenly spoke. 'I won't leave this city!' he exclaimed, the words spurting from his mouth.

Irfan sat up, staring. For the first time since they had met, Rustom's voice was strong and forceful.

'I won't go back to Porbandar.' A fire raged in Rustom's eyes. 'I don't care if my uncle throws me out. I will find a job. I will stay put here in Bombay and start a life of my own.'

'Shabash!' whooped Irfan. 'That's the spirit.'

A smile lit up Rustom's face. He was much calmer now, as if he had cast off a heavy burden and was revelling in the release that followed. 'I was terrified, Irfan. Terrified that if I became homeless, I would have to return to Porbandar. But I know now that I don't have to. I wasn't thinking. The shock of the robbery and fear of my uncle had numbed me. But I see now that there are options. I will find work. A job will take care of my needs and rid me of my nasty uncle. I will have to give up school. I don't want to, but it's a price I will have to pay. You have given me courage, Irfan. You have shown me the way. I will be brave. Being thrown to the street is not the end of the world. It is a beginning instead.'

Irfan squeezed Rustom's shoulders. 'Come with me tomorrow. I work with horses. They need people in the stables. I can fix you a job.'

The setting sun caught Rustom's eyes. 'Yes,' he breathed. 'Yes, jobs are easy to come by in Bombay. In Porbandar, everyone speaks of Bombay. They call it a city of dreams, a haven of opportunity. All who have come here have found work. Noshirbhai, a Parsee from Porbandar who had lost his leg, arrived here penniless. In five years, he has a mithai dukaan of his own and he's talking of buying another. Anyone with will and determination can do well in this city. I shall take a job . . . any job. I will live on the streets if I have to, but I won't leave.'

Irfan grinned delightedly. He waved a fist for Rustom.

The Parsee boy's mouth suddenly popped open. 'School! I thought I'd seen you before. Now I know! School is where I've seen you. Two months back, a boy came to our school who spoke English like an Englishman. That was you!'

Irfan nodded, smiling.

'Your face was familiar, but I could not recollect. I remember because it was your English that was so good, better than any of our teachers. People called you the angrez Mussulman; the boy who corrected teachers in class. Is that why you quit? Because you knew more than the teachers?'

Irfan laughed. 'I did correct teachers. Yes. But that had nothing to do with my leaving. I don't claim to know more than your teachers. I quit because I didn't like school. How do I explain? All my life my education was private. There was only Mr Hunter—our teacher—and the twins and me. Then I was pitched into this place that swarmed with children. I hated the crowds. My classmates didn't like me. They were jealous of my knowledge and kept making fun of me. The teachers kept trying to put me down. School was a bad experience and a waste of time. A horse dealer had been pestering me to take up a job. He offered me a horse and—'

A shadow fell across the stairs and the boys looked up. A man in a police officer's uniform had halted his horse at the foot of the staircase.

'Master Irfan. There you are, young man, I was searching for you.'

Mr Forjett dismounted and walked towards them, his face red in the setting sun. 'I see you have your friend with you. Excellent! What I have to say will please him, I'm sure.' He reached into a jacket pocket and removed an envelope. His dark eyes twinkled as he surveyed Rustom. 'Here, have a look at this, lad. Do you recognize it?'

Rustom leapt forward, gasping. He grabbed the envelope from the officer's hand. Opening it, he extracted a sheet of paper. 'M-mm-my receipt,' stuttered the boy. 'It is the receipt for the carriage I delivered. Where did you get this, sir? It was stolen along with the money yesterday.'

'It has been recovered from the house of a thug named Mota Modi. Hasn't your friend told you about his afternoon exploits?'

Irfan gaped at the officer. 'It was Mota Modi, sir, wasn't it? Has the money been recovered, sir?'

Forjett nodded, smiling. 'There was a pile of money in Modi's house. Even though the sum was dubiously large,

I couldn't book him as there is no law regarding how much money a man can possess. I had to prove that the money was not legitimately his. That's where you helped me out, lad. I found this envelope on his desk and he couldn't explain how it got there. Insisting on a receipt is a good practice. It is because of your receipt that I was able to arrest the man. I have placed him behind bars and I shall see he remains there. Tell your uncle his money will be returned in a few days. Tell him that the Superintendent of Police has given you his word.'

Forjett patted Rustom's shoulder and mounted his horse. 'You are lucky to have a friend like young Irfan,' he said as his mount shuffled away. 'If it wasn't for him, the thug Modi would not have been arrested and your money would have stayed lost. I too owe you a debt, master Irfan, and I shall repay it someday.'

Rustom stood rooted to the ground, staring after the departing officer. His feathery frame quivered as he turned to Irfan. Nervous energy pulsed within him.

'Irfan . . . the money . . . how did you—?'

'Don't worry about it,' said Irfan hurriedly. 'Now you can tell your uncle . . . hey . . . easy, easy, my friend!'

Rustom had grabbed Irfan. He stared wildly at his laughing companion.

'*Friend!*' Rustom's voice thundered, lion-like. '"Friend" is the most beautiful word in the world. I have no idea what you have done for me, Irfan, but you are the truest and nicest friend I have ever known.'

Children halted their play, looking on curiously. A crowd gathered below the steps of the Town Hall. But

Rustom couldn't care less. He hugged Irfan, crushing him to his chest. A flood of tears burst from his eyes. His misery and despair exited with the force of a cloudburst. Deep sobs racked his body as Irfan held him. Avoiding the gaze of thc onlookers, Irfan looked up. Though the sky was still bright, a star was visible, shining like a celestial jewel. Irfan recalled Mrs Brown's words as he stared at the evening star. Was the star shining for him? Could it be that a fresh jewel had entered his life?

Peace and quiet reigned in a Pune hospital room with white walls, a white bed and white sheets. The only noise was the soft swish of fan blades rotating slowly. Anirudh slept soundly in the bed. The upper part of his head was wrapped in a gauzy, white bandage. His countenance was calm; if anything there seemed to be a hint of a smile on his face.

Then he stirred suddenly. His cheeks tightened, his eyes shot open and a cry burst forth from his lips: 'Dost . . . friend!'

Smita Dongre, who was reading a book at his bedside, leapt to her feet.

'Anirudh!' she shrilled. 'Anirudh. Meri jaan . . . bol! Speak to your mother.'

But Anirudh's eyes snapped shut. His face muscles relaxed and the calm and smile returned—the smile even more pronounced now.

IRFAN'S PHOBIA

Having established the friendship between Irfan and Rustom, the dream abruptly steered the bystander back to where it had begun—to the grey sea, the dark clouds and the terrifying voyage. The transition caught the bystander unprepared, and the storm-tossed sea instantly triggered his sickness and misery. The bystander pulled away, fighting the dream, and surprisingly, with not a trace of opposition, the dream yielded to his protests, returning him to Bombay. But there was a difference this time. The dream had shifted gears, accelerating to a canter now, leaping from incident to incident, skipping days and sometimes weeks.

The stolen money was returned promptly to Rustom's uncle. In spite of the successful resolution of the robbery, Rustom vacated his uncle's premises. Palkhivala's family was glad to see the back of him. Only his sister tried to dissuade him, pleading he change his mind, but Rustom held firm to his decision.

The place Rustom found for himself couldn't be called a home—not by any stretch of imagination. 'Space' was a more apt description. The new abode that Rustom cheerily shifted to was a cramped space on a landing under the staircase of a narrow building, which he generously shared with any cat or dog that felt disposed to spend the night with him. The staircase and landing belonged to a kindly Bohra gentleman, who did not seek a rent. He and his wife were of advanced age and requested only that Rustom help out with odd jobs like shopping and keeping the area clean. The arrangement suited Rustom fine and shortly after settling in, he secured himself a job.

Having only recently befriended him, Irfan did not know Rustom well. Brief though their acquaintance was, Irfan was bewildered by the transformation of his friend's personality. As if his previous avatar was only a mirage; Rustom's defeated demeanour and sorrowful slant of shoulders vanished without a trace. The hesitancy and meekness that Irfan had come to associate with him exited his makeup completely, like a slate wiped clean.

In addition, Irfan quickly learnt that Rustom had a mind of his own. For one so young, Rustom possessed a singularly clear vision of his future. That future did not involve horses, and he had politely declined the job Irfan had arranged for him at Ismail's stables. Rustom's heart—from the time he had first arrived in Bombay—had been drawn to the city's bustling harbour. Fittingly, the first job he secured for himself was with a shipping company.

Champaklal First Boat Service was a company engaged in the business of ferrying passengers between Bombay and nearby towns along the coast. The timetable of the company's vessels changed frequently, depending on the weather and wind conditions, and had to be broadcast daily across the city. The task assigned to Rustom was to visit busy areas and in a loud voice announce the weekly boat schedule.

The first time Irfan heard Rustom broadcast his timetable was at the busy crossing outside the Fort's Bazaar Gate. There was a pond not far from the outer darwaza of the gate where several large trees grew. It was a pleasant area, adorned with platforms for gentlemen of leisure to gossip and idle time away. Mounting a platform, Rustom had waved his arms and shouted, 'TIMETABLE . . . BOAT TIMETABLE,' chanting his refrain repeatedly till a sizeable crowd collected around him. Then, with a voice that would have done a drill sergeant proud, he had loudly reported his schedule.

'Tuesday, 7.00 a.m. sharp, boat *Surti Jahaaz* will depart from Apollo Bunder. It will halt at Bassein before reaching Surat. Thursday, 12 noon sharp, boat *Konkan Ranee* will depart from Bori Bunder for Ratnagiri. Halts at Panvel, Pen, Murud and Harnai before turning around at Ratnagiri—'

The job entailed considerable travel as Rustom was required to publicize the schedule across far-flung localities of the city every day. Irfan helped him as often as he could, taking him along on horseback whenever he found the time.

Like a breath of fresh air, Irfan infused caring and companionship in Rustom's troubled world, and in turn, Rustom resurrected Irfan's spirit, ridding him finally of the hopeless despair of the twins' departure. Irfan's enthusiasm for life was restored. So marked was the change in Irfan that even Mr Brown, usually a reticent man, remarked on his renewal.

'I see that the old mischief is back,' he commented one morning, as Irfan led his carriage to the porch. The Englishman examined Irfan closely. 'No, not a trace of the moping and sadness we've grown accustomed to. What's up, young man? Have you found a new friend or has a young girl charmed you?'

Mr Brown was dressed for work in his jacket, tie and hat. He was a portly gentleman with a thick moustache and bald head. His face was very white in the morning sun. Over the years, Irfan, Ralph and Peter had worked out a system of foretelling the daily weather by observing the colour of Mr Brown's face. When his cheeks were flushed, the conditions were sure to be hot and uncomfortable. On that morning, the day was certain to be pleasant as his face was ivory-white in the morning sun.

'No, it is not a girl, saab,' said Mohammed Aziz, stepping on to the porch and handing Mr Brown his cane and hat. 'I will select an appropriate girl for him when the time is right. It is a friend that he has found.'

'Splendid!' declared Mr Brown, settling his hat on his head. 'I shall send a telegram to Alice. I shall tell her that Irfan is finally happy and settled. Not only has he found a friend but he is gainfully occupied with a job.'

Mohammed Aziz's face tightened. 'Job!' he snorted. 'Working for that scoundrel Ismail is no kind of job for an honourable Mussulman boy. That man has no morals or scruples. He is deceitful and ungodly. Saab, you support my son in this matter, but if I had my way, I would not allow him to work for such a man. Ismail is a heathen, an infidel. He will ruin and corrupt my son.'

Mr Brown's eyes popped as he stared at Mohammed Aziz. 'Good lord! Those are strong words, Aziz. Ismail is not a saint, I admit, but he's certainly not as bad as you make him out to be. What's come over you, my man? You always see the darker side, don't you?' Mr Brown gestured impatiently. 'You worry like a mother hen, Aziz, always believing the worst. Have faith in your son. Irfan is a good righteous boy; you have brought him up so. Think about the experience your son is gaining instead. Your son is special with horses. There's no need to consult one of your Indian fortune tellers to predict Irfan's future. It is obvious he is going to spend his life working with horses. At Ismail's stables, he is in charge of the best Arab stallions in Bombay. More importantly, Ismail believes in your son. Irfan is his most valuable employee. What better experience can he get? You must encourage your son instead of being hard on him.'

Mohammed Aziz did not reply. Though he kept silent, his body language indicated he did not agree with his employer. Mr Brown sighed. Settling inside his carriage, he waved to Irfan as he was driven away.

Irfan's relationship with his father had always been a troubled one, but of late, it had begun to deteriorate at an alarming rate and he talked about it one evening to Rustom, at Apollo Bunder. Located near the Fort's Apollo Gate, Apollo Bunder was one of many piers that jutted out like stubby fingers into the deep waters of Bombay's harbour.

Two passenger boats—one a large liner from England and the other a smaller local ferry—had piloted into the harbour and people were collecting at the Bunder to receive the travellers. Rustom intended to address the gathering shortly, when it swelled to a crowd.

It was Rustom who brought up the topic. A month had passed since their fledgling friendship had taken root, and it troubled Rustom that Irfan was spending every moment of his free time with him.

'Irfan,' he said. 'This last month has been the happiest in my life. I finally have a friend. Not an ordinary one . . . but a true, real friend. Your companionship is sheer joy for me Irfan but . . .' He looked up quickly, worried that Irfan might misconstrue his words. 'Don't get me wrong. I look forward to our daily meetings. Our evenings together are the best part of my day. But . . . don't you think you should return home early, at least sometimes, to be with your father?'

Irfan did not reply immediately. He was looking out at the sea, gazing at the ferry—a fair-sized boat with two pencil-like masts poking skywards from its deck. Though it hadn't dropped anchor yet, a fleet of smaller craft was streaming towards it, each vying for passengers to transport to shore.

Irfan dropped his head and sighed. 'How do I explain, Rustom? My father and I hardly talk. The home I once knew, the warm and happy place that I grew up in, doesn't exist any more. We were close, Father and I, very close, but that was a long time ago. Now, each night when I return, I feel I'm entering a graveyard. There's nothing there, nothing except memories and sadness. We greet each other every evening. We say our prayers together, but then we both turn silent. We are father and son, yet we are strangers. Everything I do displeases him. There is a barrier between us and it grows stronger by the day.'

Rustom shook his head. 'That's not good enough, Irfan. You have to sort things out. You are your father's son. No matter what the trouble is, it's your duty to be with him.'

Irfan's eyes turned dark. 'I've tried, Rustom. I've built bridges between us. I've reached out so often that I've lost count. Each time my bridges come crashing down.' He grimaced unhappily. 'The latest quarrel was my dealings with Forjett saab. You were there. I was thrilled when Forjett remembered my father. It is honourable to be remembered by a powerful angrez like Forjett. I was certain that I had stumbled on an opportunity to draw closer to Father. But it was not to be. Not only was he angry to learn about Forjett but he turned furious when I told him how I helped solve your robbery.' Irfan's voice turned bitter. 'Nothing I do is good enough for him.'

Rustom started to speak, but an eruption of angry voices halted him. A fight had broken out. Anticipating business, several palanquin bearers had gathered on the pier. The more aggressive amongst them were pushing and shoving each other, jostling for choice locations to win customers from. Strung on poles, the palanquins were long, unwieldy, boxlike contraptions, and as the men wrestled each other, one of the boxes crashed to the ground, generating a fresh round of shouting and swearing.

'Isn't there something you can do to make your father happy?' asked Rustom, turning his gaze away from the warring men.

'Nothing I do makes my father happy. My job offends his morals. Even my friendship with you troubles him. Yes, it does, Rustom. In his heart, he believes that I should only have Muslim friends. Any other parent would have been proud of his son for helping the police solve a robbery, but in my case, my father has hardly talked to me since that day.'

Out on the water, the ferry was turning its nose into the wind and lowering its sails. Since it was far smaller than the bulky English liner, the ferry was anchoring closer to the shore. The passengers crowding its decks were visible, many of them waving to the shore. Rustom looked around the pier. The crowd he had been waiting for had gathered.

'My father is lonely and unhappy,' continued Irfan. 'Bombay is not his home and he has never liked the city. His heart is in Mahabaleshwar. Part of the reason he is so discontented and bitter is that he has never returned to Mahabaleshwar. It's been thirteen years since we came to Bombay, but not once has he returned home.'

Rustom had risen to address the crowd, but he halted, turning. 'That doesn't make sense. You are talking in riddles. You say his heart is in Mahabaleshwar, yet in all these years your father has never gone back. How can that be?'

'The blame is entirely mine, Rustom. Father will not leave Bombay without me, and I refuse to leave the city. It is because of me that my father has never returned home.'

Rustom stared blankly at Irfan.

'It's a long story, Rustom. The boats are coming to shore. Finish your announcement. I'll explain afterwards.'

Even with just a month's experience, Rustom was already an expert at addressing crowds. The swelling throng maintained a respectful silence as in a spirited voice, he delivered the details of the Champaklal First Boat Service timetable. Afterwards, several amongst the audience gathered around him for additional details, but their queries abruptly ceased when the first of the passenger-laden canoes pulled up beside the pier.

The two friends withdrew hurriedly, moving further down the shore to where the Bunder yielded to rocks and pools of tidal water. The clamour from the pier swelled as passengers began to disembark. Coolies and palanquin bearers shouted, competing to draw their attention. Friends and families waved and called excitedly. Hawkers added to the din, loudly promoting their wares.

Rustom turned to Irfan after they had settled themselves on smooth rocks, free of barnacles. 'Go on then,' he said. 'Tell me. Why are you responsible for your father not returning to Mahabaleshwar?'

Irfan shooed a crab away. Unbuckling his sandals, he placed his feet in a pool of water. 'It's funny, isn't it?' He grinned. 'We're best of friends, but there's so much we don't know about each other.' Irfan waved an arm across the harbour. 'You see me sitting here with you on the shore, my feet in the water. It seems normal and yes, of course, it is. There's nothing remarkable about loafing near the shore, but you have no idea what kind of achievement it is for me to be able to sit here and talk calmly, as I'm doing now.

If you knew me a few years ago, the very sight of me near the sea would seem a miracle. For most of my life, even a glimpse of the sea would terrify me. I would find it hard to breathe and I would retch helplessly. That was when I was younger. As the years have passed, I've improved, but even today I cannot dream of venturing on water. I can never board any kind of boat, not even small canoes and Bunder boats, leave alone large liners and ferries. A sea journey will break me mentally, might even kill me.'

Rustom sat silently, listening raptly.

Irfan expelled air through his lips, making a whistling noise. 'I survived a shipwreck when I was six years old. My father and I were travelling by boat to Mahad—a village near Mahabaleshwar—from where our home is only a two-day walk. It was father's first holiday after taking up his job with the Browns in Bombay. We set sail right here at Apollo Bunder, and my clearest memory of that morning was the joy on my father's face. But a storm hit our boat as we left the harbour. Our vessel was overloaded, father says. I remember that there was standing room only on deck. We learnt later that the boat was old too and in her final year of service. The wind and the waves were too much for the weighed-down ferry and it sank within minutes.'

Irfan paused, swallowing. 'The sinking of a boat is the most frightful experience anyone can undergo, and I was only a child then. I clung to my father in terror as the water rose and the deck tilted. Everyone screamed, but my father stayed calm, holding me in his arms and praying. Allah made Father brave that day. Nothing daunted him. Not even the groans of the vessel or the terrible noise as the storm ripped it apart. When the waves swept us off the boat, he held me in a tight embrace. All I can remember of the disaster is the monstrous waves, the heaving ocean, the sickening taste of seawater and Father's crushing hold on me. We survived by clinging to the wreckage of the boat. Luckily, we sank not far from the harbour and rescue boats arrived soon. I lived through the storm, but the experience scarred me for life. For years, I couldn't bear even the sight of the sea. It was a mental illness. Time has eased my dread since. I can sit here comfortably beside the water, I can even get my feet wet, but I will never be able to board a boat or travel on the sea again.'

A pair of canoes laden with fish baskets paddled past, harried by a flock of seagulls. As the canoes drew away, the birds settled on the water. Their beaks flashed in the evening sun as they gulped their opportunistic meal.

Rustom pointed to the seagulls. 'Look at the gulls,' he said. 'It's as if they are sitting on land. The sea is so amazingly calm. The water is like glass. You'd never think it could toss and destroy boats.'

The swell broke with barely a whisper on the shore. Out on the harbour, it was so gentle that it was barely noticeable. Many hundred boats flocked Bombay's famous anchorage. From where the boys sat, their towering masts were packed so densely that they resembled a floating forest. In the deep water at the centre of the harbour bobbed the large galleons, liners and the warships of the Royal Indian Navy. Everywhere else, smaller craft floated. Local fishing boats were the most numerous, the largest of them equipped with several masts and the smallest with only ragged bits of cloth improvising as sails. Chinese junks floated placidly beside Arab dhows with lateen sails.

The setting sun tinged the harbour waters orange. The ferry, having discharged its passengers, was pulling away, its sails tilted to the wind. So tranquil was the seascape that Rustom found it impossible to imagine it could strike fear in the heart of his friend.

Rustom dragged his gaze from the harbour. 'It isn't possible that you can't board a boat. Years have passed since your ill-fated voyage. You are sitting here by the sea just now, something you said you couldn't do earlier. Time has healed you. It follows logically that it has healed your fear of boats too. You can travel by boat. You only have to try.'

Irfan laughed hollowly. 'People scorn me. What's so difficult about boarding a boat, they say. I have tried, Rustom. A few years after the accident, the Browns persuaded me to set foot on a boat. Mrs Brown held my hand and Ralph and Peter cracked jokes, trying to distract me. I was frightened out of my wits, yet I cooperated. But within a minute of boarding, I suffered convulsions. My mouth foamed, my legs crumpled, I collapsed and passed out. It took me weeks to recover, and so horrified were they at what happened that they never tried again.' Irfan dropped his head. 'Father's dearest wish is to return to Mahabaleshwar . . . but I can't travel with him.'

Rustom frowned. 'There you go again. What has your inability to travel got to do with your father? Why do you have to go? He can leave you behind and return when he is done.'

Irfan sighed deeply. 'I wish Father would. His bitterness and resentment towards me would disappear if he returned home. He would be a happy man. His biggest source of ill will to me would be gone. Everything between us would be solved. But my father is a man who never breaks his word. He made a vow to my mother as she lay dying in his arms. He loved my mother dearly. There was nothing in the world he wouldn't do for her. My mother's greatest concern was for me. I was her joy, her happiness, and when the snake bit her, her dying wish was that he take care of me. He swore he would and that he would never leave my side. He has been true to his word till this day.'

Rustom was impressed. 'Wow!' he whistled. 'You are blessed, Irfan, to have such a wonderful father.'

'Yes, I am blessed and I have led a blessed life till now. But it's not the same any more. Ralph and Peter are gone. My father is a changed man. His vow to my mother is working against us. Home is no longer a happy place—'

Rustom interrupted. 'Wait a minute! Why is it that you insist on going to Mahabaleshwar by sea? You can travel by land. There are even trains now. You can get there without having to undertake a voyage.'

'Yes, Rustom, there are other ways of getting to Mahabaleshwar. There always have been, but that doesn't help me. I haven't explained my failing in full to you. My dread of voyages is only part of my problem. I wish it was as straightforward as that, but my fear is not restricted to the sea. The shipwreck inflicted more damage than only scaring me off boats. It destroyed my ability to travel. I fear the very thought of a journey. I fear leaving Bombay.

'My phobia might seem irrational, but that's the way it is. You spoke of trains. My father and I were excited when they started operating a few years back. It was as if Allah had taken pity on me and had specially invented the wonderful machines so I could travel. The train would deliver us quickly to Pune and from there we could walk to Mahabaleshwar. I was thrilled. I could finally grant my father his dearest wish. I remember on the first day the train operated, Ralph, Peter and I were there to see it. There was a big crowd, and we had to push our way forward to catch a glimpse of it. The hissing and puffing engine scared us, but none of us admitted our fear. Mrs Brown bought us our first tickets. She obliged our enthusiasm by taking us on short journeys: to Byculla to visit the club, and to Parel to see the governor's mansion. Our journeys were fun and I thoroughly enjoyed them. But when my father booked tickets all the way to Pune, something snapped inside me. As the day of our journey drew closer, my convulsions returned. I couldn't breathe, and the evening before our departure, I collapsed. I discovered eventually, after booking tickets twice more and breaking down each time, that I couldn't travel. Just the thought of a journey—any journey—is enough to break me.'

Irfan raised his head, anguish writ on his face. 'I can never leave the shores of this island, Rustom. It is my destiny. I can never leave Bombay.'

'CAREFUL!' shrieked Mrs Smita Dongre.

'IDIOTS!' howled Commander Vikas Dongre. 'Clumsy buffoons! You call yourself ward boys? Can't even hold a stretcher properly. The fool who hired you should be shot!'

Commander Dongre's anger was justified. In a coma for days now, the doctors had decided to shift Anirudh to a hospital in Mumbai where the facilities were better. But as they were placing Anirudh in an ambulance, one of the ward boys holding his stretcher tripped, dropping his load. The stretcher had crashed to the ground. Although Anirudh was strapped securely, the impact jarred him. He twitched furiously, straining against the rubber straps that held him fast.

'My baby,' sobbed Smita Dongre, kneeling beside the fallen stretcher.

Her husband rushed forward and grasping the stretcher handles, lifted it off the ground. He then lowered Anirudh gently inside the ambulance.

Entering, Smita Dongre crouched beside her sleeping son and stroked his forehead. Anirudh's spasms quickly ceased. His breathing settled, and after a while, his expression turned calm once more.

THE KONKAN COAST

Without warning, an incandescent flash interrupted the dream. The burst of light sparked out as quickly as it came, leaving darkness in its wake. The darkness was absolute, all-encompassing and distinctly familiar. By now the bystander had come to recognize the darkness as a kind of way station, a signal that the dream was changing tracks. He strained mightily, battling the dream, as each time the darkness dragged him back to the misery of the voyage.

The bystander experienced a fresh sensation, as if he was being jolted. He puzzled over this, then abandoned the line of thought as the darkness had started to fade. At first, haziness fogged his vision. Then, instead of the sea and the storm, he spied a forest and green hills.

The imagery of land greatly relieved the bystander. He had been spared the horrid torment of the voyage. There was no need to pull away. He examined the new vista with interest. The thickly forested hills were certainly not Bombay. The landscape expanded and he spied a village. He corrected himself—the handful of huts was inadequate to describe as a village. The area appeared to be a settlement, a tiny shabby settlement in the midst of a forest. A stream with clear water flowed nearby, merging with a river whose banks were packed solidly with vegetation.

The dream seemed to have strayed, shifted out of sequence. Yet the bystander instantly found his bearings, identifying exactly where he had re-entered the dream. The drab skies and rain indicated that the dream was in the proximity of the voyage episode. Irfan's condition—sickly and drained—settled the matter.

The voyage was over. Irfan had survived.

I can't travel. It is my destiny. I can never leave Bombay.

Irfan's words echoed in the bystander's head. Yet Irfan had travelled from Bombay's shores, and astonishingly, the journey had been undertaken by boat. The voyage hadn't finished him off, as Irfan had prophesied it would. It had certainly come close to achieving that end, failing only because of Rustom's loving, tender care. Irfan owed his life to Rustom, his friend and now his saviour too.

There had been four of them altogether on the boat: Rustom, Irfan, Shahid and Tabrez. Just a few years older than Irfan, Tabrez was a quiet young man with dark, brooding eyes. Shahid was roughly Irfan's father's age. Hailing from Mahabaleshwar, he was a distant relative, a friend of his father. He was a big and brawny man who had worn a beard for as long as Irfan had known him. By profession, he was a sailor. Each time he passed through Bombay, he dropped by at Seawind to visit Irfan and his father. It was Shahid who had piloted the boat that had brought them to the forest. Tabrez was not a sailor and like Irfan, he had suffered bouts of sickness during the voyage too.

The journey from Bombay had taken several days. Like fugitives, they had sailed in the dark, travelling under the cover of night. At daybreak, they halted in creeks, resuming only after nightfall, voyaging ghostlike through the darkness. Finally, they had sailed up a creek until they could go no further, and when they disembarked, Shahid had sunk their boat, scuttling it on the banks of the forest.

The voyage had taken its toll on Irfan. At the very start—as they departed the shores of Bombay—he had collapsed. Mercifully for him, his bouts of consciousness thereafter had been short. Rustom's devoted nursing had kept Irfan alive, but his sickness and his lack of food—a few mouthfuls during the entire voyage, had left him frail.

It was now a week since they had come ashore. The feel of solid, immovable earth beneath his feet had improved Irfan's condition quickly and within days, he had been able to sit up and take notice of the world about him. The settlement comprised six simple huts with mud and bamboo walls and roofs made from thatch. A portion of forest bordering the huts had been cut and converted into fields. Each night, Irfan was disturbed by loud shouts and calls. Wild animals were afoot in the darkness, and the villagers stayed awake to keep them out of their precious fields.

Only a handful of people lived in the settlement, all of them short, the tallest barely topping Irfan's shoulder. To Irfan, they seemed thin and malnourished. Several were unwell. Some limped, some coughed, and many of the children had swollen eyes that oozed a sticky discharge.

Halting at the settlement was not part of the plan, but Irfan's condition had forced Shahid to cut the voyage short at this secluded shore. The forced halt had disrupted schedules and jeopardized a planned rendezvous with Mohammed Aziz. Shahid wasn't the kind of man who could sit idle, and when it became clear that Irfan would require several days to recuperate, he had decided to put his time to good use, exploring the area. His primary objective was to chart a route that would connect to the one he had been forced to abandon. He hoped to get horses too, as they would ease the onward journey for Irfan. Leaving Tabrez in charge of the boys, he departed the day after they arrived, taking with him two men from the settlement as guides.

It was clear to Irfan that they weren't welcome at the settlement. It showed in the attitude of the adults and the suspicious glances cast their way. The children, although naturally inquisitive, had been warned to stay away. If they wandered in their direction, they were shouted at and punished. Tabrez explained that the unfriendly behaviour of the settlers wasn't surprising. People in these forests had suffered often at the hands of strangers. Marauding gangs stole whatever they laid their hands upon, plundering and sometimes killing too.

Tabrez was short, just a wee bit taller than the villagers. His skin was a pale shade of brown, the colour of the bark of Bombay's coconut trees. In spite of his lack of size, he was stronger even than Irfan. Although of little help during the voyage, Tabrez had immediately demonstrated his value on land. It was abundantly clear that the forest was his home. He flitted with extraordinary agility amongst the trees and on the ground, he moved with animal lightness. His prized possession was a catapult, which in his hands was as effective as a pistol. His aim never erred. With accuracy comparable to that of a striking eagle, he could knock birds down from the air. He was a master at laying traps and snared hares and deer with rolls of twine that he spread in the underbrush. He could dress and expertly cook the game he hunted, and could coax a flame from wet soggy wood. Shahid had chosen well. Irfan and Rustom were glad to have Tabrez with them.

Persistent rain confined the boys to their hut. The enforced rest quickened Irfan's recovery, but it wasn't a comfortable experience. The monsoon is the most difficult season of the Konkan as incessant rains deluge its rocky shores. The forests of this region were infested with leeches and the damp had multiplied their number manifold. In addition, they had to deal with scorpions, millipedes and beetles, all of which swarmed cheerfully into the hut to shelter from the rain.

Though distressing, Irfan's physical discomforts paled in comparison to the mental agony he suffered. Not a night passed without Irfan weeping inconsolably. Fate had singled him out, striking a terrible blow, tearing apart his existence, snatching away what was dearest to his heart.

Bombay.

Bombay was the city that had bred and nurtured him, the city he loved, the city he had dreamt of spending the rest of his days in. But fate had dictated otherwise. One incident . . . one irreversible deed . . . that was all it had taken. His dreams had been crushed and his world turned upside down.

Rustom too hadn't been spared. But where there had been no option for Irfan, Rustom had knowingly chosen his fate. Rustom could have stayed back, holding fast to his dreams. Except for the loss of a friend, life would have been unaltered for him. But displaying exceptional loyalty, he had refused to abandon Irfan, choosing to accompany him in spite of the certain ruin of the promising future he was shaping for himself.

Irfan had no words to express his gratitude. His love and respect for his friend had grown immeasurably. Not only had Rustom ensured that he had survived, but now, in his darkest moments, it was his presence that was keeping his spirits alive. Despite everything, Rustom's enthusiasm for life was intact. Nothing could dim his smile and resolve—not the voyage, not the hardship of the forest, not even the turnaround in their fortunes. Rustom's steady and quiet strength enabled Irfan to recover rapidly, and when the time came to travel, Irfan was ready.

On the eighth morning after their arrival, a day on which the rain eased considerably, one of the men who had accompanied Shahid returned. The man's name was Bhiku. He was short and skinny, but unlike the sickly members of his clan, his frame rippled with strength and vigour. He delivered to the boys a message inked on a scroll of paper. It was from Shahid.

Shahid had decided not to return, which was not altogether surprising as he had indicated the possibility before departing. Horses had been difficult to find. Instead of wasting time doubling back, Shahid intended to scour the area for the animals and also assess the safety of the route he had selected. If Irfan was well, they were to leave the settlement immediately and make their way south. He was changing their rendezvous, as the area he had chosen earlier was unsafe on account of the movement of thugs and roving gangs. He had settled on another place, a thickly forested region rarely frequented by locals. Bhiku, the bearer of the note, knew the spot and would lead them there. Contradictorily, Shahid's very next sentence warned them to keep a watch on Bhiku. The man was not to be trusted, he wrote. But he allayed any fears that Bhiku might betray them, explaining that Bhiku's brother was in his custody and that Bhiku had been warned that if any harm befell the boys, he would never see his brother again. Shahid's letter ended on a cautionary note, instructing them to travel unobtrusively and to avoid villages and settlements.

Irfan declared he was strong enough to travel, at which Tabrez decided to set out right away. Although the settlement had enabled him to regain his strength, it was the most miserable place Irfan had spent time in, and neither he nor Rustom objected to Tabrez's haste. The rains had no doubt exaggerated the settlement's wretchedness, but it was the unprovoked hostility of its residents that was most insufferable. Irfan and Rustom were vastly relieved to turn their backs on the squalid huts and their unfriendly occupants.

They quickly discovered that their guide Bhiku was no different from his kinsmen. He was cocky and surly, and he barely disguised his contempt for them. He set a spitefully hard pace on departure, which Tabrez and Rustom had to force him to lessen for Irfan's sake.

Tramping through a forest was a new experience for Irfan. Everywhere about him rang the cries of birds and animals. Monkeys foraged in the trees. Deer hid amongst the bushes. Tabrez pointed out wild pigs, mongooses and jackals. On the ground, there were peacocks and pheasants, and in the trees, an unending variety of brightly coloured birds.

The possibility of predators worried Irfan. Their weapons—sturdy sticks with pointed tips—did not inspire confidence. They were equipped also with catapults, which Tabrez had fabricated for them. Bhiku wielded a spear tipped with metal and there was a bow strapped to his chest. His arrows were ordinary sticks with sharpened ends. All their armaments, even if wielded in concert, were pitifully insubstantial when measured against the might of carnivores like tigers and leopards that were known to prowl the area.

Luckily, except for odd, sharp showers, the weather held. Tabrez had fashioned bamboo hoods for them and had lined them with leaves and strips of sailcloth for protection. He had also stitched anklets from the remnants of the sailcloth, which he wrapped around their feet to fend off leeches.

For Irfan's sake, the first day's march was limited to a few hours. Bhiku found them a cave-like shelter halfway up a hill. Surprisingly, it was Rustom who provided their meal that evening. Having practised at the settlement, he was already adept in the use of catapults, and when they stalked junglefowl in the brush, he brought down a large bird with a well-directed projectile. He then proudly dressed and smoked the unfortunate creature on a soggy fire, which despite Tabrez's best efforts, sputtered and fizzled out before the bird was cooked. Though barely half-cooked, they consumed their meal ravenously and Irfan fell into tired sleep.

They travelled in this manner for three days, walking by day and halting before it turned dark. They camped mostly in caves, huddling to one another to keep warm. Only once, beside a holy shrine in the forest, did they spend the night in comfort, in a simple hut with a thatched roof that was kept in good repair by pilgrims who halted there.

Unfortunately, the weather turned wet and stormy after the first day, and Tabrez's bamboo hoods failed to keep the dampness out. So hard was the rain that nothing, not even the thickest and finest raincoats of Bombay, could have kept them dry. The ground softened to slush beneath their feet and often they had to ford flooded, fast-flowing streams. Leeches attacked them in droves, leaping on them from branches and the underbrush. The tiny creatures gorged on their blood, feasting till they could drink no more, falling to the ground like bloated worms after having their fill.

Thankfully, hunger did not add to their woes, as food was available in plenty. During the day, they ate berries, yam and fruit and whatever else they gathered. In the evenings, Tabrez provided for them, downing birds and tiny animals. Bhiku never partook in the evening hunt, neither did he bother with camp activities. His manner was sullen throughout. He refused even to entertain questions regarding the route. Having no recourse, they were forced to put up with his behaviour. They drew comfort though from Shahid's claim that he held Bhiku's brother in custody. It was unlikely that he would betray them at the cost of his brother's life.

On the fourth morning of their journey, when they woke, they discovered that Bhiku had slipped away during the night. He returned an hour later, slinking into their camp as unobtrusively as he had departed. He refused to explain his absence, responding with infuriating grunts to their queries.

Bhiku's excursion resulted in a delayed start and as if to compensate for the hold-up, he set a scorching pace, faster than at any time during the journey. They soon came to a wall of hills and after a steep ascent through wooded slopes, they halted on a rocky, wind-blown summit. The panorama revealed before them struck the boys to a dumb silence. A series of forested hills dimpled the horizon. Everywhere about them was the richest green Irfan had ever seen, unbroken except for outcroppings of black rock girding the slopes of the hills. Mist hung like smoke in valleys and water gushed everywhere.

Bhiku drew their attention to a distant hill, notable for a massive rock face at its summit. A thick white ribbon—clearly visible despite the distance—cleaved the vertical mass of rock. Several similar ribbons graced the slopes of the surrounding hills. The ribbons were streams of cascading water, tumbling to the earth in spectacular waterfalls, and the one that split the rock face of the mountain Bhiku had singled out was the largest Irfan had ever seen.

Bhiku delighted everyone when he announced that Shahid was waiting beneath the mountain with the vertical rock face. He was camped at the mountain's base, where the falling water spawned a river. Though it seemed just a short march, the journey to the mountain would entail a full day's travel as the terrain was hilly and several rivers—all in spate—would have to be negotiated while traversing the wooded country that stretched in between.

On that heartening news, they continued their journey, more carefree now, laughing and enjoying themselves. In their merriment, they failed to notice Bhiku fall behind. Only at the bottom of the hill did they discover that he was no longer with them. When their calls drew no response, they backtracked and searched the area. Tabrez quickly located the spot where Bhiku's tracks angled off in an unexpected direction. Ordering Irfan and Rustom to wait, Tabrez hurried after the man. He returned an hour later with worrying news. He explained that another pair of footprints had linked with Bhiku's a short distance along the trail. Running fast, he had soon come upon Bhiku and his new companion. On seeing him, they had laughed and shouted derisively. Bhiku's companion was of the same height and build as him and when Tabrez drew nearer, he recognized him as Bhiku's brother, the man Shahid was supposedly holding in custody. Keeping out of range of Tabrez's catapult, Bhiku and his brother had taunted him. Tabrez had shouted, asking about Shahid, and Bhiku's brother had confirmed that Shahid was waiting beneath the mountain with the tall rock face. Then he had laughed and hooted and had said they would never get there. There was a surprise in store for them, he cackled. Bhiku had guffawed too, as if his brother had cracked the most hilarious joke in the world. Sniggering, the two brothers had turned away, returning presumably to their settlement. Deciding it was pointless to pursue them, Tabrez had returned.

After a conference, the boys decided to continue to the mountain. They had little choice as backtracking to the settlement was out of the question. Shouldering the mantle of leadership, Tabrez opted to follow the route Bhiku had suggested—trekking to the river and tracking it upstream to its source. A swift walk brought them to the river, and they saw that it had overflowed its banks. Its waters were brown and restless, sweeping along a flotsam of branches and broken trees. Skirting the river's edge, they trekked upstream. After a while, the hills closed in around them, shutting them in a valley. The valley narrowed, turning finally into a gorge, forcing them to abandon the river and enter the forest once more. A half-hour later, as they tramped through thick forest, Irfan suddenly halted. He had heard a sound. Faint though it was, he was sure it was the whinnying of a horse. His companions stared at him, unconvinced. Tabrez suggested it might have been a wild animal. But Irfan, whose hearing was attuned to such high-pitched nickering, was adamant it was a horse.

Noting Irfan's conviction, Tabrez turned cautious. A sense of unease overcame them and they tightened their grip on their sticks when they resumed their march. The forest was dark and still. Water dripped steadily from the trees and the only other noise was the tramp of their feet.

They were on a level, wooded stretch when they heard the unmistakable pounding of hooves on wet earth. Like a scalded cat, Tabrez leapt sideways off the path.

'Don't follow me!' he hissed, as he vanished into the shrubbery. 'Keep walking. Stay on the track.'

They managed just a few strides before horsemen appeared around a bend. There were three in all and they galloped their steeds forward, surrounding the boys. Two riders were dark-skinned and wore turbans, while the third, a white man, sported a blue hat. There was a pistol in the white man's hands and it pointed steadily at the boys while the horses snorted and stamped.

'Who be Irfan?' barked the white man. Dirty brown hair hung in curls beneath the man's hat and a stubby beard fuzzed his jaw. His eyes were blue and intense, as his gaze alternated between Irfan and Rustom.

Irfan stepped away from Rustom. 'I do not understand, saab,' he said, speaking in Marathi.

'Liar!' shouted the Englishman. He raised his gun, but even as he did so, there was a scything sound and he suddenly screamed, clutching his head. His finger tightened on his gun as he slumped forward. There was an appalling burst of noise and Irfan felt a sudden wind brush his cheek. The roar of the gun spooked the horses. Neighing shrilly, they reared and flailed their hooves. The Englishman tumbled to the ground, his feet still strapped to the stirrups. The men on the other horses struggled to control their mounts. Irfan reacted swiftly. The horses were on their hind legs, off-balance. Dodging hooves, he leapt to the side of the nearest horse and lashed out with his leg, thrusting hard.

The horse screamed as it lost balance. Its rider swore loudly, crashing to the ground with his mount. As Irfan turned to the other horse, there was another scything sound and the man riding it slumped forward soundlessly.

Tabrez emerged from the shrubbery, catapult in hand.

'The horses!' cried Irfan, grabbing the reins of the animal with the slumped rider. 'Take their horses.'

The man on the fallen horse was struggling to free himself. Tabrez raised his catapult, firing a missile at point-blank range. The man screamed, clutching his head.

The horse with the Englishman was running away, dragging its rider behind it. Rustom sprinted after it and pulling alongside, yanked the Englishman's boots from the stirrups. Irfan grabbed the reins of the other two animals. Their riders were easily dislodged, in no condition to resist. Rustom snatched the gun from the Englishman's hands before mounting and Tabrez and Irfan appropriated swords from the fallen men.

Mounting swiftly, Irfan turned his horse around. 'Follow me!' he yelled, kicking his horse into a gallop. Hooves flashed on damp mud as the animals were spirited away from their former masters.

They rode hard for several minutes before Tabrez signalled a halt.

An ecstatic grin split Irfan's face. Their victory was only part of the reason for his ebullience. The feel of a horse between his legs contributed far more. Too many days had passed since he had last ridden one. His gloom and despondency were forgotten and his eyes shone with a special light. Rustom's face was bright and happy too. He gazed at Irfan, joyous for his friend. Irfan had withstood the cruel blows life had sought to knock him down with. Now there was laughter on his face and hope in his eyes again.

They completed the remaining leg of their journey on horseback. Shahid spotted them well before they reached the mountain with the spectacular rock face. He greeted them with wide-open arms, hugging each of them in turn, reserving the longest and most heartfelt embrace for Irfan. He was delighted they had managed to find their steeds as his quest had yielded only one animal. But Shahid's joy receded when he heard of their encounter with the Englishman. The news of Bhiku's brother troubled him deeply. The man had escaped a couple of days earlier, and it was obvious he had betrayed them to the Englishman.

The enemy had information of their movements. There would be no rest for them today. They had to shake off their pursuers.

'But that's not a problem,' cried Shahid, mounting his animal. 'We have horses. No one can catch us now.'

The journey by ambulance to Mumbai had been uneventful. In another white hospital room, Anirudh was tenderly lowered on to a white bed with fresh white linen. Leaving nothing to chance, Commander Dongre held one end of the stretcher this time. Anirudh's transfer to the bed was gentle, yet when the stretcher was eased away from under him, he shuddered. His mouth popped open and he rolled. Smita Dongre stroked his forehead. Anirudh tossed and turned in the bed. His father reached down and held him. Anirudh's agitation lasted less than a minute. Then he relaxed. His body turned limp; he seemed to sigh, and the semblance of a smile appeared on his lips.

MARIO AND AJIT

The dream turned patchy. The overcast skies and mountains began to fade. Annoyance rippled through the bystander as the familiar darkness descended. *Not now! Not when the action and excitement were reaching fever pitch.* He wrestled the dream, trying to steer it back to the journey and the drama of Irfan's flight. But after a brief tussle, he retracted his resistance.

What if the dream withdrew? The possibility of Irfan's story being lost forever alarmed the bystander. By now it was obvious that the dream was divulging the details of a life—not any ordinary life, but an existence that was somehow connected with his. The dream's abrupt lurches and turnabouts were vexing, but opposing them might not be prudent. The dream must have its reasons; logic that he would perhaps understand at a later stage. The bystander quieted his discontent. Barring the nightmarish voyage—the episode he was determined to oppose—he would allow the dream to determine its own course. Eventually, it would reveal the ties that bound Irfan and him.

Soon enough, after a short interval, the darkness withdrew and light appeared again. On this occasion, in sharp contrast to the gloom and mists of the previous sequence, the skies were bright and blue. There was a beach and an aquamarine sea sparkled in the morning sun.

The dream had reverted to Bombay.

Palm trees grew in thick profusion behind the beach. A cool wind swept in from the sea, noisily rustling a packed canopy. Irfan and Rustom were on the beach, seated at its very edge, under the shade of the trees. Two horses dozed behind them, eyes shut, heads drooping.

The beach Irfan and Rustom rested on was called Chowpatty. It was so named because four creeks had once converged here. There was no trace of the creeks now, but the name had survived. Located in what was known as the Back Bay area, Chowpatty was a quiet, sleepy section of Bombay frequented mostly by fishermen who beached their boats on its sandy cove.

A few fishing boats rested on the bright sands and several more cruised the blue sea. The ones on shore sprawled listlessly, like beached whales, while those on the water bobbed sprightly—masts upright, sails fluttering, each escorted by a cloud of squabbling gulls.

The weather was cool and pleasant as it always was in Bombay during February. Though it was nearly six months since the twins had left the shores of India, Irfan had mailed only two letters to his English friends. His tardiness wasn't on account of indifference, rather it had more to do with his habit of postponing laborious tasks. Ralph had corresponded regularly, and his brother Peter, who was even lazier than Irfan when it came to such exertions, had occasionally scribbled a paragraph in his more conscientious twin's letters. Mrs Brown had written faithfully to start with, her letters arriving punctually every fortnight. But with the passing of the months, her correspondence had turned sporadic before ominously ceasing. Ralph's letters had kept Irfan informed, conveying distressing news. Mrs Brown's cough had taken a turn for the worse. More worrisome was her failing strength and her inability to rise from her bed. The doctors spoke little to the twins, but Ralph reported that they departed always with grim faces, their manner indicating the seriousness of her illness.

In Bombay, Mr Brown had brushed Irfan's queries away, asserting that all was well with his wife. But Irfan's misgivings had been confirmed a few days earlier, when he had come upon the Englishman unawares one evening. Mr Brown was seated in the veranda reading a letter, head down, shoulders drooping. It was a cool evening yet his face was red, a shade it acquired during the heat of summer. Mr Brown was a man who rarely displayed emotion. He never smiled, not even on his children's birthday. At the dockyard when his family had departed for England, while Irfan sobbed, he had remained impassive, as if the parting was a routine one, no different from a weekend excursion. But on this occasion, there were deep hollows beneath his eyes and his mouth was open, lips quivering. His eyes had glittered when he looked up at Irfan and he had simply shaken his head.

Mrs Brown's failing health accomplished what Irfan's father, despite constant urgings, had failed to kindle in his son—her sickness drawing Irfan to the masjid and prayer. Each day Irfan confirmed his faith and love for Allah and appealed to him to cure his foster mother of her illness.

Irfan's new-found devotion notwithstanding, matters had not improved between him and his father. If anything, they had worsened. Irfan's refusal to terminate his association with his employer continued to rankle Mohammed Aziz and the latest obstacle—straining their ties to breaking point—was his blossoming relationship with Forjett, the English police officer, who his father held a fierce and unrelenting grudge against. Mohammed Aziz might have tolerated his son's disobedience, but Irfan's unambiguous and open loyalty to the officer deeply embittered him. Even worse, like a knife twisting in a festering wound, was his son's readiness to assist the Englishman; an act which Mohammed Aziz held as not just objectionable but one of high treason.

Irfan, in fact, owed his presence at the beach that morning to Forjett. It was on Forjett's request, seeking their aid, that Rustom and he had taken the day off from their respective jobs. The morning's undertaking was not the first time they had assisted the police officer. The errands Forjett sought were highly unusual—pursuits like eavesdropping, spying and gathering information—not exactly the sort of favours one requested of young boys. The first job hadn't been easy, but Irfan and Rustom had overcome their awkwardness and after several undercover outings, they now executed Forjett's assignments as routine chores. On this occasion, however, their task was different and far more demanding. Irfan recalled the cool evening in Forjett's large and airy office when the officer had first spoken of the matter. Forjett had been uncharacteristically tense that day. He had sat rigidly in his chair and his fingers had drummed continuously on his table. At the outset, he had warned that the task could be dangerous, but sequestered in his office, and emboldened by their past successes, the boys had readily volunteered. Now, on the warm sandy beach, as the chosen hour drew near, a mild anxiety gnawed at them as they gazed distractedly at the calm, blue sea.

Rustom stirred beside Irfan. In spite of Chowpatty's splendid beach and sea, he was sulky. 'Do I really have to come along?' he fretted. 'I have work to do. My boss doesn't like newcomers taking time off.'

Rustom had switched jobs. He worked at the docks now, boarding vessels that arrived in the harbour, inspecting and indenting their cargo, and supervising its removal. It was a job he enjoyed and was afraid of jeopardizing.

Irfan glanced irritably at Rustom. 'Your boss has granted you permission, so what's the problem?'

Rustom's expression turned sullen. 'It wasn't right of you to ask my boss. There was no need. The rest of you can do the job yourselves. You don't need me.'

'Stop whining, Rustom,' snapped Irfan. 'It was Forjett saab who requested your help, not me. You look the most innocent, he said, and you are a Parsee. The angrez trust Parsees.'

'I don't want to break that trust,' shot back Rustom. 'I'm not a thief. I don't like what I've been asked to do.'

'You are doing this for Forjett saab. You owe him a debt. He wouldn't ask if it wasn't important. You should be proud of his faith in you. He believes you are best suited for the job.'

Rustom remained silent. He stared out to sea, clearly unhappy.

Irfan looked at his watch. It was past 9.00. The others were late. He wished they would come soon. Rustom wasn't the best company when nervous.

Irfan was proud of his flowering relationship with the police superintendent. Most ordinary citizens couldn't boast of such a high-ranking acquaintance, and Irfan was flattered by the officer's attention, particularly the fondness Forjett publicly showered on him. Even on the street, in full view of everyone, Forjett would halt his carriage to inquire about his health and well-being. If they met on the Esplanade, he would buy Irfan snacks and walk with him as if he were a friend. People would stop and stare, and Irfan's chest would swell with pride. Their association had strengthened over time and Forjett had started inviting Rustom and Irfan to his office. The visits soon became a regular affair. On these occasions, he invariably sought their opinion on the city. They spoke about the state of the roads, the sanitation, the availability of water, the behaviour of the police, the attitude of the Indian sepoys, and even the gossip in the market. Forjett was particularly interested in assessing public sentiment and requested elaborate details of grievances. It was always the boys who did the talking and Forjett the listening.

As he idly watched the fishing boats, Irfan thought of his father's condemnation of his relationship, going as far as to label it as collusion with the enemy. No doubt their communications benefited Forjett, enabling him to acquire intelligence he could never have collected on his own. But what of it? Forjett employed that knowledge for the good of the city. Forjett was a sincere man, the most upright officer to head Bombay's police force. No one, neither native nor white, disputed his honesty and ability. It was only his father who thought otherwise, clinging stubbornly to a grudge about something that had taken place years before. Couldn't his father be magnanimous and put it behind him? Forjett had done so. The officer was unfailingly courteous and respectful of his father, conveying his regards for Mohammed Aziz every time they met.

The tramp of heavy feet disturbed Irfan from his musings. Turning, he saw that their friends Ajit and Mario had finally arrived.

'*Challa*! *Challa*!' exclaimed Mario, the larger of the two. 'Passing time as usual. Lazybones both of you. Come on, there's work to be done.'

'You loud-mouthed monkey!' exclaimed Irfan. 'You are half an hour late, and you have the nerve to say that we are passing time.'

The smaller boy, Ajit, halted beside Irfan. His frame was petite, skinnier than even Rustom's. 'It's your fault,' he said, helping Irfan to his feet. 'I thought you knew Mario by now. He's always late. You have to add a half-hour to any programme you fix with him. I do it all the time.' He laughed. 'That's why our friendship survives.'

'Angrez!' bellowed Mario, halting beside the horses. 'You are so kind! You have brought a horse for me.'

He opened his arms wide, but Irfan hastily backed away. 'Every day, I walk to work. Today I will ride. You are a true friend, my dear Angrez!'

Mario refused to address Irfan by his real name. He never referred to any of his friends by their actual names. He had dubbed Irfan as 'Angrez' because of his perfect English. Rustom he had nicknamed 'Parsee' and on account of his size, Ajit was 'Chotu'.

'We're travelling double,' said Irfan. 'Rustom is on Mohini with me. You two can ride Hafeez, the black horse.'

Despite his hulking frame, Mario mounted the horse nimbly, and he trotted the animal forward the moment Ajit settled behind him. Guiding the animal to the sea, he galloped across the sand.

Irfan followed more sedately, trotting Mohini on a firm strip of sand bordering the tideline. Ahead, jutting into the blue waters of the Arabian Sea, rose the forested slopes of Malabar Hill. Till recently, except for the ancient temple complex of Banganga at its distant tip, the forest cover of Malabar Hill had been left largely untouched. Deer, monkeys, wild boar, leopards and the occasional tiger had roamed undisturbed in its wooded environs. Now, however, ominously for the wildlife, wealthy inhabitants of the ever-expanding city, fed up with congested living conditions, had turned their attention to the hill, viewing it as an escape, a next-door refuge where they could build villas and mansions and lead a country lifestyle. This morning, Irfan and his friends were making their way to one such country residence on the crest of the hill.

Their destination was an opulent, freshly constructed mansion belonging to a rich Parsee businessman. So extravagant had been the man's design—fancy verandas, ornate carvings, fountains and a palatial garden—that he had spent far more money than he had planned and had been forced to rent out his mansion to recover the hefty sums he had recklessly squandered. Shortly after construction was completed, the now not-so-rich businessman had let out his home to a high-ranking English officer by the name of Cunningham. The officer's fussy wife had insisted on numerous additions inside the house and Irfan's friends, Mario and Ajit, had been assigned the job. The work was considerable, and fresh furniture had to be fabricated. The boys had been on the job for a month and their task was nearing its end. Mario was skilled both as a mason and a carpenter, and Ajit, though not in the same league, was good with his hands too. Both were keen to show their friends the quality of their workmanship. Irfan and Rustom had come along today ostensibly to admire their work.

Mario and Ajit were as unlikely a team as one could expect to meet. Not only were they physically dissimilar—one hulking, resembling a bear, and the other small and birdlike—but they belonged to different communities too: Mario, a Goan Portuguese and Ajit, a Brahmin. The boys owed their friendship to their fathers, who were colleagues, working together for many years in a construction company. Mario's father was a site foreman while Ajit's father worked at a desk, as a senior accountant. When their boys had come of age, both had been inducted into the company. Mario's father was pleased that his son was following in his footsteps, but Ajit's father, who wanted his son to apprentice as an accountant under him, was unhappy with his choice of work.

Mario had already reached the end of the beach and was exuberantly cantering up the road that led to the top of the hill.

'Slow down!' hollered Irfan.

Mario wasn't using his head. The horse bore a double load—triple, considering Mario's size—and would quickly tire on the slope. But the boom of surf on the sand drowned Irfan's voice and the unfortunate animal, tiring visibly, pushed on, stumbling up the slope.

'Don't waste your breath,' advised Rustom. 'Mario won't stop even if he hears you.'

But Irfan continued to vent his frustration, shouting till the foliage and winding road swallowed the floundering horse. Irfan cared far more for horses than he did for humans, and he was furious with himself for not having instructed Mario to slow down on the hill. It wasn't that Mario was unkind to animals, it was the exuberance of his personality that often got the better of him.

Though their acquaintance was no more than a month old, Mario and Ajit were already Rustom and Irfan's best friends. They had first met on a pleasant December evening, on one of those days when most of the Fort's populace had stepped out to enjoy the breeze on the airy expanse of the Esplanade. The evening had begun with Irfan in a bad mood, as Rustom hadn't shown up. They were scheduled to meet at the Bandstand at the southern tip of the Esplanade, at 5.00 p.m., shortly after Rustom finished work.

Though Irfan had arrived promptly, an hour had passed and there had been no sign of Rustom. Irfan had lost count of the number of marching tunes and jingles he had heard the band belt out. With mounting frustration, he had watched little children run circles around their mothers. He had been harassed by vendors trying to sell him everything possible, from mithai to miracle oils to massage his head with. Finally, fed up and frustrated, Irfan had crossed to the Fort walls, towards Church Gate, where Rustom usually exited the Fort, and had spotted a crowd beside the moat.

Curious, he had sauntered there and to his consternation, had spotted Rustom on the ground with two boys—one large and beefy, the other small and reed-like—crouched beside him. The boys were trying to assist Rustom to his feet, but he seemed in no condition to rise. There was blood on Rustom's face, his Parsee cap was trampled and torn and his clothes were streaked with mud, as if he had been rolling on the ground. When Rustom had finally been settled in a quiet corner of the Esplanade, Irfan had been apprised of the events leading to his predicament.

It was on account of a small quantity of ice—a much sought-after commodity—that Rustom had been assaulted. As ice was not manufactured anywhere in India, it was rare, expensive and available only when boats carrying the precious commodity docked in the harbour. That morning, a large boat from America—every gallon of its hold crammed with a glacier-cold cargo of ice—had arrived at the docks.

The company Rustom worked for had been assigned the task of handling and unloading the vessel, and though Rustom had known of the boat's impending arrival, he had kept it a secret. He and his colleagues had been promised free bucketfuls of the coveted substance, and he had wanted to surprise Irfan with a hoard of the prized chunks. But as Rustom burst upon the Esplanade, with two sweating jugs of ice clutched in his arms, he had been accosted by three hostile youths who had demanded he hand over the jugs. Rustom had refused and a fight had ensued. The youths had roughed up Rustom, but his battering would have been far worse if it hadn't been for beefy Mario and his tiny friend Ajit coming valiantly to his aid.

Though Mario was large and loud, his concern for Rustom indicated a warm and caring personality. Ajit was friendly and helpful in his own quiet manner. Irfan had taken an instant liking to both the boys. Deeply grateful, Rustom had expressed his gratitude with a continuous supply of ice. For the rest of the week—while the boat was being unloaded—he treated their new acquaintances every day to the sparkling substance and their friendship had been cemented on the shores of the Esplanade, as with numbed hands and mouths, they blissfully consumed copious quantities of marvellous, bracing, precious and expensive ice.

Now, on the wooded slopes of Malabar Hill, Irfan clenched his jaw in frustration as Mario, whooping gleefully, raced his mount up the slope. He had only himself to blame. A few cautionary words before they trotted off would have saved the animal.

Conscious of the double burden his mount bore, Irfan trotted her sedately up the hill, pausing whenever Mohini's breath turned laboured. As they climbed, an arresting view unveiled below. To the south, a sprawling mass of land arched into the sea with Colaba and Old Woman's Island at its distant tip. The Fort dominated the panorama, its walls dark and rounded, encircling a clutch of tightly packed red roofs. Viewed from here, the Esplanade was an enormous featureless brown expanse. The Girgaum woods—surprisingly large—were a pleasing swathe of coconut palms, their greenery offsetting the drab shades of the Fort and Esplanade. Below, the woods merged with the forested slopes of Malabar Hill and on the far side, they yielded to the brown ghats of Sonapur where the Hindu citizens of the city were cremated.

Mohini rested only twice during the climb and in a short while, they reached the top of the hill. They trotted along its ridge through quiet leafy glades. The cries of birds rang everywhere and sunlight fell in mottled patches on the rutted mud track. Presently, they came to a wall with an iron gate embellished with polished brass that flashed in the dappled light. A burly guard stood at the gate, looking important in a dark tunic and big turban. Beside him, stooped over a stick, crouched a man dressed in rags.

Hafeez, the black horse, rested beneath a jamun tree, his flanks dripping sweat. Mario stood crouched beside the animal, cloth in hand, swabbing it dry. Mario's concern for the animal stalled Irfan from passing angry remarks about his riding; he forced a smile instead when he and Rustom dismounted.

The man crouched beside the gate was a beggar. His clothes were filthy and his face looked as if it hadn't been washed for days. The guard was trying to shoo him away, but only half-heartedly.

'*Ek anna*,' implored the man, touching the guard's feet. 'God will bless you for helping the destitute. Have pity on the poor.' The man paused as the boys, led by Mario, crossed to the gate. 'Young sirs,' he entreated, turning to them, 'heed my plight. Don't ignore me like this hard-hearted man. You are kind, I am sure.'

The boys sidestepped the beggar. As Irfan entered the gate, he glanced back idly at the man and halted mid-stride. So abruptly did he pull up that Ajit bumped into him.

The guard gesticulated, waving Irfan on. 'Don't waste your money. The man has already been given alms. He is greedy and is making a nuisance of himself.'

Irfan shook his head as he entered the mansion grounds. 'My eyes played tricks on me,' he said, placing an arm around Ajit. 'Sorry, I didn't mean to stop like that, but the beggar looked so familiar, as if he was someone I know.'

'You should be sorry!' exclaimed Ajit, rubbing his nose. 'That hurt. And has anyone told you that you smell like a horse?'

THE MALABAR HILL MANSION

The mansion wasn't visible at first as it was tucked behind a grove of mango trees. Irfan pulled up once more when the cobbled path looped round the mango grove. The mansion was everything Ajit and Mario had described—grand and built like a palace—equalling, if not outrivalling, the most opulent homes in Bombay. Its striking feature was its veranda, obviously the showpiece of the edifice. Designed clearly for parties, it was broad and capacious. It wasn't only its size that impressed Irfan. Magnificent arched pillars fronted the length of the veranda, each adorned with intricate stone carvings depicting a handsome lion, its mouth frozen in a soundless roar. The veranda was protected from the elements by an enormous, tiled roof. Above rose an additional floor with several rooms. Each room had large windows with engraved lintels and outside, there were pretty balconies with baroque balustrades.

The garden matched the mansion in stateliness and size. At its centre was a huge fountain with a stone spout sculpted in the shape of a lion once again, except that this one was life-size. Its head was thrown back and its mouth was open to the sky. Several smaller lion-head spouts, identical to the carvings that decorated the veranda, lined the circular wall of the fountain. The fountain was shielded from the sun by tall trees. A grassy lawn, ornamented with bushes and flowerbeds, stretched on either side

A dozen malis toiled in the garden. One of them, a pint-sized, swarthy individual wearing khaki pants and shirt, straightened and stepped forward as the boys approached.

Brushing dirt from his hands he halted before them. 'Cunningham memsahib is busy,' he announced in a pompous tone. 'She is expecting guests and has left instructions to wait till she calls. You may rest in the garden till then.' The man narrowed his eyes. 'Mind you, no wandering. Memsahib gets very angry and so do I. No plucking flowers, no breaking branches, no spitting. You will behave yourselves or I will throw you out.'

Mario never took kindly to being spoken rudely to. Irfan expected him to react, but surprisingly, he nodded meekly. The mali stood aside and they crossed into the garden.

Rustom's face was flushed as he settled with the boys beneath the shade of a mango tree. 'This is a truly beautiful house,' he whispered, gawking at the mansion. 'It's the grandest home I have ever seen.'

Ajit rested an arm on Rustom's shoulder. 'It jolly well should be,' he said. 'Shiploads of money and effort have been sunk into it. My father's company took four years to build it.'

Rustom continued, almost as if he hadn't heard. 'The veranda . . . those arched columns . . . they are fabulous.

Whoever designed them is a genius. Look at the carvings. All those lions. They are so real . . . so dignified.'

Ajit made a face. 'I'm not sure I like the lions, but Jehangir saab . . . the man who owns the mansion . . . has a thing about them. His granddad used to hunt lions in Kutch and Jehangirbhai has childhood memories of accompanying him. That's why there are so many.'

'It's clear now why Jehangirbhai ran out of money,' said Irfan. 'What a home! No wonder you and Mario went on about it.' He turned to Rustom, looking quizzically. 'Why this interest in a house?' he asked. 'The only architecture that excites you is the sort associated with the sea—docks, ships, cranes—those kinds of things.'

'It's beautiful,' whispered Rustom. He sat still, as if entranced. 'It excites me . . . I don't know why. It's the nicest home I've ever seen. When I grow up and make my money, I'm going to build a house like this one.'

Mario clapped his hand against his thigh. 'You!' he hooted. 'You're going to build a house like this?' He stared incredulously. 'Do you have any clue of the kind of fortune it takes to build such a house? Even if you live a hundred lives, you won't make a fraction of that money as a dock assistant. You are some dreamer, Parsee baba.'

Rustom gave Mario a withering stare. 'I'm not an assistant any more,' he said, pride palpable in his voice. 'I'm a *chitti-wallah* already. Soon I will be an inspector. I am learning the trade and shall have my own boats one day. I will ship consignments all over the world and when I make my money, I will build such a house.'

Mario threw his head back and laughed uproariously. Ajit looked amused too.

Irfan rose to his friend's defence. 'Stop it, you two. Rustom has a dream. Unlike many of us, he has set goals for himself. You won't be laughing when he invites you to his home twenty years from now.'

Mario sniggered loudly. He opened his mouth to mock Rustom further, but was distracted as a horse-drawn carriage rolled into the driveway. Its polished frame sparkled in the morning sun as it drew to a halt at the veranda. The smartly dressed driver opened its door and two fair-skinned ladies in pretty summer dresses alighted.

While the carriage was being driven away the dark-skinned mali crossed to where the boys sat. Though even smaller than Ajit, he drew himself up, staring arrogantly at them. 'Memsahib's guests have begun arriving. I want silence now. No chit-chat. Memsahib gets angry. Sit quietly till she calls you.'

The boys fell silent. Ajit plucked grass absently and Mario sharpened a knife. Rustom stared infatuatedly at the mansion. Irfan was thankful that the house engaged his friend's attention, diverting his thoughts from the task ahead.

The purpose of their visit was not a pleasant one. They were not here, as Mario and Ajit believed, to marvel at their workmanship. Mario and Ajit had often pestered Irfan and Rustom to visit the mansion and see for themselves the excellence of their work. As luck would have it, their long-standing invitation served finally as a convenient cover-up for visiting the mansion.

Unknown to Mario and Ajit, Irfan and Rustom were here on a mission to retrieve stolen papers that Forjett believed were stashed in the mansion. Rustom's agitation was the fallout of the task of recovering the papers being entrusted to him. Rustom had never entered a house with criminal intent nor had he ever stolen anything in all his life. Yet Forjett insisted that it was he who was best suited for the task, selecting him over Irfan.

Five more carriages arrived bearing English memsahibs dressed in their finest. Fancy umbrellas, stylish headgear, expensive jewellery and the latest attire from London were paraded before them. An elegantly costumed butler, clothed as ornamentally as the memsahibs, received and directed them to the veranda where they were seated on plush sofas. Several servants in crisp white uniforms stood beside the sofas, waving fans. A posse of additional servants waited obsequiously on the ladies, traipsing up and down the veranda with trays laden with food and refreshments.

Mario always drew pleasure passing comments on the fancy hats British ladies wore. Irfan had never known him to let slip an opportunity to ridicule their ornate headgear, but this morning he displayed surprising restraint. His effervescent features were unusually deadpan.

Irfan wondered what his reaction would be if he were to discover the purpose of their visit. Although it would have only been appropriate to apprise his friends, Forjett had specifically requested that their mission be kept a secret. Respecting his wishes, Irfan had not mentioned a word.

A string of carriages discharged several more splendidly outfitted memsahibs before Mario stirred and rose. 'Come on,' he said, pointing at the bossy mali who now stood on the cobbled pathway, gesticulating at them. 'On your feet everybody, we've been summoned.'

The mali wagged a finger at Rustom when they halted beside him. 'Don't stare at the memsahibs,' he snapped. Rustom had been admiring the veranda and not the memsahibs and he opened his mouth to protest, but the mali cut him off. 'No backchat,' he glowered. 'Look smart and follow me. Cunningham madam is with her guests now and her room is available.'

The pathway circled round the mansion and the mali trooped the boys to its rear, where an open door led inside. They entered a large room with a wooden floor with expensive-looking rugs draped across it. Grand bespangled chandeliers hung from the ceiling and there were tables and chairs and more stone lions. A long-haired angrez gentleman was seated at one of the tables, dressed in a robe, reading a book. He looked up briefly when they entered and then returned his gaze to his book. The boys filed quietly past the man, following the mali through a door into another room.

It was obvious the moment they entered that this was Mario and Ajit's workplace. An assortment of semi-finished furniture—couches, desks, tables and chairs—was scattered about the room. On the far wall, two large windows framed a view of the distant harbour and Fort.

The mali addressed them before leaving the room. 'You will be quiet today. No hammers, no saws; nothing that will make noise and disturb the guests.'

'Memsahib informed me of the party,' said Mario. 'We will only scrub and polish today. There is a lot of finishing to be done. I have brought two additional hands to help.'

The mali nodded. 'Memsahib knows,' he said. He turned to Rustom and Irfan, his eyes narrowing again. 'No loitering and wasting time,' he warned. 'You will not stir from this room. If I see you staring at the guests, I will personally throw you out.' He glared threateningly at Rustom and then marched out.

Mario was all business once the mali departed. He handed everyone a quantity of wax polish and a brush. He directed Irfan and Rustom to work on two flat tables while he and Ajit selected pieces that were carved and required skill to polish.

Duties allocated, Mario rolled up his sleeves and immersed himself in his work. The odour of polish pervaded the room as the others followed suit. Irfan shot perplexed glances at Mario as he worked. This was a completely different Mario from the happy-go-lucky youngster he knew. His attitude had been transformed the moment they had entered the mansion grounds, his playfulness replaced by an out-of-character industrious disposition.

Irfan leaned towards Ajit who sat beside him. 'What's up?' he queried, whispering so that Mario would not hear. 'Has Mario lost his tongue? I've never seen him so quiet or this earnest.'

'He's always like this at work,' murmured Ajit. 'He takes his job very seriously. Give him an hour or so, he will ease up then.'

Irfan saw Rustom looking at them. His face was taut and troubled, his earlier anxiety back. Irfan made a face, trying to ease his friend's nerves, but he looked away. They would have to make their move soon, thought Irfan. Rustom was betraying signs of crumbling under the pressure.

Returning his gaze to Ajit, he whispered, 'Where is the safe Mario has installed?'

'It's in the study room. We'll have to wait till Cunningham saab leaves. Let me check on him.' Ajit turned. He was sitting beside the door and pushing it slowly, he edged it open. He poked his head into the drawing room and quickly withdrew it. 'He's still there. We'll have to wait.'

Of all the fittings and artefacts Mario had worked on, the piece he drew the greatest pride from was a secret safe he had installed in the mansion. The task was not a routine one, requiring an extraordinary degree of skill, and despite the availability of older and more experienced masons, it was Mario who had been chosen to install it. The safe was a vault with a special spring attachment, designed specifically for concealment within the brickwork of a wall. Jehangirbhai had imported the vault assembly from England and had ensured absolute secrecy during its installation. No one except Mario and Ajit knew where it was fitted. Mario's work had apparently been outstanding. So flawlessly had he embedded the safe that Jehangirbhai had rewarded him with an imported toolset from France.

Though the gift had gratified Mario, a sense of discontentment had lingered, as he couldn't share what was unquestionably his most outstanding success with anyone. But Irfan and Rustom were his friends, they could be trusted, and in keeping with his irrepressible nature, he had trumpeted his triumph to them. He had badgered them to visit and admire his handiwork, but since the mansion was far away and the boys were busy with their jobs, they had been unable to take up his offer. Now they were finally here, but Irfan hadn't been entirely honest with Mario. He couldn't possibly tell him that they were here to steal the contents of the very object that was Mario's pride!

Forjett was convinced that stolen documents were being stored inside the safe. He had explained that a few weeks earlier, documents had been thieved from the office of Lord Elphinstone, the governor of Bombay. The robbery was not public knowledge as the matter was sensitive, involving an internal security lapse. As governor, Lord Elphinstone was the most powerful man in the city, his authority second to none, and the loss of the papers was not only embarrassing but also a threat to security in the region.

Forjett had been assigned the task of retrieving the documents and had immediately arrested a British official of high rank. He had searched the officer's house, but the papers had not been found. Unfortunately for Forjett and Lord Elphinstone, the detained officer had powerful connections. He had raised a stink about his arrest; his complaints quickly reaching London, where, to Lord Elphinstone's embarrassment, his Lordship's detractors in the Parliament Houses discussed them with great interest. Stung by vengeful criticism from England for apprehending an innocent man, Lord Elphinstone had commanded Forjett to find the papers at all costs; move heaven and earth if he needed to.

The detained officer was the brother of Mrs Cunningham and it was common knowledge that his closest confidant was his sister's husband, Tim Cunningham, who was therefore a prime suspect. Forjett had earlier sent a spy to the Cunningham residence. Masquerading as a servant, the man had searched the mansion but had found nothing. He had learnt, however, of the existence of a secret safe from others who worked there. But no one had any idea as to where it actually was or any clue of how to open it.

It was during a recent social call on the police officer that Irfan, chatting idly about his friends, had let slip that they worked at the Cunningham bungalow. Forjett had been dumbfounded to hear that it was Mario who had installed the safe and, in a trice, had enlisted their help.

The visit had been speedily arranged. Forjett's need was critical and Mario had been delighted to finally have them along. Mario had warned that they would have to come prepared to work as he could only sneak them in as his helpers. Irfan had laughed off the prospect, thinking nothing of it, but polishing, as he quickly discovered, is a tedious task, and as he toiled in the stuffy room, Irfan soon grew tired and restless. Beside him, Rustom worked half-heartedly, his mind clearly not on the job.

In the drawing room outside, Cunningham stayed fast in his seat and as time passed, Rustom's nervousness percolated to Irfan. He started to worry about Cunningham, whether he would ever leave the room. He wondered why Cunningham wasn't joining his wife and her friends. Was he suspicious of something? In truth, Irfan was uneasy about the mission too. He wanted to get the job over and done with. But Cunningham, like a bear guarding his den, sat unmoving in his chair.

Ajit's forecast about his beefy mate was accurate, as after an hour of sincere toil, Mario eased the tempo of his work. His workmanlike expression wore off and he turned cheerful again. His ebullience resurfaced, but this time there was the added excitement that his friends would finally be seeing his work. He spoke proudly of the skill the job had demanded and the degree of precision required to fit the vault in the wall. He challenged Irfan and Rustom to search out its location. 'Stare at the wall as long as you want,' he bragged. 'Inspect every tile. You still won't find it.' That had been the hardest part: embedding it so seamlessly that it would be impossible to detect.

Irfan promptly took up his challenge. He and Rustom would take turns, he said. He scoffed at Mario, needling him deliberately, saying each of them would separately discover the vault's location; it would be child's play. Mario turned indignant. Though the risk increased the longer they stayed in the study, he pledged them ten minutes each. He even swore that he would abstain from enjoying ice for a year if they located the vault.

Irfan winked at Rustom. Mario had fallen for his ploy. Like a child eager to show off his most treasured toy, he had yielded to manipulation. It had been Irfan's intention all along that Rustom and he visit the study separately. Forjett had insisted on it. The police officer had mandated that Rustom should enter the study alone and retrieve the documents. The matter was far too crucial to take needless risks, he had said.

Outside, as if on sentry duty, Cunningham refused to budge. Mario, excitable as ever, quickly turned impatient. Irfan distracted Mario, asking him to explain in detail the mechanism of the vault, even though he had done so several times before.

Finally, Cunningham stirred. Wooden boards creaked in the drawing room and when Ajit stuck his head out, he caught sight of the Englishman disappearing up the stairs. Irfan felt a tightening in his stomach. It was time. There wasn't a moment to waste. The Englishman was in nightclothes and hadn't shaved. It would take a while for him to freshen up.

Rustom swallowed when Mario nodded at him. Ajit checked the hall and signalled the coast clear. Rustom's heart beat faster as he rose to his feet, clutching his cloth bag. Irfan squeezed his shoulder as he passed, but Rustom ignored him.

Rustom detested this assignment with every fibre of his being. Stealing was against his principles. He had not wanted to be any part of the affair even though the mission's purpose was just. His throat turned dry as he stepped into the drawing room. The hall, for some reason, seemed larger now than when he had first entered. Mario had said that the study door was at its far end, beside the exit to the garden. Rustom walked as softly as he could, sneaking like a frightened schoolboy from rug to rug.

The uneventful passage to the study did nothing to calm Rustom's fears. His hands shook as he opened its polished mahogany door and entered. The study was a large room with windows overlooking the garden. Rustom was thankful that the window curtains were drawn. But on closer scrutiny, he saw they were white and cut from a light fabric. They weren't entirely opaque and he could detect the shadows of the malis working in the garden. Rustom caught his breath. The mission was impossible. The malis would see him! They would catch him and thrash him like a thief. But as he backed away, it struck him that the sun was shining on the garden. The study was dark. Noticing movement from outside wouldn't be easy. The study would be a shadow.

Rustom's heart felt as if it had come unhinged in his chest. It thudded painfully against his ribs and his lungs heaved, sucking at the stale air inside the room. He surveyed the study as he waited for his breathing to steady. Several sofas and chairs were neatly arranged in its central area. Rustom flicked his gaze about the walls, searching for the fireplace Mario had said he should locate first. He found it on the wall opposite the windows, beside a large work desk. He had been instructed to search for a band of tiles on the lower section of the walls—a feature he couldn't miss, Mario had said. The tiles were there, cladding the wall at hip height. The vault was embedded behind the tiles. Mario had said it was concealed in the region above the fireplace and the desk; the challenge was to locate it.

Mario had explained the mechanism that prised open the vault and had also told them where the knobs that activated it were located. But they were not to press the knobs. Mario wanted them to save the opening for the last.

Irfan and he had to first discover the vault's exact location, a doomed effort according to Mario, given the quality of his work.

Regrettably, for Mario, his challenge was not on Rustom's agenda, it was in fact the furthest thing on his mind. His only desire was to open the safe, appropriate its documents and leave as quickly as he could. Rustom stared at the wall, recollecting Mario's proud discourse. Mario had said the mechanism was hidden behind a painting above the study desk. Sure enough, a fair-sized canvas hung there. Rustom crossed and halted before the painting, an image of a horse set artfully against pretty countryside. The tiles caught his attention next. Now that he was only an arm's length away, he saw that they were not ordinary tiles. Each was embossed with a blue design and at their centre was the impression of a lion; the same lion carved on the veranda pillars, with identical features and open mouth.

The room was silent. The only sound was his heartbeat, which ticked as audibly as a Ghadiali clock. The painting had to be removed first. He grasped it and lifting it off its supporting hooks, he placed it on the ground.

Mario had said that there were two metallic knobs flush with the wall, painted over so that it was impossible to detect them. The knobs when pressed together, activated the mechanism of the vault. Rustom quickly ran his fingers along the wall. The knobs had been cleverly hidden. No more than a foot apart, they were tiny rounded bumps. Rustom would never have found them if he hadn't known they were there, detecting them only because their texture was harder than that of the wall.

Placing his thumbs against the knobs, he pressed. There was a grating sound from the wall and suddenly three tiles, at chest height, thrust forward. Rustom stared in fascination. The tiles hung before him, solid and blue. On the wall, amidst the tiles, a cavity had appeared—a perfectly edged cavity with rims so smooth that no one could ever have guessed there was a vault hidden there. Mario certainly had reason to be proud of his work.

Rustom reached forward with trembling hands, but even as he did so his stomach lurched. His ears detected noise from the hall—the unmistakable thump of footsteps on its wooden floor.

His friends heard the footsteps too. The colour drained from Irfan's face. Mario and Ajit tensed, but having no idea of Rustom's true objective, their fear was a fraction of the panic that seized Irfan.

The footsteps halted outside their workroom and the door was thrust open. The tiny, dark-skinned mali stood there.

His lips curled in a snarl. 'Only three! Just as I thought! Don't bother pretending your friend has gone to relieve himself. The little rascal is in the study. I saw him moving there. The sneaking low-down son of a thief! First, he stares at memsahib's guests, next, he disobeys my orders! I will thrash him with a stick . . . oh yes, I will. He will regret his rashness for the rest of his life.'

Turning swiftly, the mali marched towards the study. Irfan sprang to his feet. As he raced out of the room, he heard a call and the pounding of footsteps on the stairs. The mali's ranting had alerted Cunningham.

Irfan rushed forward. The little gardener had no idea that Irfan was behind him and he was caught unawares when Irfan sped past.

'STOP!' shrilled a loud voice. Irfan glanced behind as he ran. Cunningham was on the stairs and there was a pistol in his hands. Ignoring him, Irfan dashed for the study, the mali hot on his heels.

'HALT!' screamed Cunningham. 'Halt or I will shoot!'

Irfan reached the study and flung the door open. Rustom stood frozen beside a desk. A section of tiles beside Rustom protruded from the wall. Rustom had opened the safe!

'The papers!' shouted Irfan. 'Take them and run. I'll hold the others back.'

Rustom snapped out of his trance. Scooping out the contents of the vault, he stuffed them into his bag.

The mali was only a few strides behind Irfan. Irfan spotted a poker propped beside the fireplace. In one swift motion, he seized it and swung it at the mali. The dwarfish man screamed and fell to the ground as the metallic rod slammed into his shoulder.

Cunningham was shouting and sprinting across the hall. The man had a gun.

Irfan grabbed the study door and slammed it shut. There were latches on the door and Irfan quickly bolted them. 'Open up!' howled Cunningham. 'Open or I will shoot.'

Irfan pushed Rustom to one side. His eyes fell on the windows.

A gunshot boomed thunderously and a hole appeared in the study door beside the knob. The door shook as Cunningham tried to open it, but the latches held it fast.

On the floor, the mali was stirring and attempting to rise.

Irfan ran to the windows and heaved one open. He saw a flowerbed below and the cobbled path beyond. Rustom needed no prompting. He leapt and Irfan followed.

Stumbling to their feet, the boys dashed along the path. Distracted from their work by the commotion, the malis in the garden stared in confusion at the fleeing boys. But a roar from their headman from the study window stirred them to action.

'STOP THEM!' howled their diminutive chief. 'Stop the thieves! They have robbed Cunningham saab.'

The men sprang to their feet.

Rustom and Irfan pelted past the veranda in full view of the ladies. The turbaned bearers gaped blankly. Their memsahibs chatted shrilly.

'So young and already thieves—'

'No different from the blacks at Cairo. Doesn't matter where they come from. These natives are all crooked.'

'Look, there's Tim. Goodness gracious! He has a gun in his hand. He's not going to shoot at them, is he? They are only boys.'

A gunshot boomed. Tim Cunningham swore loudly. 'STOP THEM!' he bawled. 'Guards, malis, bearers! Everybody. I want them captured.'

Rustom's eyes were white and round. The bullet had struck a tree only a yard to his left. His heart quailed when the gun boomed again.

'Keep running!' yelled Irfan, as the bullet tore through the foliage beside them. 'Follow the path.'

Irfan looked back as the path curled towards the mango trees. A horde of men was chasing them. The malis were in front, waving sickles and pickaxes. Cunningham followed, gun in hand, long hair streaming in the wind. Behind ran the bearers and the servants, turbans toppling from their heads.

Though the men were far behind, Irfan suddenly went cold. A horse was being galloped on the cobbled path. Cunningham had heard the drum of its hooves and was frantically gesturing its rider to halt.

Ahead, the gate had appeared. It was latched shut and the burly watchman crouched before it, his hands raised like a boxer.

'STOP!' yelled the watchman as the boys approached. He looked more than a match for both the boys together.

'Leave the guard to me,' panted Irfan.

'He's too big,' protested Rustom. 'We'll rush him together.'

'No!' hissed Irfan. 'You keep going. You have the papers. Slip out of the gate and run down the hill. I'll tackle him.'

The drum of hooves grew louder as they neared the gate. Irfan glanced back. Cunningham was seated on the horse now and was galloping forward.

Irfan refused to let despair overcome him. 'Keep going!' he shouted as he reached the gate and leapt fearlessly on the guard.

Rustom veered sharply as Irfan and the guard went down in a heap. A huge sliding bolt held the gate in place. Rustom unfastened it and shoved. The gate swung ponderously and stumbling through it, he passed into the clearing beyond. The beggar they had met earlier stood there. But the beggar was no longer stooped. He stood tall, staring at Rustom and shouted when he caught his eye.

'This way!' cried the man, gesticulating. 'Come to me.'

Rustom almost fell when he heard the beggar. The man had spoken in English. Not broken native English but perfect angrez English. Implausibly, his voice seemed familiar too, as if belonging to someone he knew. But the man was a beggar . . . Rustom paused, unsure. The gate crashed open and a horse charged into the clearing. Rustom ran to the beggar, flinging himself into his arms.

'Unhand the boy,' commanded Tim Cunningham, spurring his mount forward.

The beggar looked up. Shielding Rustom behind him, he shook his head.

Cunningham's face, a rosy red already, turned purple. 'You dirty, filthy swine. Release the boy this instant or my horse will trample your scrawny bones.'

Men poured through the gate, assembling in a circle about the beggar and Rustom. Though he was cornered with no possibility of escape, the beggar remained unruffled. Staring Cunningham in the eye, he spoke, his tone startlingly authoritative. 'I command you, Mr Cunningham, to lay down your gun. With the powers vested in me, I arrest you on behalf of the governor, Lord Elphinstone.'

The crowd pulled back, a ripple running through them. A beggar. A man dressed in rags. How could he speak like an Englishman?

Cunningham was taken aback too. He stared at the long-haired mendicant, not knowing what to make of him.

The beggar placed a whistle in his mouth and blew it loudly.

Cunningham recovered his bluster. He leaned forward threateningly on his horse. 'Whoever you might be, I've had enough of your games. I warn you not to test my patience any further. If you don't hand me the boy, I will command these men to beat you black and blue.'

The beggar smiled. He plucked the cloth bag from Rustom's unresisting hands. Reaching into its folds, he retrieved the papers stashed inside and waved them. 'I believe it is these documents you seek. They were stolen last month from Governor Elphinstone's office. I am curious as to how you propose to defend yourself when the judge seeks to know why they came to be found in your home.'

Cracks surfaced in Cunningham's bearing. Blood drained from his inflamed features. His arrogance seemed to shrivel. He stared blankly at the beggar. Recovering, he raised his pistol and pointed it at the old man. 'Give me those papers. They are mine and were stolen from my house. Hand them over or I will shoot!'

The beggar smiled. 'You disappoint me, Cunningham. I was mistaken. I credited you with far more intelligence than you have. You have admitted before this gathering that these papers were taken from your house, evidence that will seal the case for the judge.'

As the beggar turned away, the ground trembled and in a cloud of dust, a company of mounted troops swept into the clearing. A bearded officer on a big brown horse broke away and halted his mount beside the mysterious Englishman masquerading as a beggar.

'Arrest the man,' commanded the spurious beggar.

Ashen-faced now, Cunningham turned to his gathered servants babbling unintelligible orders. But his men backed away as the troops advanced.

Rustom suddenly found his tongue. 'Sir . . . Mr Forjett, sir . . . is it you?' he asked tremulously.

'Fooled you, didn't I?' Forjett laughed, his dark eyes gleaming. He squeezed Rustom's shoulder. 'You did a great job, young man. I knew I could depend on you. Where is Irfan?'

Rustom pointed at the gate.

Irfan was trooping through it with Mario and Ajit behind him. There were bruises on Irfan's face and his nose was bloodied. But his eyes lit up when he saw Rustom and Forjett.

He ran forward, joy all over his face. 'I knew it was you, sir. Your voice and eyes reminded me of someone I knew. But your disguise, your begging . . . it was so real, you had me fooled.'

Forjett's eyes twinkled. 'My Hindoostani is good, isn't it?' He laughed. 'No one recognizes me.' He turned to Mario and Ajit who were standing dazed behind Irfan. 'I take it these are your friends—the safe expert and his helper.'

Mario, for once, was struck dumb, unable to respond. Ajit gaped numbly.

'They helped us, sir,' bubbled Rustom. 'We would never have gained entry without them and Mario told us how to work the vault mechanism.'

Forjett inclined his head. 'I am in their debt. They will be rewarded for their assistance.'

Rustom was feeling light-headed. 'We would have got away with it, sir,' he prattled, his cheeks red, eyes gleeful. 'Then something went wrong and they discovered us, but you stepped in and saved us.'

Forjett smiled. 'It was never my intention to leave you alone. My men were hidden in the forest and we were prepared.' He gazed at Rustom and Irfan with his dark eyes. 'The governor will reward all of you. You have saved him from a terrible embarrassment. You two boys, in particular, have shown exceptional courage. My heart stopped when I heard gunshots. I would never have forgiven myself if either of you had been harmed. I shan't forget, masters Rustom and Irfan, not for the rest of my life. I owe you both a debt. A debt I hope I can repay someday.'

TRAGEDY

The Cunningham affair was not reported in any of the local newspapers. Bombay's dailies sidestepped the issue, although it was vastly more exciting than the dreary accounts they described in their columns. Irfan and his friends were sworn to silence too and ordered not to speak to anyone about the incident, not even their parents. Not that they cared, as they were rewarded generously, the governor, Lord Elphinstone, personally handing them a purse of cash each. In addition, Rustom was the recipient of special benevolence from Forjett, on whose unreserved recommendation he secured a senior position in a shipping firm owned by a wealthy Parsee gentleman.

Mr Ghadiali, the shopkeeper, expressed his happiness at the change in Rustom's fortune. He filled Irfan's ears with praises when he stopped by to spend a portion of his reward money on one of Ghadiali's 'wonderful' watches.

'Your friend Rustom visited yesterday to buy a watch for his sister, Naheed,' he beamed, scattering an impressive array of timepieces on the counter. 'It is Naheed's birthday today and he wanted to surprise her. I'm proud of the boy. Everyone is talking about him. Rustom's new boss Dhanesh Lowjee and his son visited my shop the other day. Mr Lowjee is a rich man, one of the richest in Bombay.' Mr Ghadiali drew himself up and puffed his chest, reminding Irfan of a pigeon. 'He has good taste, Mr Lowjee, and like all Parsees of distinction, he buys his *ghadials* only from my shop. It didn't surprise me when both Lowjee and his son spoke warmly of Rustom . . . Honestly, nothing surprises me any more about the dear boy. They said his work is excellent and they find him dependable and trustworthy.' Mr Ghadiali leaned forward conspiratorially. 'It is a secret still, don't let Rustom know, but they plan to promote him and give him more responsibility.'

Mr Ghadiali beamed again, looking up to the sky. 'Who would have dreamt this of our little Rustom? Just the other day he was penniless and had nowhere to go. Now he lives in a good home. He told me he has rented a spacious bungalow in Cavel, and he has money to buy expensive gifts for his sister. But one man surely isn't happy.' Ghadiali sniggered delightedly. 'Aha! Your smile tells me you have guessed. That's right! His spiteful brother-in-law. Oh ho, Palkhivala is jealous! You can see it in his face, the way he squirms when Rustom's name is mentioned. People praise Rustom in his presence—purposely, just to anger him—and he hates it. Serves him right. It was unforgivable, the way he treated the boy. When he grows up and makes a lot of money, Rustom should buy out Palkhivala's miserable business, just to teach him a lesson.'

Significantly, the turnaround in Rustom's circumstances did not have any influence on him. At heart, he remained the same simple boy Irfan had first met. He spoke nothing of his success and he continued to spend his every free moment with his friends. Yet, though inwardly his personality remained unaffected, the fair winds favouring him wrought conspicuous outward changes, radically recasting his appearance. A wardrobe of exemplary quality replaced the tattered clothes poverty had forced on him. Endowed surprisingly with a highly pedigreed taste, he selected for himself only the best fabrics. As with all his pursuits, he ensured that the subsequent tailoring fitted to perfection. His pale face was scrubbed clean at all times. His imported footwear was polished till it shone even by lamplight. Although only a boy, the Rustom who reported punctiliously each day at work was a man of the world—intelligent, smartly dressed and replete with confidence and ability.

Unfortunately for Irfan, the upturn in Rustom's fortune coincided with a sharp downturn in his. The slide began one fine morning when without any intimation, Mr Brown announced he was leaving for England. A steamer was departing the next day and he had bought himself a ticket. Biting back tears, he explained that his wife's condition had deteriorated suddenly and the doctors had lost hope. Irfan had been expecting the worst, yet the confirmation was a crushing blow. He poured out his grief that evening in a letter to the twins.

Dear Ralph and Peter,

Your mother will be mourned by three sons, not two. I am not of her blood, it is true, but she was the only mother I knew. She was the kindest, most loving and wonderful person I have ever known. Never once did she say why she cared for a simple native boy like me. I asked often, but she always hushed me, telling me not to bother myself with such questions. Now that she is gone, I will never know. It is Allah's will and maybe it is better that way.

I owe everything to her: my education, my English, my status in life. She will always be my mother and I will miss her as much as you.

Your brother,
Irfan

Mrs Alice Brown passed away a few days later, while her husband was still in transit, on board a steamer. Barely a fortnight later, when Mr Brown had finally reached England, news arrived in Bombay of a disaster in his shipping business. A storm in the South China Sea had destroyed two boats belonging to him. Their loss was a terrible catastrophe for Mr Brown as the cargo stocked in their holds had been purchased with borrowed money. Compounded with the grief of his wife's passing, the shock of his financial disaster broke his spirit. Shortly afterwards, Mr Brown's office in Bombay received word that he had suffered a stroke in England. The series of tragic events continued, and a fortnight later, a letter arrived from Ralph.

Dear Irfan,

With inconsolable grief, I write this letter to convey the passing of our father. Mother's death broke his heart. Her loss, followed so closely by the failure of his business, was too much for him to bear, and he gave up on life. Both Ralph and I are shattered. Father was not an expressive man. Though he rarely betrayed his feelings, it was clear that he loved us.

Amidst all this misery and heartbreak, it is hard to believe that just a few months ago, we were carefree children. Now we are orphans. Our dreams of returning to India are crushed. We are in the custody of our aunt and uncle, but only for now. There are other uncles and aunts who say they can also look after us. Our future is uncertain. You, dear Irfan, must be worried too. I have overheard talk that Father's financial situation is not good and that our beloved Seawind will have to be sold. I pray that the new owners are decent, that they will be kind, and that you and your father will continue to be happy there.

There might be no letters from Peter and me for a while as our lives are unsettled. I beg you to excuse us, Irfan. When we have a home and order returns, I will write. Don't trouble yourself with letters, as they will surely be lost. We are moving home and are unsure of our future address.

Dear Irfan, you and Bombay will always be in my heart. I shall never forget the wonderful childhood we shared. One day, when I am older, I will return and we shall be united again. You have my word.

Your loving brother,
Ralph

Events sped at a bewildering pace thereafter. The sale of Ralph's beloved Seawind took place barely a fortnight after Irfan received his letter. The mansion's disposal was imminent, the subject of much speculation amongst the servants who lived there, yet when word finally came, something snapped inside Irfan, as if another of the fast-dwindling crutches that had propped him all his life had crumbled.

It was Forjett who broke the news when he dropped by unannounced on a warm April morning. Irfan was exiting Seawind's gate—unmanned since the departure of Mr Brown—when the police chief arrived on a brown stallion, a strong, finely boned animal, which Irfan had personally selected for him from Ismail's stable.

Preoccupied with work, Forjett hadn't met Irfan for weeks. He greeted the boy warmly, and hitching his mount to Seawind's gatepost, entered its spacious compound. Like an invisible cloud, an air of sadness pervaded everywhere, escalated by the neglect that had befallen the estate.

The winding cobbled drive that led inside was overlaid with a month's debris of leaves and branches. On either side of the drive, flowering canna plants had shrivelled and fallen. An ornamental bamboo grove had yellowed, and a heap of dead leaves had collected below.

Forjett surveyed the mess with disgust. 'Who's the mali here?' he demanded. 'Only a scoundrel would allow a beautiful place like this to descend to such shambles! The rascal needs a hiding. Has he no pride in the upkeep of his estate?'

A wry smile hovered on Irfan's lips. 'Not this mali, sir. Balu has never cared much for his work. He's the head mali, but only in name. He is bone lazy and drunk half the time. The Browns retained him only because his wife was the children's maid.'

Forjett snorted. Unbuckling his hat, he strode forward, boots scrunching on leaves and bird droppings. The drive curled between rows of trees whose branches arched umbrella-like above, dappling the morning sun.

Around a bend, they came upon the mansion. Forjett halted, surveying it.

The erstwhile Brown residence consisted of a pair of twin bungalows with steeply sloping roofs. In-between there was a porch and a spacious veranda. It was a pleasing structure, lacking flashy ornamentation. Its simple elegance reflected the sensibilities of its former proprietors.

Forjett's jaw tightened as his eyes swept the garden. The lush grass that Irfan had played on as a child had been scorched lifeless by the unforgiving sun. The flowerbeds sprouted only weeds, and the once neatly trimmed hedges were a tangled mess. Forjett's outraged gaze fell upon a man who was sleeping at the edge of the dried lawn, beside a bougainvillaea bush.

'You there!' shouted Forjett, striding forward.

The man stirred, raising his head. His eyes were red and bleary, but they snapped into focus when they spied a wrathful white man in police uniform advancing. The man pulled himself to his feet, staggering. He was the gardener, Balu.

'Are you the mali here?' demanded Forjett.

Balu nodded, swallowing. He was a short sallow-complexioned man, thin and slightly stooped. His hunch was not a result of hard work as some mistook, but a consequence of an unquenchable love of liquor. His brow twitched as he stared nervously at the angry Englishman who had halted before him.

'This garden is a bloody disgrace!' ranted Forjett. 'The worst I've ever seen. Do you have no shame, you miserable man?' Forjett raised a threatening hand. 'Listen to me, you . . . you lazy blackguard. You have one opportunity to redeem yourself—just one. I want the garden swept, watered and restored to its original condition, starting now—this instant. I will have you jailed and I will personally throw away the key if it isn't.'

Balu rocked on his feet.

'Irfan here will report to me tomorrow. Heaven help you if he finds even a single leaf on the driveway. I will return and have you dragged by your hair to jail.'

Balu noticed Irfan for the first time. A look of contempt veiled his eyes. Irfan wished Forjett hadn't taken his name. Balu's entire family held a grudge against Irfan. His humiliation would drive the wedge between them deeper.

'Move!' raved Forjett. 'Get cracking!'

Balu threw a vengeful glance at Irfan. He took to his heels as Forjett hurled a string of abuses behind him.

It was a while before Forjett's breathing settled. He shook his head, as if clearing it. Then he turned his gaze on the mansion and sighed. 'I find it hard to imagine that the Browns are no more. I was never very close to them, I must admit. We were no more than acquaintances.' Forjett's fingers toyed with the strap of the hat in his hand. 'Craig Brown was a permanent fixture in Bombay. You could always depend on him being here, much like a priest at a church. They say he never once returned to his home in England; he loved India that much. He was a bit of a bore actually, never socializing, always serious and immersed in his work. Alice was different. She was one of many English women who came down from England to marry wealthy men here. She was warm and effervescent, charming all of Bombay's society. So dissimilar were her and Craig's personalities that there were misgivings as to their union. But they proved their detractors wrong, didn't they? You would know, Irfan. They lived contentedly together and reared a happy family.'

'I was part of the family,' said Irfan simply.

Forjett's eyes turned soft. 'Yes, you were, and I understand how you feel.'

Dust popped in tiny clouds as Forjett and Irfan walked on the wasted lawn.

Forjett frowned. 'The mali will lose his job if he doesn't spruce up the garden. Seawind has been sold.'

Irfan caught his breath.

'Word has arrived that a businessman from England, a Mr Colvin . . . Alexander Colvin, if I remember correctly, has purchased the mansion.' Irfan's face had shrunk, but Forjett hadn't noticed. 'This Colvin has bought out Craig Brown's business. The news is that he is already on board a steamer from London. He is new to India . . . a griffin. I have no idea what kind of a man he is, but one thing is certain, Irfan, you know what I'm talking about, don't you? Yes, it concerns you.' Forjett turned his gaze on his companion and finally registered his undisguised dismay. His voice softened. 'Life for you is not going to be the same any more. You cannot expect people to treat you the way the Browns did. Colvin will not. For that matter, I don't think any Englishman will.'

Irfan attempted to nod but managed a shudder instead.

Forjett placed a hand on Irfan's shoulder. 'I want you to know that you have no need to worry. I will ensure that Colvin treats you well. You can count on me, and if you desire, I can help you secure a better job like I did for Rustom. The same applies to your father. If he finds that he cannot get along with Colvin, I can help him find alternative employment too.'

Irfan's throat quivered. 'Thank you, sir,' he said. Speaking was an effort. His tongue felt sluggish, as if gummed to his jaw. 'Your kind offer is very dear to me, especially at a time like this. I . . . I never dreamt I might one day have to leave this place. Seawind has always been my home—' Irfan's voice trailed away. Tears fogged his eyes.

Forjett patted Irfan's shoulder. 'It's all right,' he comforted. 'I will manage Colvin, don't worry. It won't be so bad. You have my word. It is to reassure you on this that I have come here.' He changed the subject. 'Is your father home? It's been a long time since I saw him last. Fifteen years or so . . . I cannot remember. I would like to renew our acquaintance.'

Irfan dropped his gaze, refusing to look Forjett in the eye. With bowed head, he spoke. 'Father doesn't want to meet you, sir.' He paused, wiping his face with the sleeve of his kurta. 'He holds a grudge against you, sir. I have tried to change his attitude, but he ignores whatever I say. I'm terribly sorry, sir, but he will not meet you.'

Irfan had held back the truth about his father's sentiments from Forjett, speaking now only because he was forced to. But instead of reacting, the police officer remained composed, surprisingly with not even a hint of resentment on his features.

Forjett tapped more dust clouds from the dried earth. 'Tell your father that I respect his feelings,' he said. 'Tell him also that my offer of assistance holds. His animosity notwithstanding, he can always come to me.'

Irfan's respect for Forjett soared even higher. He blinked tears. 'Why . . . why does my father behave like this, sir? He does not talk, but he is bitter and angry. What happened in Mahabaleshwar? Please tell me, sir.'

Forjett paused in thought, then patted Irfan's shoulder again. 'Your desire to know what transpired there is understandable, but since your father has not spoken, it is not right for me to do so. I can venture only that your father suffered terrible tribulations there. His anger is justified. Do not be harsh on him. I know why he has not spoken. There are sound reasons. When the time is right, he will reveal all. Have faith and patience.'

Forjett departed shortly afterwards. An hour later, a messenger arrived from Mr Brown's office, officially announcing the sale of Seawind. The tidings of the impending arrival of a new English saab unsettled everyone and a pall of uncertainty fell upon the servants. The only silver lining, as perceived by Balu and his family, was the certainty that Irfan and his father would soon lose their 'special' status. Balu's wife, Radhabai, had served as Ralph and Peter's maid. More than anyone else, it was she who detested Irfan. She had never accepted his 'special' status in the Brown household, hating the fact that Irfan was the apple of her memsahib's eyes and not her precious sons. Her malice had ripened like a fruit over the years, and she had planted its seeds in her offspring. Within hours of the announcement, derisive statements about Irfan were openly aired, and it was Radhabai's children who were the rudest and most offensive.

Nitin was the elder of her two boys. He was the same age as Irfan and had once been his best friend. Of all the servant children, it was Nitin who had maintained his friendship with Irfan, even after Irfan's 'special' status became evident. Ignoring his mother's constant railing, he had remained steadfastly loyal to Irfan and the twins. But all that had changed when Mr Hunter, the tutor, had arrived and Nitin had been shut out of the classes. Unable to understand his rejection, and goaded by his mother, Nitin's camaraderie had switched overnight to outright loathing. Like a wound that refused to heal, his enmity had festered for years. Now it raised its ugly head.

Among the milder of Nitin's taunts was his morning pantomime, which he performed daily as Irfan left for work. Bowing low as Irfan rode to the gate, he would snigger loudly: 'Hail, prince Irfan! Here rides the English-educated nawab who, like a bloodsucking leech, clings to power through friends in high places. But sadly, his patrons are no more.' He would pause here to giggle, before concluding with a salute. '*Hail*! Hail, the angrez nawab who will soon be stripped of his title.'

His younger brother Ravi would take up the cue immediately after: 'Come one, come all. Everybody is invited to the event of the year, when young prince Irfan will sweep the floors and scrub the tiles and wash dishes like a common man. No need to rush for the first show. The tamasha will be enacted every day for the entire year, and from then on for the rest of his life.'

Their lampooning would conclude always with hooting and derisive shouting.

Irfan ignored their mockery. Inured to their jealousy from childhood, their jeering—even in its heightened zeal—failed to bother him, but his friends were appalled when they heard about the ridicule he was subject to. So intense was Mario's anger that he swore to storm into Seawind and thrash the brothers. Irfan's pleas for restraint fell on deaf ears, and it required all of Rustom's and Ajit's persuasive skills to hold Mario back. When alone, Irfan often wondered whether he could have coped without his friends. Their unstinting support was a ray of sunshine in a rapidly darkening sky, helping him maintain his sanity, as fragment by fragment, his precious world was being dismantled.

It wasn't only Irfan's future that was being recast during the fateful summer of 1857. Winds of change were sweeping across India, shaking the very foundation of English rule. The scorching heat afflicting the northern plains had sparked a bloody uprising. The discontent that had simmered for years burst into a flame and spread like wildfire across the entire subcontinent.

Tremors of unrest from the north had trickled into Bombay during February and March. The disquiet stemmed from the native regiments of the Indian Army.

After several years of loyal service, resentment amongst native sepoys had brewed to a boil against their English masters. Displeasure over the high-handed treatment at the hands of their foreign officers had been accumulating for years. A flashpoint was reached when the sepoys were forced to load their muskets with cartridges that offended their religious sentiments.

By April, news of the first revolt arrived from Barrackpore, when a sepoy by the name of Mangal Pandey boldly confronted his officers, accusing them of insulting his faith. Though Pandey was apprehended and sentenced to death, the revolt he initiated spread rapidly through the native ranks. In a few weeks, the uprising had spread to Lucknow and Meerut.

An atmosphere of unease settled over Bombay as news of insurrections and ruthless reprisals arrived daily. The eruption finally took place in May when the revolt turned into a full-fledged uprising. Hostilities spilled out into the open. There was carnage in Delhi as sepoys and their officers fought a pitched battle against each other. No one was spared. Horrific stories of the death of women and children alarmed the populace of Bombay, particularly the British. There were whisperings on the street. Rumours spread that the bloodshed would soon engulf Bombay; that the native sepoy regiments of the city were readying to rebel. The administration responded by clamping curfews on the town. Sepoys were relieved of their key duties and vigilance on them was stepped up. European soldiers replaced the native guards who manned the gates of the Fort. Leaders of the Indian population of Bombay were summoned and spoken to by the governor and the police chief. Troops marched conspicuously around the town and gallows with large nooses were erected in the crowded areas of the city. It was into this charged environment that an unsuspecting Alexander Colvin arrived on a humid summer's day on the shores of Bombay.

PANKHA DUTY

Colvin's steamer anchored on a warm afternoon in the placid harbour waters. Fending off a determined band of coolies at Apollo Bunder, Mohammed Aziz collected Colvin's belongings and drove him to his new home in Mr Brown's favourite carriage. The servants of Seawind, sweating profusely in their finest uniforms, had gathered respectfully to greet him. Colvin's complexion was an unnatural shade of pink, approximating that of a rose. His skin glowed as he stepped off the carriage, flushed possibly by the unforgiving sun. He was tall and bespectacled, with a protruding beaklike nose. During his brief address, his voice was silken and sweet, and Irfan's first impression of the new ruler of Seawind was that of a well-bred, industrious man with a peaceable disposition.

The impression of a sedate temperament proved to be an illusion, however. Distressingly for the servants, Colvin was possessed of a fierce temper and did not hesitate to berate anyone who ran foul of him. Balu, the mali, was pulled up if even a single leaf was found on the lawn; the sweeper was rebuked if the barest trace of mud sullied the veranda; the dhobi was reprimanded for the smallest of creases; and the hapless cook was berated daily, as Colvin, fresh from England, could not stomach his fare. Even Mohammed Aziz was not spared. Colvin scolded him if he was late and he never let slip an opportunity to criticize his uniform, which in truth, though the Browns never objected, was unsightly and never fitted properly. But, to the chagrin of his detractors, Irfan was spared his wrath. Although Irfan's special privileges, like entering the house and enjoying the garden were withdrawn, Colvin never spoke roughly to him nor did he trouble him with work.

Forjett's hand in the matter was obvious. Yet, Irfan received confirmation of his role only weeks later, as disconcertingly, the police officer turned inaccessible despite Irfan's best efforts. The reason was all too clear—a fallout of the turmoil scorching the subcontinent. The uprising had exploded into outright war. Fear stalked the land, afflicting all, but particularly the British, as the fury of the rebellion targeted them. Forjett, as the police chief, was a key member of the council entrusted with the maintenance of law and order in the city. Unlike in the past, he was only rarely available in his office, and on those occasions, he was too busy to spare time. Finally, towards the end of May, when monsoon clouds shadowed Bombay's skies, Forjett summoned Irfan to his office.

Forjett's vastly altered appearance staggered Irfan. The police chief had aged. There were creases on his forehead that hadn't been visible before. Hardly perceptible earlier, the streaks of grey in his hair had multiplied into prominence. His impeccably trimmed moustache was in disarray, overgrown, with ragged and untended borders, much like the hedges of Mrs Brown's garden. His face was haggard, eyes puffy, as if he wasn't managing enough sleep. He smiled, however, when Irfan asked him about Colvin, affirming he had spoken to the man, warning him—not very subtly—that if he spoke harshly to Irfan, or laid hands on him, he would have to face his wrath.

But significantly, Forjett had not spoken up for Mohammed Aziz. 'I deliberately did not stand up for him,' he said. He leaned forward on his desk. 'Irfan, the time has come for me to speak to you about your father.'

Irfan's heart leapt. Could it be that the events in Mahabaleshwar, suppressed for so long, were about to be revealed? But Irfan was disappointed, as Forjett restricted himself to the present.

'It is because of your father I have summoned you today.' Forjett drummed his fingers on the table. 'This is a bad time for everybody, Irfan. The whole of Hindoostan is under siege.' His jaw tightened. 'Unrest, killing and pillage are sweeping the land, as you know. Under the circumstances, I should be taking action instead of doing what I am just now, which is offering your father one more chance. I have known your father for many years, and in addition, I owe you a debt, Irfan, so it is only right that I should speak to you first.' Forjett's fingers turned silent. 'Your father is associating with people he should not. He will know of whom I allude to when you speak to him. Tell your father that unless he stops meeting these men, I will have no choice but to arrest him. Warn him to take my cautioning seriously. He is in grave danger because he is plotting treacherous, unpardonable ventures. Unless he desists, he will be arrested and if found guilty, he will be sentenced to death.'

Irfan was thunderstruck.

Forjett continued grimly. 'Maintaining the security of Bombay and its citizens is my duty. The sepoy mutiny is spreading. Bombay is untouched so far, and I intend to keep it that way. I will allow nothing to impede my efforts to ensure peace in this city. This is not a time when the administration will indulge in leniency. Those found guilty of plotting to disrupt the peace of the city will be dealt with harshly. It is not for nothing that we have erected gallows in the prominent areas of the city. We intend to use them. Mutineers will suffer the ultimate penalty and their execution will be public so that all can see that we mean business.'

The meeting ended shortly afterwards when two European officers marched into the room, saluting Forjett smartly. Irfan rode home in a daze. Forjett had never addressed him so abruptly before. His tone hadn't been harsh, but neither did it have the warmth Irfan was used to. It was his face that had disturbed Irfan the most—cold and distant—unrecognizable for the absence of its smile. Striving to justify the officer's behaviour, Irfan attributed his blunt manner and aloofness to the heightened tensions of his job. It was stupid to expect Forjett to be cordial when rumours abounded of a bloody uprising. Irfan had heard them himself. In the coffee shops and local bars, people openly discussed the downfall of the English, adding darkly that they had it coming. Irfan was also aware that not everyone held the same view. His employer, Ismail the horse dealer, hoped that peace would prevail. There were several who wished the same, most from Bombay's business community, those who had prospered under English administration, conducting their businesses under their strict but orderly regime.

The revelations about his father shocked Irfan. It was true he stepped out every night, in itself an extraordinary deviation in his habits, for Mohammed Aziz was a simple man who rarely ventured out after dark and went to bed early. But ever since Colvin had taken charge of Seawind, Mohammed Aziz saddled his horse each evening and rode away, returning late, well after midnight. Though curious about his nightly jaunts, Irfan had never inquired as relations between them were still strained. Now he knew and the knowledge horrified him. His father . . . a rebel. There was wild talk of people meeting and plotting . . . but not his father. It wasn't possible. Mohammed Aziz was a God-fearing man, non-violent and law-abiding. Forjett had got it wrong. The police chief was confusing him with someone else. He would speak to his father and the misunderstanding would be cleared once and for all.

But distressingly for Irfan, Forjett's aspersions were chillingly accurate.

Mohammed Aziz snorted derisively on hearing of the police officer's threat. 'Tell your dear friend Forjett that I do what I desire and meet whomsoever I choose. Like every Englishman in this country, he believes he can bully and order us natives around. He can threaten me, jail me and hang me if he likes, but I will not bow before him.'

Mohammed Aziz's anger was such that Irfan quailed before him.

'But, Father, tell me that the treason he accuses you of isn't true. That you are not plotting a revolt in Bombay.'

Mohammed Aziz's eyes flashed. 'You have always lived in your own little world, Irfan. First, you were pampered by the Browns, now Forjett is your guardian. Never have you opened your eyes to how the English treat the rest of your countrymen. The uprising that has spread across India—what they choose to call a mutiny—is a revolt against their vicious, shameful and cruel behaviour. They care nothing for our religions or our sensitivity. To them, Hindu, Mussulman, Sikh and Rajput are the same—people of a lower class. It was because Brown saab was kind to me that I tolerated their injustice. Have you seen now how Colvin behaves with me? I would treat a dog with more kindness and dignity. That is the contempt with which all English people view us. I will not tolerate their attitude any more. The war has begun in the north. The English are on the run and in Bombay, their day of reckoning draws near. I am proud to be associated with the revolution, and no intimidation, not even the threat of death will deter me.'

Another of Irfan's diminished props crumbled. 'Father,' he implored. 'I beg you not to bring danger upon yourself. I will do anything you ask. I will even travel to Mahabaleshwar if you desire. I will overcome my fear of the sea for you. I will swear never to meet or speak to Forjett saab again if you insist. I will give up my job and stop associating with Ismail. Ask anything of me, but do not pursue the perilous path you have chosen.'

Mohammed Aziz laughed hollowly. 'So now you are prepared to travel to Mahabaleshwar. After turning a deaf ear to my pleas, finally you have decided to heed my wishes. I thought I would never hear these words you speak, Irfan. But they have been spoken too late. You are a young man now and you earn your own living. My duties to you as a father are over.'

Irfan goggled at his father. No . . . it wasn't possible. Mohammad Aziz couldn't be uttering such words.

'Yes, Irfan. My duties to you are over. In the same breath, I admit that you have defeated me. You are not the boy I dreamt to be my son. You are more an English saab than an Indian child. You are one of the thousands who refuse to join the revolution because it suits you. Like the wealthy businessmen, the brokers and the shopkeepers, you turn a blind eye to the injustices perpetrated by the English. You have no pride and see nothing wrong in being treated as lower-class citizens in your own land. Their wrongdoings never bother you because your life is comfortable. But there are hundreds of thousands who bear the brunt of their villainy. They are the ones who have started the revolution. I am part of that rebellion. Nothing you say will change my mind. Your friend Forjett is the biggest liar, the most shameless of his ilk. Ask him about his trickery and the empty promises he made me. You want me to heed his word? Say to him that I laugh at his threat. Deliver him a message from me. Tell him the days of English rule are over. He and his people will be toppled and we shall rightfully rule our destiny once more. That is all I will speak on this subject.' Mohammed Aziz held up his hands when Irfan opened his mouth. 'Silence! We have spoken enough. I command you not to trouble me with your foolish talk any more.'

Irfan hardly slept that night or any night thereafter. From then on, his sleep was always troubled by fear. He would lie awake, tossing and turning in his bed, till his father returned from his nightly excursions. Mohammed Aziz never spoke of the matter again, reverting to his reserved self, withholding information from Irfan as he had done all his life.

Irfan did not speak of his father's clandestine activities to anyone, not even Rustom. In a telling reversal of mindset, reflecting the vastly altered reality of Irfan's life, the possibility of an encounter with Forjett, once a much-anticipated affair, now haunted Irfan. There would doubtless be inquires regarding his father and Irfan would not be able to lie. He actively avoided Forjett and was thankful at not being summoned again to his office.

Depression claimed Irfan. Life ceased to be enjoyable. This despair was even more profound than when Ralph and Peter departed India. The world he knew and loved had all but ceased to exist. The Browns were no more. The twins weren't coming back. His father had virtually disowned him and could soon be arrested for treason. The uprising was spreading and threatening to overrun his beloved Bombay. Divisions were becoming increasingly sharp between the Indian populace and the English. He was torn between his loyalty to his father and to Forjett, and he knew that the day would soon come when he would have to choose between them.

Irfan's only solace was his friends. Their meetings were a ritual that instilled stability in his splintered world. He drew pleasure in listening to Rustom's dreams and in his touching conviction that he would be rich one day. Mario's wisecracks never failed to lighten his mood. Ajit was always serious and quiet and yet, oddly, it was he who delivered the only good news of that period, announcing one day that a bride had been selected for him and that his marriage was imminent. He would be turning fourteen and his father had decided it was time. He had met his bride once, he blushingly admitted. She was nine years old and had been too shy to even look up at him. She was from a good family and his parents were satisfied. A date would soon be announced after consulting the temple priest.

The arrival of the monsoons brought no joy to Irfan either. The skies turned gloomy, wind assailed the city, and rain fell in torrents. One day, when the initial fury of the rains had abated, Irfan returned home to discover that his father had had a nasty spat with Alexander Colvin. Barely had he settled Mohini in her stable when he was summoned to Colvin's study.

Colvin's rosy complexion had tanned considerably since his arrival a month earlier. He was noticeably thinner too, a sure sign that the cook's food wasn't suiting him. There was a second man in the study, draped casually on Mr Brown's favourite chair, reading a book. His hair was blonde and long and was combed neatly with a centre parting. Except for thick sideburns, his features were clean-shaven, handsome in a sort of cavalier way. He raised an eyebrow when Irfan entered, then turned his attention to his book.

Colvin was in a temper, his rage sputtering to a boil when Irfan halted respectfully before him. 'Listen to me, boy!' he roared. 'I have put up with your father, despite extreme provocation, but no more. His behaviour was shocking today. *Outrageous*! How *dare* he insult me, and that too in public? Wallace here is my witness. First, he ignored my order to hold the door open for Wallace and me. Then he refused to drive the carriage. He turned his back on me'—Colvin frothed at the lips—'and he walked off . . . just walked away—' His voice choked and trailed away.

Wallace stirred from his chair. 'Calm down, Alex,' he said, looking up from his book. 'No point working yourself into a fit. You can harm yourself if you're not careful. Farfetched as it might sound, I have this feeling that it was because of me that your coachman behaved so bizarrely. He was perfectly normal till he saw me. Then his face went purple; he looked as if he was about to faint. I can't recollect meeting him before . . . yet I have this distinct impression he went crazy after seeing me. Very strange.'

Colvin was in no mood to entertain speculations. 'This has nothing to do with you, Wallace. The man is disobedient and insolent. At the office, he keeps me waiting every day, always loafing somewhere when I want him. He chews that disgusting white substance even when I tell him not to. Time and again, I have asked him to smarten his appearance, but he refuses. It is only because of this boy—his son who is Forjett's pet—that I have not kicked him out. But this time he has gone too far. He has humiliated me. Your father is dismissed, boy. Tell him to pack his bags and leave this instant.'

The room swirled before Irfan.

'Mr Colvin, sir,' he babbled. 'Have pity on us. We have no other home. Give us time, sir. I will be your coachman. I am good with horses. I will work with you till we find another place.'

Colvin crashed his fist on Mr Brown's study desk. 'Get your father out of my house! OUT! This instant!'

Wallace whistled softly. 'Calm down, Alex,' he soothed. He uncurled himself from the chair and crossed to Colvin's side. 'You said this lad knows Forjett well. It might not be wise to upset Forjett. Not while I'm around . . . you understand. Besides, this boy could be an asset. He speaks English better than any native I've met and he seems smart and intelligent. Hold on to the boy, at least till my steamer leaves for London. You have no one in any case.'

Colvin's chest heaved. His anger blazed furnace-like inside the room. 'All right,' he said, lifting a shaking finger. 'All right . . . I will allow you to stay. You will take over your father's job, and as for your father . . . he will not stay free on my land. He will work. Wallace is here for a fortnight. Your father will turn the *pankha* in his room every night, turn it all night long.'

'But, sir,' protested Irfan. 'My father is old. He cannot—'

Colvin's voice turned high decibel again. 'You heard me, boy! Your father either works or leaves. The choice is his. His duty starts tonight when Wallace retires to his room. You report here tomorrow. On time! Not indolently like your father. Now leave.'

Colvin waved Irfan out.

Irfan found his father sitting quietly in the veranda of their tiny home. It was raining and Mohammed Aziz was gazing sightlessly at the ground as shafts of water drummed puddles in their yard.

Mohammed Aziz did not look up when Irfan confronted him.

'Do you know what you have done?' sobbed Irfan. 'You have lost our home. My home . . . now we have to leave. Why . . . why in Allah's name are you bent on destroying my life?'

Mohammed Aziz averted his face.

Irfan leaned against the wall, crying silently. The rain pelted harder, smacking noisily against the roof. After a while, Mohammed Aziz rose silently and slipped his sandals on.

'Yes, walk away from me,' wept Irfan. 'Go about your business of plotting to kill Englishmen. Nothing matters to you any more except death, killing and revolution. The welfare of your son is no longer your responsibility. Your duty to me is over. I have to fend for myself. I need a roof over my head . . . so I have taken over your job.'

Mohammed Aziz paused as he reached for his turban.

'I will drive Colvin every day to work,' went on Irfan. 'I will take over the stables and the horses. You go about your business whatever it is. I will see that we have a roof over our heads.'

Mohammed Aziz finally looked up. His face was in darkness, but his eyes were ablaze. 'Today I saw a murderer.' His voice was low and Irfan had to strain to hear him. 'I saw a criminal . . . a killer who committed a murder most foul. Yet he is a free man. Because his skin is white, he walked away as if he had never done anything wrong. The English talk so highly about their justice, as if it is the greatest gift they have presented us, but like everything they have brought to our land, it favours only them. This afternoon I witnessed with my own eyes how shamelessly unfair they are to us, and I have vowed that never will I work for them again. I will raise not even a finger in their service.'

Mohammed Aziz placed his turban on his head. 'When I was young and you were a baby, I would dream of you becoming a coach driver like myself. Maybe it is Allah's will that you tread the same path your father did. Years have passed since those days when I used to dream. You are grown up now and I dream no more. Today I am finally a free man. I have no job, no commitments to white men or to anybody. I can pursue the destiny I have chosen. I must leave now. Tonight, our roles are reversed. It is because of you that I have a home to return to. I shall return tonight and maybe for a few more nights hereafter, but I know Colvin will soon not allow me here.' Mohammed Aziz's eyes grew soft. 'You and I have differences. I know you disagree with the path I have chosen. One day maybe you will understand. I give you my blessings, Irfan. I shall pray for you and your happiness.'

Mohammed Aziz reached forward and wrapped his arms around his son. Then, umbrella in hand, he stepped out, melting into the darkness and the rain.

There was to be no rest for Irfan that night. Pankha duty hung before him, poised like a guillotine blade, ready to destroy his self-esteem, slice it to shreds. Irfan hadn't broached the subject to his father, knowing that he would only have laughed in scorn. In all his years, Irfan had never performed servant duty. Today would be a first. There was no choice as the consequence of disobeying was too terrible to contemplate.

The agony and shame of that night seared Irfan's soul, etching forever in his consciousness the memory of the wretchedness of those hours. Although an ordinary monsoon night, driven with rain and wind, it marked the transition of his status at Seawind from favoured sibling to an ordinary servant.

For his detractors, it was a momentous occasion. Radhabai's family queued up to witness Irfan's humiliation. Balu's jubilation was especially satisfying, as he had often worked the pankha in the children's room while Irfan had slept inside, alongside the twins. Balu's insults struck deep, piercing Irfan like flaming arrows. Holding fast to the remnants of his mangled self-esteem, Irfan reined in his emotions. He worked the pankha rope rhythmically, suppressing the terrible hopelessness inside him. It was only late in the night, when his tormentors had retired satiated to their quarters, when there was no noise except the creak of the gently swinging pankha, that his wretchedness had finally come pouring out. Tears gushed in unstoppable streams and his body heaved as sobs racked him.

Wallace enjoyed the night, sleeping restfully, while Irfan toiled unflaggingly at the rope. Retiring at dawn from his task, Irfan snatched an hour's sleep before it was time to ready the carriage for Colvin and ride him to office. Later, while Colvin was at work, Irfan searched out Rustom, whose office was nearby, beside the bustling Customs House.

Rustom's jaw dropped when Irfan, in a tired voice, informed him of the developments. 'You can't live like this, Irfan. Look at you, you can hardly stand. You are swaying like a drunken sailor on Bazaar Gate Street. It isn't possible to stay awake the entire night and work during the day also. Life at Seawind is done for you. You cannot stay there any longer, even a fool would tell you so.'

Rustom pressed Irfan to come and live with him at his new home at Cavel. It was large and roomy, the entire ground floor had been leased to him. Both he and his father could live there. But Irfan refused.

'I cannot endanger you, Rustom. Not while my father engages in treasonable conduct.' Swearing Rustom to secrecy, he told him of Forjett's revelation of Mohammed Aziz's activities. 'If my father is thrown into jail, those who shelter him will also be arrested. Forjett has warned that even he will not be able to help. I cannot drag you into my troubles.'

Rustom grasped Irfan's shoulder, digging his fingers in. 'Do not insult our friendship, Irfan. You helped me when I was in trouble. Do you think I will turn away in your hour of need? Your father's problems are mine too. We will deal with them together. If you go to jail, so will I.'

Irfan's eyes blurred. 'I cried so much yesterday I thought I had run out of tears. But your loyalty drags fresh tears.' He wiped his eyes and forced a distorted smile. 'Just the other day it was I who offered you my home.'

'That offer came from your heart, Irfan. From deep inside. You didn't even know who I was. I will never forget.'

Irfan sniffled. 'Strange are Allah's ways. Now you have a home and I will soon lose mine.'

Rustom grabbed Irfan by the shoulders. 'Remember that day? My face was dirty, my clothes torn and filthy. The strap of my sandals was broken and I couldn't afford to fix it. I had nothing, no future . . . yet you told me to be brave. Face up to life, you said. I did that, Irfan. I managed with your help. It was you and your love that saw me through. Now you take up my offer. Come. Come and live in my home.'

Irfan gazed at Rustom, taking in his shining face, his stylish jacket, his polished brass buttons, his carefully combed hair, his clipped fingernails. Their roles were reversed. It was Rustom who was settled now and he virtually homeless. Everyone was equal before Allah, his father always said. How true his words rang.

Irfan shook his head. 'I will take up your offer, Rustom, but not now. I cannot leave Seawind overnight. Give me time. In the meanwhile, request Ismail to grant me leave. Invent an excuse.'

Rustom eyes darkened. 'What do I tell him? That you have discovered a fresh talent; that you now wield a pankha rope more skillfully than horse reins? Stop wasting your time, Irfan. Forget Seawind once and for all. Come and live with me.'

Irfan attempted to smile but managed only a grimace. 'Pulling a pankha rope is not so bad.'

'It is a servant's job,' said Rustom scathingly. 'Remember Mrs Brown's words. The words you spoke to me at the

Green . . . that even in the darkest moments, a star always shines. That star won't shine for you, Irfan, unless you search for it. Tugging a pankha rope is not going to find one for you. You are not a servant.'

Irfan lowered his gaze. 'Give me time,' he said. 'Don't speak about this to anyone. Not even Ajit and Mario. I will find strength somehow and live through this difficult time.'

For three days thereafter, Irfan toiled beneath a double load, keeping Wallace comfortable during the night and chauffeuring Colvin by day. On the fourth night, Colvin visited Wallace's room for a nightcap and Irfan overheard a conversation, which he discussed with his father the next morning.

Though Colvin's coach was no longer his responsibility, Mohammed Aziz still took pride in its appearance and was scrubbing its brass fittings when Irfan spoke to him.

'Father,' said Irfan, halting beside him. 'Did you know that Colvin's guest, Wallace, once knew Mrs Brown?'

A look of disgust came to Mohammed Aziz's face, as if the very mention of Wallace's name offended him. 'Yes, he did,' he acknowledged curtly.

'You don't like Wallace, do you, Father? Even I dislike him after the way he mocked and made fun of Mrs Brown. He said he knew her in England. He said that she had loved him and that she had once been engaged to him.' Irfan's lip curled in distaste. 'He spoke of her as an object: something you use and when you grow tired of, you discard. He kept her hanging, he said, refusing to marry her, and that her family—he called them stuck-up because they never approved of him—sent her to India to forget him and marry respectable Mr Brown.'

Mohammed Aziz suspended his work. He looked intently at his son. 'What else did he speak of?'

'Not much about Mrs Brown thereafter. Both he and Colvin were enjoying their drinks. They were in a happy mood. They spoke of things they shouldn't have. They weren't aware I could hear them or maybe they had forgotten that the servant who turned the pankha was not a typical native and could speak and understand English. From what I heard—their voices were slurred from drinking—Wallace had come here to India to get rich and now after fifteen years in the country, he had achieved his goal. He spoke of a treasure—rubies, diamonds and gold—that he had collected during his travels through the country. He spoke of a band of men that once worked with him. But now, those men are dead and everything belongs to him. All that remains is to get his treasure across to England. Once there, he said, he will be wealthy for the rest of his life.'

Mohammed Aziz grabbed his son by his shoulders. 'Where is his treasure?' he barked.

'On a boat in the harbour. The boat came in last night—that's why he was celebrating.'

'Where is the boat?'

'I don't know, Father. It is a sailboat from the south, not a big one, he said. He is a thief, Father. I heard only snatches, but he spoke openly of having robbed people. He robbed Indians—"filthy black sorts", he called us. He robbed Englishmen too. But the bulk of his loot he acquired only now. The sepoy war turned out to be a golden opportunity, he said. Pretending to be English officers, he and his men would accuse princes and rajahs of sedition. They were easy bait, according to him. The frightened rulers would willingly part with their wealth and jewellery to avoid the execution he threatened them with. I must speak to Forjett about Wallace—'

'You will do nothing of the sort,' interrupted Mohammed Aziz harshly. 'You will not breathe a word about this to Forjett. I forbid you. Vow to me you will not.'

'But—'

Mohammed Aziz suddenly turned wild. His nostrils flared. His fingers dug like claws into Irfan's shoulders, prompting him to cry out in pain. 'Vow to me this instant. Now!'

Irfan gazed in terror at Mohammed Aziz. 'I promise, Father.'

'In the name of Allah.'

'I promise in the name of Allah, Father. I will not speak to Forjett.'

Mohammed Aziz let go of his son. He stared at Irfan, eyes smouldering. Then he turned and stalked away, leaving Irfan more terrified than he had ever been of his father.

Irfan was spared from Colvin duty that day. As expected, Wallace and Colvin overslept, having made merry through the night. Irfan caught up instead on much-needed sleep, and in the evening—fresh and energetic after a long time—he rode to the Esplanade to meet his friends.

The rains had paused. Storm clouds darkened the skies, but they spared the island, jetting their soggy load to the mainland. Crowds thronged the Esplanade, enjoying the moist evening breeze. A military band played at the bandstand. Irfan found Rustom sitting on rocks at the water's edge beside the bandstand. Mario arrived shortly after, but Ajit, his faithful shadow, for a change, did not accompany him.

'Marriage commitments,' explained Mario. 'Also, the poor fellow is embarrassed. He doesn't want to face either of you. It's got to do with the wedding, which is later this week.'

Rustom and Irfan gazed blankly.

Mario sighed. 'You haven't been told because neither of you is invited. Ajit is very upset. He pleaded with his father to have you attend. He even threw a sulk, but his father would have none of it. It is a Hindu marriage and his father will not allow any Parsees or Muslims. That's the tradition, and he's not about to break it. My dad and I aren't attending either. We've been invited to the function afterwards, but we are the only ones who aren't Hindu. We're acceptable because his father and mine are colleagues.'

Irfan spoke disdainfully. 'Tell Ajit I'm not going to invite him to my marriage either.' But his laugh took the sting out of his words.

Rustom looked up sharply. Expecting laughter from Irfan these days was like hoping for clear skies during the monsoons. But Irfan's face was as radiant as a bright blue sky.

A thought suddenly struck Rustom. He turned to Mario. 'You got me thinking after what you said about Ajit,' he said. 'We four are a strange set of friends. I never thought of it so, till you spoke. We are a rare combination, the four of us, each of different religions: a Muslim, a Hindu, a Christian and a Parsee.'

Mario stared. 'Funny, I never thought of it like that. But what you say is true, Parsee. There can't be many like us . . . Probably none.'

'Yes,' nodded Rustom. 'None. Just us. It's weird isn't it, a little frightening if you ask me, how religion and community divide every aspect of our lives.' Rustom laughed. 'Except at work that is. Religion doesn't seem to matter when it comes to business and money. At the docks, everybody—Christians, Hindus, Jews, Muslims, Parsees—we make no fuss and work together. Even at places where they deal with money, Gujaratis, Parsees and Englishmen sit together. At your construction sites, you have workers from everywhere. But take away the work hours, and you will see that at all other times, we live and socialize with only our *jaat-wallahs*. You only have to look around to see the proof.' Rustom swept a hand across the Esplanade. 'There . . . beside the Church Gate. Look at the Parsees, they are sitting together in their private groups. Next to them is a bunch of Hindus, all by themselves. Those Baghdadi Jews, the ones wearing those long robes, walk only with one another. We four are different. We belong to different communities, yet we are always together.'

'And we're going to keep it that way,' said Irfan. 'Always together, right?'

'Of course,' smiled Rustom. 'We shall keep it that way. Friends forever!'

Mario grabbed Irfan and Rustom, crushing them in his huge arms. 'You boys make me cry,' he wailed, pretending to shed tears. 'For you, I will forget my religion. I'll be friends . . . but I have my conditions.' Releasing them, he turned on Irfan. 'My companions have to be fun-loving, not sad and spiritless. Stop behaving as if the world has come to an end, Angrez, as if you've been thrown into prison, like poor Cunningham. You have problems, but so have others. If I start describing what my mother puts up with every day just looking after me, I'd be talking all day! But in spite of her woes, my mom isn't miserable. She laughs and smiles and keeps us all happy. You have no excuse for your behaviour, Angrez. You can't be my *dost* if you go on like this. You had better laugh and learn to enjoy life again.'

Irfan folded his hands together in a gesture of plea. 'Spare us, Mario. Not another of your "mother" stories. Anything but that. I promise to be a happy boy. See.' He flashed the most brilliant smile he could conjure. Then he burst into tears.

Rustom and Mario looked on in concern. But Irfan laughed through his tears.

'I'm fine. I am happy today, truly happy. I've finally made up my mind. I am quitting Seawind. It's going to be hard. Giving up a home isn't easy, but it is time. I've decided. It's a burden off my shoulders . . . you can't imagine how big. I am relieved, filled with joy, and I can smile once more.'

'Shabash!' cried Rustom, springing to his feet. 'This is the best news since Ajit announced his wedding.'

Mario squeezed Irfan in a bear hug and only when he protested, as the embrace threatened to suffocate him, did the beefy boy let go.

Irfan laughed, wiping wetness from his eyes. 'Today I slept well for the first time in days. I've been tired and miserable so long that I had forgotten what it feels like to be cheerful. This evening I am fresh, energized and happy. There is a life beyond Seawind, and I have decided to live it.'

In a mood fuelled by the heady optimism of the moment, the boys discussed their fantasies of the future, expressing their desires forthrightly, holding nothing back. Rustom spoke once more of his ambition of owning boats that would ply the seven seas. He was certain he had discovered the path to success in business. Simply put, honesty and hard work were the key, he said. His primary goal was to earn a reputation as an honest and reliable trader. His task would turn easy once he established his trustworthiness and dependability. People would clamour to do business with him and he would earn a fortune and build a beautiful home near the sea.

Irfan dreamt of having his own stables. They would be the best in India. His horses would be prized by Maharajahs, by Europeans and all the rich of India. Mario desired fame as the best mason and carpenter in Bombay. He aspired to design great furniture and build wonderful homes. Money was not important to him. The work, the skill, the challenge and customer satisfaction were more precious. Mario spoke for Ajit, sharing his friend's goals. Regretfully, though Ajit hated accounting, he had resigned himself to the certainty that his father would force him into the vocation. Fortunately, his father's meddling didn't matter, as Ajit did not harbour any great ambition at work. Home and family were more important for him. He dreamt of being a good father and bringing up a happy family.

Irfan enjoyed the evening immensely. He was light-headed and happy. He savoured the company of his friends and the pleasure of the Esplanade. He delighted in the crowds, relished the music of the band and basked in the wind that swept in from the stormy sea.

The three friends bade goodbye to each other as the evening faded to darkness. Irfan rode Mohini back to Seawind for the last time. He should have been heartbroken, but he wasn't. Instead, on a rebound from the clutches of dark despair, Irfan was in an exceptional mood. This day was a turning point in his life. Already it had incited a critical change, inspiring him to reconsider his outlook on life. As the night fell like a curtain about him, Irfan extended his optimism to his luck. Yes, his luck would turn too, and his future would be cheerful and happy. That was Irfan's cherished desire, but fate and reality were about to cruelly dictate otherwise.

REVENGE

Irfan entered Seawind's gate and trotted Mohini along the well-worn path that led to the stables and his home. His mind was made up. There would be no more pankha duty. His absence tonight would serve as notice of his intentions. He and his father would pack their belongings and leave at first light. But his plan did not shape up the way he intended. On reaching home, he found his father waiting for him with another man beside him, half-hidden in shadow.

Irfan was stunned by his father's reaction when he spoke of his decision. Blood surged to Mohammed Aziz's cheeks. His face swelled alarmingly. He slammed his fist on a table beside him with such force that it almost splintered. 'You will attend duty tonight!' he thundered. 'It is an order. You will not disobey.'

Shocked at the ferocity of his father's voice, Irfan stumbled backwards, almost falling.

Mohammed Aziz's eyes had puffed up. They bulged till they were the size of doorknobs. His entire frame trembled.

'You heard me?' he roared. 'You will perform pankha duty tonight! Is that understood?'

'Ye-yes, Father,' stuttered Irfan.

Mohammed Aziz raised a hand. Irfan backed further. Then he remembered that this was the way his father calmed himself. After every bitter quarrel concerning Mahabaleshwar, his father closed his eyes and glided his hand back and forth, suppressing his rage.

Irfan recognized the man beside his father. It was Shahid, his uncle, his father's first cousin, who hailed from their home village of Mahabaleshwar. Shahid was a frequent visitor. A sailor, he stopped by every time his boat dropped anchor in Bombay.

Mohammed Aziz lowered his hand. The swelling on his face had diminished. His breathing had eased and he no longer quivered. Yet there was an animal edginess about him, like a deer at a waterhole.

'Forgive my anger, son,' he said, his voice heavy with remorse. 'You are not to blame. You know not the reason for my wrath, and I cannot share its cause with you. Your decision to leave Colvin's service gladdens my heart. I am relieved, profoundly so. You must quit. But you must report for duty just for one more night. That's all I ask of you. One night and then you are free.'

Irfan remained silent; afraid that if he spoke, he might enrage his father again.

'We have waited for you to return, Irfan, both Shahid and I. We must leave now.' Mohammed Aziz paused and Irfan saw wetness in his eyes. 'This is the last time you will see me.'

Irfan stared at his father in alarm.

'It is not that you will never see me again,' clarified Mohammed Aziz. 'We may meet, Irfan, but it will be up to you. This is certainly the last time you will see me in Seawind, or here in Bombay, for that matter. I leave tonight, never to return. Don't ask where I go, for I shall not tell you. But your uncle Shahid will stay behind for you. His boat will leave tomorrow from Apollo Bunder, at night, when the Bunder is deserted. The time has come, Irfan, for you to make decisions, for if we are to meet again you will have to overcome your fear of the sea. Only Shahid knows where I am going. To set your eyes on my aged face again, you will have to travel on his boat. Shahid will spend the day at the room he rents beside the docks. It is your choice, Irfan, whether you want to travel with him or not. You must convey your decision to him tomorrow, before nightfall, so he knows whether to wait or leave without you.'

Irfan stood as if paralysed. He registered his father's words, but he couldn't bring himself to believe them.

Mohammed Aziz opened his arms. 'Come to me, my son. Let me embrace you one last time in the home we have shared for so many years.'

Mohammed Aziz swept Irfan into his arms. In spite of his despair, in spite of the shock . . . in spite of everything, Irfan's heart leapt. This couldn't be . . . his father displaying love. It had been so long that he had forgotten. Tears surged to his eyes. Emotions, buried so deep that he wasn't aware, broke free. The hurt, the years of accumulated bitterness, all blinked out in one cleansing moment as his father crushed him to his chest.

Father and son stood locked together, faces pressed, cheeks wet, eyes tightly shut. Shahid averted his gaze, embarrassed at witnessing an intensely private moment.

'Father . . . don't go. Don't leave me,' whispered Irfan.

'I must,' replied Mohammed Aziz. He pressed his lips to his son's ear. 'Trust me, son, I have to go. Do not ask me what I do tonight because I cannot speak. People will tell you I have committed a crime, but I want you to know that all I am doing is righting a terrible wrong. You must have faith in me, Irfan. This could be the last time I hold you, but I am certain it is not. I know that you will come to your father and we shall be united again. Goodbye, my son. May Allah be with you.'

And just like that, with only a small cloth bag slung on his shoulder, Mohammed Aziz departed the humble abode that had been his home most of his adult life. In his heart, Irfan had known the moment would come one day. Yet the stark reality was impossible to bear. Crumpling on his bed, Irfan sobbed his heart out. When his tears dried, he prayed for his father's well-being, for success in the venture he planned that night. Then he washed his face, snatched a meal and tramped across to the mansion.

Thankfully for Irfan, Wallace retired early and after reading for a while, fell asleep. Irfan worked the pankha rope numbly, his brain stricken with fear, a single thought echoing inside his head, consuming him. His father was committing an act of sedition. An unpardonable crime. Forjett had warned that nothing would save his father. Although the police chief hadn't spoken further, it was clear Irfan would have to bear the consequences. He too would become a fugitive. He would have to flee Bombay.

Prayer helped Irfan pass the night. He begged Allah for the fortitude to face the coming days. He sought strength to overcome his fear of the sea. He prayed for his dearest companions. He prayed for his 'brothers' in England. He prayed for Rustom, for Mario, for Ajit and for his horse Mohini, bidding each of them goodbye. Finally, he prayed that Allah allow him to return to the city that was so precious to him and reunite him one day with the ones he loved.

At dawn, he saddled Mohini, and with a heavy heart led his horse away. It was a grey morning, laden with cloud. The mansion shone like a lustrous pearl in the gloom. A strong wind buffeted the trees bordering the drive. They moaned as the wind whistled through them. Like tears, they shed leaves on the winding cobbled path, as if already mourning his loss. Mounting Mohini at the gate, he rode away with bowed head and blurred eyes. Riding along the familiar tree-lined track, he emerged finally on Colaba's rocky northern shore.

The causeway that connected the island of Colaba to the Fort was long and narrow, barely wide enough for two buggies to pass. A salt-laden wind strafed the causeway, plucking at Irfan's clothes and tousling Mohini's mane. Breakers smashed thunderously against the causeway wall and spattered its cobbled surface with fizzing seawater. Irfan shuddered. The sea was in a temper, stormily protesting its confinement. Convulsed with a terrible anger, it pitched and heaved, churning the harbour into a cauldron. Boats strained at their anchors, masts rocking violently, scything the sky like jousting swords.

Irfan's throat tightened, throttling his breathing. He wrenched his gaze away as the hated giddiness spread acid tentacles in his gut. How could he travel tonight? The sea was at its ferocious worst, its condition chillingly similar to that frightful day when it tore apart the boat he had travelled on. He would surely die.

Yet, surprisingly, Irfan's resolve did not crumble. From somewhere within, another of Mrs Brown's sayings came to him: 'When there is no place to run, nowhere to hide, even a timid deer battles like a lion, a dove turns to an eagle'. Exerting a will he didn't know existed, he forced his gaze upon the sea, and in a rousing instant of clarity, he knew he was ready. A calm descended on him, spreading like a healing balm. If he had to confront his worst nightmare, so be it. The time for weakness had passed.

Soon, they were upon the Esplanade. In stark contrast to the cheer and bonhomie of the previous evening, the area was wet, windy and desolate. Waves licked hungrily at its rocky shore, surging far across its flat expanse. It was as if the sea and the clouds had conspired to lay a siege upon the land. There was no horizon, just a band of stomach-wrenching grey. The Fort walls stood grim and tall, an unconvincing line of defence against the monsoon onslaught.

The dismal conditions failed to dampen Mohini's spirits. She tossed her head and strained at her bit. Irfan loosened her reins and she streaked forward, mane rippling in the wind. Irfan let her run. She snorted in delight when, jockey-like, he leaned forward. The heaviness smothering Irfan's chest lifted. He was a wild carefree boy again, revelling in the speed and power of his mount. Mohini would have surely dashed on to the palm glades of Gamdevi, but Irfan checked her, turning her to the puddle-strewn streets of Cavel.

Rustom lived in a pleasant double-storeyed bungalow with thick wooden walls and a fine veranda. A small yard, overgrown with weeds, fronted the house and Irfan let Mohini loose inside. He found Rustom kneeling at prayer, in his *kasti* and prayer cap. Rustom greeted him with a delighted smile, but his elation was short-lived.

His eyes popped as Irfan related his story. 'No!' he exclaimed. 'No . . . you're not serious. Tell me you're joking. You're not leaving Bombay.'

Irfan looked his friend in the eye. 'I am leaving, Rustom. Tonight.'

Panic fanned like wildfire on Rustom's face. 'But you are terrified of the sea and boats, and look at the weather!'

Irfan's face was set. 'I cannot abandon my father.' There was a resoluteness to him that shook Rustom. 'I will lose him if I don't go. The day has come when I must brave my nightmare. I am prepared.'

Rustom clutched at straws. 'But what about the dreams we spoke of last night? What about the stables you want to own? What about your friends, what about Mohini and me? You can't just leave like that.'

Irfan's resolve wavered. 'Mohini . . .' he breathed, blinking. 'I will need your help with Mohini. Ismail is a trader. He will sell my horse if I return her to him.' Irfan's eyes had moistened. 'I have enough money to buy her from him. Besides, he owes me a month's salary. Pay Ismail tomorrow. Keep Mohini with you or hand her to Mario. I know both of you love her.' His voice cracked. 'She will be safe.'

'Yes, Irfan, safe she will be. Mario and I can assure you of that. But happy . . .' Rustom shook his head. 'No . . . not without you. Never.'

Irfan reached forward, seizing Rustom's hands. 'Do you think I will abandon my horse? Forsake my friends? What do you take me for, Rustom? Bombay is my home. Do I have to tell you that? You are my best friend. I can't imagine life without you or the city. I will be back, I promise.'

Irfan's assurances were of no comfort to Rustom. He left for work in a daze. He returned unexpectedly before noon, storming in, chest heaving, as if he had run all the way.

Words spilled from him at torrential speed. 'Forjett summoned me,' he babbled. 'A constable came to the docks and escorted me to his office. Your father stole a boat last night. Yes, a boat! The crime was reported this morning. The police have searched the harbour. The sea is stormy, near impossible to navigate, so the search took time. They found no sign of him. He has fled, taking the boat with him. Since they cannot find him, they are looking for you. Forjett has delayed the search as long as he can, but he can't any more. His men are at Seawind just now and the next place they will hunt is this house. Forjett knows you are hiding here. He wants me to move you elsewhere, where you cannot be found.'

Irfan digested the news calmly. 'How do they know it was my father who stole the boat?' he queried.

'He was seen casting off in a canoe from Bori Bunder last night. There were three men with him. They overpowered the tindal who slept in the boat. The description the tindal gave of the leader matched that of your father. In any case, your father made no attempt to hide his identity. It was Wallace's boat that he stole. Your father left word with the tindal to tell Wallace that it was he, Mohammed Aziz, who had stolen his boat. He went on to say that he was avenging a crime, a crime that had been committed in Mahabaleshwar, and that Wallace would know what it was.'

Wallace!

Finally, it was Wallace. In hindsight, the signs had been obvious. It was on the afternoon he first laid eyes on Wallace that his father had gone wild, abandoning his employer, recklessly storming off, and losing his job as a result. His bizarre behaviour had continued thereafter, the morning he assaulted Irfan when he shared the conversation he had overheard between Colvin and Wallace. It was clear his father hated the Englishman. Now he had evened his grudge, hitting back at Wallace, stealing what was dearest from him.

Irfan shook his head, clearing it. 'Where do I go?' he asked.

Rustom held the door open. 'A senior colleague lives down the street. He is on leave, gone to his village to attend his brother's wedding. I have the keys to his house. No one will guess you are there.'

It wasn't safe for Irfan to ride the streets any more. Rustom's hired carriage was waiting outside. Irfan had unfinished business before boarding, a heartbreaking task. With bowed head, he bid goodbye to Mohini. The mare whinnied softly as Irfan petted her, fingers lingering on her neck. Kissing her gently, Irfan turned away, eyes glistening. Rustom handed him a handkerchief as he boarded the carriage. He sat with his head buried through the short journey. Rustom comforted him, arm across his shoulder.

The carriage halted beside a big ornate house, with thick lintels that were embellished with carvings, mostly of animals, but also of men with long, strict faces. There was a grass lawn in front with pretty flowers in pots. Two fat pigs were penned in its backyard.

Rustom unlocked the door and ushered Irfan into a large sitting room.

'The man who works here will get lunch for you,' said Rustom, returning to the door. 'I have to get back. Forjett has instructed me to work normally, as if today is just another ordinary day. But I have to hide Mohini first. I'll stable her at a livery for now, the one where Mario keeps his horse. We'll decide what to do with her later.'

'Look after my horse—' Irfan's voice faltered. 'She . . . she is a noble animal.'

'I will,' assured Rustom. 'It isn't just me. There's Mario and Ajit too. We all love her as much as you do.'

Irfan brushed fingers across his eyes. 'You do . . . I know you all do,' he whispered. He looked up. 'Don't forget to tell Shahid I will sail with him. He must wait for me at Apollo Bunder tonight.'

'His room is near my office, I'll speak to him.' Rustom made to leave. Then he halted and faced Irfan. 'Your father has turned you into a fugitive. You know that, don't you?'

'My father has his reasons, Rustom. He is not a thief. He was driven to it.'

Rustom's heavy silence conveyed his feelings. Closing the door, he hurried away.

It was dark and gloomy when Rustom returned in the evening. A light rain drummed the roof, spiralling to the ground in silvery streams. Rustom stood at the door but did not enter.

'Come,' he said, holding an umbrella. His face was tense. 'We have to leave for the Fort. Forjett says it is safe to enter now, while the gates are crowded and busy. It might not be so later. Wallace and Colvin are searching for you.'

Irfan protested. 'But why are you moving me? No one knows about this place. I feel safe here.'

Rustom removed his hat, brushing wetness from it. 'Forjett knows you are leaving. I've told him about Shahid and your plans. You'd like to meet him, wouldn't you?'

'Yes,' nodded Irfan. 'I would like that.'

'Forjett wants to meet you too. But he can't come here because his every move is being watched.' Rustom gesticulated with his hands. 'Your friendship with him is common knowledge. Colvin has been spreading the word that he is stalling your arrest. The problem is that Colvin has friends in high places and Forjett has been spoken to by people who matter, urging him to apprehend you. I told Forjett about Ghadiali's shop and he agreed it is a good place to hide you. He will send for you when he thinks it is safe and he has promised you safe passage to Apollo Bunder.'

The black carriage of the afternoon was waiting outside and they barely managed to board it before the skies opened and rain came pelting down. Crouched beneath a leaking umbrella, the driver urged his reluctant horse forward. Inside, there was a gap between the doors and the panel on the ceiling. The box was stuffy and Irfan glued his face to the gap, looking out on the flooded streets. Bumping along potholed roads, they soon came to the Fort's Bazaar Gate and its three massive darwazas. People hurried across the bridge over the moat, heads bowed, huddled under umbrellas. The carriage clattered past the darwazas and entered the Fort. Two boys, sheltering under umbrellas, stood beside a paan shop at the domed gate. Irfan sucked in a breath, recognizing them. Nitin and Ravi, Radhabai's children. Nitin glanced idly at the carriage, but Ravi stared searchingly and Irfan thought he saw him stiffen as they rolled past.

'Do you think he saw you?' asked Rustom, who was watching.

'I don't know,' said Irfan uncertainly.

'He was certainly staring.' Rustom looked thoughtfully about the carriage, then shook his head. 'I doubt he could have seen anything. It's gloomy outside and even darker inside here. There's no need to worry.'

'It is Colvin, isn't it?' asked Irfan. 'Colvin stationed them there.'

Rustom nodded. 'Yes, it is Colvin. There's talk that he and Wallace are recruiting people to search for you. They've even offered a reward, Forjett says. We have to be careful.'

Rattling through drenched, rutted streets, the carriage rolled to a halt outside Mr Ghadiali's shop. Neither the dismal weather nor the news of Irfan's plight had dampened Mr Ghadiali's mood. Beaming brightly, he stepped out and escorted Irfan into his shop. His only concession to Irfan's changed circumstances was to refrain from pestering him to buy a watch. 'I won't bother you today,' he assured, squeezing Irfan's shoulder. 'Rustom has told me about your troubles. But I have set a condition for sheltering you.' His eyes twinkled. 'You have to buy the finest watch in the shop when you visit next. Is that a deal?'

Irfan favoured him with his first smile of the day. 'I'll buy two of the best!'

Mr Ghadiali clapped him on the back. 'That's my boy. We have a pact. I'm holding you to your word, so don't you forget.' He led Irfan behind the counter. 'I've made space for you in the area where we repair watches. One of the boys is absent, so there is room. Move the chair to the corner, where there isn't much light. No one will see you.'

Rustom excused himself once Irfan had settled. 'I have to speak to Forjett. He has to be told you have reached safely.' He dropped his gaze, not looking at Irfan. 'Also, there are errands I have to run. I'll be back soon.'

Surprisingly, the inclement weather had no effect on the shop's patronage. Customers crowded its counters, keeping Mr Ghadiali busy.

'The rains are always good for me,' explained Mr Ghadiali, during a lull. 'The Almighty is kind during this season. People forget about their watches and water enters them. We have our hands full repairing spoilt watches. Of course, most cannot be repaired.' He winked. 'So I get to sell new ones.'

The bustle and noise comforted Irfan, a welcome change from moping all by himself, as he had done the entire day. A young man with thick spectacles hunched over a table not far from him. The light from his lantern failed to illuminate Irfan's corner. He felt secure, certain he was not visible from the road.

An unexpected visitor dropped by. It was Naheed, Rustom's sister. Like all married Parsee women, Naheed spent most of her time at home. Irfan had met her only twice before. First, during Nowruz, the Parsee New Year, when Rustom had smuggled her out of her house to meet him. The second occasion was during the hot season, when water was scarce, when she had stood in a long queue at the well beside the Fort wall, waiting patiently to fill her buckets. At both meetings, she had been shy, veiling her face and not looking him in the eye. This time, however, she lowered her veil.

There wasn't much room in the corner and though Irfan pressed himself against the wall, only a few inches separated them. A faint fragrance wafted from her, like that of roses. She was small and delicate, like her brother. Her complexion was fairer, as pale as the paper on which Irfan wrote his letters to the twins.

'My brother loves you,' she said, lowering her shawl, wrapping it around her shoulders. 'He loves you more than he loves me.'

Irfan nodded uncertainly, not sure what she was getting at.

Her features bore a distinct likeliness to Rustom, only that she was pretty and that her skin was smooth and childlike. Her face was round and beautiful, except for her eyes, which were puffy and red, as if she had been crying.

Naheed dabbed a handkerchief to her face. 'My Rustom is very dear to me. My only brother. I want you to look after him. See that no harm comes to him. Bring him back safely to me.'

Irfan stared blankly.

'He hasn't told you?' Naheed shook her elegant head. Tiny, studded earrings flashed in the lamplight. 'That's my brother. Always noble . . .' She swallowed, her voice cracking. 'Maybe . . . maybe it is right that his sister should tell you.' Her eyes were candles in the darkness. 'Wherever you are going, Irfan, Rustom is coming with you. You are his friend . . . his best friend. He says that in your time of trouble, his place is by your side.'

Irfan fought back a rush of tears. 'No,' he said, eyes swimming. 'No . . . his place is with you. You are his sister . . . his blood. Tell him not to. He has responsibilities, a job, a dream, a life . . . he cannot leave.'

Naheed attempted to smile but gagged instead. 'His mind is made up.' She sniffled, her lips quivering. 'I tried and I failed. He won't listen, not even to you.'

Irfan gazed at her, his throat lumping, unable to speak.

Naheed looked nervously over her shoulder. 'I must leave now. My husband will beat me if he knows I am here. I slipped out on the excuse of buying vegetables.' She grabbed Irfan's hands. 'My brother is all I have, a thousand times dearer than my husband. I cannot live without him. Bring him back to me. Swear on your God that you will.'

Emotions raged inside Irfan. He couldn't cry in front of a lady. It wasn't gentlemanly. Naheed was gazing at him, beseeching him with her eyes. He had to say something, anything to allay her fears. Words flowed from him, assurances he knew he couldn't guarantee. 'Your brother is strong. Far stronger than you or I can ever imagine. He will look after both of us. It isn't only blood that binds the two of you. He loves you deeply, Naheed. He will return . . . I promise.'

Naheed's eyes drilled into Irfan, reaching deep, probing for truth. They flickered momentarily and Irfan knew that she knew. Knew that his words were hollow, that his assurances were only wishful words.

'Take care,' she whispered. 'May God be with you.' She departed, trailing a memory of tender hands and an aroma of roses.

Rustom returned after darkness fell, Mario and Ajit accompanying him. There was no space to accommodate Mario's large frame, so Irfan stepped out. The rain had halted and Rustom selected a dark building with boarded windows to stand under.

'Don't argue, Angrez,' said Mario, when Irfan heatedly confronted Rustom. 'You need looking after. Have you seen the condition of the sea? It makes me sick just looking at it. What will happen to you? You will not survive the voyage on your own. Be grateful you have a friend like our dear Parsee—someone willing to give his life for you . . . sacrifice his job . . . do anything for you.'

'That's just it,' argued Irfan. 'How can he give up his job? Not after the hard work he has put in. He'll have to give up his house too. It's too much.'

Ajit spoke up. 'You are missing the point!' he explained in his gentle voice. 'Rustom cares more for you than for his job. You should be counting your blessings having a friend like him. He knows you will not survive on your own. He loves you, Irfan. And when there is love, nothing can stand in the way. Don't you see . . . his is a rare friendship.'

Irfan stared at Rustom, swaying.

Rustom's face turned tender. 'Did you really think I would let you go on your own, Irfan?' His voice was soft, like the murmur of a quiet sea. 'Our bonding isn't ordinary. It never was and will never be. You stood by me during my troubled times. Do you think I will turn my back on you during your time of crisis? We are more than friends, Irfan—we are family.'

Irfan's face crumpled. Tears spurted from his eyes. Mario held him, his own eyes turning wet.

Ajit wiped dampness from his cheeks. 'We'll be waiting for you, Irfan.' The smile he attempteded failed, succeeding only in twitching his cheeks. 'My bride wants to meet you. Come back quickly. I've spoken about you and your skill with horses. She wants to learn to ride.'

'We'll have to wait for her to grow up first,' said Rustom, laughing and then choking.

'And you have to find a girl for our Parsee friend,' grinned Mario, steadying Irfan. 'You are family to him, remember? You have responsibilities now.'

A warm sensation spread inside Irfan, triggering a fresh bout of tears. Ajit put an arm around Irfan. Rustom couldn't help smiling at the amusing sight of his friend propped between the monstrous bulk of Mario and Ajit's pocket-sized frame. But even as he grinned, he noticed movement on the road.

People were running down the dimly lit street.

'THERE!' yelled a triumphant voice. 'There he is. I knew he was hiding somewhere here. GET HIM!'

FORJETT'S STORY

'Ravi,' breathed Irfan, recognizing the voice. 'It's him and the others from Seawind.'

Mario bunched his fists. 'So this is the lot who give you a hard time, Angrez. You didn't let me bash them earlier, but today I will.' He crouched, licking his lips.

There were several men in the advancing group. Irfan counted six, but the numbers did not bother Mario as he hunched bull-like in the centre of the road.

Nitin, Ravi's elder brother, barked instructions as the group drew closer. 'Dhanaji, Dhondiba, find Wallace saab. Alert him. We won't let him get away now.'

Two figures peeled off, racing down a side street.

'We'll have to go, Mario,' said Rustom urgently. 'Hold them off while we escape. Come on, Irfan, RUN!'

'Goodbye, Angrez,' said Mario, wrenching his eyes from the advancing men. 'May Jesus be with you, my friend. Ajit and I will hold them off. Go with Rustom. God bless.'

Irfan stared ashen-faced at his friends. The knot of attackers burst forward, whooping and shouting.

Mario pushed Irfan, thrusting hard. 'GO!' he bellowed.

Rustom was already running. Irfan sprinted after him.

Mr Ghadiali was on the road too, striding with a stout stick in his hand. 'May God be with you, Irfan,' shouted the shopkeeper as Rustom and Irfan raced past. 'I'm holding you to your word. Don't forget the watches you promised to buy when you return.'

Irfan followed Rustom, running blindly, feet splashing through puddles. The streets were virtually empty. The hour was late. Rain had kept people indoors too. Irfan accelerated, drawing level with Rustom as they burst on to Church Gate Street. Rustom turned left, but Irfan grabbed his shoulder.

'Shops are open,' he panted. 'I'll hide in one of them. You go and warn Forjett.'

'Forjett is here on Meadows Street,' panted Rustom. 'His friend Remington is throwing a party down the street. We have to meet him there.'

'Right,' said Irfan, nodding. 'Lead the way.'

The entrance to Meadows Street lay a short distance ahead. But as they ran, there was shouting and the clatter of hooves on stone. Their way ahead was suddenly barred.

'Got you, you little scum,' snarled an English voice. 'Now you will tell me where your thieving rascal of a father is.'

Irfan looked up. Two men mounted on horses obstructed his path. The man who had spoken brandished a pistol. His long, blond hair and handsome features were unmistakable. For a change, instead of their carefully braided finery, his tresses flopped in a tangled wet mess. His elegant features were twisted in a hideous snarl.

Wallace.

Irfan turned. But any possible escape was blocked. A mass of men, with Balu in the lead, was rushing forward.

'That's right, you little scoundrel. You're trapped. You are going to pay, my young friend. I'm going to whip you. Whip you till you beg for mercy. You are going to regret ever crossing my path.'

'Let us pass,' blustered Rustom. 'Stand aside. Police Commissioner Forjett has sent for us. We are on our way to meet him.'

Wallace chuckled nastily. 'There is no Forjett here to save you,' he spat. 'Not now, not ever.' He holstered his weapon and dismounted. Shoving Rustom aside with a force that sent him stumbling to the ground, he advanced on Irfan, eyes smouldering. His face glowed crimson with barely controlled rage.

'Thought you would rob me, did you, you slimy black cur? I'm going to thrash you to a pulp. And when you tell me where your brigand of a father is, I will kill you both.'

Irfan swayed as Wallace aimed a savage blow at him. Stepping aside, he clenched his fist and swung at the Englishman with all his strength, smacking him squarely on the chin and sending him crashing to the ground.

There was a sharp intake of breath from the gathering as Wallace, his face contorted with a terrible rage, staggered to his feet, yanking his pistol from his holster.

'Go ahead and shoot!' goaded Irfan, in his perfectly accented English. 'I dare you to kill me.'

For a heart-stopping moment, Irfan thought he had pushed the man too far. Such was Wallace's fury that he frothed at the mouth. His face flashed gaudier than any sunset Irfan had ever seen. The hand that held his gun trembled with violent anger. But his blazing eyes seemed to blink. Their colour paled and he shook his head.

'Good try, young man,' he scoffed. 'I almost finished it for you, didn't I? But unfortunately for you, sense prevailed. Your end will come, but not so fast. You will live to regret your indiscretion. You will wish tonight that I had pulled the trigger.' Turning to his men, he shouted, 'Grab him!'

Irfan felt himself being lifted off the ground. A swarm of spidery arms clutched at him. His turban was swept from his head and he heard the fabric of his shirt tear. Although resistance was pointless, Irfan struggled gamely. Amidst the press of bodies, he spied Balu's face. It shone with glee, as if this was the happiest night of his life. Balu's delight hardened Irfan's resolve. He would not give in. He would deny them the pleasure of begging mercy from them. But as he strained and grappled, Balu's euphoria flickered and dimmed. The hands that held him loosened their hold and he fought free of their vile clasp.

He saw now that instead of two horses there were several more, and the men mounted on them wore blue clothing with yellow hats—the uniform of the police.

'Unhand the boy,' shrilled a commanding English voice. 'Back off. Leave the boy be.'

'Move aside,' ordered another. 'Now, or I will use my whip.'

The crowd backed away. Irfan searched for Rustom. To one side of the mounted policemen, there was an additional troop on foot. Rustom's hand waved from their midst. Irfan stepped forward, but Wallace barred his way.

'The boy is mine,' he hissed. 'He stole my boat last night. He stays with me.'

A red-faced Englishman with a large moustache eased his horse forward, halting it before Wallace. 'The boy doesn't strike me as the sort who would steal a boat. If he did, he would be intelligent enough to be with the boat and not here beside you. More to the point, you have no right to confine anyone; only we are authorized to do so. Your conduct, sir, is disturbing the peace and order of the city. If you persist with your behaviour, I will be forced to take action against you. You will stand aside and let the boy pass.'

Wallace did not move, but Irfan stepped around him. The Englishman made no attempt to halt him, yet Irfan winced, as if singed by his wrath, as he passed him.

The officer waved Irfan on. 'No one will harm you, boy. My men will look after you. March with them.' He turned to Wallace. 'As for you, sir, I will escort you back to where you came from.'

Wallace protested fiercely. 'So now you protect black pirates. I will have you reported. Forjett is behind this, I know. The governor shall hear of this outrage. I will get that thieving black rat. I will kill him. I shall tear his skin off him, and as for his father—'

'If I were you I would mind my words, sir,' interrupted the officer. 'I can jail you if I wish to for issuing such revolting threats.'

But Wallace continued to rant. Irfan's escort pushed forward the moment he drew level with them. Rustom squeezed his hand. They hurried forward, side by side.

The Remington residence lay just a short distance ahead, around the next corner. Even a minute would have saved them from the encounter with Wallace.

'We've reached!' exclaimed Irfan, as they entered a shoulder-high gate. He grabbed Rustom's arm. 'It was you who called the police!'

A smile flashed on Rustom's face. 'No one saw me when I slipped away. The policemen were standing here beside this gate. Forjett had left word with them. They came rushing the moment I informed them.'

Blazing lights and a clutch of carriages indicated that a party was in progress. They were escorted across a modest-sized garden to a porch where a smartly dressed man with a white hat frowned at them. A brief chat with the constables accompanying them followed, after which they were ushered down a passageway to a room at the rear of the bungalow. Light from a lantern on a table revealed a small chamber, almost bare, except for a table and a few chairs.

Forjett arrived quickly, looking smart in a brown jacket and tie. His features crinkled into a smile when he saw Irfan. 'You look fine,' he said, 'no worse for your experience. I was worried when they told me Wallace's men had got hold of you, but it seems Rustom alerted my men in time.'

He turned a chair so it faced Irfan and settled on it. 'I'm not going to hide the facts from you, son. You are in trouble. It has been established beyond doubt that your father stole

Wallace's boat. If ever a thief is to be commended for his handiwork, then your father surely should, for he has netted himself a fabulous catch. The boat he has commandeered contained all of Wallace's possessions, everything he owned and had appropriated during his sojourn in India. Wallace . . . naturally, has gone crazy.'

Forjett allowed himself a small laugh, then his face turned grim. 'Your father's absence does not bode well for you, Irfan. Wallace stormed into my office this morning demanding that I deploy my men to search the city and find you. He didn't like it when I told him the security of the city was a far more important obligation than looking for you. What I said was the truth. Perhaps a convenient truth, but I wasn't lying. Ever since the mutiny has flared, my men—under instructions from the governor—are exclusively on security duty. Robberies and petty crimes are largely being ignored. Wallace stalked angrily away when I told him I couldn't help him. I had hoped the matter would end there, but then Colvin got into the act, contacting people he knows.'

Forjett exhaled loudly. 'I am under pressure to arrest you, Irfan. I have consulted Governor Elphinstone who hasn't forgotten what you did for him. He gave the matter some thought, but concluded finally that your father has committed a crime and that we cannot stall justice. He doesn't want to make an issue out of this matter, especially at a time when our countrymen are being killed and our provinces are under siege. The governor doesn't want you to be jailed, but at the same time he cannot hold off your arrest for long. You have been asked to leave the city, Irfan.

Rustom told me of your plans. I will provide an escort for you to Apollo Bunder and you must leave tonight.'

'I know I must go,' said Irfan quietly. 'I beg you to thank Governor Elphinstone on my behalf, and I am indebted to you, sir, for your help. My father does not trust Englishmen. I hope he will change his impression when I tell him of your kindness.'

Forjett sighed. 'Your father has his reasons and I respect them. Did he tell you why he stole Wallace's boat?'

'No, sir,' replied Irfan, after a brief hesitation.

Forjett smiled. 'I don't think you are being entirely honest with me, Irfan. But I shall not press you. I will share with you, however, what I know of Wallace. I'm sure his dubious antecedents will be of interest to you.'

Forjett regarded Irfan with his dark eyes. 'You probably aren't aware, but in England, tales abound of young men coming to India and striking it fabulously rich. Many have come and have acquired a hoard of money, very often by questionable means, but back home, the means have hardly ever mattered; it's only the extent of their staggering wealth that counts. Their success has spurred many young Englishmen to cross the seas to India. Wallace is one of those who came here to seek his fortune. By sheer chance, or should I say ill luck, I met the man in Mahabaleshwar.'

Forjett stared searchingly at Irfan. 'Has your father spoken of what happened in Mahabaleshwar?'

Irfan shook his head. 'Not yet, sir. He says he will, but that is only if we meet again.'

'I see,' said Forjett. He rocked his chair, silent for a while, then ploughed on. 'As I said, I met Wallace in

Mahabaleshwar and I quickly discovered the dark side of his personality. He is a man without scruples; the kind who would murder even his own mother if an inheritance was involved. I didn't meet him again after that, not till he came to stay with Colvin here in Bombay. I did hear talk of him, however, over the years. Nothing has ever been proved, but there have been rumours, rumours of him amassing a great fortune. It is said he robbed Maharajahs, duped Englishmen and tricked businessmen. He is suspected to be the man behind a band of thugs who roamed the northern provinces, raiding villages and robbing travellers. There are several stories of Wallace, all of them distasteful, but the man is shrewd and though people talk, there is not a shred of evidence against him. When he arrived here in Bombay, I heard he was planning to return to England for good. He claims that the boat your father stole contains all his possessions. If that indeed is the case, your father has struck Wallace a virtual death blow. He has appropriated from him his entire ill-gained fortune.'

Irfan's eyes flashed in the lamplight. 'Sir. You have known my father for years. Do you believe he is an ordinary thief?'

Forjett considered before replying. 'I will say that your father is an angry man. His anger has driven him to dangerous company. I know also that your father is a kind man. He is kind to beggars. Just as I tricked you that day on Malabar Hill with my disguise as a beggar, I have fooled your father too, squatting beside him in dirty coffee bars, while he sat with his friends discussing frightful acts that could seriously have threatened the peace and security of Bombay. Your father's anger is so deep that it has allowed him to be misled. But thief he most definitely is not.'

'Then why did he rob Wallace?' Irfan's voice rose. 'Why would he stoop to something so low? Why would he commit a crime that would ruin his name, makc him a criminal and his son a fugitive? Why must I suffer without knowing?' Irfan wrung his hands. 'Will somebody please tell me!'

The last was uttered with such feeling that Rustom stared in astonishment at Irfan. There was a bitterness in his friend's eyes that Rustom had never seen before.

Forjett rocked his chair. He drummed his fingers on the table. 'I can set the matter straight for you, Irfan, if you desire. I have not spoken on this subject out of respect for your father. It is his place to speak of such matters, not mine.'

'I may never meet my father again, sir,' Irfan's voice was weighed by feeling. 'Truth has been withheld from me all my life. No one has answered my questions—neither the Browns nor my father. I am a hunted person now and I may never return here to Bombay. I must know now before I leave.'

Forjett gazed long and hard at Irfan. 'Very well,' he said finally. 'I will tell you what I know, and I hope your father will forgive me.' He looked up, staring at the peeling rafters overhead. 'It was a long time ago. You were but a baby. I was a young man then, serving as the officer in charge of the Satara region, near Mahabaleshwar. As you know, we Englishmen love Mahabaleshwar's cool climate, escaping there at the first opportunity, especially during the summer, when it is hot and miserable in Bombay. Back then, the Browns were recently married with twin children. They were regulars at Mahabaleshwar in those days, spending the entire hot season there. Your father worked for them whenever they visited. It was a good arrangement as your father was excellent with horses and served as their liveryman, while your mother worked for Alice as an ayah, helping her with her twin sons who were babies like you. I would also get away from the heat of Satara and slip away when I got the opportunity, and as Mahabaleshwar was a small place, I would meet the Browns at the marketplace or in the evenings at a common friend's home.

'One summer, I forget the exact year, a man by the name of William Wallace arrived in Mahabaleshwar.' Forjett shrugged. 'Many young Englishmen visited the hill station and the appearance of Wallace was hardly a notable event. I didn't know the man and I would never have learnt of his presence there if it weren't for his beastly behaviour and the tragic consequences of his actions. That tragedy involved you, Irfan, striking at the very heart of your existence.'

Rustom, who was watching Irfan, saw him wince, as if struck by a blow.

'I can stop here, Irfan,' suggested Forjett. 'Knowledge of the events that followed can hurt you deeply. It is possible that your father and the Browns never spoke because they felt you would not be able to bear the knowledge of the catastrophe of that fateful summer.'

'Go on, sir,' mumbled Irfan, his face pale in the lamplight. 'Please.'

Forjett nodded, pursing his lips. 'Maybe it is best that you know. All your questions will be answered. You will understand why the Browns adopted you and why anger consumes your father so.' Forjett paused, toying with the buttons of his fancy dinner jacket. Dropping his hand, he continued, 'Wallace apparently had a relationship with Alice Brown in England. The story I heard is that her parents sent her to India to get away from him. The ploy worked as she met Craig in Bombay and married him and started a new life here. But Wallace never forgot her. He came to India a few years later and pursued her to Mahabaleshwar. Alice was shocked when he came to her house to renew their acquaintance. She threw him out, wanting nothing to do with him, but he harassed her, stalking her on the streets and lurking around her home. The Browns complained to me and I had a word with the cad, warning him to keep away from their home. I threatened that he would be physically removed from Mahabaleshwar if he did not. He seemed so timid and scared when I admonished him that I believed the matter was over and done with when he swore he would leave Alice alone.

'I was horribly mistaken. I was a raw recruit in those days and a poor judge of character. Wallace hoodwinked me. A few nights later, he broke into Alice's home. Craig was having a drink at a neighbour's home at that time. Alice had stayed back to look after her twins, one of whom was running a fever. Your mother was with Alice that night helping her with the children. I was informed later that you were present too, fast asleep in a cot in a corner. Wallace was in a drunken state. He demanded that Alice leave her husband and come away with him. She refused, of course, and ordered him out of her home. But Wallace was dead serious. He pulled out his gun, threatening to shoot her if she did not come with him. Alice reacted furiously. She lashed Wallace with her tongue, disparagingly comparing his character with her husband's. She laughed at Wallace, daring him to shoot, telling him he didn't have the nerve. Alice underestimated Wallace's resolve and ruthlessness. Your mother, however, spotted the danger signals. She came to her mistress's side, trying to calm her, but Alice had lost her temper by then and she did not heed your mother's caution. Only Alice survived to describe what happened later. Wallace screamed and shouted. Alice yelled back. Wallace raised his gun. When he pulled the trigger, your mother threw herself between them. The bullet pierced your mother's chest. She died a few hours later.'

Irfan's breathing had turned to tortured gasps, yet Forjett plodded on. 'Bonding between ayahs and their English memsahibs is common, but the relationship between your mother and Alice Brown was unparalleled. Alice said they were exceptionally close because their children—the twins and you—were born just a few months apart, enabling them to share the joys of motherhood. They discussed everything women do, keeping no secrets from one another. It mattered not that they belonged to different communities; they were both deeply attached to one another, and your mother made the ultimate sacrifice to save her dear friend.'

Irfan's eyes were dry. But his shattered countenance betrayed the turmoil inside him. He gasped. 'No one . . . No one ever told me . . . why?'

'Craig Brown confided to me that Alice swore your father to secrecy. She was afraid you would hold your mother's death against her. She wanted you to love her as you would have loved your own mother. She was determined to bring you up as one of her own. She reasoned that if you learnt of your mother's death, there was a chance you could turn against her and blame her for it. She dreaded that possibility and so, the past was kept a secret from you.'

Irfan was silent. Beads of sweat had collected on his brow and his breathing was tortured. Then his eyes flamed. 'Wallace!' he exclaimed. 'Why was he allowed to go free? He killed my mother.'

Forjett dropped his gaze. His fingers, at rest since he had commenced his story, drummed the table again. 'Wallace's escape was a low point in my career.' His drumming grew louder and his eyes remained fixed on the table. 'I took the swine into custody immediately after the incident, promising your father that the man would be brought to justice. He was held in jail for a week or more, I can't remember. During that period, I had to travel on an assignment and when I came back, I found his cell empty. I learnt later that Wallace hadn't broken out of jail; he had been permitted to go free. My senior had let him out. He washed his hands off the affair when I questioned him. Instructions had come from higher up, he said. After all, it was a native woman who had died; the crime could be overlooked. My protests and anger fell on deaf ears. I was told to shut up and get on with my work. The case had been dropped and I was warned not to attempt going after Wallace. Your father then learnt about Wallace's release. The day he came to me ranks amongst the most shameful of my career. There was nothing I could do. I had to express my inability to help him.'

Forjett finally raised his gaze, looking Irfan in the eye. 'Your father's scorn for me is deserved. I let him down. I can argue that it was the system—its bias against native people—that cheated him, but in my heart, I know I am to blame too. His hatred for Englishmen and their ethics is justified. As an individual, I applaud his enterprise in stealing Wallace's boat. It is his way of striking back at Wallace, and his revenge must be especially sweet as he has sailed away with the man's entire fortune.'

Forjett's hands fell from the table. 'It isn't easy for you, Irfan, I know. Learning about your past can be very painful, especially in a case like yours. Your father has never approved of anything I do. I hope when you meet him, he won't be angered at my having spoken. You sought to know and the time had come for you to learn.'

Forjett rose. 'I must go now. My host will be wondering what mischief I have got to. I shall arrange for dinner for both of you. You are safe here, and you will be escorted to the Bunder when it is time. I will be back before you leave.'

Food arrived shortly after Forjett departed. Though the meal was excellent, Irfan consumed it absently, hardly noticing what he ate. Rustom kept silent, respecting his friend's need to be left alone.

Forjett returned shortly before 10.00 p.m., accompanied by the same red-faced, moustached officer who had confronted Wallace. 'This is Constable Campbell,' he said, introducing the officer. 'He will escort you to Apollo Bunder.' He turned to the officer. 'Your arrangements are in place, Campbell?'

'My men have checked the Bunder,' replied Campbell in a clipped voice. 'They say a boat is moored there. Wallace suspects something is planned tonight. I am afraid he could be a problem, sir. He is waiting outside and refuses to leave. He has stationed his men—mostly servants from Seawind—at all the Fort gates.'

'Is the carriage ready?' queried Forjett, unperturbed by Campbell's revelation. 'It is time now.'

'But what about Wallace, sir?' asked Irfan.

Forjett winked. 'We have made arrangements,' he said. 'Don't worry, he will be handled. The carriage is waiting behind Remington's residence, on a back street. Come, I shall escort you there.'

Passing a crowded kitchen and a dirty backyard, they emerged on a dark, ill-lit street. Forjett halted beside an elegant black buggy with brass trimmings and a hood ornamented with expensive velvet lining.

Forjett's face had turned grave. 'For your sake, I must warn you, Irfan, before you leave. Today, you are safe from Wallace . . . but I cannot guarantee the future. Wallace will hunt you down. Both you and your father. His fortune is gone. He is not the sort of man who will give up. He will move heaven and earth. Prepare your father for battle. I must caution you also from returning to Bombay soon. I hate saying this, but I must. A white man has been robbed. The legal system will be against you despite your innocence. You must spare me the embarrassment of arresting you.'

Irfan's eyes flooded once more. He nodded, unable to speak.

Forjett looked away. He turned to Rustom. His eyes widened with amazement when Rustom bid him goodbye.

'I leave with Irfan, sir,' said the boy.

Forjett stared blankly. 'But you don't have to. There is no case against you. I am here to protect you. Your employers admire your work. They have told me so. You have a job with great prospects.'

Rustom shook his head. 'Irfan is my friend,' he said simply.

Forjett gazed at Rustom. After what seemed an interminable time, he extended his hand. 'I will shake you by the hand, young man,' he said.

Embarrassed, Rustom raised his hand.

Forjett shook it, solemnly. 'I understand your sacrifice. Your selflessness is rare. I know what you are giving up and for that, I salute you.'

Forjett then turned to Irfan and embraced him. 'My wife says I don't know how to deal with partings, so I will keep this short. You are blessed, Irfan, to have a friend like young Rustom. I dearly wish I too had a friend like him. The two of you are good for each other. You make a fine team as I have discovered in the past. I have grown very fond of both of you and I shall miss you. I hope your troubles will end soon. I wish you the very best. Have a safe journey. May God be with you.'

With bowed heads, the boys entered the carriage. Campbell fastened the doors and directed the driver forward. The last Irfan saw of Forjett was a vision of a strong, upright man, hand raised in farewell, a warm smile on his face—an image he would cherish and remember.

As the carriage pulled away, six horsemen drew up alongside, keeping pace with it, three on either side. The Fort's Apollo Gate was nearby. They reached its guarded fortifications without incident. A sentry armed with a musket saluted the carriage and commanded the gates to be opened.

Fear seized Irfan as the carriage rolled across the dark expanse of the Esplanade. He hadn't prepared himself for the terrible voyage ahead. Forjett's stunning revelations had occupied him, keeping at bay his dread of the sea. But now, as the moment of departure drew close, a dreadful anxiety overcame him.

'We have company,' announced Campbell, looking out of the carriage window.

Irfan and Rustom looked. A lone horseman was tearing across the Esplanade towards them.

'Wallace,' said Campbell grimly. 'Don't worry yourselves. There's nothing he can do.'

The horseman drew level with the carriage as it halted beside the Bunder. The night was dark and a strong wind buffeted the carriage. It wrenched the door from Irfan's hands and tore at his clothes as he dismounted.

Campbell had guessed correctly. The horseman was indeed Wallace. An overpowering rage flared inside Irfan. His breath turned to furious gasps as he stared at the man who had killed his mother. Sensing his anger, Rustom held his arm. But Irfan shook himself free and strode to the Englishman.

'You,' he choked, struggling to control spasms of the most terrible fury ever to have afflicted him, 'you killed my mother.'

Wallace stared at Irfan with an expression of utmost scorn. 'And I will kill your thieving father too,' he said, in a voice so cold that it chilled Rustom's heart. He kicked his horse forward, halting it beside Irfan. 'You think you escape me now, but you are mistaken. There will be no Forjett to protect you when I come after you. Your father committed the biggest blunder of his life when he went after me. I will not rest till I cut him down, shred his flesh and feed him to the vultures.'

A terrible scream tore from Irfan's gut. He lunged forward, arm raised to strike, but Campbell caught him and held him tightly.

'You will leave now, Mr Wallace,' ordered the officer. 'Leave or I will set my men on you.'

Wallace retreated. Halting his horse at a distance, he looked back. 'There will be no one to save you next time,' he spat.

A cold fury had replaced Irfan's anger. 'It won't be helpless women you will be up against,' he seethed. 'We will be waiting for you. Your crime will be avenged.'

Wallace spat once more. Turning his animal around, he calmly rode away.

Rustom caught Irfan when Campbell released him.

The officer and his men stayed back as Rustom led Irfan to the Bunder.

A sprinkle of rain fell from the skies. Waves heaved against the railing, spattering the boys with saltwater. Irfan shut his eyes and clung to Rustom. His feet trembled as he was led down a flight of slippery stairs. There was a shout. It was Shahid, but his words were lost on Irfan. A giddy blackness overwhelmed Irfan as a wave swept over his feet. He tottered, unable to stay upright. There was another shout and he felt himself being lifted off the ground. The world turned unstable. Everything shook and swayed. He was on the boat. The nightmare he had evaded for years was finally upon him. The world reeled, spinning at an incredible speed. Darkness engulfed him and he knew no more.

ACKNOWLEDGEMENTS

Sharda Dwivedi was a noted Bombay conservationist, historian and friend. This book would not have been possible without her encouragement and support. Deepak Rao is a Bombay historian and an expert on the history of Mumbai's police force. His guidance and assistance were invaluable. My thanks also to Saaz Agarwaal, for her literary inputs and encouragement.

Don't miss the exciting conclusion to
Sahyadri Adventure: Anirudh's Dream*!*

Read more from the next book
in the series.

Sahyadri Adventure: Koleshwar's Secret

Searching for the remnants of Mumbai's fort is a futile exercise, for not a wall or battlement of the edifice survives today. But waking from his dream, Anirudh inexplicably knows every gate, contour and detail of the vanished fort. Fascinated by Anirudh's revelations, Vikram explores Mumbai with him.

Far out in the Sahyadri rises a mountain known as Koleshwar. Striving to make sense of his dream, Anirudh stumbles upon a forgotten legacy that leads to the mountain. Buried on its ancient slopes is a secret that only he has the power to decode.

Journey to the Sahyadris in the concluding instalment of this riveting tale where history meets adventure in one of the most beautiful locales of India.

READ MORE IN THE SERIES

Ranthambore Adventure

THIS IS THE STORY OF A TIGER

Once a helpless ball of fur, Genghis emerges as a mighty predator, the king of the forest. But the jungle isn't just his kingdom. Soon, Genghis finds himself fighting for his skin against equally powerful predators but of a different kind—humans.

The very same ones that Vikram and Aditya get embroiled with when they attempt to lay their hands on a diary that belongs to a ruthless tiger poacher. Worlds collide when an ill-fated encounter plunges the boys and their friend Aarti into a thrilling chase that takes them deep into the magnificent game park of Ranthambore.

Journey through the wilderness, brimming with tiger lore, with a tale set in one of India's most splendid destinations.

READ MORE IN THE SERIES

Ladakh Adventure

On their visit to the Changthang plateau of Ladakh, Vikram and Aditya find themselves on the run along with Tsering, a young Tibetan boy they meet while camping on this grand yet barren frontier of India. Determined to protect Tsering from the mysterious band of men chasing him, the three boys traverse the majestic land beyond the Himalayas in search of answers.

Who is Tsering? Why is he being hunted with such fierce resolve? Follow Vikram and Aditya across the remote frozen plateau to the mountain city of Leh—through a land of startling contrasts and magnificent mountains—as a perilous game of hide-and-seek unfolds.

Journey to the roof of the world with an enthralling tale set in one of India's most splendid destinations.

READ MORE IN THE SERIES

Snow Leopard Adventure

Vikram and Aditya are back in magnificent Ladakh. Having finally freed their young friend Tsering from the hands of dangerous men, they've set themselves up for an even greater challenge: to track down the grey ghost of the Himalayas, the snow leopard. The boys join a team of ecologists and explorers in their search for this rare and beautiful creature.

Here, Vikram befriends a troubled and unhappy girl called Caroline. The soaring peaks of the Himalayas hold no attraction for her, yet she is driven by an overpowering desire to spot a snow leopard. Set amidst majestic mountains and plunging valleys, *Snow Leopard Adventure* is a satisfying finale to a chase that began in *Ladakh Adventure*.

Journey in search of the elusive snow leopard with an enthralling tale set in one of India's most splendid destinations.

READ MORE IN THE SERIES

Lakshadweep Adventure

Far out in the Arabian Sea, where the waters plunge many thousands of metres to the ocean floor, lies a chain of bewitching coral atolls—the Lakshadweep Islands. Vikram and Aditya dive into lagoons with crystal-clear water and reefs that are deep and shrouded in mystery. But when they stumble upon a devious kidnapping plot, their idyllic holiday turns into a desperate struggle for survival.

Forced out into the sea in the eye of a raging storm, they endure a shipwreck, only to be marooned on a remote coral island.

Journey through these breathtaking islands with a tale of scuba diving and sabotage, set in one of India's most splendid destinations.